ALWAYS BE A
WOLF

Also by Mima

Fire
A Spark before the Fire
The Rock Star of Vampires
Her Name is Mariah
Different Shades of the Same Color
We're All Animals

To learn more go to www.mimaonfire.com

ALWAYS BE A
WOLF

MIMA

ALWAYS BE A WOLF

iUniverse books may be ordered through booksellers or by contacting:

iUniverse
1663 Liberty Drive
Bloomington, IN 47403
www.iuniverse.com
1-800-Authors (1-800-288-4677)

Because of the dynamic nature of the Internet, any web addresses or links contained in this book may have changed since publication and may no longer be valid. The views expressed in this work are solely those of the author and do not necessarily reflect the views of the publisher, and the publisher hereby disclaims any responsibility for them.

Any people depicted in stock imagery provided by Thinkstock are models, and such images are being used for illustrative purposes only. Certain stock imagery © Thinkstock.

ISBN: 978-1-5320-2179-4 (sc)
ISBN: 978-1-5320-2180-0 (e)

Library of Congress Control Number: 2017906102

Print information available on the last page.

iUniverse rev. date: 04/24/2017

ACKNOWLEDGEMENTS

I would like to thank the West Prince Arts Council of PEI for their continued support of my work. Please visit them at: www.westprinceartscouncil.ca

CHAPTER ONE

If there was a crazy train, Diego Silva drove it. He did so with no apology, no care; he was like the devil himself, plunked into the middle of a society that insisted on conformity while resented it at the same time. It was the world that both hated and admired the 40-year-old Colombian man who had a certain charm that was impossible to deny but he was a joker dressed in an Armani suit, a firecracker that was always ready to explode; you could see it in his black eyes, the same ones that occasionally warmed into a gentle brown but very few people saw that side of him. He was dangerous and the moment Diego sensed your fear, he would invade it with both guns blazing. Others discomfort rarely phased him. He fed off it.

Chase Jacobs knew this all too well but had fortunately grown resistant to the world around him after dealing with much turbulence in his own life. Diego and his games were nothing new; he challenged his young employee on a daily basis, often in the form of an unscrupulous or overtly sexual comment, he seemed to enjoy watching Chase's reaction, his eyes glazing over in pleasure, a suppressed grin on his lips, as if holding back from saying something that pushed things just a little too far.

But he liked to push things far; the question was when would Chase fight his stubborn side that refused to meet the challenge; the boxer in him wanted to prove that none of Diego's games affected him, no words intimidated him and nothing, absolutely *nothing*, would get the best of him. But that was a challenge Diego was only too happy to take on.

It was at the moment when Chase thought his heart was about to explode, that he felt things had finally gone *way* too far. Feeling the blood pumping through every inch of him, from the tip of his toes to the top of his head at an exhilarated pace, knowing Diego's dark eyes were occasionally, gingerly glancing toward his face, hoping to find some sign of emotion, it was getting increasingly difficult to fight those natural impulses from being exposed. This was like nothing he had ever felt before; his hand gripping on the smooth material while his eyes began to water, his throat too dry to speak, he struggled with not reacting but deep down, he knew Diego was already seeing the subtle hints that gave him away.

"Stop! You have to stop!" Chase attempted to scream and yet, his voice was the hushed tone of a child, barely escaping his lips. And that's when he heard it; the gentle, almost unnoticeable laugh that Diego was attempting to confine, that pleasurable moment when he knew he had finally won.

"You're going to kill us both," Chase finally managed to regain his normal, deep voice as he watched the empty road ahead of them, the gears shifting in Diego's hand, as he only increased the speed of the brand new Gran Turismo that he had driven off the lot earlier that day. What had started out as a simple drive out of the city limits to show off his new car was now turning into a horrifying adventure, as they flew past other cars and road signs indicating that they were driving at a speed that was almost twice the acceptable limit.

"Nonsense, *amigo*, this is *living*," Diego replied, followed by a devilish laugh that made Chase wish he hadn't said a thing. This would only entice him to go faster, with no regards for life, he wouldn't care if he killed them both in a brand new car; one that would make most people scared to drive at a normal speed because of its value, let alone flying down the 401 as if they were part of a NASCAR adventure. "You worry too much. That's the dad in you talking."

A mischievous smirk caused the Colombian's lips to pucker into a stiff smile, his eyes hidden behind dark sunglasses, fortunately, they stayed focused on the road ahead. Shaking his head and letting out a short laugh, he began to gear down and Chase felt his body start to calm. He now felt the tightness in the back of his neck, an ache in his chest that replaced the intense fear as he caressed his sweaty palms, his fingers feeling powerless and weak. When he glanced into the side mirror, he saw panic in his dark brown eyes, his tanned complexion appearing unusually flushed, as his hand ran through his short, black hair as a form of self-comfort. Relief also brought with it something very unexpected; a beautiful elation that he had only previously experienced after sex. It made him wonder if this was Diego's plan all along.

"Chase you don't understand," Diego continued to focus on the road as the car, now at a normal speed, pulled to an exit; not that Chase had any idea where they were at that moment. New to Ontario, he had only moved to Toronto a week earlier after Diego turned his private sex party business legit and decided to take their Canadian office to somewhere more central. "If you've never felt intense fear ripping through your body, then how would you know that you ever truly lived? Can you tell me that? You're what? 23? 24? You should thrive on this kind of thing."

Chase remained silent, hating to admit that there was some truth to Diego's statement. Regardless of how crazy it sounded, hadn't this experience awakened his senses in a way nothing else had in a long time? Only months earlier, his life had fallen flat. That was until Diego Silva walked in the door at the former office in Calgary. Nothing had been normal since that day.

Up until that point, Chase worked for Diego's younger sister, Jolene. The beautiful Colombian woman who showed no apprehension when it came to flaunting her curves, nor did she downplay her exceptional beauty. In fact, it was probably her strong confidence that made her more enticing to men around her and yet, she often appeared unaware of the looks of longing and attraction, absorbed in her work, she was always thinking ahead and ready for anything.

She wasn't, however, ready for her impulsive and fanatic brother. When he first announced closing the US and Calgary offices and moving everything to Toronto, Jolene calmly listened with interest, as if he were a child telling her about his new imaginary friend. She nodded, calmly asked questions that brought out more points, then bit her bottom lip as Diego paced the room, excitedly talking about his new 'master plan'. Chase didn't say anything, merely noting the occasional glances in his direction; Jolene with questioning eyes and Diego for his few, brief moments of vulnerability, as if Chase's opinion mattered.

It was only after he left that Jolene shrugged and said, "He will not do," Then opening her laptop and starting back to work, she continued, "He will talk talk talk, but he won't do. That's just Diego."

But he did. A couple of months later, after traveling to Toronto and 'meeting some people' and 'having some conversations', Jolene was left to organize the big move, frustrated and angry, often stuck taking care of the tedious details while still running the business. Chase bent over backward to help her, often working late into the night, weekends and getting calls at all hours. And just when they were both about to lose their minds, Diego returned to Calgary and sauntered into the office, calm as could be, a relaxed smile on his face.

"Everything going ok?" His dark eyes darted through Jolene who looked as if she were about to snap, instead, she calmly asked Chase to go get them some coffee while she talked to her brother. He did so and although apprehensive to return, he found everything was fine when he did. Jolene looked defeated while Diego, who rarely appeared stressed, was sitting cross-legged in Chase's seat, swinging his foot back and forth, his arm resting on the back of the chair, his black eyes darted in the young assistant's direction.

"I hope I didn't return too soon," Chase announced, unsure of what else to say as he entered the room with the tray of coffee in hand. Jolene showed no expression but thanked him, while a smirk crossed Diego's lips as his eyes inspected Chase carefully, from head to toe.

"And Chase," Diego spoke up, "He will be my assistant now. You will have to find a new one."

Appearing crestfallen, for the first time after many frustrating weeks and problems, Jolene looked as if she was going to snap. Her eyes filled with tears which she quickly blinked back. Her expression turned cold as she glared at her brother.

"Fine! Take him away from me, take everything," she snapped, jumping up from the desk, she grabbed her coat, purse and finally the coffee from the tray that Chase held, as he stood in the middle of the room, dumbfounded. Her heels sharply hit the floor as she rushed across the room and flew out the door, slamming it behind her. Diego, meanwhile, appeared unfazed.

"I wish she would listen to me and hire someone to help with her English," he continued to sit cross-legged, swinging his foot around excitedly, his eyes big and innocent, as if unaware of why his sister was so furious with him. "Can I have my coffee."

Chase passed him the Americano and silently sat down beside him with the last remaining coffee. Taking a drink, he realized Jolene had, in a fit of anger, grabbed the wrong one, leaving him with her overly sweet blend. Reluctantly drinking it, he opened his mouth to say something but decided against it.

"Ah.....now *that* is good coffee. I knew that I could finally teach that *dama* how to make it right," He pointed in the general direction of the coffee shop that Chase and Jolene often frequented. "I just flirt, you know, it works sometimes."

Chase exchanged looks with him.

"I know but she can live with the fantasy that I like women and I can get a decent Americano," Diego had been so flippant about it that Chase grinned in spite of himself. "As for Jolene, do not worry, she will cool off."

"Are you sure it's a good idea?" Chase inquired and to that, Diego merely shrugged.

"You were never hers to have." His grin was suggestive as he took a sip of his coffee and Chase looked away. "Besides, I need a big, strong, intimidating man like yourself."

Chase licked his lips and stared at his cup, feeling too awkward to reply. His height, as well as his regular boxing workouts and diet, gave him the physique that some viewed as intimidating. Half native, he had a mix of features that emphasized his strength and inner pride. By contrast, Diego was shorter, smaller but his dark gazes were probably more powerful than every muscle in Chase's body.

Time flew by quickly, only allowing Chase a short visit back home to Hennessey to see his three young boys one last time before the big move. Although happy to see him, it was clear that they no longer viewed him as their father, replaced by his ex-wife's fiancé; the man who tucked them in at night and took them for ice cream on Sunday afternoon. Chase was the occasional visitor that they had to talk to on Skype a few times a month.

"They know you are their father but Albert is here all the time," Her excuse was feeble, but he didn't blame his ex, in fact, despite a terrible marriage, he now held no animosity toward Audrey. He would learn to accept this new reality. But wasn't that what life was about, accepting difficult truths?

Diego didn't think so. He thought life was about expanding your limits, pushing things as far as they would go, then pushing them a little further. He was exciting, fascinating and even in the most normal moments, often surprised Chase.

It was as they left a convenience store after the insane car ride that Diego surprised him once again. Sipping his coffee, his legs feeling a bit wobbly as they walked outside, Chase noted that two teenage boys were admiring Diego's new car. Upon seeing the two men return, they quickly scurried away.

Turning up his nose after taking a drink of coffee, Diego's eyes fixated on the car and shrugged as Chase made his way to the passenger side.

"I don't like it, I'm taking it back."

Chase opened his mouth and then closed it again. He knew he wasn't talking about the coffee; although, he probably didn't like that either.

"It's just too, I don't know, *flamboyant*," he ran his hand over the roof of the car. "You know, kind of like a horny bridesmaid at a wedding who hits on all the men, looking to get her.."

"I think I got it," Chase cut in as he uncomfortably got back in the car while Diego did the same, a mischievous smile crept on his lips. "You think it's flamboyant."

"Yes, but not in a cool, homosexual way," He raised his eyebrow, suddenly serious, he took another drink of his coffee. "I'm talking in an obvious way, 'hey look at me, I'm dying for attention' kind of way." He curved his lower lip up and made a face. "I don't like it."

"So you're taking it back. You haven't had it a day and you're taking it back?" Chase exchanged looks with him.

"It's, you know, not practical," He spat out his words in reply, his lower lip stuck out in rebellion.

"So what, you're going to take it back and get a Corolla?" Chase snickered.

"I use to drive a Lexus a few years ago," Diego spoke thoughtfully. "I did enjoy that car."

"Unbelievable," Chase muttered as he looked out the passenger side.

"I'm a man of prestige," Diego insisted thoughtfully, looking around the parking lot. "I don't need this car to show that I'm important. What was I thinking? Must be a mid-life crisis."

He started the car and moved to the edge of the parking lot.

"Can you at least let me drink my coffee before you start breaking speed limits again?" Chase boldly asked something that seemed to humor Diego as he glanced in his direction with a twisted smile on his lips.

"Then you better drink fast my friend."

CHAPTER TWO

"Ah, springtime! It gives us all hope, doesn't it?" Diego made this impromptu statement as he pointed toward the beautiful flowers unnaturally erected from the concrete on the outside of the downtown building. It was the home of their new office. Feeling slightly awkward and lost, Chase followed his boss toward the entrance while people rushed all around them but few seemed to notice the two men wearing expensive suits. He felt insignificant.

"I never looked at it that way," Chase awkwardly replied as they entered the building, immediately heading toward the elevator.

Once inside, Diego hit the button for the third floor and the two silently waited. Removing his sunglasses, Diego wasn't paying attention to his assistant but glancing at his phone. He sniffed, shrugged and finally replied. "Maybe you should."

Arriving on the third floor, the two stepped into the dimly lit hallway and Diego rushed ahead toward their office and then abruptly stopped. Chase was on his heels and immediately discovered what he was looking at; a beautifully engraved sign that said, 'Diego and Jolene INC' with gold lettering against a black background. Diego reached out, his fingers gently slid over their names, his lips drew into a satisfied smile as he shared a silent look with Chase before opening the door.

Inside, a small staff barely glanced in their direction but it was impossible to miss the tension. Chase noticed office supplies scattered everywhere while a lone chair and parts of a table sat in the reception area. A young Filipino man and an Italian woman he vaguely remembered from the interviews were repositioning a desk while simultaneously attempting to work around an older man, who stood on a ladder, as he inspected a camera directed toward the main door. Three garbage cans were overflowing with clear plastic, empty coffee cups, and a donut box. The place was a mess.

Diego appeared unfazed, barely giving them a glance, he headed down the hallway. The aroma of coffee met them as they slowly passed a room crowded with cubicles, making everything seem very cramped and uncomfortable while across from it was the boardroom, which in contrast, appeared roomy and professional. The two continued to Jolene's office at the end of the hallway, just beside Diego's and across from the staff area. She was mid-sentence with her new assistant Beverly when the two walked in the room.

"Well, it is nice of the two of you to show up, *finally*, at almost lunchtime," Jolene's eyes darted from Diego to her former assistant. Feeling shameful, Chase averted his eyes and said nothing.

"Calm down, Jolene, I had to take my car back," Diego spoke casually and glanced around the small office, cluttered with opened boxes and piles of papers on her desk beside a cup of coffee and a half-eaten breakfast sandwich. "God it's a mess in here."

"It is a *mess* in here because we are trying to organize all morning," Jolene's accent grew heavier as her anger increased, while her assistant awkwardly shuffled beside her. Jolene stood tall in her heels, a stylish dress fell just above her knees, she took a deep breath. "While you were off, taking a car back? Didn't you just get that expensive car yesterday? What is wrong with you, Diego?"

"It wasn't for me," He made a face and shrugged, continuing to inspect the room. "You know, too fast..."

"Did he take you for a drive in the car?" Jolene abruptly cut him off, focusing her attention on Chase. "That crazy, I don't know how you say, *sport* car?"

Chase nodded and remained stoic.

"He took me, almost killed me, he go so fast!" She pointed in Diego's direction and not surprisingly, her brother's face fell into a relaxed grin, his eyes glazed over in pleasure. "Diego, you cannot drive that way, you will die."

"Nonsense, I have the angels on my side." Diego was flippant, shoving a hand in his pocket while the other one played with his tie.

"*Ay caramba!*" Jolene shot back, her dark eyes blazing, she muttered, "More like the devil."

"I think we need a meeting," Diego announced and glanced at Beverly, who appeared awkward as she bit her bottom lip, her large blue eyes seemed to amplify her discomfort. "You, clean up this *mess* and Jolene, we will go to the boardroom."

Chase opened his mouth to ask what they wanted him to do but Diego was already flying toward the door, Jolene snatched up her laptop and phone, her face in a scowl and rushed to catch up. Just as they reached the door, Diego abruptly spun around, almost running into her, something which he ignored, his large eyes focused on Chase. "*You,* come with us."

Glancing briefly toward Beverly, who looked as if she wanted to cry, Chase immediately decided that it was perhaps better to enter a room of hostility than stay in one full of tears. That's the last thing he wanted to deal with.

The yelling started immediately after the boardroom door closed. Jolene was furious that Diego wasn't 'stepping up' to help, too busy with the details of his own life, leaving her to carry more than her share. "We are supposed to be partners, Diego, not me doing everything while you run out to get a manicure."

"Who says I got a manicure," Diego appeared slightly irritated for the first time since Chase met him, he sat with his legs crossed, turned toward his sister, who was towering over him. "I was getting a car and today I returned it and here I am! Chase and I are here to help, so you stop yelling and tell us what you need."

Diego suddenly shifted gears, clearing his throat, he calmly fixed his tie before removing his jacket and in a relaxed voice said, "It's warm in here, don't you think, Chase?"

Not replying, Chase glanced down at his own suit and sensing the fury coming from Jolene, decided it was best to keep quiet.

"Diego," Jolene took a deep breath and sat down beside him. Her eyes softened as her long, dark hair fell forward. "I'm overwhelmed, I need your help. You're all over the place, I don't know what I should do."

"Well, first your assistant should organize your office and be ready to drop everything when you need *anything*," Diego forcefully insisted. "This isn't the old days where you had Chase be everything from your errand boy to the doorman at the parties. You need to hire people to do all those things. Get what's her name hiring, give her a list of what is expected right away. If she can't cut it then replace her."

"You make it sound so easy as if I can find the ideal person with a snap of a finger," Jolene countered. "It's not that easy."

"Then make *her* be what you want," Diego sat forward in his chair. "We have a business to run, Jolene. We still need to plan the parties, as well as get organized, so your assistant must balance her work. It is up to her to figure out how to get the job done."

"Which ones, you talk of so many things," Jolene seemed to lose some of her original steam as she opened her laptop, "We have two party planners starting tomorrow."

"Make a list of what they need to do."

"And the others? You want boy parties? Ones for straight people? I don't know anymore, Diego," She referred to the various sex parties that had caused their company to grow rapidly in a short period. Originally geared toward women interested in experimenting with the same-sex in a safe, confidential environment, the underground events were extremely popular prompting Diego's decision to expand their business. An important investor was backing them and wanted everything up and running immediately.

"Eventually, yes," Diego agreed. "First we are going to reestablish ourselves then raise the prices next month. These new party planners will work on their own schedule but will be responsible for all the details, keeping this business running. There's no more of you planning everything, Jolene, you will oversee and oversee only. In the future, you will only watch the others, watch the numbers and look at ways to expand what is working and decrease what is not. Jolene," He leaned forward and touched her hand, his voice softened. "I want to make your job easier, not more difficult. I'm not saying there won't be stress but you won't have to do *everything* anymore."

"But right now, it's a lot," She sighed as her eyes watered, her voice softened as did her whole disposition. "I don't know where to start."

"I understand," Diego clasped her hand. "Chase," his voice grew stronger as he looked toward his assistant. "Can you go get what's her name, Jolene's assistant, we must talk to her," his eyes returned to Jolene's face, "Together, we will talk to her."

Chase rose from his seat while Diego spoke to his sister in Spanish. Leaving the room to return to Jolene's office, he found Beverly looking out the window, her voice hushed, she spoke on a cell phone.

"....to do, it's crazy, maybe I can't-

"Excuse me," Chase interrupted and she swung around, her eyes large and frightened, she quickly ended the call.

"I'm sorry, I.."

"I don't care," Chase spoke honestly, his voice gentle. "Jolene and Diego want to talk to you."

She appeared apprehensive. "Are they going to fire me?"

Chase studied her face and although he knew he should show kindness, he also knew that women sometimes misinterpreted that as an invitation to bond. He didn't want to become her confidant. "Not if you do your job." His words were direct and to the point. "They're in the boardroom."

She didn't reply but walked ahead of him and he noted how painfully thin she was; he had never found really skinny women attractive but viewed them as unshapely and weak. He could already see that her frailness reflected her personality.

Returning to the boardroom, Diego shot him a look that was almost pleading. Jumping up from his chair, he almost ran into Beverly as he focused his attention on Chase. The new assistant sat down while Diego squeezed out the door and in a hushed voice began to speak, "Oh *amigo,* I have to sort out this shitshow before my sister loses her *mind.* Can you look around the office to make sure everyone is doing something? Just, you know, check in, try to look intimidating. Well," his eyes glanced over Chase's body. "Be yourself. You know what to do."

With that, he slipped back into the boardroom and closed the door. Chase turned around and glanced toward the reception area where the remaining three people worked together. Running on a skeleton staff, they only had the essentials hired; someone to take care of accounting and payroll, another person for marketing, and one more to handle reception and customer service; they were all jobs he had once assisted Jolene with, at least to a degree, but this was a whole other level.

He couldn't remember their names and therefore felt awkward approaching them, only vaguely recalling each from the interviews he sat in on, something Diego insisted that he do to make sure Jolene didn't hire someone who was 'terrible'; It was probably better he hadn't been available to interrogate the interviewees.

Deciding that the new staff didn't need monitoring, he instead headed toward Diego's office. Even at first glance, he could see that the room was substantially more organized than the rest, with only a MacBook and lamp on his desk, both still in boxes. As Chase entered the room, he saw that there were no overflowing garbage cans, no papers piled but then, he stopped in his tracks. There was a second desk; his desk.

For the first time since moving to the new city, Chase felt overwhelmed. A sudden tightness grasped his chest and began to squeeze and he broke out in a cold sweat, as if his body were attempting to send an intense message. It took him a minute to calm down, his legs still heavy as he walked to the new desk and sat behind it. Closing his eyes for a moment, he struggled with the million thoughts that were taking over his mind.

They would be together all day. Not only was Chase sharing an office with Diego, until he was able to find his own apartment, they were also sharing a living space. Granted, his boss lived in a beautiful, luxurious condo in the downtown area, so it wasn't exactly a hardship. However, as much as his brain attempted to rationalize it, his body continued to send waves of anxiety through him as if to scream a message he wasn't yet able to understand.

Diego suddenly breezed into the room, whistling a top 40 song they had listened to on the way to work that morning, as if he hadn't a care in the world. He shot Chase a humored glance as he passed by and headed for his own desk.

"Sitting on the job already!" He teased and focused on the new laptop on his desk. "Ah! My new MacBook! It's a beautiful day! Too bad Apple didn't make cars, that would make my car decision much easier."

"I think they are,"

"Ha?" Diego turned around, his eyebrows shot up and he appeared defenseless. "Oh yes, that's right, but it won't be on the market anytime soon."

His smile was sincere and he quickly looked away.

"Everything out there," Diego asked as he walked around his desk, "Is it okay?"

"Yes, from what I can tell."

Diego nodded and opened the box and pulled out the Macbook, carefully inspecting it.

Replacing the computer in the box, he looked at Chase, "This is for you. It's your new computer."

"Thank you but, it's not necessary. I already have one."

"That piece of shit," Diego glanced at the laptop bag that sat in the corner. "Nah, we can't have the best and give you a cheap toy from the bargain store. Take it to your desk and see what you think."

"So this is my desk?" Chase asked as he rose from the seat.

"Yes."

"In your office?"

Diego studied his face for a moment, his brown eyes appearing defensive as Chase approached. "You shared an office with Jolene, did you not?"

"Yes, I mean, I thought you would want some privacy for meetings or whatever," He replied hesitantly and took the MacBook that Diego passed him. "I don't want to get in the way."

"Nonsense, you'll be at the meetings," Diego insisted.

"Ok," Chase spoke uncertainly and glanced down at the new computer in his hands, "Thanks for this, Diego."

With an impish grin, Diego didn't reply but merely sat down.

CHAPTER THREE

The pace at the office increased as the days moved forward; interviews were held, meetings were had and Chase saw his job duties change day-to-day; sometimes hour to hour. It felt like he was on a never-ending, frantic merry-go-round that didn't stop for a second, only slowed down from time to time. His work days were often long and followed by a trip to a gym on the way home. Although his body was often exhausted at that point in the evening, Chase welcomed a few minutes away from his new coworkers and for that matter, Diego.

His comfortable living arrangements and busy schedule made it difficult to search for a new apartment. By the time his days ended, the last thing Chase wanted to do was more research, even though it was to his benefit. Then again, was it? He lived in a luxurious condo, comfortable and beautiful, with large windows in the living room that looked out over the city's downtown and filled with new, plush furniture that was simple, yet refreshing after living in homes that mostly consisted of second-hand offerings. The kitchen was clean, compact, his bedroom small, yet inviting and both he and Diego had their own bathrooms, something that Chase appreciated.

Although he thought living with Diego would be awkward, the first two weeks were so busy, that he actually spent very little time with his new boss. He noted that Jolene hadn't extended an offer for him to stay with her, something that stung a bit when he considered it but at the same time, it made sense. She was a private person and although they were close, sometimes he felt as though he didn't know her at all. Her private life was a mystery.

Diego was similar. He didn't discuss many areas of his life unless they involved a good story. He loved telling stories. Although they were sometimes saturated in exaggeration, there was something in his enthusiasm and energy that drew you in and always made you smile. Diego had a charisma that many could only dream of; a personality that made him easy to be around, even when he was mad. His passion toward life never ended nor did his appreciation of 'the small things'. He would notice the sun setting at nighttime and comment on it or the details in a simple meal at a nearby, family restaurant. He was observant and always reached for the positive, even when he was tired, even when frustrated, even when he had a hint of sadness in his eyes.

"It has been a successful week, has it not, my friend?" Diego asked Chase as they were preparing to leave the office on the first Friday night after opening. Most doors were locked; except for Jolene's office, where she continued to work. "We made great strides, we sorted out our plan for the business and the website, you know, except for minor details and we already have a few new parties booked. We will be, as they say, a *hit*."

His enthusiasm was contagious, Diego's devilish smile settled into more of a pucker as he glanced toward his sister's office. "Jolene, are you coming with us? We need to go out and celebrate!"

"Celebrate, Diego, I still have work to do and I-

"Leave it!" He insisted and strode toward her office while loosening his tie. "Jolene, it's after 6, you've been here since before 6 this morning, time to go!"

"I just-

"No no no! Do it later. Take it home. I don't care, you need a break," His voice was calm for a man that rarely relaxed. Everything fell silent. "You've done well this week, come out for dinner with us. It'll be fun."

She reluctantly agreed.

After making sure doors were closed and locked, that lights were turned off and the alarm turned on, the three headed to a downtown bistro that Diego insisted was one of the best in Toronto. Unfortunately, he hadn't anticipated that the restaurant would be full on a Friday night, requiring a reservation, so they settled on a pizza place that was nearby. Although Diego turned his nose up at the idea, he gave into Jolene's insistence that the intoxication aroma that escaped the establishment as they passed was enough to encourage her rumbling stomach.

The three sat next to a window at the back, fortunately away from the family with the three small children who were loud, obnoxious, not to mention messy. Jolene had to step around a slap of pepperoni on the floor as they passed, her heels barely missing a string of dried up cheese. Fortunately, the family left shortly after their arrival.

"My God, people and their children," Jolene's forehead wrinkled as she talked, the three of them watched a hapless waitress cleaning up a mess around the table, her expression displaying the frustration that Chase greatly understood. Having three young children of his own, especially after a period where he stayed home with them, he was sympathetic to her situation. "Do they not understand that not all of us finds them as....I don't know, how you say, *enjoyable?*"

"Oh, who cares, they're gone," Diego waved his hand in the air, his eyes searched the room. "Where's that waitress? I want to get some wine. We can celebrate Jolene not breaking her neck on her way to the table as well as our success this week."

"*Dios mío!*" Jolene shook her head and seemed to relax in her chair, taking a deep breath, her eyes suddenly overwhelmingly exhausted. "I do not understand this culture sometimes. It can be so...difficult... different. Yes, different, from how we were brought up."

"We were brought up in a very different country, Jolene," Diego injected as his focus returned to his sister. "A dangerous area, our parents had to be strict so we were safe. Plus religious," his focused turned to Chase. "Our mother? Catholic. Read the Bible every day, so we were not to misbehave. If we were bad," he rose his hand as if to slap an invisible figure on the table. "There were consequences."

"*Sí,*" Jolene nodded vigorously. "We would not be like those children." She pointed to the now, abandoned table, as the young woman finished cleaning it. "We would get a slap in the car. Not that this one," She pointed toward Diego. "ever listened. He was crazy."

A smug grin covered Diego's face as he avoided eye contact with both, his eyebrows rose and fell and he muttered, "Still am, I'm told." He cleared his throat, his eyes suddenly pouncing on an approaching waitress like a cat on its prey. He ordered them each a glass of wine and within minutes, she returned with their beverages.

"Ah! Here we are! Thank you, *señorita*." He smiled and winked at her.

The waitress blushed and shyly replied. "You're welcome. Are you ready to order?"

"I think so," he glanced around the table. As it turns out, the menu was quite extensive and although Chase went for the healthy option of chicken and a salad, Diego and Jolene decided to share a pizza.

"And," Diego added as he passed her their menus back. "We would like a shot of something, I don't care what at this point," his attention jumped from Jolene to Chase, who merely shrugged, for he rarely drank.

"Tequila," Jolene answered and the three agreed as Chase took a small sip of his wine, something that didn't get past Diego, as he took a long drink of the red liquid. "So Chase, tell me something, do you avoid drinking because you are health conscious or is it because you're native and have a drinking problem."

"*Diego!*" Jolene snapped, her eyes suddenly wide open. "That is racist! You cannot say such things!"

"I'm not being racist, Jolene," He insisted, turning to face her and away from Chase, who was on his other side. "But you know, they do say that the aboriginal community has a problem with alcohol, I just thought he was being...cautious."

Chase laughed while Jolene's eyes continued to darken.

"It's okay, Jolene," Chase replied and relaxed in his chair "It's actually neither of those reasons, I've never been much of a drinker." He smirked and while Diego appeared intrigued with his answer, Jolene gave him an apologetic look. "And I'm only half native from my mother's side. My dad was white."

"Still, he should not ask these things," Jolene muttered. "You have to be careful, Diego. People get offended sometimes, you know?"

"Ah, he don't care," Diego casually pointed at Chase, who shook his head just as the waitress returned with three shots on her tray. "Honestly, my friend, I'm not seeing the 'white' in you except when you talk."

Chase merely grinned, glancing down at his tanned hands, he noted that he was almost the same color as Jolene, while Diego's skin tone was lighter.

Almost as soon as the shots touched the table, the three friends made a toast and sunk back the tequila. Chase made a face but followed Jolene's instructions; licking the salt from his hand and sucking on a piece of lime.

Diego didn't flinch but giggled as he watched Chase's expression, while Jolene's eyes watered. "This one, they do not make a good tequila. It was just, you know, okay."

"You got that right," Diego pushed his shot glass aside. "It was mediocre at best."

"What's mediocre?" Jolene asked as she checked her phone.

"Jolene, you need to improve your English, it's not good," Diego let out a sigh. "You need someone to help you."

"I'm doing fine," Jolene snapped back. "I am learning, every day, right Chase?" She turned toward him and before he could reply, "What is mediocre?"

"It means, it was ok, not great."

"Well, that is what I said, is it not?" Jolene complained. "I said it was *just ok*. Why do you have to be all fancy talking, Diego? You want to make me feel stupid?"

"Don't get so defensive, Jolene," Diego appeared frustrated and changed the topic. "So Chase, how did your meeting with the Italian go today?"

"Sylvana? She was...ok, I guess."

"*Mediocre?*" Jolene spoke up and flashed a look at Diego.

"Doesn't really work in this context, Jolene." He countered.

"Hmm..."

"She's not exactly friendly," Chase spoke honestly. "But she gave me a list of places to check out, message boards where people talk about their fetishes, some that specifically talk about our parties, some from other countries, where they already have the same parties as us, it is pretty interesting."

"Very good," Diego nodded. "I had the Italian checked out, she's good. I don't know, though, I'm still cautious, she asks a lot of questions."

"Her name is Sylvana not 'The Italian' and we do not have to provide her with answers, you know," Jolene spoke up as she sipped from her glass. "We do not have to tell her about things before this. We were experimenting at first, just doing some work to see what took off. We did not have a 'real' business necessarily so, it is ok. We pay our taxes, right? That is all your government cares about, I think."

Chase nodded.

"The next problem we have with the government is me becoming citizens," Diego insisted. "Even if I were to marry, apparently the Canadian government can be picky. I don't understand, I bring work here."

"Maybe that will help?" Jolene suggested.

"I don't know," Diego spoke honestly.

"I think I will be fine. I must wait." Jolene admitted. "You, Diego, *you* may have trouble."

Chase watched a look between them and took another drink of wine.

CHAPTER FOUR

Diego disappeared later that night. He gave no indication where he was going, only sending a text after the fact, instructing Chase to put his Tahitian Lime on the balcony during the day and bring it in before nighttime. The dwarf tree was awkward to move and wasn't even producing any limes but Diego had obsessively fussed over it since bringing it home earlier that week. He enthusiastically researched every detail, carefully inspecting the leaves and in his text, making it clear to Chase exactly how much water to put on it and when. His attachment to the plant was somewhat unusual but humorous at the same time.

Chase spent the weekend feeling drained. As much as he wanted to meet new people, his ambitions were lacking. Other than going to the gym, running errands and talking to his kids on Skype, he spent much of his weekend looking for an apartment. The options were endless and yet, limited at the same time. He didn't know the city well enough to live too far from work but their office was located in a pricey area. For something that seemed so simple in a vast city, it proved difficult. It wasn't just looking at the attributes online, he was also researching the location in relation to work, commute times and transportation. His frustration grew and on Sunday afternoon, as he slammed the laptop shut and pushed it aside.

Having sold his car before moving, Chase was itching to buy a new one but his budget and lack of parking in the city made it undesirable. It was an expense that could be put on the back burner until he was more settled. At least he had a drive with Diego; who seemed to have no difficulty finding his way around any place and certainly wasn't intimidated by a new city.

By Sunday evening Chase's apathy fell into a depression and he dreaded Diego's return home. Knowing that he would fly in the condo with a roaring energy that should've been inspiring, it would most likely have the opposite effect. Although Chase knew he should've been happy; living in a new city, working for a thriving company with endless opportunities ahead, something inside of him felt stagnant. It was the same part of him that succumbed to a lackluster life while still a teenager, after getting a mere stranger pregnant at a party. Although that probably would've been a difficult journey for anyone, being forced into a loveless marriage drove away his joy.

It didn't matter that those days were long gone or that divorce proceedings had started, a part of Chase was still caught in a web he couldn't get out of and even though he was free of those old chains, he remained restricted. That was one of the reasons why he loved his job. Lost in an office environment, busy with endless tasks, he felt valuable again; as if his life had meaning. Diego and Jolene counted on him and neither took his loyalty for granted.

It was only at nighttime, as he lay in bed that Chase's mind traveled to that secret place; his former best friend Maggie, whom he once fell in love with was now just a memory, their journey together complete. Her younger sister Kelsey, who lived a trainwreck lifestyle was infuriating and yet her sexual prowess had never escaped him. His fantasies of both often appeared in the dead of the night when he felt most vulnerable, his body sensitive to the yearnings he avoided throughout the day.

His loneliness ran deep. Disconnected from his family, Chase felt like the lone balloon that escaped the group, floating away, rising in the air with vigor until one day he realized that he had drifted so far away. Would he suddenly pop or would he float around aimlessly until forgetting where he started?

In many ways, Jolene and Diego were his new family. They included him in everything and like a set of parents, they protected him. There were details that they circumvented when talking about the business, details that didn't quite add up; such as why they recently decided to disassemble the former American office. Always led to believe that it was a thriving business, it seemed to fold as soon as Diego decided to move to Toronto. Now, there was no talk of American parties and although questions were burning in his throat, something told Chase it was best to not ask.

When Diego did get home late Sunday night, his primary concern was the lime tree. Rushing through living room, barely saying hello to Chase, he touched the soil and carefully inspected the leaves of the plant. Once satisfied that it had been well taken care of, Diego joined Chase on the couch and let out a loud, exhausted sigh as he sat down.

"Busy weekend?" Chase assumed this was probably the safest way to broach the topic and yet, he felt like Diego's personal life was well-guarded. He suspected his weekend away was with a lover because he hinted at having many but yet, this was a side of his life that he kept very quiet. He didn't kiss and tell.

"I had to go to the American office and make sure everything was closed, *terminado,* all loose ends tied up," He rubbed his closed eyes with one hand while loosening his tie with the other. "I'm fucking beat."

"I could've helped out," Chase cautiously offered and for a long moment, it didn't appear that Diego would reply. He sniffed loudly, his eyes still closed, he suddenly sat up straight and yawned.

"No no, that's fine, I took care of things" he spoke airily, his eyes barely opened as he stretched. "Everything is fine and besides," Diego's gaze fixated on Chase. "You had to look after my lime tree."

A grin crossed Chase's lips and he nodded.

"And you, how was your weekend?" Diego turned toward Chase and leaned against the back of the couch. "Do anything fun? Wild? Did you get sex?"

Chase laughed in spite of himself. "No to all of that, I did laundry, went to the gym, bought groceries and looked for an apartment." He noted Diego raised an eyebrow at the last word and sat up a bit straighter. "Nothing very exciting this weekend."

"You should be out," Diego pointed toward the patio doors. "Out having fun! Living life, learning about new people, fucking your brains out and why you stay here, locked away in a condo like some *Stepford* wife, cleaning all weekend. We have a maid."

"I'm hardly a Stepford wife and I didn't clean all weekend, I just did laundry," Chase laughed. "I did normal stuff that people do on the weekend."

"Maybe your people but for me, I work hard all week, I want to play hard when I can," Diego insisted and jumped up from the couch and rushed back to the door, grabbing his suitcase. "That is what life is about."

"From the sounds of it, you worked all weekend," Chase commented as he turned just fast enough to see Diego roll his suitcase across the floor, behind the couch and toward his bedroom.

"Not it all, I played too," Diego sang out as he went into his room and closed the door. Chase didn't see him again until the next morning when he found him sitting at the island in the kitchen, his laptop already opened. Squinting, he leaned in looking at something as Chase walked behind him and toward the coffee pot.

"Morning," Chase quietly said as he poured a cup of coffee and went into the fridge to find the cream. For a minute, Diego didn't reply, appearing caught up in whatever was on the screen. He finally looked up and gave a quick smile.

"*Buenos días* my friend," His eyes roamed over Chase's body as he approached the island with a coffee in hand. "You look very dapper this morning."

Chase glanced down at his suit. "I look the same as I do every morning."

"Maybe you look dapper every morning," Diego spoke seductively then returned his attention to the laptop. "I see here that Jolene has worked steadily all weekend. The parties are booking fast and soon, we will need to hire more people to take care of them, this is good news for us."

"Definitely," Chase agreed and took a sip of the coffee that was more satisfying than what he often bought on the run. Diego was as picky about his coffee as he was to the care of his Tahitian lime tree. He was particular about details and expected the same of everyone else.

"This," Diego said as he closed his laptop, "This will be a beautiful day."

"You say that every day."

"But I am right, am I not?" Diego reminded him as he pushed the MacBook aside and grabbed his own cup of coffee. "It is what you make of it. It is what you believe."

Chase envied his enthusiasm, his endless optimism toward life and in a way, wished he would someday be able to do the same. It was getting to that place that wasn't so easy.

"So what is this about you finding an apartment," Diego asked, his eyebrows crinkled. "What is your rush?"

"I don't want to overstay my welcome," Chase spoke evenly, taking another long drink of coffee and checking his phone for the time.

"What do you mean, overstay your welcome?" Diego interrupted, his eyes narrowing in on Chase. "Who says you are overstaying your welcome? Did I?"

"No, but.."

"Then do not worry," Diego shrugged and twisted his mouth. "Do I look worried?

"No, but come on, you probably want some privacy."

"There is no privacy with family."

Chase opened his mouth to reply but hesitated. He knew it would be disrespectful if he pointed out that he wasn't family, that really, he hadn't known Diego all that long and that he didn't particularly want to live there when he started to bring home boyfriends. That would be awkward.

"Chase," Diego leaned forward on the table, his eyes doubled in size while his expression grew serious. A faint scent of cologne filled the air as he moved a little closer. "You're welcome until you are ready to go. Just get used to the city, see what you like, where you prefer to live. You haven't been here long. There's no rush."

"Thank you." Chase quietly replied.

"Besides, if I'm not here, who's going to look after my lime tree?" A lopsided grin twitched his lip, his eyes full of mystery as if words were hidden deep inside but he would not allow them to breathe. There was a certain temptation that lurked beneath the surface, a sign that he wanted more from Chase than a chaste 'family' relationship but yet, he kept it carefully placed in a corner, unopened.

When the two had originally met the previous year, Chase had been quite intimidated by Diego. He gave the impression of this tough, mob-like personality from the movies, a real life Tony Montana, a ladies' man but his first impression quickly evaporated when Diego kissed him. Stunned, Chase was at a loss for words. He had never had a man hit on him before and felt slightly idiotic for not sensing the attraction since in retrospect, hadn't it been obvious? Hadn't he been entranced by the atmosphere, the bliss of being wanted by someone in a way that had only rendered disastrous when it was women? He was briefly playing with the concept that maybe he was bisexual but the idea quickly slipped away. He was just paranoid. Still, it left an elephant in the room.

Although most days, it was easy to ignore, there were awkward moments when the question lurked around, veiled in silence, there were some things that were too difficult to discuss unless you are ready. This was one of them.

Not that Diego brought it up either. His eyes hinted at it. His gestures were smooth, graceful and silently reminding Chase that if allowed, he could have a different kind of life than if he left the condo and moved into his own dank, little apartment. There was a certain vulnerability that could be seen now that they shared a place; something he never would've guessed when they first met. It was something the rest of the world rarely saw and it was a side that Diego was slowly allowing to seep into their days together, both at work and at home. There were many secret. There was so much he didn't yet know.

CHAPTER FIVE

The office environment began to relax over time. The staff grew comfortable with one another as their duties became more clearly defined, their roles within the company more deeply understood. There was a sense of pride and bonding that formed after getting through the first couple of weeks together, having set up the office from scratch, the staff worked as a team with the same goal in mind.

Where Jolene's assistant Beverly became more confident and serious as the days moved forward, Sylvana appeared more aggressive and vocal, proving herself a leader. The original secretary quit and was replaced by a woman in her early 20s, Deborah, who wore glasses and dressed quite conservatively compared to Jolene and Sylvana; both of which loved to flaunt their curves and regularly wore high heels to work. Deborah wore flats, dress plainly and although was friendly, she was also eerily quiet.

The accountant Benjamin was a Filipino man whom Diego admired for his diligence. Always keeping everything on track, aware of government forms and rules for business with knowledge beyond his position, he was able to make recommendations to both Jolene and Diego on other elements of business. Smart, savvy, Benjamin was also quiet and professional, never appearing stressed or frustrated.

The party planners, Cleo and Raymond were rarely in the office but kept the events running smoothly and to Jolene and Diego's satisfaction. Since their hours were quite erratic, they mainly worked remotely.

Although Diego and Jolene originally talked of hiring more staff, they were hesitant to move ahead too quickly. Things were still pretty new and there would be an adjustment period even though their plans were well beyond the current situation.

"Where we once had larger parties directed only toward women, we now have more smaller, intimate parties where the customer have more say in what they want," Diego insisted in a regular Friday afternoon meeting. He stood at the head of the boardroom and spoke to their small staff. "It's not the direction that I thought we would go in, but here we are...give the people what they want."

"There's still a huge demand for the original parties with just women," Sylvana jumped in, her eyes glanced around the table before returning to her laptop screen. "People know us as the company that does the '*girl on girl*' parties." She briefly made eye contact with Chase, who remained silent, as he often did in the meetings.

"Yes, but through time, people will learn we are so much more," Diego insisted as he gestured toward his own laptop. "That's *our* job, to make them see us differently. Specifically, it's *your* job, Sylvana. That's why you are in charge of marketing, it's for you to decide how to do this."

She frowned and avoided his eyes while Diego ignored her reaction and turned to Jolene. "Our numbers, they aren't good with the gay men yet?" he shrugged. "I would've thought the complete opposite, to be honest. I thought that would be our biggest demographic as soon as we expanded. I don't understand."

"We are in *competition* with another company," Jolene spoke slowly, something she did when concerned about her English. Chase bit his lip anxiously, sensing her discomfort. Jolene occasionally struggled with finding the correct English words, especially when she was nervous or not having a good day. "There is another place that has these type of parties, Diego and they are well-known, unlike us. We need to do something to bring that business here."

"Undersell them?" The suggestion came from Benjamin who leaned ahead in his chair, taking everything in stride. He sniffed, his lips fell into a frown. "Maybe we have one big blowout to introduce ourselves to their community, have a cheap night or something that the other parties don't have and see what happens."

"I say stick with what we know and put a hold on all that," Sylvana spoke up, her eyes glued to her laptop, she ignored Benjamin, who appeared unfazed by her comments. He merely shrugged and shared a look with Diego, who was taking it all in. He silently nodded.

"Beverly and I will research this," Jolene piped up and closed her laptop. "Maybe we should wait, maybe we need to do now, I don't know."

"All right, well I guess that's something we have to look at a little more closely and decide next week," Diego abruptly stuck his hands in his pockets and walked toward the window, quickly pivoting around. "Deborah, I invited you to this meeting as well because you are, in many ways, the face of the company. If someone comes through those doors or calls, you are the first person they talk to or see and the person dealing with customer service."

Nodding, her eyes flickered between Chase and Diego, unlike the others, she had no laptop or notebook with her for the meeting.

"I need you to be the eyes and ears," Diego pointed toward the door. "What's going on in the office? Who's calling? What are they asking? What kind of emails are coming in? I want to know everything that seems relevant. I want you to be on top of everything."

His eyes were dark, pressing as they narrowed in on her and she silently nodded, appearing nervous and quickly looked away.

"And the rest of you," Diego abruptly continued, "I expect the same. Loyalty is important to me and I want to know if you see or hear anything that concerns you, then you must bring it to my attention. If you have any thoughts, any new ideas, you bring it to me or Jolene. We all want the same thing here and that is for this business to be a success. It has been so far but let's make sure it's not a novelty that passes. We have to keep on top of things, be inventive with new ideas. We can't fall behind or someone else will move in and swallow us up."

There was silence around the table. Chase could sense a discomfort, it was something he also knew Diego thrived on. He enjoyed making people uncomfortable and in fact, seemed to believe it kept staff on their toes, a bit on edge, which made perfect sense. He had that effect on Chase at first too but that faded over time. He somehow doubted it would with his coworkers. He sensed their intimidation. He saw it when he glanced around the table; the sheepish looks, the nervousness as they shuffled in their chairs. Deborah's face was flushed, as it often was, he suspected she was having difficulty with this particular setting.

The meeting ended and the others left. Chase remained in his chair, as did Jolene while Diego stomped toward the window, taking a deep breath, he suddenly seemed unexpectedly vulnerable, tired, for the first time since their move to Toronto. It was a fleeting moment but it hadn't gone unnoticed.

"Diego, you must relax," Jolene spoke up and reached for her bottle of water. "Be careful, they may not like, how you say? Scare them."

"They have to know who's boss, Jolene," Diego swung around and shrugged. "You can't let them get too comfortable or nothing will get done around here. We can't afford for them to get lazy."

"I don't think they are going to get lazy, Diego but you got to not, I don't know," She stopped and her eyes shifted toward Chase. "What do you say? Scare?"

"Intimidate?" Chase attempted to guess what she meant. "Is that what you mean?"

"That's it, that's what I mean," Jolene spoke excitedly. "Intimidate. You intimidate, Diego."

"I do not," He made a face as he edged back to the table and sat in his chair. "I'm just being a boss. You got to be tough if you want something done. You need to put a fire under people or they do nothing. They cannot get too comfortable."

"That's why so many businesses fail," Diego continued, his ring finger tapped on the table. "They don't listen to their customers and they get lazy. We are not to do either. We are going to push ahead even when we don't know where to go next. We have to be strong and listen to what the customers say then give them what they want. That's what we have to do."

"I agree," Jolene sigh. "I agree. I guess you are right about that one. I just assume that we all want this to succeed but yes, we need to make sure to move ahead."

"Chase, you're the quiet one," Diego turned his attention to the opposite side of the table from Jolene. "You don't say much in the meetings, why not?"

"I don't have anything to say."

"Ah, the strong silent type!"

"Diego, Chase never has much to say. That's a good thing because he observes," Jolene commented and pointed toward her eyes. "He sees everything."

"Chase, what did you see today, I must know." Diego pushed his chair ahead and placed his elbows on the table. "What did you observe in this room?"

"I...I guess what Jolene was saying, people are intimidated."

"But tell me your impression of each person at this table."

"Well," Chase cleared his throat and thought for a moment. "I think Sylvana is controlling, tough, determined. I think Beverly is compliant. I think-

"Wait wait, what?" Jolene cut in, waving her hands in the air. "What is *compliant?*"

"Ah, Jolene!" Diego waved his hands in the air, frustration rang through his voice. "You have to learn English better."

"I am trying!" She snapped and turned her attention back to Chase.

"Compliant means to kind of go along with whatever people want and not question anything."

"She's soft." Jolene nodded and pointed to her chest.

"Yes, I suppose that is another way to put it."

"And Benjamin?" Diego asked, his eyes darted in Chase's direction.

"I like him. He's a smart guy. He's calm, easy to talk to and I think he could do pretty much anything. He seems resourceful and hard-working."

Jolene nodded and smiled, while Diego gave a stiff smile.

"And Deborah?"

"She's...I don't know," Chase thought for a moment. "There's something odd about her but I can't pinpoint it yet."

"I think emotion problems," Jolene answered. "Maybe she break up with boyfriend."

At the end of the table, Diego cringed as his sister spoke. Chase couldn't help but wondered if she did it on purpose to irritate him but agreed with Jolene.

"Maybe, I don't know. I guess it's too soon to know."

"It'll come out," Diego insisted and stood up. "It always does."

Jolene agreed. "It does."

Chase remained silent.

CHAPTER SIX

"Are you still living with the gay man?" Angel's question was predictably sharp, automatically making Chase paranoid that Diego could hear, even though he was on the other side of the room. However, one glance proved that he was much too preoccupied with something Benjamin was showing him on an iPad. Holding the phone tighter to his ear, he slipped out of the room and into the staff room.

A new girl who was appropriately his age sat at the table. He hadn't had a chance to meet her but assumed she was one of the two new party planners that Jolene hired in a panic, when business suddenly took an unexpected spike the previous week. Although dressed professionally, if not somewhat bohemian in nature, she wore her hair it two small, blonde pigtails and was cute, reminding him more of a teenage girl than an adult woman. He didn't really want her to overhear his conversation but felt it would've been awkward to suddenly leave the room.

"Yes, but not in the way you're suggesting," He spoke in a hushed voice as he sat at the end of the table, turning away from the new girl.

"I wasn't suggesting anything," Angel snapped and he could immediately picture his sister's brooding face. Her personality was heavy, always bordering on dreary. The two never had much of a relationship and in fact, it was the first time they had spoken in months. "I was asking because when you have your own place *if* you get your own place, I would like to visit."

Chase frowned. He sensed that her interest in visiting had more to do with his location than actually seeing her younger brother. Rather than comment on that, he instead attacked her insinuation that he would stay at Diego's forever.

"I will be moving as soon as I can find a new place," Chase spoke evenly, not allowing himself to fall into her trap.

Angel always degraded his lifestyle. In high school, she put down his relationship with then-girlfriend Lucy Willis, suggesting he only used her, to get his 'rocks off' then tossed her aside; even though she had dumped Chase, not the other way around. When he accidentally got Audrey Neil pregnant after a post-breakup romp at a party, his sister suggested that he was merely an animal who didn't prepare for the consequences. Now that he was living in the same condo as a homosexual, he assumed she was implying that he was gay.

"Right...sure," she was clearly mocking him but Chase refused to play her game. There was no sense. His relationship with Angel had always been strained and at that point, he saw little reason to make any effort.

He took a deep breath. "Is there anything else, Angel?"

"Have you talked to mom lately?"

"No."

"*Will* you talk to mom *sometime?*"

He ignored her question. "Is there anything else Angel?"

A vulnerability snuck in her voice. "No, I guess not, I just-

"I have to go," Chase cut her off. "I'm at work."

"Ok....I....have you talked to your kids lately?"

"Did you just call to take inventory of my fucking life?" He snapped and the new girl let out a smothered laugh and quickly covered it up by taking a drink of her coffee. Chase caught himself and cleared his throat. "Of course I did. I do every week. I have to go."

Disconnecting the call, he gave an apologetic look to the new girl. "Sorry...family stuff."

"No, I'm sorry. I didn't mean to listen in." She spoke with a French accent and her lips lifted into a smile. Her hazel eyes shone as she turned slightly, to face him. "I just caught that last comment and it made me laugh. Are you Italian?"

"I- no, do I *look* Italian?" He asked evenly, sliding the iPhone into his pocket.

"No, it's just that my ex, he was Italian and his family were always in his business and he said that was normal," She shrugged awkwardly and began to stutter. "You know, calling, checking in on him. I don't know...I just thought..or assumed maybe you were too."

"No," He shook his head and stood up, "I don't think that's just an Italian thing."

"Ummm," She blushed and nodded.

"I'm Chase, by the way," He reached out to shake her hand and a relieved smile crossed her face as she did the same. Her fingers were small, soft, her handshake gentle as she appeared to relax.

"I'm Gracie."

"Gracie?"

"Benoit. Gracie Benoit."

Chase slowly let go of her hand and merely nodded.

"It's French."

"You're French? From Quebec?"

"Actually from the Maritimes," She referred to Canada's east coast and Chase continued to nod, regretting he hadn't paid more attention in high school geography class. He didn't know much about the Atlantic provinces outside of the fact that many people from that region traveled to Alberta to work. "New Brunswick."

"Interesting," Chase awkwardly commented.

"Is it?" Gracie asked skeptically.

Chase shrugged. "*I* think it's interesting."

"Not really, I'm from some little community nobody has heard of," Gracie said and gave him an awkward smile. "Or cares about."

"*I'm* from a little town that nobody's heard of or cares about either," He offered and grinned, "in Alberta."

"People like Alberta, lots of oil," she seemed to warm up as Chase made his way toward the door.

"Not where I come from," Chase reached for the doorknob and cleared his throat. "There's nothing there. Trust me, that's why I'm here."

"Ditto." She giggled and his smile grew.

"Nice to meet you, Gracie," He left the room and turned toward the office to find the door closed, something that seemed to happen more and more often, which in turn left Chase wandering around like an idiot. He decided to peek into Jolene's office. She was working on her laptop.

"Hello Chase," She called out glancing up from the screen. "Did you need to speak with me?"

He shook his head.

"Ah, he has the door closed again?" Jolene didn't even wait for his answer but rolled her eyes. "Come, sit!"

Following her instructions, he noted that Beverly wasn't around. As if reading his mind, Jolene was quick to reply.

"I send her out for a latte," Jolene shrugged. "Sometimes, I don't even want the latte, I don't want to see her, you know?"

"Maybe that's why Diego has the door closed," Chase said with a grin.

"Oh, he like you, that's why you live together," She raised her eyebrows.

"We don't *live* together, live together." Chase corrected her and noted the confusion on her face. "I mean, not, we aren't, you know…"

"I know, I know, you are not his boyfriend," Jolene let out a sharp laugh and pushed her chair back from the desk. "But you know, people might think if you stay there too long. Not that it matters and let's face it, my brother values your company."

"He does?" Chase asked. "I feel bad I haven't found a place yet. I'm sure he's just being polite."

"Have you ever known Diego to be polite?" She countered.

"True," Chase considered her question. "I mean, It is kind of nice being new in a city and having a roommate. If you want to call him that."

"You know, he likes you a lot Chase," She pushed her chair forward again and spoke in a hushed tone. "I don't say you should leave but, I think you must be careful. He might feel differently than you know. Like a boyfriend?"

She said the last word louder than the rest of the sentence and Chase glanced over his shoulder to make sure no one was near the door.

"Has he said that?" Chase muttered awkwardly suddenly feeling a sense of dread.

"No, I just know him," Jolene replied and gave him a sympathetic look. "I'm not saying to pack your bags tonight and leave, I mean, be careful. I know Diego comes across as this tough guy and nothing bothers him but, he holds a lot inside, you know? He doesn't talk much about anything serious. He just..he hid a lot in his life so that's normal to him."

Chase didn't know what to say and decided to remain silent.

"I'm sorry, I should not say, I don't know," Jolene spoke in a more hushed tone. "I feel he likes you a lot. I know you don't see him that way and you are not trying to mislead. But sometimes people like a companion even if it's not the way they want, you know?"

"Yes," Chase nodded. "I think so."

"Don't be scared away," Jolene continued. "I don't mean that either. I just...I know my brother. He's jumped from boy to boy to boy...but you, at first I think, I thought maybe he like the challenge, you know? Now, I think differently. I feel there's something more.."

"Chase!" Diego's voice bellowed out from the next office and Jolene clasped her mouth shut. The two of them exchanged looks.

"I don't think he hear," Jolene pointed toward her ears. "We talk low."

Chase didn't think so but still briefly considered her words as he returned to Diego's office. Inside, the same Colombian man who once represented excitement and power now seemed vulnerable and small as he studied Chase's face, his dark eyes were full of questions. He heard something, there was no doubt.

"Chase, can you close the door?" He spoke sternly and a chill filled the room. Without replying Chase followed his instructions before sitting across the desk from Diego. "I think we have a problem."

"Ok."

"The parties, they are doing good but I just went over the numbers with Benjamin and he thinks we may have to let someone go."

"Already?"

"Unfortunately, yes,"

"But shouldn't we wait and see?"

"We could but the problem is Jolene freaked out and hired those extra girls and we aren't consistently busy enough yet."

"Maybe we should focus on getting more business."

"That's Marketing and Sylvana's job and I'm not impressed with her lately," Diego made a face. "We should be on fire, especially with the gay men and we're not."

"It doesn't seem right that one of the planners get let go because Sylvana isn't doing her job efficiently."

"That's business," Diego shrugged. "So the new girl, Gracie, she's got to go."

Chase opened his mouth and looked away.

"What? You don't agree?" Diego asked letting out a loud sigh.

"I was talking to her in the break room and...I don't know."

"You *like* her?'

"Not in *that* way," Chase quickly replied. Thinking on his feet, he quickly added, "Look, she's bilingual, so that could be an asset."

"Oh," Diego made a face and opened a file on his desk, his eyes scanned a piece of paper and he nodded. "You're right. She speaks French, we better keep her then...the other girl hired the same day? I forget her name. Can you send her in?"

"Do you...have to talk to Jolene about this first?" Chase muttered and saw Diego's lips formed an O.

"Oh *amigo*, good point, she won't be happy with me if I make this decision without talking to her first. I'll go talk to her." He grabbed the file from his desk and hastily rushed toward the door. "What would I do without you, Chase?" He asked with a boisterous laugh before exiting the room.

Chase studied his hands and bit his lower lip. Jolene's words resurfaced and a heaviness filled his heart.

CHAPTER SEVEN

Jolene's words haunted him for the rest of the afternoon. When his own sister had suggested a cohabitation between him and Diego, Chase merely laughed it off but when Jolene made the same comment, it suddenly had more legitimacy. Was he comfortably settling into a life with Diego that was more than he intended? Was Diego content with having Chase close to him in any way he could, even if not in the intimate situation that he would've preferred? Was this obvious to everyone other than himself?

Suddenly he was very conscious of how people looked at him at both the office and the complex he lived in; did others assume they were together? Did people at work know that they lived together? Did they know that Diego was gay? He didn't discuss his personal life and in fact, gave a heterosexual vibe when he was out and about; flirting with women, his eyes preying on them from across the room as if he were desiring their company when in fact, he had no interest.

It was confusing and in a way, Chase wished Jolene hadn't broached the subject because it opened a whole can of worms that he couldn't deal with. Diego was his friend and of course he cared about him and enjoyed his company, but was he also sending him the wrong message? Should he be doing something differently? Bringing women home? Then again, Diego didn't bring men to the condo. Was that weird?

It was on the way home after work that night that Chase felt as though he should say something; but what? He didn't want to bring up what Jolene said but then again, had Diego overheard their conversation? If he had, there was no clear sign when he called Chase into his office.

In fact, he had seemed preoccupied with the information Benjamin had given him about the numbers.

"I think I need to look for a place this weekend," Chase broke the news while they sat in traffic, as the bright sun poured through the window. Up until that point, Diego had been unusually quiet, sunglasses hiding his eyes and his face expressionless. "It's been weeks and I-

"*Amigo, come on*, I've told you there is no rush," Diego replied in a tone that didn't carry any emotion. His fingers played with the buttons for the radio and 70s rock suddenly poured through the car. He sniffed and ran a hand through his dark hair, his lips shuffled uncomfortably. "You Americans worry too much about proper etiquette and stuff like *overstaying your welcome* as if there is such a thing when it's family. Come on! Don't worry! We've talked about this before."

Chase couldn't help but grin at Diego's flippant answer and his ability to cram Canadian and American culture into one group. It was funny how the two North American countries saw themselves as being so different and yet, to someone like Diego, they were exactly the same.

"You Canadians, always so polite all the time," Diego said with a frown and continued to play with the radio, "if you wish to leave, it's fine. Just say so, it's OK." Suddenly, Lynyrd Skynyrd filled the entire car and interrupted their conversation. "Hey Chase, you're from a redneck town, you must know this song." Diego teased.

"Diego, I didn't mean-

"You're probably too young," Diego continued and suddenly traffic moved forward and Diego returned his concentration to driving. Feeling his stomach turn, Chase reached forward, his fingers touched the buttons to lower the volume.

"Look, I wasn't trying to politely say anything," Chase said, hearing a rigidness in his voice that he hadn't intended. Suddenly, he was full of remorse for even bringing up the topic and wasn't sure of what to say. "I really *do* feel that maybe I've overstayed my welcome. I don't want to take advantage of your kindness."

"Chase, you're not taking advantage of anything," Diego replied and shrugged casually even though his body looked stiff and awkward when he did so, he seemed to jerk involuntarily, his attention pulled toward the left. Then like a tsunami, his words came flowing out rapidly.

"Look, Chase, I could hear some of your conversation with Jolene today and that's her ideas, it's not my own. I'm happy having you there and there's nothing strange about us living together and let's not make this weird, ok? It's not weird, just...just don't listen to her." Diego spoke so fast that he appeared to run out of breath. He was clearly agitated.

"Okay, its fine, I'm sorry and please," Chase replied and took a deep breath. "Don't get mad at Jolene. She didn't tell me to leave."

"But she *did* say something," Diego expressed some emotion in his voice. "I know my sister, she gets involved when she shouldn't. She always has."

"That's family."

"Does your sister get this involved in your life?"

Chase considered his conversation from earlier that day. "Not really, I mean, she takes a lot of stabs at my life but I, unlike Jolene, it's not from a loving place, it is cause she's miserable with herself. But I don't have a normal family."

Diego seemed to contemplate what Chase said and remained silent as the song ended and another Lynyrd Skynyrd one replaced it.

"Having a normal family isn't always great, my friend," Diego injected. "They want to look out for you even when you don't need it."

Chase didn't reply at first and when he finally did, his tone was soft. "Take it from someone who's pretty estranged from his own family, having an overprotective sister sounds kind of nice. My family? They didn't care when I left Hennessey. They didn't care when I left Alberta. Probably because in their minds, I was already gone."

The original tension seemed to evaporate after Chase spoke from an honest place. He knew Diego appreciated directness, for people to be candid with him and immediately became defensive when he suspected anything else. Jolene had been right, there was a vulnerable side to him that wasn't immediately clear; but it was definitely there, carefully placed in a corner but visible for those who bothered to look.

"You're right, yes, I am fortunate," Diego spoke evenly as they moved closer to where they lived. "I do love my sister, she is my only family. I know she wants what is best for me. I know she worries but I don't want her to say things to you about me. I don't like that."

There were clear emotions in his voice and Chase could hear his accent slipping in as he spoke from the heart. Perhaps, he considered, that's who he really was at the end of the day. He could be 'American' in how he dressed, acted or in thoughts but in his heart, he was still very tied to his Colombian roots.

"I understand," Chase replied and glanced in Diego's direction. His face looked old, a sadness could be felt, his words suddenly having a more intense impact from even a moment earlier. "I didn't know it was just you and Jolene. Your parents, they...."

"I'm no longer in their life," Diego replied as his fingers touched the volume to turn it down while *That Smell* continued to play in the background. "My father, when he learned I was gay, said I was dead to him. That what I did, it was unnatural and the church did not accept my lifestyle. And so, he hasn't spoken to me since."

"I'm sorry to hear that," Chase replied, his thoughts jumped to his friend Maggie and the struggles she faced when first coming out as a lesbian. Her family hadn't disowned her but simply decided she was confused. Then again, didn't he too? Hadn't he lusted after her, secretly wishing she would change her mind? Was that what Diego was doing with him now?

"It's, you know, it's the past," Diego spoke with some hesitation. "I think, I knew that would happen but it was when my mother said it that really killed me. The worst part was that she had no issue with me being with men but it was because she had to agree with my father to keep the peace, that broke my heart. My own mother disowned me because she chose my father over me. She said, 'your husband is in your life before your child and you must concede to his wishes'. I was 19 and we haven't spoken since that day."

"I..I don't even know what to say," Chase spoke honestly and thought for a moment. "I guess, I kind of relate. My mother hasn't accepted me either but in my case, is kind of mutual."

"Family, it's complicated," Diego replied and made a face. "I think that is why Jolene worries extra for me but she needn't. I'm fine."

Chase didn't reply.

"How come, with your mother, how come you're estranged?" Diego gently asked. "I mean, with me, I was gay but with you, what?"

"I don't know, it was building over time," Chase said and bit his bottom lip. "She kind of turned against me more and more when I was a teenager. It was almost like she didn't like me anymore. She hated that I was in sports, she said they were barbaric. She didn't like my girlfriend, she thought she was a tramp."

Diego let out a laugh.

"Then I got Audrey pregnant and she hated me because I was so irresponsible and basically forced me to marry her, which was something they *both* wanted."

"And you didn't?" Diego asked as he turned onto their street.

"No," Chase replied and took a deep breath. "I hooked up with Audrey at a party. I wasn't even interested in her. I was depressed cause my first girlfriend just dumped me and Audrey gave me some pill, whatever it was, fucked me up and the next thing I knew, we were having sex. *Unprotected* sex and she got pregnant."

"Wow!"

"And my mother basically kicked me out and forced me into Audrey's home, we got married and were miserable most of the time and then finally, one day, she saw that I would never be the husband she wanted."

"That's when you moved to Calgary and met my sister?"

"Yes, I haven't really spoken to my mother since then and my father is dead."

Diego nodded. "That's pretty harsh, my friend."

"It was, but I survived."

"Me too," Diego's voice was barely a whisper and he fell silent as they drove into the parking garage below the condo and found his spot.

"Me, I never had unprotected sex, not that I could get anyone pregnant." Diego let out a laugh and his usual, flippant self returned. "But ah, that was also because of my father, the last thing he ever said to me was that I would get 'The Aids' and die."

Chase felt his mouth drop open.

"But you know, probably the best thing he could've ever said to me because it made me more careful." Diego turned off the car and lifted his sunglasses. His eyes were unusually gentle. "I slept with a lot of men in my day but I was always careful because I didn't want to prove him right. I've never had a thing."

They shared a silence and Chase nodded.

CHAPTER EIGHT

Diego was once again off on a mysterious trip that weekend. Whether it was a rendezvous with a lover or something business related, Chase wasn't sure, only learning of his departure through a messy note stuck to the fridge on Saturday morning. He grinned at the old-school way of communicating in a time when it would've been easier to just text or for that matter, simply tell him in person since they lived in the same place.

It was a quiet weekend for Chase. Other than running a few errands, talking to his kids on Skype and going to the gym, there wasn't much for him to do. Of course, the lime tree would need the usual, lavish attention but other than that, the condo was immaculate. An older Latino woman cleaned every Friday afternoon, usually finishing up about the same time that the two men arrived home, she would have a long conversation with Diego in Spanish before slipping out the door with some cash in hand. She would shyly smile at Chase but didn't attempt to speak to him in English.

When Diego took off for the weekend, he usually returned early Sunday evening and his first priority was always looking after the lime tree. He would barely say hello but instead rush to inspect the leaves, checking the soil to see if it needed any water and would lug it back inside if it was still out. It was almost comical for Chase to watch a grown man fuss over a miniature tree the way most would over a child or pet. It was harmless, if not a little weird.

However, when Diego didn't rip through the door with a suitcase dragging behind him, a laptop bag over his shoulder and a mischievous smile on his face on Sunday evening, Chase began to worry. Although his habits were slightly erratic and mysterious, they were still quite consistent. Unsure if he was crossing any kind of line in the sand, he decided to text him just to check in.

I'm stuck at an airport. Big fuck up. Call Jolene to see if she can pick you up in the morning.

Although this hadn't been his primary concern, he followed Diego's instructions and received a quick reply from his other boss.

Of course Chase! Diego already text me. I will see you in the morning.

He felt like a child who had two parents looking after him and although it was somewhat comforting, it did feel slightly unsettling. Of course, Diego was in his early 40s whereas Jolene was not far behind him in age, he reasoned that it probably was natural for them to feel somewhat protective of their young employee.

Chase woke to a quiet condo the next morning and immediately knew that Diego hadn't arrived home in the night. There was no muffled sound of either the radio or television coming from his room, no razor buzzing, no whistling or phone conversations but rather, silence. It did briefly cross his mind that perhaps he had returned and was getting some sleep and would turn up at the office later, but if he was home, there were no signs.

Jolene was early picking him up. Unlike her brother, she drove a modest car in comparison, a bright red Honda Civic which she purchased after much consideration a few weeks earlier. In fact, she had taken Diego to the dealership to help negotiate. Chase didn't have to be there to know he would've been relentless to the car sales rep until he got the price he felt was deserving.

"Where is he?" Jolene asked almost immediately after Chase got in the car. "He did not say when he text me."

"I don't know," Chase said with a shrug. "I don't ask and he doesn't tell."

"Hmmm," Jolene replied and made a face as she inched onto the street and remained silent for a few minutes. "He's a mysterious one at times. I don't even know where he goes or who he is with but he will not tell. And, I guess that's fine."

Chase didn't reply. He bit his lower lip and looked out the window as they drove through downtown Toronto, making their way toward the office. He liked his new home and as the weeks moved forward, he was slowly starting to familiarize himself with Ontario's capital. For some reason Chase felt more accepted than he ever had in Calgary; where he often felt like a stranger in a strange land.

"Hey, do you like it better here or in Calgary?" Chase asked and glanced at Jolene. Deep in concentration, sitting stiffly, her eyes carefully scanned everything around her.

At first, she didn't reply then slowly tilting her head to one side, her lips curved in a similar fashion as Diego's when he was in thought.

"I do not know," she finally said and made a face. "It's still very new to me. I do not like the people. I think Calgary was friendlier to me. But maybe it's too early to say."

"I actually find people friendlier to me here," Chase remarked as they headed more toward the area of the city he was familiar with, close to the office. "I never really felt like I fit in Calgary."

"You sound like Diego now!" Jolene said and let out a loud laugh. "He say 'too many cowboys' all the time. Diego, he don't like cowboys. Says they have no class. He like Toronto better, he said it is more distinguish? Distinguished? Yes, that is it, distinguished. Classy, you know?"

"I feel more comfortable here. I never did in Calgary."

"Maybe, a little too close to home, ah?" Jolene said and he could see her raise an eyebrow behind her huge sunglasses. "I once moved from my town to another city in Colombia, not far from home and I never really felt comfortable. We need distance sometimes. I think you, Chase, you needed distance too."

He nodded upon hearing her assessment.

"I think you might be right," He agreed as she pulled into the underground parking for their office.

"Chase, have you not noticed that I am always right," She teased as they got out of the car and made their way to the elevator. "I miss this, you and me together like the old days. Now it's usually you and Diego but it's not the same. You know?"

"I feel like my time in Calgary happened so long ago," Chase commented as they stepped into the empty elevator. "It wasn't of course, but it feels like forever. Everything is different now. I feel like I'm on vacation from my life."

"Cause your responsibilities, they are far away," Jolene remarked as they arrive on their floor and walked out of the elevator. "Your little boys, do they miss you?"

Chase shrugged. "I'm not so sure but that's nothing new, I-

Just as she opened the door, Jolene put a finger to her lips to indicate silence, as they quietly entered the office. Pointing toward the alarm, he realized that it wasn't on. Slipping off her heels, her eyes quickly scanned the area, she seemed to hold her breath. Chase was about to step ahead to inspect the office when her hand rose to stop him. She shook her head and reached into her purse and pulled out a gun.

Stunned, Chase held his breath and stepped back.

Without thinking twice, he stayed behind her as she slowly walked down the hallway, making her way toward Diego's office, where the door was open ajar and with one sudden move, she shoved it opened and rose the gun, her loud voice alarming even Chase.

"¿Quién coño es aquí?"

"Jesus Christ, Jolene!!" Diego shouted out in response. "Put the fucking gun away. Don't you recognize your own brother? For fuck sakes!"

"Oh, Diego!" Jolene's voice softened and she placed her left hand between her breasts and slowly lowered the gun. Suddenly appearing emotional, she blinked back tears as Chase reached the door to see Diego, who was white as a ghost. "I was so scared. I thought somebody broke in and was here going through your office. I only saw your head down."

"I was wiping the coffee from the floor," He continued to yell, his voice full of emotion as he pointed toward the brown liquid dripping from his desk. "I knocked it over and Jesus Christ, Jolene, we're not in Colombia anymore. Put the gun away."

She quickly did so and gave a pleading look to Chase, as if suddenly remembering he was there. "Sorry did not mean to scare you."

"Why you apologizing to him," Diego shouted out as he rose from his chair. "I'm the one you had the gun pointed at, not him."

"I'm sorry, Diego, you are right, I shouldn't have done," Jolene commented and walked into the office and Chase followed, stunned by the chain of events he had just witnessed. "I was just so scared. No one is ever here in the morning before me."

"I came here from the airport. I figured I didn't have time to go home and I needed to check on some things," Diego pointed toward his MacBook pushed to the edge of his desk, away from the coffee that he was now wiping up. "Then I will go home later, take a quick shower and change...maybe get another cup of coffee."

"Did you sleep?" She asked as she approached Diego. "The dark under your eyes. You did not sleep."

"I slept on the plane but not much," He looked away and glanced toward Chase. "Did you look after my lime tree, Chase?"

"Yes, I...." He glanced from Jolene to Diego and back again. "You carry a gun? Have you always carried a gun?"

"Yes," She replied, dragging out the word, she nervously shrunk back. "I usually have a gun."

"What if you go somewhere there's a metal detector?"

"I leave in car."

"In fairness, Chase, that's not many places," Diego calmly replied as he finished wiping up the coffee. Throwing the tissue in the trash can, he quickly pumped some Purell in his hands and sat down. "It's good to have but *not* good to point at your brother." His eyes made a sharp turn toward Jolene. "I hope you at least had the safety on."

"Yes, of course!" Jolene replied and sat down on a nearby chair. "I sorry. I did not mean to scare either of you."

"Especially me, right, the person you had the gun pointed at?" Diego asked, still clearly agitated by the incident. Chase sat down and didn't say anything. Noting his reaction, Diego turned his attention back in his direction.

"See, you don't understand, Chase," He started to speak and Jolene took out her gun and inspected it as her brother spoke. "We come from a different country, Colombia. It's not like Canada where you walk down the street at any given time and are relatively safe if you stay away from certain neighborhoods or certain times of the day. It wasn't like that when we were growing up, we had to be....proactive."

"It is true," Jolene chimed in while putting her gun back in her purse. "I love my home country, don't get me wrong but it can be dangerous. Not always. It's not as bad as you make it sound here on the news or whatever but you have to be..."

"Vigilant," Diego cut in while his hand ran down his tie. Wearing a white shirt with a few wrinkles in it, his face had a dusting of dark stubble and much to Chase's surprise, a few gray ones were in his sideburns. His hair was slightly disheveled but still, he looked pretty polished; just not for Diego. "We are from a beautiful country but unfortunately, not the safest especially back in the day, so we look after ourselves, you know?" He shrugged and sniffed.

"Do you know how to use it?" Chase asked as he pointed toward Jolene's purse.

"Of course, yes!" Jolene said. "I shoot well."

"She could've had me between the eyes," Diego pointed toward his forehead. "I would be dead in a second if she had shot. She's *that* good."

"Really?" Chase asked and his mouth fell open.

"I can, yes," Jolene nodded. "I'm a good shot."

"I teach her," Diego piped up. "But she's better than me."

"So you have a gun too?" Chase asked.

Diego nodded.

"He has more than one," Jolene muttered as the main entrance could be heard opening.

"I have a few," Diego said with a nod. "One can't be too safe."

"But you just said Canada is relatively safe," Chase said, unsure of how he felt about this new information. "Why do you need any here?"

"You just do," Diego replied as Sylvana stuck her head in the office and said a quick good morning before heading into the staff room, lunch bag in hand.

"You do not talk about this by the way, Chase," Diego instructed. "It is a *family* thing, this information."

"I won't," Chase replied. "Don't worry."

The two Silva's exchanged looks and Diego quietly replied. "Here in Canada, you have guns to go out and shoot defenseless animals for sport. In Colombia, we had guns so that we don't *become* the defenseless animal."

Before he had a chance to respond, the door to the staff room could be heard opening and Sylvana stuck her head in again. "There's a pair of shoes by the door. Are they yours, Jolene?"

"Ah, yes, they are mine," Jolene said with a little laugh, jumping up from her seat. "My feet, they hurt, you know?"

Chase glanced back at Diego, who, in turn, winked at him.

CHAPTER NINE

It wasn't a surprise that Diego didn't listen to Sylvana's advice to focus on their original format and hold off on parties for gay men. Rather than taking a slow, comfortable journey with their new business, he instead continued to gamble and expand Diego and Jolene Inc. with fierce determination. It made everyone nervous but regardless of how much backlash he got in their regular meetings, he refused to listen. He thought the company had to be proactive and unless they were running full speed ahead, they were sinking.

"People want companies that are always expanding, always reaching for the stars and aren't afraid to take chances, that is the way of the world Sylvana," Diego walked around the boardroom and spoke excitedly, his hands dancing in the air, his eyes wide open and full of vigor, the excitement of a child and yet, the dark secrets of a man. Diego didn't seem to care that he was constantly undermining Sylvana's opinions and in fact, it almost seemed as if he thrived on it. "You have to get out of your comfortable, safe, little world."

Her face turned crimson and she didn't respond. Fortunately, Benjamin calmly jumped in.

"I think what she means, Diego, is that people get nervous when companies are moving too fast. They prefer a more conservative approach to business," He spoke calmly, leaning back in his chair, his fingers tapped the armrest and he gave a slight shrug and continued. "I know that it's not your vision and I understand what you're saying too but maybe we have to meet in the middle here. As much as we would love to expand quickly, we're still a very new company and we should be cautious. We also have a lot of expenses."

"Exactly, that's why we need to make more money," Diego replied, his eyes full of fire as he waved his arms in the air. "Why am I the only person who sees this? We can't afford to be overly cautious right now, we have to go full steam ahead."

Everyone looked at Jolene as if she were the only hope of talking sense into Diego but she didn't appear to be listening. Instead, she was reading something on her laptop. Chase was probably the next person Benjamin, Sylvana and Beverly glanced toward; something he ignored. Although he saw everyone's point of view, he wasn't quite sure what the answer was in this case and therefore, didn't add anything to the conversation.

It wasn't until after the meeting ended and they were alone that a sense of insecurity moved in and Diego asked his opinion.

"You, do you think I'm crazy?" Diego suddenly looked defeated, exhausted as he slumped over his desk. A rare vulnerability filled his voice and for the first time, Chase felt concerned about his job and the company in general. Without responding at first, he rose from his chair and closed the nearby door before walking toward Diego's desk. He noted that the larger than life character from the meeting earlier now resembled one of his children at the end of the day, as they struggled to keep awake, frustrated and depressed.

"Is this about the meeting earlier?" Chase quietly asked as he sat across from Diego, who's dark eyes appeared gloomy. He leaned against his hand, an untouched cup of coffee sat beside him and papers were all over his desk.

A knock at the door interrupted before Diego could reply, as his face tightened up and he muttered, "The door is fucking closed for a reason." He didn't attempt to hide his aggravation and called out, "What?"

The door opened and Deborah stuck her head in. "There's a man here to see you. Jesse? He said he spoke to you recently?"

This seemed to bring Diego back to life as he automatically sat up straighter in his chair, his face full of light again. "Tell him I will be right out in a moment. Thanks, Deborah."

She beamed and closed the door.

"I got a meeting with this guy, he could be the answer," Diego jumped up and grabbed his suit jacket and rushed past Chase. "He used to work with our competition for the gay men parties, the company Jolene mentioned once? He can tell us what we need to do to win Toronto over and once we have Toronto, we can get any city."

Chase opened his mouth to say something but it was too late. Diego was already out of the office, his voice could be heard booming down the hallway. "Jesse! You finally made it! Let's go out for a cup of coffee and conversation."

By the time Chase got to the doorway, the two were already gone, the main entrance closed. He stood with his own thoughts for a moment just as Jolene walked out of the staff room with a raised eyebrow as if to ask him what was going on.

"Some guy was here to see Diego and he rushed out," Chase commented and saw her roll her eyes. "I mean, you know, to talk about the parties he wants to have for gay men."

Moving close to Chase, she muttered, "The only gay man party he's probably interested in right now is his own. Did you see the man he left with?"

Chase shook his head and she ushered him back into Diego's office and closed the door. "I didn't have a chance. By the time I got to the hallway, they were already gone."

"I just bet." Jolene retorted. "He will be gone for the afternoon. I will drive you home."

"What?" Chase was confused by her comment. "I think it was just a meeting, Jolene. It's not...."

"I think you are wrong," Jolene said with a shrug. "I love my brother but he's impulsive. He doesn't think normal sometimes, he just jumps from idea to idea, boy to boy and that's what is going on here. He will try to seduce this man, get his answers, it's how he is."

Chase remained silent but wasn't sure Jolene was right. He had lived at Diego's place for over a month and hadn't seen that side of him. In fact, Diego's life seemed quite tame compared to what he would've expected.

"I don't know, Jolene, things are pretty normal at the condo," Chase commented, feeling the need to defend Diego in this matter. Perhaps she was speaking of how her brother once was but maybe it was no longer relevant. "Other than going away on the weekends..."

"Exactly," Jolene said as she leaned up against his desk. "You have no idea but you probably don't want to know. Trust me. I was his roommate at one time. He lived a very...adventurous lifestyle. I used to worry that he was a little too...how do you say? You know, when a person sleep around a lot?"

"Promiscuous?" Chase quietly asked, almost as if Diego was going to come charging through the door any minute, his dark eyes glaring at both in accusation. "I don't know. I don't want to say, Jolene. I haven't seen that side of him so I don't know."

"You do not see that side because he does not want you to," Jolene pointed out. "Diego, he has a thing for you and I know you do not want to hear but it's true. He's not going to do anything to give you a bad impression. He will be a saint around you. He will charm you and do anything he can to get you to...you know."

"I don't think so," Chase said and laughed self-consciously. "It's really normal, there's nothing going on and he doesn't try anything."

"Yet!" Jolene said, her eyes widened and she raised her finger in the air. "I think it's important you move."

Chase opened his mouth to respond but instead let out a sigh.

"Chase, trust me please," Jolene spoke with a pleading tone. "I do not know where he goes or what he does when he's away on weekends. I know it is not good. If it's not something with the boys he dates then it's something...it's something you don't want to get in the middle of, that is all I say."

Chase studied her face. "Jolene is there something that I need to know here?" He asked and she hesitated for a long time before responding and when she did, it was to shake her head while her eyes suggested otherwise. He studied her face in silence and nodded.

"Ok, I will make more of an effort this week. I promise."

"Good."

It wasn't until after she left that he felt guilty. He wasn't being completely honest with her. As much as he wanted his own place, Chase didn't look forward to living alone again. His months in an empty apartment in Calgary were unbearable to him; the silence was crippling as depression crushed him. It was hard enough now when Diego was away and he was alone but there was some comfort to the fact that it was only a short time. He wondered what made him so reliant on having company. There was a time when he lived for those few quiet moment, free of his family, free from the women he had affairs with, free from clients at both the gym and nightclub he worked for in Hennessey. He loved those silent moments in his secret place, a small room behind Bud's bar, where he could be alone with his thoughts. Now, he didn't want to listen to his thoughts. They were unbearable.

As Chase worked on research that afternoon, he started to see a connection between Jolene's comment about Diego's promiscuous behaviour and what he was reading on message boards. He viewed many posts that suggested that gay men were very sexually open and revealed their fetishes as well as their interest in having many partners; but was that really different from straight men? Perhaps, he considered, straight men felt more boxed in like they couldn't reveal their needs and lust as openly without appearing perverted. Women didn't like it when you were overly open unless it was a topic that pleased them and when it suited them to hear. There were so many complicated rules with women and Chase felt like he had to hold back until receiving the right sign that it was safe to speak honestly without being ridiculed or unfairly judged.

Of course, the other side revealed that gay men weren't really different from straight men or women; their message boards were full of topics that could be seen in various places on the Internet and overheard in local coffee shops; opinions about politics, television, and music. Some revealed problems they were having and asked for advice and one man spoke honestly about being attacked outside a nightclub in an east coast city. It opened his eyes to some of the issues that perhaps Diego had dealt with in his life and he wondered how much harassment and discrimination he had faced over the years.

Much to his surprise, Diego bounced back in the room shortly after 5, full of energy and light with a spring in his step that could've been revealing, depending on what he had done for the hours away.

"Great news Chase!" Diego spoke excitedly as he clapped his hands together and briskly moved across the room and sat in his chair. Turning off his laptop, he started to unplug it as he continued to talk. "This afternoon you are looking at a man with a plan! I know exactly what we're going to do for the gay men parties and they're going to be the biggest thing that ever hit this city!"

"That's great," Chase started to turn off his own laptop and slowly mirrored Diego as he gathered his bag from the floor. "Was this guy you met with helpful?"

"*Very* helpful. It was a productive afternoon."

"That's good," Chase replied, ignoring the insinuation hidden in Diego's voice, the familiar mischievous grin lifting one side of his mouth, his eyes focused on the items on his desk as he shoved various papers in his bag. "So, what did you find out?"

"Work is done my friend, we'll discuss it in the meeting tomorrow." Diego insisted as he zipped up the bag and waited for Chase to do the same. "We must go celebrate now!"

"I don't know if I can," Chase spoke honestly. "I made plans with Audrey to talk to the kids after work. She's pretty precise with her schedule for the boys."

"Do it now," Diego shrugged and gestured toward Chase's desk. "See if they are available now. I will wait for you. I have to go talk to Jolene anyway."

"Oh...ah, ok," Chase said and reached back in his bag to pull out his Macbook. "I guess that would be okay. I won't be long."

"Ah, take your time," Diego said and twisted his lips into an odd shape as he walked out of the office, pulling the door closed behind him. He could be heard hollering to Jolene in the hallway and loudly speaking to her about the 'success' of his afternoon meeting.

Chase felt anxiety as he signed into Skype. It was a familiar feeling of vulnerability that made him more and more awkward with each conversation; he wanted to talk to his children and felt a longing to see them face to face and yet, their conversations grew weaker each time. There was a distance between them that had nothing to do with the fact that they lived a few provinces away but that they no longer saw him as a father figure but merely the man who checked in from time to time, someone they felt obligated to speak to. He sensed their disinterest and Audrey's sincere attempt to reel them in was with much struggle.

That day was no different. His ex-wife managed to gather his young children together in front of the computer. His oldest, Leland, was 4 while the twins were about to turn 3, so harnessing their attention was always a challenge. As they grew restless, the children would often hit and bite one another, followed by hugging, as if it was the most normal thing to do.

"They are tired today," Audrey warned in a stiff smile before leaving the children to talk to their father. And although their conversation was pleasant enough, it wasn't long before they were practically spinning in their seats, clearly ready to erupt if they had to sit still any longer. He felt powerless and disappointed as Chet rushed away followed by his twin, Devin.

It was just then that Diego flew back in the room with an apologetic look on his face as he rushed toward the desk, grabbed a piece of paper off his desk, his eyes fixated on Chase as he made his way toward the door. On Skype, Leland called out "Daddy's home!" in a loud voice and suddenly, the screen only revealed an empty wall that had previously been the background to his three sons. Now, they were gone.

Diego halted his step as Chase slowly closed the laptop. He felt crestfallen as if the last bit of life in him was drained and he was left an empty shell sitting at his desk. He normally would've wished that Diego hadn't witnessed that moment but as he sat there feeling helpless and worthless, Chase didn't really care. Perhaps it was best he knew the truth.

At first, he didn't say anything. Instead, Diego stood still as if assessing the situation, he silently watched Chase, who avoided eye contact. He couldn't do it. He couldn't share this moment with anyone and yet, it was too late to hide it. Although Chase had never concealed the estrangement he felt with his children, it was a whole other thing to have it witnessed. It was a whole other thing to show anyone this side of his life; a side that was breaking him a bit each day.

"I'm sure, I'm sure it meant nothing Chase. Children, they don't understand their words. I once had a neighbor's kid call me 'grandma'," He let out a self-conscious laugh, clearly hoping to remove some of the tension in the air. "Children, they don't understand what words mean sometimes, it means nothing."

"No, it means something this time," Chase spoke evenly and shot Diego a compassionate look. He appreciated the effort his friend was making to relieve some of his disappointment but he also knew that his kids saw Albert, their step-father as their *real* dad. He was with them daily to help them learn, to feed them, to care for them, in a way that Chase barely could when he *did* live in their family home. He was a father in name only.

Diego looked helpless as he shook his head and glanced toward his feet. "I'm sorry Chase, I don't know what to say. I wish I could help but I don't know children. I don't know how to fix this situation with your kids."

"It's okay, Diego," Chase said as he took a deep breath and stretched in his chair. "I know how things are but it still doesn't make it easy to hear."

Diego grimaced and shook his head just as Jolene rushed in the door.

"Come on Diego! Show me what it is you want me to see, I want to go home," Her words were abrupt, as they often were with her brother but this time she suddenly stopped as if sensing the tension. She glanced from her brother to Chase. "What is wrong?"

"Chase was talking to his children and they," Diego hesitated as if to pick out the right words. "They called this other man their 'father'. The man his ex lives with."

"Oh Chase," Jolene shook her head. "You can't take that to heart. They are children, they don't mean it to be hurtful."

"I know," Chase replied.

"I know, I know," Jolene piped up. "It does not make it easy to hear but you have to take with a grain of salt. It does not mean anything.

They know you are their father. *You* know you are your father, that is all that matters."

Chase exchanged smiles with Jolene.

"You and me," Diego jumped in, pointing toward Chase. "We will go have a nice dinner, some drinks, it will cheer you up."

Jolene shot her brother a dirty look.

"What?" He replied jovially when he caught her expression. "You can come too!"

She grabbed the papers from Diego's hand and walked out of the room. Diego scratched his face and shrugged. "I don't know what her problems is."

Chapter Ten

Diego chose a restaurant that wasn't too far from where they lived, an upscale establishment that appeared to cater more toward business class; something that suited Chase since the last thing he wanted to see was a happy family joined together for a meal. It wasn't that he begrudged anyone their own happiness but at the same time, he didn't want to have it shoved in his face. Chances were good that Diego's choice had nothing to do with sensitivities for his friend but his lack of patience for children; he said he couldn't fully enjoy a meal at a restaurant if someone's kids were crying, throwing food on the floor and being 'obnoxious'. In fact, he often referred to McDonald's as 'hell's playground' when Jolene suggested they pop in for something quick.

It was a quiet setting with few patrons when they first arrived and Diego requested they sit away from the others, supposedly because they were having a business meeting. Once seated and the waitress left them to look at the menu, Chase cleared his throat and raised an eyebrow.

"Business meeting?" He asked and grinned for the first time since leaving the office. "What's that about?"

"They treat you better if they think you're having a business dinner," Diego insisted as he squinted and held the menu away from his face. "They think, you know, that you're important."

"I assumed you always thought you were important," Chase teased as a slow grin rose on one side of Diego's face.

"I am *amigo*," Diego had a hint of humor in his voice and he scrunched up his lips. "But sometimes, they have to be reminded."

The waitress returned to see if they were ready to order.

"Let's start with some drinks," Diego insisted and glanced at Chase who shrugged in response. "What's good?"

"Well, I'm told mojitos are the best in town," She replied with a smile.

"Told? You don't know?" Diego teased.

"I don't drink," She replied and tilted her head with a faint smile on her lips.

"Ah, you're like this one," He pointed toward Chase and winked at him. "He's a good boy but me, not so much. I would love a mojito." His tone was seductive as his eyes scanned her body.

The waitress appeared to enjoy the minor flirtation as she nodded and then turned her attention to Chase. "And you, sir?"

"Actually, I've never had a mojito but it looks good in this picture," Chase pointed toward the menu.

"You've *never* had a mojito?" Diego asked and let out a laugh. "Oh my! The drink virgin here! Give us two, *señorita*." His eyes preyed on her as he passed the menus back.

"Very good," She nodded. "Anything from the kitchen?"

"I ate earlier but Chase, how about you?" Diego asked and then added. "You should eat."

"I'll have the chicken caesar."

"Great! I will return with your drinks."

The waitress left and Chase shook his head.

"Why do you flirt with women?"

"They like it, why not?"

"You're gay," Chase reminded him. "It's not like you're going anywhere with it."

"I probably wouldn't anyway but you can tell she likes it," Diego pointed out. "And it makes her happy and why not make someone happy?"

Chase considered his words and shrugged. "I guess."

The waitress returned with their drinks and quickly rushed away again.

Glancing toward the drink as Diego took a sip, Chase grinned. "Is this why you're growing a lime tree, to make mojitos?"

"Oh! My lime tree. *Shit!*" Diego said as he made a face. "I should've swung by the condo and took it in. I hope it doesn't get too cool before we get home."

"What is your obsession with that tree?" Chase asked and took a mouthful of his drink. It was more favorable than he expected and he quickly followed it up with a second drink.

"It's my thing. I like plants."

"That's one *hell* of a big plant."

"I like limes. *Good* limes. Not that shit you buy in the grocery store that sit in a van for a week," Diego replied dismissively. "I had that in Colombia and I had that in California. Here? I get that crap at the store."

"You just seem obsessive about the tree."

"I love plants. It's a living thing. People and animals, they are messy. Plants aren't and they give back," Diego considered his words and sipped at his drink. "It's hard to explain."

Chase nodded. He felt his thoughts suddenly drift back to his earlier conversation with his kids and immediately took another drink. By the time the waitress returned with his food, it was gone.

"Get him another," Diego suggested and the waitress rushed off while Chase turned his attention to his food. He ate and listened to Diego talk about his meeting with Jesse earlier that day.

"He has an ax to grind with his old company," Diego said and raised an eyebrow, a faint smile on his lips. "They did not separate on good terms so he was happy to reveal all their secrets to me, especially after a few drinks. Turns out he might come work for us. I'm not sure, maybe as a freelancer. Although, he likes the idea of competing with his former boss. That's the kind of passion I need now plus he has connections to the community."

"That sounds great," Chase replied in between bites. "That could be beneficial to us."

By the time the waitress brought his second mojito and took Diego's order for another one, Chase was almost finished eating his food. The alcohol was helping him to relax and although he normally didn't drink, he couldn't see anything wrong with having a few for a change. It was a rare step off the usual track for him but wasn't that part of life?

"So, your research, how did it go today?" Diego asked.

"Good."

"Did you learn anything interesting on the message boards?" Diego inquired.

"I learned that gay and straight men aren't so different except, well the obvious thing," Chase said and took another sip of his drink. Across from him, Diego nodded his head. "I was surprised to read that a lot of gay men were actually with women at some point. Some even married women. I think it would be a bit of a shock to find out your spouse is leaving you because he's gay."

"It happens sometimes. People are confused or for religious reasons, they try to hide it," Diego spoke honestly, his fingers stroked the side of his glass. "It was like that when I was growing up in Colombia. People didn't accept the lifestyle and it was back before the Internet and all that, so we didn't have anywhere to connect with others in our community. Plus my family was very religious. They didn't even want us to have premarital sex, forget with someone of the same sex."

"My mom was kind of like that too," Chase confessed as he continued to enjoy his drink. He felt lighter, more relaxed, calm. "Big time. That's why I ended up married with a kid before I was 20."

Diego merely grinned, listening attentively.

"So how did you know you were gay?" Chase asked.

"How did *you* know you were *straight?*" Diego asked back and the two shared a smile.

"Fair enough."

"Ah, don't think it wouldn't have been simpler for me if I had been straight back then," Diego added as he finished his drink and he took a sip of water. "But not much. My mother would've been like yours, insisting I get married. Actually, she did. I was dating a girl in high school and she assumed we were to marry."

Chase replied by raising his eyebrows.

"Obviously, that wasn't going to happen," Diego said as he caught the waitress's attention to order more drinks. "She was a sweet girl, though. Never knew that we broke up cause I was gay. I mean, she might now, I don't know but probably not."

"Ever talk to her now?"

"Nope," Diego answered. "It was good though because she didn't want to have sex before getting married or till things were serious, so I didn't have to delve into those waters for a long time."

"Did you even want to try."

"I was already *trying* lots of things with my best friend when we had *sleepovers*," Diego let out a laugh as the waitress arrived with more drinks. She quickly and smoothly grabbed the empty dishes and disappeared. "My mother would've died if she ever walked in the room late at night when he was there. Fortunately, she never did. Almost did once, but we managed to fool her."

"So, your friend was gay?"

"I don't know, I actually think he's married to a woman now....I guess it's normal to want to experiment."

"I guess that's an advantage to being gay when you're a teenager. No one is suspicious of sleepovers," Chase said and laughed, suddenly feeling extra giddy. "My best friend back home was a lesbian and even then, we couldn't spend time together without people assuming we were hooking up. They thought it was an act."

"People! They believe what they choose, am I right?"

"Definitely," Chase said and his thought drifted back to Maggie; her smooth curves that always beckoned his attention, those lust-filled times together when he would've done *anything* to touch her.

"You wanted her, didn't you?"

"What?" Chase was surprised by his comment.

"I can see it on your face," Diego spoke quietly, his eyes fixated on Chase as he took another drink.

"Yeah, I really wanted her."

"But she wasn't interested in men?"

"No."

"Ah, welcome to my life," Diego teased with a mischievous grin.

Chase didn't respond but awkwardly took another drink.

"So did you ever sleep with this girlfriend in Colombia or any woman?"

"I did."

"And?"

"Ah!' Diego said, shrugging, his face twisted in a sour expression. "It was frustrating. Women are complicated machines. Nothing seemed to really work for her until one day on a whim, I shoved my dick up her ass. As it turns out, we were into the same thing."

Chase almost choked on his drink. Laughter quickly followed - both his and Diego - heartily, so much so, that people from a nearby table stopped their conversation to look over.

"You know, I don't get that, I don't get why that's a turn on," Chase spoke candidly. "I don't get why people are into it."

"Anal?" Diego asked, his eyes glowed as the lights lowered in the restaurant, while Chase suddenly felt comfortable asking the questions he wouldn't normally ask.

"Yeah, I don't get it."

"Have you ever had it done to you?"

"No."

"That's *why* you don't get it."

"So you're saying if I had a dick in my ass, I would like it?" Chase couldn't help but to feel humored by this suggestion and although he knew it was probably not smart to get into this area with Diego, he had to ask. All his research online had peaked his curiosity.

"Yup."

"Nah," Chase replied and shook his head.

"Ok, so tell me this," Diego leaned forward. "You're in a passionate moment with a spectacular woman, say that waitress over there," He pointed toward the woman who had serve them throughout the night. "She wants to shove something up your ass, you going to say no?"

"I somehow think I would."

"Ok, then tell me this, have you ever had your prostate milked?"

"What the fuck?" Chase asked as he burst into a fit of laughter. "I read about that online when I was researching one day. That sounds... intense..."

"It is," Diego seemed to get a charge out of the conversation and barely breaking eye contact with Chase, he signalled the waitress for more drinks. "Not at your doctor's office but in bed, it is."

"Really?"

"It would blow your *fucking* mind. Way more than the best blowjob," Diego spoke excitedly. "You think you died and went to heaven."

On some level, Chase knew Diego was trying to tempt him, trying to entice him in much the same way he would've with Maggie back in the day, had he been more courageous. He could feel himself lighten, his defenses down while his desires were suddenly on high alert. Had Diego purposely set the scene for this to happen?

"I take it you've-

"Done it, had it," Diego spoke evenly, his dark eyes stared into Chase's until the waitress returned with their drinks. He opened his mouth as if to say more but hesitated and instead took a drink before a satisfied grin crossed his face.

Chase sat in stunned silence. Neither said a thing. Around them, people ate, drank, talked and laughed. A gentle flow of Black Sabbath streamed through the room while outside, the day slipped into night.

Not knowing what to say, he stared across the table at Diego who showed no signs of discomfort unlike Chase, who suddenly felt his lips become dry, his throat ached and he took another sip of his drink and awkwardly looked away.

"You've done lots of research, Chase, so I assume that you probably already know what a 'daddy' is?" Diego asked casually, as his fingers lightly ran over the tablecloth and then he suddenly stopped and looked back up. "In that gay community, that is?"

"I think so," Chase quietly replied and felt his face flushed.

"Well, back when I first moved to America, I had one. Very rich, powerful man, probably in his early 40s. He looked after me, guided me, taught me many things including what we were just talking about," Diego stopped and looked up as the waitress passed by. Chase noted she winked at him. "He looked after me even when he knew I was cheating."

"Jolene is nervous. She thinks that because you stay with me, I am trying to do the same with you," Diego spoke honestly, tilting his head slightly to the side. "I have told her again and again that this is not the case. Even tonight, she thought I was trying to get your drunk so I could try to take advantage. I want you to know that I would never do such a thing. I don't know if she's said that is a possibly but I need to have the air cleared between us."

"She seems to think I should move," Chase admitted in a quiet voice, feeling as though he was betraying a trust. "I don't think...I mean, I think she's just scared for you. Scared you'll get hurt."

"Chase, I'm fine," Diego spoke with sincerity, the usual veil of ego lowered, his eyes full of warmth and purity. "Do not worry about such things. I like you. I think we are good friends. I think it's nice to have someone to share a place with and someone to look after my lime tree."

Chase snickered and took another drink.

"I'm not trying to seduce you. I'm not trying to trick you. I won't die of a broken heart if you never see me as anything more than the gay guy you live with," Diego's words were gentle, smooth, humbled. His eyes grew, the light gently touched them as he licked his lower lip. "I hope we are friends, though."

"Of course we're friends," Chase spoke earnestly, his eyes glanced quickly at his drink and up again. "You're probably the only friend I have now."

"And Jolene."

"Yes, of course," Chase nodded. "It's not the same, though."

"Jolene, she has a bit of a wall up."

"I've noticed."

"But Chase, I'm not going to lie," Diego's words were full of warmth as he leaned forward across the table. "If you ever told me you wanted to, I would have us both naked before you even had the words out."

Chase couldn't help but laugh as he shook his head.

"So, drink up my friend," Diego let out a hearty laugh that captured everyone's attention; their waitress, the couple at the nearby table, but most of all, he had Chase's attention.

CHAPTER ELEVEN

The last time Chase got wasted, he was a naïve 18-year-old that had just gotten dumped by his girlfriend. Heartbroken, he had been open to anything that brought him some temporary relief from his misery and so, when Audrey Neil offered him some hope in the form of a pill, he gratefully took it. Shortly after, he felt as if he was floating. His heart and mind drifted into a state of bliss that was beyond any physical sensations, his body erupted into a level of satisfaction he had never felt before in his young life.

It hadn't taken long before reality set in. The woman he had no interest in was lying naked beside him as he shamefully rose from the bed and slunk out of her room, only to later learn that they had conceived their son Leland that night. He would never take pills again and on the rare occasion he drank, it was generally a modest amount of alcohol.

At least, that had been the case. Stumbling home after a few too many mojitos with Diego, another demon had erupted in his soul, reminding him that he was far more vulnerable than he wanted to admit. He felt an uncomfortable combination of shame and depression as they returned to the condo, met by the bright lights and a deafening silence, he wanted nothing more than to curl up in a corner and die. The blissful satisfaction had already started to slip away and he was left feeling heavy in spirit, as he sat on the couch, head in hands.

"Want another drink?" Diego asked casually as his voice moved toward the kitchen.

"Oh God! No!" Chase shook his head and closed his eyes, his heart suddenly filled with sorrow. He briefly wondered if the liquor had caused it, created it from a small fragment of sadness that had been there all along. The same sadness that returned every time he spoke to his children. "What the hell was I thinking?"

Hearing the refrigerator door open then close, he looked up in time to see Diego walk in his direction with a bottle of water in hand. His face was crestfallen, his eyes helpless as he handed him the plastic container. Chase took it and struggled to smile.

"I'm sorry, I should've cut you off sooner," Diego solemnly commented, sitting beside him on the couch, his cologne drifted past Chase and with a slight breeze, it became pungent, causing him to make a face. "I know you aren't a drinker but in my defense, you're a big guy, so I figured, I don't know, you would be fine." He cleared his throat and started to loosen his tie and crossed his legs. "You did knock them back pretty fast, though."

"I know," Chase quietly admitted, feeling somewhat defeated as the room seemed to spin after lifting his head from his hands, causing him to close his eyes again. "Why do people do this to themselves?"

"The key is to find the *right* amount of drinks," Diego offered encouragingly as Chase turned his head to look at him. "Enough to relax you, let your guard down a bit but yet, you know, not too much that you feel like fucking dying." His dark eyes studied Chase longingly. Leaning his arm against the couch, his finger placed over his lip, as if to hold himself back from saying anything, his eyes continued to probe Chase, who's main concern was to not get sick.

Suddenly feeling as though his tie was strangling him, he immediately reached for it. His hands worked quickly to loosen it, followed by unbuttoning the first few buttons on his shirt, a sudden heat enclosed his body, causing his clothing to feel tight, restrictive, uncomfortable like sandpaper on his body. He rose from the couch, his head spun as a result of the sudden, abrupt movement but he took a deep breath as Diego jumped up beside him.

"Are you okay?" His voice was soft, gentle and Chase realized Diego's hand was grazing his arm, as if hesitant to touch him but as a sign of compassion. "Are you going to be sick?"

"No," Chase shook his head, not completely sure if this was true. He turned toward Diego and recognized the look in his eye and hesitated for a moment before continuing his thought. "I just...I just need to go to bed. Sleep it off. I'll be fine."

"Are you sure? Maybe you need to eat?"

"No, I'm fine," Chase insisted with a quick smile. "I'm sorry, thanks, I had fun, Diego. I really did."

An undeniable sense of misery filled his body as he headed to his room and behind the closed door, he quickly removed his clothes until he was only wearing a pair of white boxers. His mind searched for an escape route, something that would take him away from the many thoughts that continually rolled through his head but if that night had proven anything, it was that it was impossible. The demons that haunted him were never far away; especially when trying to avoid them, instead they cropped up even larger than life at your most weak, vulnerable moments.

He crawled into bed, attempting to deny his discomfort, he wouldn't give into it. Chase briefly wondered how he had come to this moment in his life. The 18-year-old version of himself had been naïve, living in a world of misplaced hopes and dreams, illusions of a simple, uncomplicated life that held some meaning and yet, he had been so wrong. Talking about Diego's youth had surprisingly erupted some ghosts of his own past; ghosts he had thought were quietly locked away, slowly dying but instead, they returned, stronger than ever and he didn't know what to do with them.

He drifted into a disruptive sleep, interrupted by sounds that he first thought was a dream but as he lifted his head from the pillow, glancing at a nearby clock, realized that the noise was coming from the living room. Jumping out of bed, he ignored a dull pain that grasped the crown of his head and rushed toward the door. He opened it in time to see Diego, wearing a slightly ruffled version of the same clothes, letting someone out the door; a woman. Blinking rapidly, he realized it was the waitress from the bar.

Neither noticed him, the woman quietly scurrying out the condo while Diego closed the door behind her. Turning around, his eyes double in size when he saw Chase watching him from across the room. Diego's shirt unbuttoned to show his bare chest, his hair disheveled as a bashful smile on his face told a story that didn't make sense.

"Oops, you weren't supposed to see that," Diego let out a gleeful giggle as he made his way toward the kitchen, where a bottle of gin sat on the counter. Pouring himself a shot, he quickly lifted it to his lips and sank it. His eyes watered as Chase approached him, feeling as though he was having a strange dream.

"What's going on here?"

"That girl, from the restaurant, she came over."

"Yeah, I got that part," Chase replied as Diego's eyes didn't hide the fact that they were scanning his semi-naked body. "Did you suddenly decide you're not gay?"

"Trust me, right about now," He gestured toward Chase's smooth abdomen, his eyes continued to drift down. "I couldn't be more positive that I'm gay."

It took a moment for Diego's words to process, Chase still feeling as if he were in a bit of a fog, he finally asked, "Why was that woman here?"

"What? Gay men can't have women friends too?"

"You looked...more than friendly," Chase countered and realized he was being too confrontational.

Diego shrugged. "I was feeling.....you know, lonely and she slipped me her number at the restaurant so I called her up."

"She knows you are gay, right?"

Diego shrugged. "It didn't seem important to mention at the time."

"She probably thinks you're interested in her."

"I was," Diego said, his dark eyes earnest and his voice turned soft, "There was one, specific moment in particular that I *really* liked her." A smile eased across his lips with such grace that it was intoxicating to watch. "But, you know, I think she caught me when I was weak. I told her that, I'm sorry but I couldn't return the favor. She was actually somewhat gracious, all things considered."

"Why would you even bother, I don't understand," Chase asked pointedly. "Why would you lead someone on like that?"

Diego studied his face in silence, his pupils widened and his lips fell open and into a gentle smile. "I didn't mean to *amigo*, as I said, it was a weak moment and our conversation tonight, it made me wonder, maybe I would like women too? You know, it's been a long time and I do think women are attractive and sexy but it's not, it's not, quite.... quenching that fire, if you know I mean."

Chase was too stunned to talk.

"So, I can honestly say I tried it with women again and it's not for me," He spoke with certainty, his eyes continued to search Chase's, an unspoken question filled the air as he moved away, walking toward his bedroom. "Good night, *amigo* and oh," He abruptly turned around and gestured toward the ceiling. "Can you get the lights before you go back to bed?" A faint smile touched his lips as he walked into his room and shut the door.

Chase suddenly felt exposed and uncomfortable. Glancing toward the lime tree beside the patio doors, he suddenly had the urge to go outside. The cool June evening was an unexpected treat since it had been so hot in recent weeks. He was left with his thoughts, suddenly feeling both very sober and awake, unsure of how to process the day.

He didn't understand Diego but he felt like he was in quicksand, his body slowly starting to sink just as it had many times before in his young life. Jolene's warning suddenly felt so prevalent and yet, did he want to leave this condo? Wasn't there a part of him that enjoyed the unpredictability and vigor of life with Diego, didn't it, in some way, make him feel more alive? Was there something to learn here?

A chill crept up on him and he turned to go back inside. Closing and locking the doors behind him, he glanced at the lime tree before turning off the lights and heading back to his own room. The apartment was silent again. Unfortunately, the voices in his head were not.

CHAPTER TWELVE

"Have you ever noticed that there's a certain beauty in music?" Diego's question came out of nowhere as the two drove to work the next morning. Still feeling slightly hung over, both physically and spiritually stagnant, Chase barely acknowledged it with a shrug, noting that unfamiliar music flowing through the car. Of course, Diego being Diego, he was picky about the sound system and when he finally 'settled' on buying another Lexus, his next project was to make sure music was crystal clear and 'clean'. He was adamant about it. Chase felt a sweeping sense of relief that he didn't work in direct sales because people like Diego would drive him over the edge. So picky, so precise but on the other side, he was a man who knew what he wanted.

"What do you mean?" Chase finally responded, his mouth dry, his lips felt as though they would stick together, regardless of the bottle of water Diego shoved in his hand on the way out the door that morning.

"What do you mean, what do *I* mean?" Diego asked as he concentrated on traffic in downtown Toronto. "You really don't know what I mean *amigo*, do you?"

A haunting song surrounded the two men and a quick glance at the dash told Chase it was "Frozen". He briefly closed his eyes as the music and lyrics gently touched him and although Chase wasn't about to admit it, the song contributed to his already somber mood. Glancing out the passenger window, he watched people walking on the sidewalk, going in every direction, a multicultural collection of people from every continent and yet, everyone mixed together in their own small worlds.

"The music, it speaks to us. It speaks to our soul," He paused and sniffed before gesturing toward the dash. "Take this Madonna song for example, without realizing it, do you think this song maybe came to me today for a reason? Do you ever wonder that? Is it a coincidence when a song comes on at just the right time?"

His words made sense and yet, Chase wasn't able to focus. He thought back to his days in Hennessey, as he flew down the road in his old Civic and the music that would blare through the speakers. He preferred classic rock, often drawn to Pink Floyd along with a lot of heavier songs from both past and present. Did he even listen to music anymore? Why was it so relevant at one time and now almost completely insignificant?

"And this here," Diego continued and shook his head. "The last *real* album Madonna ever made. I mean, I love her work but this one had so much meaning, at least it did to me. It still does. It was so long ago at a different time, a different place. How young and naïve I was back then, *amigo*, how young and naïve we all were once."

His voice hinted of sadness and Chase noted a slight smile on his lips as he turned toward the mirror outside the car. "I think we all feel like that when we think of our past, Diego."

"Nah, you're still there," Diego attempted to assure him but Chase wasn't so convinced. He somehow felt as if he was long past that time and place but when you're young, no one ever believes it. They think you are exaggerating your trials and darkest moments as if they were minor compared to what was ahead.

"I'm not so sure," Chase admitted and opened his bottle of water, taking another sip. Was it possible it tasted worse and worse with every drink?

"Trust me, if we knew what was ahead at times, we would cherish each day," Diego insisted as they pulled into the parking garage and swung into an empty space.

Chase remained silent as they got out of the car and entered the nearby elevator. Neither said a word until they were in the office and even then, it was Diego that started to talk, letting Deborah know of her duties for the day, ordering Sylvana to meet with him in his office later that morning and finally, he turned his attention toward Chase.

"You, me and Jolene need to talk now."

"Ok."

Walking toward the boardroom, laptop bag swung over his shoulder, it suddenly felt heavy and uncomfortable as he passed Gracie, who slid out of the staff room, coffee in hand. Diego immediately stopped, his finger pointed in her direction while she remained relatively calm, if not guarded.

"You, I have something for later this morning. We're planning a big blowout for gay men, I want you to oversee it. I know you're new, so Chase will help you," He glanced back at Chase, who simply nodded. "There's a guy named Jesse that might be helping too. We will see."

Gracie simply gave a quick nod as Diego continued to move toward the boardroom, his voice boomed out, 'Jolene!' and his fingers pointed toward the empty room as he opened the door and stepped inside with Chase following behind. Immediately making his way to the head of the table, a position Jolene often took when she made it in the room first. It seemed like a competition between the two of them to see who would be in 'charge' of the meetings. Today, there was no mistaken it was the older of the two siblings.

"Yes, Diego, you called," Jolene asked as she swept into the room, her voice carried a hint of annoyance, although her expression suggested it was more teasing than anything else. "You beckon?"

"I have some ideas," Diego spoke in a low voice as he opened his laptop bag and pulled out his Mac. "I'm going to reach out to Jesse later today, I want to see if he will step in for this project, work with us and I have chosen Gracie to work with him. I think this is her domain, if she's good, that is."

"She has experience in party planning, event planning, so she will be good," Jolene spoke with confidence as she sat down, opening her own laptop and turned her attention toward Chase. "Have you talked to her yet, Chase?"

"Once," he admitted reluctantly, remembering the conversation but not able to recall the details. "Just small talk in the break room, I don't know her."

"She's a nice girl," her comment was slight but hadn't gone unnoticed by Diego.

"Jolene, we work here, not try to make friends or boyfriend and girlfriend stuff, this is work," His comment was sharp as he shook his head. "I need a coffee."

He rose from his chair and rushed out of the conference room.

"What's with him?" Jolene glanced over her shoulder while making a face. "And what is with you and the water? How much did the two of you drink last night?"

"Enough," Chase replied and felt his stomach turn slightly, as he recalled the entire evening.

"Did something..happen..."

"Not with me," Chase said and let out a small laugh.

"I do not want to know."

Not that she had to ask because shortly after Diego returned, he jumped into a quick preview of the previous night. He talked about how much Chase drank, the laughs they had and he even hinted at his flirtation with the waitress, something that immediately caused a skeptical expression on Jolene's face.

"You missed out on a fun night, Jolene," Diego insisted as he took a hearty drink of his coffee and then made a face. "Jolene, I think you should be in charge of the coffee. This stuff is terrible."

"Hey, I make that," She spoke up. "You don't like it, *you* make it!"

"When did you make it, three hours ago?"

"Maybe if you come to work in time, you would have it fresh," She retorted, her forehead wrinkled as her voice boomed through the room and Diego hid a smug smile behind the cup.

"So you have fun?" She asked skeptically, glancing in Chase's direction.

"Oh don't mind him," Diego insisted. "He's a little *hungover.*"

"Ah, did you feed him a lot of drinks?"

"I didn't force it down his throat. If that's what you're suggesting Jolene," Diego continued to sip his coffee before putting it aside. "He had fun at first."

"Diego, you are a bad influence."

He merely shrugged at her comment.

"You make people do things that are bad for them," She commented and Diego merely looked up from his screen with a raised eyebrow. "I know you."

"I think Chase would agree with you on that one," He suggested as his eyes drifted toward the topic of their discussion, creating more confusion for Jolene.

"What did you *do*, Diego?" She leaned in and challenged his eyes.

"To him?" Diego glanced toward a silent Chase. "I did nothing."

"What did you do?"

"I may have had relations with a woman."

"*What?*" Jolene asked, her mouth fell open in shock. "You've been with how many men and now, you think you might like to try women too? Diego, come on? What is that about?"

"You know, I thought I would try but I didn't like it," Diego sniffed and glanced toward Chase who remained stoic. He wasn't about to get into this conversation.

"People who are gay, Diego, don't just decide to *try* being straight," Jolene lectured him. "Why you do this? Why do you do this to a woman? Make her think you are interested when you're just trying to satisfy your curiosity."

"Hey, it's no different from men who've experimented with me even though they were pretty sure they were straight," Diego calmly pointed out and shrugged. "Who cares? It happened. Not my best decision but I did it, can we move on."

"Diego, other people, they have feelings, you know?" Jolene continued to lecture him. "You can't lead them on."

"I didn't lead her on," Diego corrected her. "I was very clear when she left that I wasn't interested."

"Did you tell her why?"

Diego started to appear irritated, his eyes suddenly wide open. "Did I tell her that I would rather a man go down on me than a woman? No, *Jolene,* I didn't feel the need to get into those details. I think she probably figured it out."

"Diego, you do not have to be vulgar. You can talk to people and be honest and *nice*," She spoke calmly, with emphasize on her last word. "That is all I'm saying."

He didn't respond but glanced at Chase.

"So you, you don't think this is smart either," Jolene directed her question at Chase. "Did you?"

"I think it's none of my business," Chase responded evenly.

"Look, he already gave me the guilt trip last night, I don't need one from you too," Diego spoke abruptly, his eyes fixated on Jolene. "He thinks it is wrong. I think you both are overly worried about this girl. Neither of you knows her but you know me and don't seem to care what I think about anything, do you?"

No one responded.

"Exactly!"

The meeting ended up being productive, Jolene and Diego actually agreed on the idea of moving ahead with the party for gay men. They were in agreement on how to proceed as well as the smaller details, something that rarely was the case when it came to anything between the siblings. Within an hour, they had mapped out the specific duties; Chase was on top of research and overseeing both Jesse and Gracie, whom Diego felt confident could run with it but still insisted on a full report by the end of each day, showing him where everyone was at when it came to planning and organizing a party that would, in his words, 'make or break' them with homosexual men.

Although he said nothing at the time, Chase was a little uncomfortable with one idea; Diego wanted him and Jolene to go to the party, to 'observe' and come back the following Monday with their 'impression' of everything. Although he had no issue with the homosexual lifestyle, he wasn't quite sure he was ready to enter that world to see what was a normal part of life to someone like Diego. His imagination and research had suggested that it wasn't something he would be comfortable with but then again, his one experience entering the women's parties had proven that his discomfort was possibly connected to sexuality in general, not just that of gay men.

At any rate, Diego made it sound pretty painless. A walk through, so that they wouldn't be invasive but still, aware of what was taking place; after all, this was his profession, wasn't it? Jolene looked skeptical.

"I do not want to," Jolene surprised him towards the end of the meeting, her face wrinkled up. "I do not want to know what you're doing with other men."

'You won't be seeing what *I* do with other men," Diego corrected her as he closed his laptop. "Look, this is part of the business and I'm not putting it out there to make either of your uncomfortable, I'm saying you have to see it with your own eyes. That is all."

"I don't know." Jolene made a face.

"Look, if I can hook up with a woman when I prefer men, then you two can get over your heterosexual narrow-mindedness and show up for this and see, that is all I ask. I don't want either of you hanging around to make others uncomfortable. Do you think these men want you both standing there, judging them? It goes both ways."

Neither Chase or Jolene responded. Not that Chase ever did when not necessary. He didn't offer his opinion but merely nodded. Jolene briefly made eye contact with him and then looked away.

CHAPTER THIRTEEN

Chase met Jesse on Friday. Much to his surprise, he wasn't the flamboyant homosexual he had, for some reason, expected. Instead, Jesse stood well over 6 feet tall and was dressed quite conservatively in a casual shirt and jeans. His eyes were a bland shade of blue, something that went well with the light shades of blond in his hair and when they shook hands, Chase noticed that he was wearing a wedding ring.

Quite modest, he was pleasant, if not overly friendly when introduced to Jolene and Gracie. Jolene said hello while Gracie gave a quick smile before flipping through her notebook to find an empty page. Chase noticed that the newest employee was dressed more conservatively than her first days at the office but continued to wear her trademark pigtails.

Diego, of course, took over the meeting in his usual, aggressive style, the same one he used when anyone other than just Chase and Jolene were in the room; it was only those times when he would fall out of this dominant role and feel free to jump to a more personal topic, to tease or joke around. He didn't do this in any other meeting but merely took charge in a direct and precise manner, which showed why he was perhaps a better business man than Chase originally thought.

Within 90 minutes, most decisions were made, with Jesse suggesting many factors that would make up this first party, appropriately called 'Coming Out'; a title that apparently had many layers. Diego seemed genuinely pleased with all the thought put toward the premier party for men as well as Jesse's ideas, allowing him to take over to a certain degree.

A potential venue had been viewed earlier in the week and Jesse insisted that it be organized in such a way that those who attended could explore within their comfort levels. "It's very important to set a tone from the beginning. If everyone feels your parties are inclusive, word will travel quickly and that's what you want." Jesse pointed out as he tapped his fingers on the table, his laptop sitting in front of him but it remained closed as if it were only a prop. "For example, you want the transgender community to feel welcomed, you want everyone to feel safe and not judged."

"But why judge? I don't understand?" Jolene spoke up for the first time in the meeting, her face scrunched up.

"There's sometimes a lot of judgment within the LGBT community," Jesse answered her question while nodding. "It's unfortunate since we get enough judgment *outside* our community but you would be surprised how much we judge one another too."

Chase remained silent but shared a knowing look with Diego. They had this discussion only days earlier with some surprising revelations.

"That's unfortunate," Jolene muttered while glancing at her laptop. "Do you think this will be a problem?"

"Nah, it's just a matter of trying to extinguish any potential issues in advance," Jesse replied and leaned back in his chair. "The main thing is that everyone has fun and walks out with a good impression."

"True that," Diego jumped back in and glanced at Gracie, who was taking notes but remained silent. Chase was a little concerned that she was given more responsibility than she was ready for when the weight fell on his own shoulders, but she showed no sign of hesitation.

"All right," Diego continued and stood up. "Now that we're all on the same page, I think I will leave it to Jesse and Gracie to spend some time together and come up with more details. If you have any questions, run them by Chase and give me a full report at the end of the day. I want this to happen soon, so maybe look into some prices, give me some numbers. How much will this cost? How much should we charge? I want a breakdown of the what and when. As many details as you can give me."

With that, he gathered his laptop and Jolene started to do the same, while Chase hesitated to get up.

"Do you want me to-

"No Chase, you come with me," Diego pointed toward their shared office. "We're going to plan for what we will do after this party. How much of our business will focus on this kind of party, where to go next, how we will promote."

"Social media," Gracie said something for the first time in the meeting. "We can target ads but for the most part, posts are free. We can build excitement as it draws closer."

"Get together with Sylvana about this, she can do up some images or whatever," Diego made a face and waved his hand in the air. "Whatever she does."

"Diego, we need to hire someone to help her out, she's got a lot on her plate, you know," Jolene spoke quietly, her voice somewhat hoarse. "It is not fair to throw everything at her."

"She can handle it," Diego assured his sister.

"I can help," Gracie spoke up while raising her hand. "I have some background in marketing from college and my last job. Wherever you need me."

Diego gave a satisfied nod. "Very good."

By day's end, Diego seemed satisfied that a venue was chosen, checked and already booked. Most details were decided, if not finalized, yet and it seemed the next big obstacle would be to find a good DJ, something that both Jesse and Gracie were confident could be done with ease.

Just before they left the office on Friday, Jesse informed Diego that he might have more good news. A popular rum company had expressed interest in sponsoring the party, which would not only cut down on costs but would provide an opportunity for them to test sample a new cooler that was about to hit stores, in a way, giving the attendees a 'sneak peak' to something that was not yet available to the public. Diego loved this idea and talked about it on the entire drive home.

"We save money, they get to show off this new product and they will post information about our party on their site and social media, getting the word out about our company," Diego spoke excitedly as he loosened his tie, a broad smile on his face. "Life is beautiful my friend, if you believe, it all works out."

"That's pretty awesome," Chase offered. "This Jesse guy seems to really know the industry. I can't believe he lost his last job."

"Ah...I think that was more of a personal thing with him and someone in the company," Diego offered and wrinkled his nose. "That's why I frown upon work relationships cause you know, it often ends up badly. That was the case with Jesse and one of the company owners. Trust me, I find out before inviting him in our doors, he seemed too good to be a true but after a couple of drinks, the truth, it poured out of him."

"I thought he was married," Chase said as he thought back to the wedding ring on Jesse's finger.

"Oh, the ring?" Diego asked. "Not married, some people, I guess they wear them to let people know they are in a 'dedicated' relationship." He let out a laugh. "I know, I know, you think that's nuts, I can tell. I know you."

"I didn't want to wear a wedding ring when I had to," Chase replied and glanced toward the window. "Of course, my marriage wasn't my idea and I certainly wasn't committed."

Diego let out a hearty laugh and raised his eyebrows. "To some, it is like a noose around their neck but to others, it makes them feel safe, I guess? I don't know, Chase, you and I, we are not marrying types."

"You don't think so?" Chase asked, surprised by his statement. He wasn't sure if he necessarily agreed.

"No, you aren't at this time, for sure and me, I'm too dangerous. People don't marry dangerous, they marry safe," He replied as the car slowed in rush hour traffic. "What they find exciting to date or to fuck isn't who they would marry. You know that right? I'm sure your ex found that out the hard way."

"I guess you could say that," Chase agreed as he thought about Diego's words. It didn't bring him much comfort to realize he wouldn't be viewed as 'safe' on the dating scene.

"I bet now, she's with some man who is nothing like you," Diego asked and lightly tapped Chase's arm. "Like the polar opposite, am I right?"

"Yes."

"See, that is what I am saying," Diego insisted. "People marry safe. Dangerous cheats. Dangerous hurts. Dangerous has no bounds and isn't scared to break conformity. If people marry it, they only do so once and never again. People want safe; safe mortgages, safe cars, job security, safe lives. People like you and I, we aren't that."

"That's kind of depressing," Chase quietly admitted. "I mean, I didn't want to get married the first time but I don't necessarily want to be single for the rest of my life either."

"The key, my friend is to find someone else who's also dangerous," Diego assure him as traffic picked up again. "You understand one another, there's a confidence that even if things were to not work out, you can handle it cause you're not the type to play by the rules anyway, to color inside the lines, so you are fine. You get it. You understand it. You can be honest with one another and know the other can handle it."

"I guess?"

"You will never be judged as harshly by someone who is dangerous because they are dangerous too. They get it, my *amigo,* they understand," Diego insisted as he tapped his steering wheel. "Safe judge harshly and try to make you feel shame every time you even look at someone else and in turn, make you resentful. No one likes to be judged."

"That's true," Chase considered the possibility. His first girlfriend had been dangerous and he was not, so she left him for another man who was dangerous. When he grew into a different kind of person, promiscuous and as Diego said, 'coloring outside the lines', he attracted Kelsey, who was the most dangerous woman he knew. As much as she was crazy, he got her. He got her more than any woman he had ever met.

"Anyway, this Jesse, he's safe. That's why he isn't married but still wears a ring on his finger." Diego replied as they got closer to the condo. "I don't care as long as he works well. He's asking for some serious cash to work for us, a high commission from the parties and hey, if he can pull in the money, I got no problem with that."

"Seems fair."

"As fair as anything in life is," Diego said and twisted his mouth into an awkward smile.

Unlike most weekends, Diego didn't take off with a suitcase on Friday night but instead lounged around the condo, laptop in hand until around 11, when he jumped up and said he was heading out for a 'date'. It was the most he had ever given away about what were usually secretive weekend plans. Chase merely nodded, telling him to have fun, as he headed to bed.

It wasn't until early the next morning as he walked out of his room, that Chase abruptly stopped in his tracks. Wrapped in a blanket on the couch, Diego looked small and frail, as he glanced up at Chase, a dark bruise was below his left eye. There was a moment when he looked startled by his roommate's appearance, as if he had forgotten where he was or what happened the previous night. Blinking quickly, he sat up and opened his mouth to say something but no words came out. There was shame in his eyes like he was caught doing something wrong, his usual strength depleted, leaving him vulnerable.

Chase felt his heart begin to race, as anger slowly burned through his veins, he remained stoic. "Tell me what happened."

CHAPTER FOURTEEN

Despite how he tried to downplay it, Diego was clearly shaken up. Reluctant to tell the truth, he huddled in a blanket, as if attempting to hide a part of himself that he didn't want Chase to see. It was clear that it was never his intention to fall asleep on the couch the night before or an assumption that Chase wouldn't be up so early to find him; whatever the reason, the truth didn't come out easily.

"Look, Chase, don't worry, I'm fine," Diego spoke in a hoarse voice, he cleared his throat and pulled the blanket closer, his bare legs slowly eased out of his personal cocoon, his feet carefully touched the ground as if in hesitation. His dark eyes carried a hint of guilt, suggesting he had done something to welcome a black eye but this didn't give any comfort to Chase, who hesitantly sat down on the nearby chair.

"Diego," Chase finally spoke. His eyes jumped to the floor and back to Diego, who was now sitting up, the blanket still wrapped around him, his bare legs were thin, resembling those of a teenaged boy, a hint of t-shirt could be seen above the blanket, making it clear he wasn't naked underneath. "I know its none of my business but the last thing you said to me before you left last night was that you were going on a date. And now," Chase hesitated for a moment before continuing. "You're sitting here with a black eye."

"Chase, I'm fine," His reply was quick, a slight change in tone caused Chase to flinch. "I know you're concerned but please, don't worry. I can look after myself."

With that he rose from the couch, pulling the luxurious white blanket tighter against his body, he silently walked away. It was only after he reached for the doorknob to his room that the blanket slid slightly just below his hairline to show more dark skin. Although Chase couldn't be sure, he thought it was bruising. It took a few minutes after Diego's quiet escape to his bedroom before Chase slowly stood up and left for the gym.

Even though he was full of anger when he left the apartment, by the time Chase stood in front of the heavy bag at the gym, his heart was instead full of sorrow. Although his voice was booming and his presence was larger than life, Diego himself was physically not a large man. It was true that he carried a gun but there were many situations when a weapon wasn't helpful.

After his workout and a quick shower, Chase changed and immediately headed home. He had errands to run but he had an unsettling feeling and wanted to check back to see if Diego needed anything. He arrived home to find the lime tree on the patio, the aroma of coffee in the air, but no Diego. Upon closer inspection, Chase noticed that his roommate's bedroom door was open and with some hesitation, decided to go inside to check things out.

The musky scent of cologne filled his lungs upon entering the room, indicating that Diego had left quite recently. The room was completely neat except for the white blanket from that morning and some clothing that was tossed on the floor. Diego's adjoining bathroom was empty, a white towel hung over the rack, a variety of hair and face products sat around the sink and a pair of boxer shorts were thrown in the corner. There was a heaviness in the air; a feeling that made Chase stop, hesitate for a moment before heading back into the living room.

Although the morning had been less than settling, he decided to carry on with his day and gage Diego's mood later. However, when he returned home around 4 to find an empty condo, he began to worry. Chase decided to send him a quick text to ask what he was doing for dinner as an excuse to check in.

I am tied up amigo. Talk later.

For some reason, this message didn't give Chase a sense of comfort. Where did Diego go? He was so secretive, so mysterious and although Chase briefly considered that this might be on purpose, something told him that Diego was naturally cautious about what he shared with people. Then again, hadn't Jolene always been the same? How much did Chase know about her life? The two had worked together for months in Calgary but she rarely talked about anything outside of the office; he had no idea what she did on weekends, who she spent time with or even if she was in a relationship. Perhaps being secretive was a family trait.

Chase fell to sleep early on Saturday night and found Diego in the kitchen the following morning, hastily ripping open cupboard doors.

"Ah, good morning, Chase!" Diego sang out as he abruptly stopped and glanced back, his black eye appearing worse than the previous morning. "Do you know where the sugar is? I need something sweet for my coffee this morning."

By sugar, he meant a specific raw brand that he insisted was the only one worthy of his gourmet coffee. Chase only used almond milk or cream in his and had no idea. "I haven't noticed."

"Shit, you know, I think I ran out," Diego said and rushed toward the garbage can, quickly opening it and looking inside while his long-sleeved t-shirt moved slightly, confirming what Chase had viewed the previous day was a bruise. It was difficult to tell if there were any other marks without staring too much. He wasn't sure how or if to approach the subject and finally eased into it after Diego announced that his raw sugar was, in fact, gone.

"I thought that was at work that I ran out," Diego said with a loud sigh and finally shrugged. "It's been a crazy weekend."

"Yeah, Diego, about that.."

"Look, I know what you want to say and I'm fine," Diego replied as he turned around, his hand rose in the air as if to show that Chase should stop. "It's okay, I'm okay."

"You didn't seem okay yesterday," Chase said with some hesitation. "You know, I can.."

"Chase, I do, I *do* appreciate your thoughtfulness," Diego said, his eyes suddenly lit up and he moved closer to him, his hand lightly touched Chase's arm. "But I am fine, as I said before. I know your loyalty is strong and we are family. But this is something I'm going to take care of myself."

A flicker of darkness ripped through his eyes as he moved away and returned his attention to the cup of coffee that sat on the counter. "Chase, my friend, the coffee is fresh, no need to waste any time. Have a cup!"

Accepting the fact that Diego didn't need his help, Chase respectfully stepped back and carried on with his day. He talked to the boys, made a half-hearted effort to look for an apartment and took a long nap. Feeling groggy when he woke, his stomach rumbling, Chase headed to the kitchen. Seeing Diego dressed in a shirt and tie, Chase assumed he had plans to go out for the evening so decided to heat up some leftover chicken and rice from the previous night.

Busy in the kitchen, he heard Diego rattling around in the closet next to the door, he assumed to find an umbrella for the rainy evening. Thinking of the weather, Chase glanced toward the patio and was relieved that the lime tree was already inside therefore he wouldn't be stuck dragging it in during a rainstorm. He placed his food on a plate, stuck it in the microwave and hit a few buttons. In the living room, Diego continued to dig in the closet and Chase stared into space, feeling oddly calm and tranquil.

The microwave beeped, grabbing Chase from his daydream and he quickly pulled his hot plate of food out. Sitting at the island where him and Diego usually dined, he heard the buzzer for the door and ignored it, assuming Diego was expecting company. Attempting to be inconspicuous, he dug into his rice and started to eat when he heard voices.

"*Hola!* Do come in, please," Diego sounded overly pleasant toward the stranger with a hint, just a whisper of something else; something that made Chase's heart pick up the pace just a tad. He ignored this instinct and continuing to chew his food and looked up to see a large Latino man walking in the adjoining living room, his dark eyes glared at Chase.

"Hey, who is that?" His words were abrupt as his face tightened into a brooding frown. Diego casually sauntered up behind the stranger, his lips scrunched up in a tight pucker of anger, a baseball bat in hand and with one, abrupt swing, hit the stranger in the back of the legs, knocking him to his knees. Loud, animal-like cries filled the room as the man fell to the ground. Chase dropped his fork.

CHAPTER FIFTEEN

It took him a few seconds to register what had just taken place. A stranger was face down on the living room floor while Diego stood over him with a baseball bat, rapidly bellowing out a series of Spanish words. It wasn't until he raised the bat again, that Chase instinctively jumped off the stool and rushed over.

"No No No! Wait!" Chase called out as he rushed toward the two men, his heart racing like a jackhammer. He assumed Diego wouldn't listen so was surprised to see him hesitate. It reminded Chase of when he would catch one of his children attacking the other; a sudden realization that they were not alone in the room. It briefly made Chase wondered what would've happened had he not been there.

"Yes?" Diego calmly asked, the baseball bat now swung over his shoulder, his eyes jumping between Chase and the victim that lay on the floor. The stranger was moaning in pain, awkwardly shuffling around but his movements were slow, reminding Chase of a dying animal.

"What the hell is going on here?" Chase muttered, his eyes darted toward the stranger, his brain rapidly searching for a way to resolve this issue. He had nothing.

"This, this piece of shit," Diego angrily replied, lowering his baseball bat, using it to point at the stranger who continued to make attempts to get up but with no success. "This is the man who did this." He gestured toward the bruise below his eye. "Nobody, and I do mean *nobody*, fucks with me, *amigo*."

With that, he fiercely lifted the bat, his eyes blazing as the stranger immediately raised one hand, signaling for him to stop. The same man who smugly entered the condo was now as helpless as a child, as he begged Diego to not hit him again. His eyes briefly sprang to Chase, as if silently begging for help than nervously jumped back to Diego.

"Give me one *fucking* reason why I shouldn't beat your skull into the ground *hijo de puta*," Diego replied with a surprisingly calm voice while his eyes continued to glare at his victim. He slowly lowered the baseball bat and proceeded to lean on it as if it were a cane. He made a face and his eyes softened slightly, but the tension in his face did not go away. "And it better be a good one because I'm not feeling particularly generous today."

"Alright," The visitor slowly turned around, his eyes jumped from Diego to Chase and back again. Now sitting up, Chase noted that the middle-aged man had hints of white in his black hair and some faint lines on his forehead. His movements were awkward and his eyes indicated his fear of the two men that stood over him. "I think, I think we can work this out."

It happened so fast that even Chase didn't notice until the baseball bat came down on the stranger's arm with a thud. He yelled something in Spanish and he tried to slide away from Diego, his eyes watering in obvious pain. It was Chase's natural instinct to stop this commotion before things accelerated to a level there was no coming back from; he reached out and gently touched Diego's arm. As if suddenly coming out of a trance, his eyes flickered toward Chase, a glaring darkness dimmed and his expression relaxed as the man on the floor continued to cry in pain.

"My arm! You broke my arm!" The stranger cried out as his opposing hand touched the upper arm and he leaned forward, his eyes closed.

Diego lowered the bat. His lips puckered and his face showed signs of satisfaction. He glanced to his right and he started to walk away but then abruptly turned around, immediately putting Chase on high alert.

"You!" He snapped at the man on the floor. "You're lucky that my friend is here to stop me, otherwise, I would've bashed your head in. You're lucky if it's just your arm broken. You go tell the *policia* and I will break much more next time."

"*No policia!!! No policia!!! I fell downstairs!*"

"You are *very* clumsy, *amigo*," Diego said with a cold tone. "Let me suggest that you be much more careful in the future." He tapped the baseball bat on the floor and puckered his lips.

The man started to rise, although it was slow and under Diego's narrowed stare, he did so once again moving away from them both, his eyes inflamed in fear, there was no doubt that he would be true to his word as he stumbled to his feet and slowly made his way toward the door. It wasn't until he was gone that Chase suddenly felt weak as if he was going to collapse on the floor.

"What the *hell* was that about?" Chase anxiously snapped, surprising both himself and Diego. It wasn't like him to probe into things that were none of his business but this time, it was unavoidable. His heart was suddenly pounding so hard that Chase was afraid that it was about to explode as adrenaline shot through his veins. Diego shrunk slightly, dropping from his powerful pose.

"*Amigo*, I am sorry you had to see that," Diego said and made his way to the door, where he peeked out the peephole and locked it before turning toward the closet and gently placing the baseball bat inside before closing the door. "I was hoping you wouldn't be here."

"It's a good thing I *was*," Chase said breathlessly, feeling a rush of anger fill his body while Diego, in comparison, appeared relatively calm. Maybe too calm, all things considered. "I wouldn't exactly want to return to a murder scene."

"Ah, Chase!" Diego said with a humored voice as he walked by and patted his arm casually before heading into the kitchen and Chase absently followed. "You're so dramatic! Are you sure it isn't *you* that is the gay one?"

"I'm serious Diego!" Chase replied, his throat suddenly feeling completely dry, he reached for his glass of water and took a gulp. "You could've killed him if you hit him in the head."

"I wasn't going to bash his skull in Chase," Diego said with a shrug, briefly making eye contact before looking toward the stove. "Any more of that chicken, *amigo*? It smells good."

"What? No, but look...can we talk about this?" Chase stuttered through his words and Diego stopped and leaned against the cupboard.

"We can talk about anything you wish." His eyes were serious, full of compassion as if nothing out of the ordinary had taken place moment earlier. "Anything, always." He appeared slightly vulnerable and Chase felt his defenses lower.

"Ok, I...I know its none of my business. I just want to know what happened here," Chase asked calmly, his body suddenly exhausted. The smell of his food caused his stomach to gurgle, something that hadn't gone unnoticed by Diego who pointed toward the plate.

"Eat my friend, this is not a concern anymore," Diego replied with a shrug.

"I was just a witness so," Chase stuttered and shook his head. "It kind of is."

"Like I say, it was that man who gave me these bruises." Diego pointed toward his eye then down toward his torso as his accent started to slip in. "I had to teach him a lesson. An eye for an eye, yes?"

Chase nodded in understanding and said nothing.

"I'm fine, you don't need to worry about me," Diego's comment was breezy as he drifted toward the fridge and opened the door.

"I do, though," Chase quietly replied and Diego turned, the door still opened, his eyes full of warmth.

"I am fine," He insisted and closed the door. "Really, I am. He left some bruises on me and it was honestly, a bit scary but you always look your enemy in the eye and let them know that you will not be their victim. You know?"

Chase nodded.

"How many bruises are we talking?"

Diego looked away, a glimmer of shame crossed his face as he silently removed his tie and unbuttoned his shirt. The bruises were painful to look at, appearing as though a hand had squeezed just below his neck on each side. Slowly removing his shirt, Diego's eyes expressed both vulnerability and humiliation, as he turned to show his upper back, covered in various shades of black and purple. His lower back also had some bruising and a small gash. It sent a shiver through Chase to see the wounds. He found himself look away as Diego put his shirt back on, his face dispirited as he turned around.

Pointing toward Chase's face, he quietly replied. "See, that is why I did not want to show you. I don't want your pity."

"I don't pity you," Chase spoke earnestly. "But I'm glad you showed me now because if I had seen all that before that guy came here, I mightn't have been so quick to stop you from hitting him."

A light filled Diego's eyes and he stood a little taller as if Chase had given him back some of his pride in a single comment. He looked as if he wanted to say something but instead patted his arm affectionately as he walked away and into his room.

Chapter Sixteen

Chase wasn't certain if Diego's bruises were the result of a business or personal relationship but he assumed the latter. They never spoke of it again and although Jolene attempted to find out some information, Chase refused to get involved and Diego simply made a joke of it.

"It is nothing, Jolene," Diego said with a quick shrug on Monday morning when the two stopped by her office shortly after arriving at work. "You know, boys will be boys, sometimes things happen."

"I do not like!" Jolene loudly replied as she rose from her desk and crossed the floor to inspect his eye closer. "Who do this to you?"

"Jolene, you really need to improve your English," Diego casually attempted to change the subject and made a face. "You know, it's been long enough that you've been in Canada, you have to start speaking like an American too."

Glaring at her brother, Jolene made a face similar to her brother's expression. "I am starting to see why they hit you." She showed only temporary frustration which quickly melted away to concern. "Seriously, Diego, who did this to you?" She asked with a hint of sadness in her voice, as Jolene moved forward and pulled her brother into a hug.

"Jolene Jolene!" Diego sang out her name in reference to the Dolly Parton song, causing her to let go of him and glare. "I'm fine. You worry too much. If you don't believe me, ask Chase?"

"I'm not getting into this," Chase replied with both hands in the air.

"You think I look bad, you should see the other guy," Diego spoke boldly and turned toward Chase once again, despite his disinterest in getting involved. "Am I right, Chase?"

Although he briefly hesitated, Chase reluctantly nodded in agreement as Jolene studied his face. Just then, Beverly entered the room holding a cup of coffee, she appeared slightly apologetic as she sat at her desk.

"Is this true, Chase?" Jolene asked pointedly, ignoring her assistant's arrival into the room. She crossed her arms over her breasts and tilted her head. "Is he *bullshitting* me?"

"No, he's not, Jolene," Chase felt confident in his answer. "He's *really* not."

Diego nodded proudly, a mischievous grin on his face. Crossing his arms over his chest like Jolene, he turned his attention back to her.

"Do I want to know more?" Jolene asked and immediately shook her head. "No, I do not."

Turning, she returned to her desk and Diego immediately followed.

"Hey Jolene, do you have any makeup, the kind that covers dark circles or anything like that, you know?"

Turning just as she was about to sit down, Jolene made a face. "I do not think my makeup can cover that, you know, it's not exactly dark circles under your eye."

"But even, you know, a bit," Diego asked and turned toward Chase, his lips squeezed together as he glanced in a nearby mirror. "Just to make it less *obvious*."

With a loud sigh, Jolene reached for her bag on the floor and muttered, "I cannot believe I have to put makeup on my brother."

"Thank you, Jolene," Diego sang out and turned toward Chase, who simultaneously noted the humored look in Beverly's eyes. "I will meet you next door."

Chase merely nodded before heading out of the room and toward their shared office, he quickly unlocked the door, dropped off his laptop and turned on the light before heading toward the staff kitchen to grab a coffee.

Gracie was leaving the staff room just as he arrived. He was surprised to see her hair a dark shade of blue and unlike most mornings, it fell loosely to touch her shoulders rather than in her usual pigtails. She also traded in her long, frumpy skirts and hippie blouses for a fitted black skirt and white blouse. He also couldn't help but notice the dark blue bra underneath but he quickly averted his eyes and pretended not to see.

"You look...nice," Chase said, careful of how he worded this compliment. He couldn't exactly tell her that she was sexy and that her new wardrobe was springing his desires to life but it was certainly a reality.

"Thanks, I decided to get some new clothes this weekend, maybe try something new with my hair." She let out a soft giggle that only caused his desires to climb. "Diego probably won't like the hair."

"You mainly..ah, deal with people on the phone anyway, don't you?" He asked, almost stuttering through his words. "I'm sure he won't care."

"Yeah, you're probably right," She shrugged and gave him a quick smile, as he awkwardly reached for the door and she followed him in the staff room. "I guess we have a meeting later."

"*We* do?"

"Yeah, that's what Jolene said, to talk about the party," She commented and didn't break eye contact with him for a second. "I'm not sure if Jesse will make it, though. I think Diego is sending me a list of things for us to do."

He nodded and she gave him one last, seductive smile before easing out the door. He was left feeling dumbfounded but quickly shook away his thoughts and moved on with his day.

Later that morning, Diego flew through the office, shooting off demands to everyone, as the last details of their first party for gay men rapidly came together. He excitedly announced that everything was 'perfecto' and that he would spend most of the afternoon out with Jesse and Jolene, first to meet with reps from the rum company and then drop by the venue to nail down the final details with the owner.

The black eye, although still there, was slightly toned down from that morning, so clearly Jolene's makeup was somewhat helpful. Diego seemed satisfied and quickly forgot about it as he excitedly rushed through his day. It was only as Jolene and Diego left to meet Jesse that Chase remembered his meeting with Gracie.

"Now, the two of you," Diego instructed as he and Jolene stood in the doorway and Gracie entered the room. "I want the two of you to go through the list that I sent Gracie earlier, get me some prices. We will order first thing tomorrow morning. Whatever it is we need. Also, we need to start thinking about a bigger storage area for the stuff we aren't renting. That big closet off the staff room just isn't going to cut it any longer."

"We figure that later, Diego. Come on, we must go," Jolene cut in and ushered him toward the door. "You two, research prices, try to think of anything we are missing and we will return later."

Gracie appeared slightly apprehensive, if not shy, as she closed the door and walked toward Chase's desk. Grabbing a nearby chair, she pulled it close and sat her laptop down and proceeded to open it.

"I've already got a list of prices, so there isn't much for us to talk about," She said, appearing bored, as her fingers rapidly clicked on the keyboard while Chase felt his desires from the morning melt away. "I sent it to you if you want to look at it."

"Sure."

A quick glance at the document proved that Gracie was on the right track and Chase couldn't think of what else was left to discuss. They quickly reviewed the other upcoming parties but since most were in other cities, the details would be prepared by the two planners who worked remotely. Fortunately, they were reliable, working independently, receiving a commission rather than a pay cheque.

"As much as I hate to say it, Diego does run things well although he's kind of crazy, you know?" Gracie said as she closed her laptop, a smile on her face. "So he's your boyfriend?"

"My what? No," Chase replied with a laugh. "Wait, do people think that he is?"

"No, I'm sorry, I misspoke," Gracie muttered, her eyes looked down and a tinge of pink filled her cheeks. "Someone said this morning that you lived together? I'm probably wrong, though."

"He's gay but I'm not," Chase quietly confirmed. "As for me living with him, it's just because I haven't found an apartment yet. I've been so busy with work and when I first got here, I guess I was a little overwhelmed."

"I can understand," Gracie said as she sat back in her chair. "It can be scary."

Chase silently nodded.

"Do you have friends or family here?"

Chase shook his head. "The only people I know work in this office."

"It can be difficult to meet new people in a city this big. I was lucky because my sister was here in university when I arrived."

"That's good," He quietly replied and they both fell into an awkward silence.

"Well, I think I'm going back to my desk to work on some other things if that's ok?"

Chase nodded but felt disappointment to see her leave. They had barely met for fifteen minutes and already she was ready to find a reason to go.

"Sure," Chase replied, not sure of what else to say.

Gracie gave a hesitant smile and left the office. It was when she hastily returned a few minutes later and stuck her head in the door that alarmed him slightly.

"There's something....*going on* in the bathroom."

"Going on?" Chase asked with some hesitation as he started to stand. "What do you mean, *going on*?"

"I think you should come...see," Gracie spoke slowly, almost stumbling over her words as Chase got up and rushed toward the door. He watched her scurry into the staff room and he followed her. It was immediately clear what she was referring to; a banging noise could be heard from inside the ladies room, as he exchanged alarmed looks with Gracie, he was hesitant to enter. He wasn't sure if she clued on what was taking place until the animal like moans started. The moment she did, her face turned a hot pink and she stepped back slightly.

"Who the hell is in there?" Chase whispered.

"I don't know," Gracie said with an apologetic shrug.

"Sylvana? Benjamin?"

"Sylvana told Diego she was going to a dentist appointment and Ben's out running an errand this afternoon," Gracie spoke in a hushed tone. "I saw them both leave."

"Beverly? Deborah?"

Without uttering a word, as the moans got louder, Gracie rushed out the staff room and quickly returned. "Deborah isn't at her desk and Beverly has the door closed so she's either in there or left the building."

"Maybe," Chase said and looked from Gracie to the door and back again. The noise stopped.

"You aren't going to make me go in there, are you?" Gracie asked as she shrunk back. "I can't..."

"No, no that's fine," Chase said and let out a loud sigh. "Just go back to your desk and I will take care of this."

"Ok," Gracie said in a little voice. "I still have to pee. Can I use the men's room?"

"Sure, yes, that's fine," He awkwardly replied and watched Gracie make a beeline for the door.

Just as the men's room door swung shut, the ladies' room door opened and Deborah walked out followed by the young delivery guy from a well-known courier company. It was a toss-up which of the two appeared more shocked to see Chase waiting for them, as he stood with his arms crossed over his chest.

"I thought you said everyone was in meetings," The delivery man muttered with some resentment as he passed Deborah and merely shrugged at Chase. "Sorry man, I..."

"Just go, please," Chase spoke firmly and then turned to Deborah. "You, the boardroom, *now*."

No longer standing as tall as she was when departing from the washroom, she followed Chase's instructions as he followed. Once the two of them were in the room behind closed doors, he turned toward her and shook his head.

"Really? I mean, during work hours, at *your* workplace, you pull this shit?" Chase snapped at her before she could even sit down, she instead stood awkwardly with tears in her eyes.

"I'm sorry, I didn't think anyone was here. I thought everyone was in meetings..."

"You do realize, that doesn't make it okay, right?"

"I know, I can't help it," She continued while nervously picking at her nails. "I have a...I have a problem."

Chase raised his eyebrows and didn't respond.

"I am a sex addict."

He shook his head in disbelief.

"I know everyone thinks it's an excuse for bad behavior," She attempted to joke but Chase wasn't in the mood. "But it's true. I have a therapist who would vouch for me and I go to a regular group. It's not helping."

"I see that." Chase dryly replied.

"I'm sorry...it won't happen again," She continued as her eyes seemed to grow behind her dark glasses. "I promise. Please don't tell Diego and Jolene."

Chase didn't respond.

CHAPTER SEVENTEEN

Their voices could be heard booming through the hallway as soon as they returned later that afternoon. Jolene's heels sharply clicked on the floor, rapidly growing louder while Diego's voice dominated the conversation, much like an excited child that was on a sugar high, he was talking a mile a minute as they entered the office.

"I can think it's sexy without being straight," Diego was insistent as he walked toward his desk and Jolene leaned in the doorway making a face. "It's the same with men and women, we all like watching half-naked, sexy people dancing around. Come on, the entire music industry is built on it these days. Do you seriously think that some of those talentless morons on the TV channel, what you call it, with all the music?"

"I did not realize there was such a channel anymore," Jolene said as a smooth grin crossed her lips. "Besides, that's not the same Diego."

"It *is* the same," Diego insisted as he sat behind his desk. "Do you think some of those women would be famous if they didn't have the hair, the makeup, the tits, come on! Sex sells and it's the same with men. Half-naked men, with the abs, the," he paused and turned his attention toward Chase. "Like this guy over here. Did you ever see his abs. Phew! To die for! Get him dancing on a stage, the men at the party would lose it!"

"*Really??*" Jolene turned her attention to Chase and raised her eyebrows. "I could always see that, you know, he had muscles and was strong but I did not know he was like...the belly, all flat and ah, what do you call?"

"Washboard abs."

"Yes!" Jolene said enthusiastically and then her expression fell. "Why do they call them that? Washboard? I do not understand."

"It doesn't matter," Diego said with a shrug.

"Ok, you know I would do a lot for this business," Chase suddenly spoke up as he shifted awkwardly in his chair. "But I'm not taking my clothes off at one of these parties. No way!"

"Did I ask?" Diego asked innocently, his eyes widened and he made a face. "You're family, we don't want our family treated like that, am I right Jolene?"

"Of course not," Jolene insisted and hesitated for a moment. "Your abs, are they like, I don't know, are they like David Beckham's abs, you know?"

"Ah no, they're way better," Diego insisted and sat up straighter in his chair, his eyes wide while he nodded his head. "Like way better but he's like 20 years younger. Isn't Beckham my age? Everything is easier when you're 23."

"This is true," Jolene said with a quick nod. "Me, trying to keep in shape now, it is not so easy."

"I don't think my abs as good as David Beckham's," Chase added, finally able to get a comment in, unsure of why they were even discussing this in the first place. "I think that guys got a lot more going for him than me."

Jolene shrugged and Diego seemed to ignore his comment as he read something on his laptop.

"Why are we talking about my abs?" Chase quietly asked.

"Oh, we were talking about stuff to add to parties and Diego thinks we need strippers," Jolene commented as she leaned in the doorway.

"We've done that before," Chase reminded her.

"I know but I do not know if we needed that, you know? It's an extra cost."

"But for this first boy party, we need to go all out," Diego piped up again as he squinted over the keyboard as he leaned back in his chair. "Why is the print on this laptop so small lately?I can't seem to get it the right size."

"You need glasses, the ones you read with, I tell you that," Jolene sharply reminded Diego and turned her attention toward Chase, as she edged out of the room. "My brother, he does not want to admit he is getting old."

"I'm not old, Jolene."

"You need reading glasses."

"I don't," He insisted. "I just need to fix the print size is all. That's it."

She didn't respond but winked at Chase on her way out.

When left alone, the room was suddenly silent. Too silent.

"What's going on Chase?"

"What?"

"I can tell something is wrong," Diego said as he looked up from the laptop. "Did something happen? With your kids? I don't know? You seem unusually quiet."

"I'm always quiet."

"Nah, not this kind of quiet," Diego insisted, his face twisted into a seductive smile. "You forget, I know you."

Chase thought about it for a moment before he slid from behind his desk and gently closed the door before crossing the room. "There was an...incident while you and Jolene were out."

"An incident?" Diego asked, his eyes widened as Chase sat on the other side of the desk. "Like what? I think our idea of an incident might be a little different."

Thinking about the violent attack on the weekend, Chase grinned in spite of himself and nodded. "This is true. It wasn't serious but it was....weird and I'm not sure of how to handle it."

"What?" Diego appeared intrigued. "What happened? Was it something with Gracie?"

"No, not directly, anyway," Chase said and hesitated. "I'm not sure how to put this delicately...."

"Chase, come on, you know I'm not someone you have to be *delicate* with," Diego let out a laugh. "After this past weekend, do you think that anything shocks me? Come on!"

"Ah....Gracie came to get me because she heard some strange noises coming from the ladies room," Chase started and kind of hoped Diego clued in to where he was going but he continued to look puzzled. "I went into the staff room and it was clear that someone was having sex in the bathroom."

"Someone was having sex in *our* bathrooms?" Diego said and although he briefly looked stunned, he quickly began to laugh. "Are you teasing me, Chase? Who was left and you and Gracie had a meeting. Sylvana and Benjamin were gone and..."

"Yeah, it was Deborah and some delivery guy."

Diego let out a hearty laugh and clapped his hands together. "Well, it sounds like he certainly delivered."

Chase opened his mouth to reply but wasn't sure what to say. He had assumed Diego would be mad and wasn't even sure if he should let him know the truth.

"You will have to point this delivery guy out next time he's here," Diego continued to snicker. "I know I'm gay but come on, you're the straight one here, do you think Deborah...I don't know, she doesn't seem like the type."

"She said she's a sex addict." Chase dryly commented.

Diego let out another hearty laugh and leaned back in his chair. "That one," he pointed toward the general direction of Deborah's desk. "That one with the glasses and dresses like an old lady? Seriously? *Wow!*"

"You're not mad?" Chase was genuinely surprised. "I was scared you would fire her."

"Nah, that's Jolene," Diego corrected him and regained his composure. "Now she would fire her for that and say it's unprofessional but me, I'm easy. I don't care."

"I won't tell Jolene."

"Now me, I think when the inspiration hits you, you got to go with it," He raised his eyebrows seductively and Chase awkwardly stood up from the chair and was about to return to his desk when Diego made another comment. "I know you're not different."

The room suddenly felt suffocating, his body tense as he observed the taunting expression on Diego's face; his eyes were challenging, his lips were tight and the insinuation behind the words could not be missed. Diego entwined his fingers and leaned back in his chair. Chase felt his stomach churn nervously and sat back down.

"I know you aren't exactly opposed to pleasure at work," He said with a mischievous grin easing on one side of his lips, almost as if he was fighting it off. "A couple of encounters with a young woman, maybe there was a camera involved?"

Chase froze. His brain rushed through some less than stellar moments from his past when he was full of anger and driven by passion, a bad combination when offered the opportunity to record a quick hook up at work. Bud, his former boss at the bar, had surprised him when confessing that he had a side porn business and offered Chase an opportunity to make extra money through a voyeurism movie that wouldn't require his face onscreen. He accepted.

Jolene had learned about this shameful part of his past after Kelsey, a friend from Hennessey, allowed the truth to slip out during her visit to their former Calgary office. Jolene hadn't cared and insisted it had no bearing on the work he did with her; until that moment, he had assumed it was in the past and she hadn't told anyone.

Feeling his face burning now, Chase took a deep breath and nodded. "Jolene told you."

"Of course, Jolene, she tells me everything," Diego smirked and appeared to have a new wave of confidence take over him. "Tell me something Chase, did you think I wouldn't find out? I know everything."

"It's not exactly the proudest moment of my life," Chase commented in a low voice that indicated his shame.

"No need to be embarrassed. It was a very impressive performance," Diego replied with a raised eyebrow. "Oh yes, I saw the movies."

Chase opened his mouth to respond but couldn't talk. He felt physically ill as his entire body grew warmer, his clothing suddenly felt tighter and yet at the same time, he felt small, almost as if he would sink into the floor. The humiliation was stronger than it had been when Jolene learned the truth; partly because she handled it with more sensitivity while Diego was mocking, appearing to enjoy watching him squirm.

"Don't be like that, come on," Diego teased and let out an innocent laugh, eliminating some of the tension. "I'm just giving you a hard time. I thought it would be fun to point out the irony of *you* coming to me with this story."

"Diego, I..."

"You regret it, I know I know," Diego said and waved his hand dismissively. "Look, it's the past, you wish you hadn't done it, I know I know...its fine. I just thought I would let you know that I like your little movies."

"How did you get them, I thought they would be destroyed or hopefully forgotten by now," Chase asked, immediately feeling incredibly naïve, vulnerable in Diego's eyes.

"They're out there, not easy to find, but they're out there," His reply was casual as if they were merely talking about Chase's graduation photo, not a few movies that had him participating in a sexual act.

"How did you find them?"

"I can find anything my friend," Diego insisted as he raised his eyebrows. "This was before I met you so of course, I was a little concerned especially when you worked so closely with my sister."

It suddenly made sense. Chase had worked many months with Jolene before actually meeting 'the boss', which turned out to be Diego. His surprise appearance in their Calgary office one day months earlier had started off on the wrong foot and now that the truth came out, Chase understood Diego's original hostility toward him.

"So you came to see if I was a dirty pervert?"

"I was kind of *wishing* you were a dirty pervert but with me, not my sister," Diego teased and raised one eyebrow.

Sensing Chase's discomfort, Diego let out a boisterous laugh and clapped his hands together.

"No no, there were a lot of reason plus I was worried about my sister. She always sounded so stressed and of course, to meet you too," Diego insisted as he shuffled some papers on his desk, his attention briefly diverted. "You were harmless, I could see that right away. I liked you and here we are." He waved his arms in the air

"I regret those movies," Chase continued to feel shame regardless of the fact that Diego was making light of the situation. Although his face wasn't exposed in the movies, everything else was; the scenes shot through his mind like rapid fire.

"Why? It's your past," Diego seemed oddly nonchalant about it. "Who cares? Lot of people make these movies. It's not like people would know it was you. I only did because I went to this old boss of yours about it."

"And he gave them to you?"

"They were online amigo, he sent me the links."

"Great! How many other people knows about them. He didn't even know you and…"

"Hey hey, calm down," Diego put his hand up in the air. "He didn't at first, I gave him an offer he couldn't refuse."

"You paid him?"

Diego shrugged, his eyes rolled to the heavens. "Something like that," he was dismissive and leaned on his desk. "We talked, business man to business man. Don't worry, Chase, these movies, I can make them disappear if you like."

"Just like that?"

"Just like that."

"On the Internet? Seriously?" Chase asked skeptically.

"It can be done."

"Please!"

"I'll take care of it," Diego replied as Chase slowly rose from the chair, his legs feeling shaky as he crossed the floor to his desk. "But I'm keeping my copies, amigo."

Chase didn't reply as Diego laughed.

Chapter Eighteen

The days flew by, leading up to the night of their first party for gay men. Diego was anxiously fluttering about all week to make sure everything went off without a hitch while Chase felt anxious as the party drew closer. Although he understood why Diego wanted him to take a 'walk-through' to get a feel for their sex parties for homosexual men, Chase felt awkward. It wasn't that he had an issue with gay men or their lifestyle, he just felt uncomfortable viewing it in person. In the end, his worry was for nothing because a last-minute emergency with the scheduled doorman forced Chase to take over his duties for the night.

It felt strange doing the same job he had back in Calgary, when he first worked for Jolene and her skeleton crew. In comparison, it definitely was the busiest party he had ever worked the door for and it went on until past 4 a.m. Exhausted when the party finally ended, Chase was surprised that Diego was hyper, insisting the night had been a wild success.

"Perfecto!!" He exclaimed on his way out the door with an exhausted looking Jesse by his side. The two had overseen everything at the party as the roles of host and organizer to see what did and didn't work. "Gracie did good with the details, didn't she?"

His attention turned toward Jesse, who took a minute to reply.

"Yes, she did great for her first, big assignment. I think from this point on, it will be all downhill."

"Not *too* downhill, though," Diego quickly injected. "We don't want her to get lazy."

"Oh, of course not," Jesse replied with a yawn. "But now that we know the perfect formula. You should add a suggestion area to your site to learn what the customers wants and build on it."

"Ah yes!" Diego agreed enthusiastically as they headed toward their cars in the back of the building. Boldly walking ahead as if he had no worries in the world, despite the fact that they were in a dark parking lot in the middle of the night. "Ah, I'm in the mood to dance or have some fun, are there any after hours clubs around?"

"We *were* the after hours club tonight," Jesse said and followed his words with a laugh. "Most of those places are probably about to close if they haven't already."

"There must be a place? Maybe someplace that isn't so known about?" Diego muttered as the two of them walked ahead of Chase, who would've been happy to crash at that point but didn't say anything. "With your connections, if there's a party, you would know, right?"

"Hmmm...." Jesse stopped in front of his car and started to tap on his phone. "I can't think of anything but if there is, I know the girl who will know."

Diego rubbed his hands together excitedly, his eyes sparkled in excitement as he glanced at Chase. Jesse was scanning through his phone when it beeped and he started to nod.

"Yes, it's not far from here actually," Jesse said as he glanced at Diego. "Wanna go?"

"Yes please!" Diego spoke excitedly, his eyes appeared to double in size as he turned to Chase and slapped his arm. "Come on Chase, it'll be fun!"

Before he could respond, Diego was already getting in his car and Jesse was still tapping on his phone. Chase walked around to the passenger side and climbed in.

"This is exactly what I need!" Diego commented as he fastened his seatbelt and stared ahead at Jesse climbing into his own car. After the break lights came on, Diego started his Lexus and followed him out of the parking lot into the quiet Toronto streets. Although Chase secretly didn't want to go, he knew that it was easier to go along with Diego.

Down the street, through the lights, they continued to drive until Jesse pulled onto a side street and his break lights came on and he signaled right. Diego did the same and they pulled into a dingy little parking lot and drove around for a while until Jesse stuck his arm out the car window and pointed toward the next block. They followed him until they finally found a lot with some empty spots. After parking, the three of them were left walking a bit of a distance before arriving at the back door in a sketchy alley.

A doorman that was substantially larger than Chase opened the door and nodded when he saw Jesse, letting the three of them in without saying a word. His eyes searched Chase's face momentarily before looking away.

Inside there was a full on dance party with a crowd so thick that Chase could barely move but he noticed Diego slid through with no issue, while Jesse was far ahead and at a small bar, where someone was pouring three shots. The main bar was full of people dancing on it; mostly women around his age while people continually were climbing on the tables and doing the same, as dance music poured through the room, the smell of sweat and alcohol filled his lungs. It probably would've been an ideal spot for someone who liked to party all night but that definitely wasn't Chase. In fact, the atmosphere made him feel awkward and lonely.

As he walked by one of the tables full of women dancing, he was suddenly alerted when one went over her ridiculously high heels and stumbled sideways. Although her friend attempted to grab her, she was already falling to the side and toward Chase. His eyes widened, suddenly very alert and awake, he instinctively reached out and grabbed the screaming woman just as she was about to awkwardly fall to the floor. Thrust into his arms, Chase wasn't sure which one of them was more surprised as she clasped his shoulder in a panic.

"Oh my God!" She yelled, wiggling around in his arms like an annoyed cat, her blue eyes full of panic, as he slowly sat her down. After wobbling in her heels for a moment, leaning up against Chase, she appeared embarrassed as she shared a small smile with him. Pushing a strand of her blonde hair aside, she apologized before rushing off while another young lady followed her toward the other side of the room.

Back at the small bar, Diego was looking in his direction, laughing hysterically. Jesse was also watching with a grin on his face, a drink in hand as Chase slowly made his way through the crowd to join them.

"Chase!" Diego yelled over the music and enthusiastically grabbed his arm. "The superhero! Catching falling damsels in distress."

Jesse laughed at the comment while Chase merely smiled and shyly looked away, slightly embarrassed by his part in the situation.

"She was cute though, right?" Diego sang out as he glanced toward the table she had fallen from. "You better stay away from over there or all the women will be trying to fall in your arms, am I right Chase?"

Letting out a high pitch, sharp laugh, he turned back toward the bar and held up a shot for Chase. "Here's one for you, superhero!" His comment was jovial. "We were waiting for you."

Before he could respond, both Diego and Jesse grabbed their own shots and sank them back. Chase did the same, the bitter taste burned his throat and his face grimaced as the liquor continued to burn all the way down.

"Hope you liked it!" Diego called out over the music. "I had to pay triple since it's after hours and technically, I think it's illegal."

"Thanks," Chase replied and glanced around the room. "I didn't need a shot, you know I don't drink much."

"Ah, once in a while won't hurt you, Chase," He spoke dismissively as if his mind were already in another place. Across the room, a group of men stood together looking in their direction and specifically at Diego. "I'll be right back, my friend."

The crowd continued to grow thicker and Chase couldn't help but feel claustrophobic as he watched Diego get lost in it. Easing back into the corner, he turned to talk to Jesse but he was gone too. Looking around, he realized that he was now alone, in the middle of a party that he didn't care about after having a shot that he hadn't wanted in the first place.

Taking out his phone, he glanced at it briefly and considered sending Diego a text that he was going to grab a cab home but then again, was he not giving this place enough of a chance?

"Chase?" He heard his name and turned to look at a woman who looked slightly familiar and it took a moment for him to recognize Deborah. *Deborah?*

Although there were small fragments of his coworker, without the dark framed glasses and boring, bland office attire that made her look unappealing, she was a whole other woman. Her dark hair hung loose, gently caressing her shoulders that were barely covered with any material, her cherry red dress reaching above her knees and hugging every curve, highlighting her thin frame. As the alcohol kicked in, he couldn't help but feel a shot of desire as he remembered her recent hookup with the delivery guy, followed by the confession that she was a sex addict. Was that why she was at this party? Was she looking for someone to take on her strong desires?

"Deborah? What are you doing here?" Chase asked casually even though yearning was building up inside of him as she stood extremely close to him, her scent filling his lungs.

"I could ask you the same," She commented, her hand suddenly touched his arm, although briefly, the flicker of her finger sent a wave of sensations through his body as he quickly glanced around the room.

"I was here with Diego," He replied evenly, "And Jesse but...they disappeared."

"Do you really want to know where they are?" She spoke directly into his ear, her hot breath sending a shot of arousal right to his groin. "They are on the other side of the room snorting coke with some guys. I saw him. He told me you were here."

"What?" Chase asked, feeling completely shocked and immediately after, completely naïve. "Are you kidding me?"

Deborah shook her head no, her chocolate eyes staring into his. "Maybe you need a ride home?"

The insinuation was there. He didn't hesitate to say yes. It didn't matter that they worked together. It didn't matter that he normally wasn't at all attracted to her. It didn't matter that he was leaving Diego at the party without telling him. These were all secondary thoughts as they rushed out of the building and to her car. Sitting on the passenger side, he was surprised when she glanced around the parking lot before leaning inside the open door, her lips abruptly grasping his as her fingers reached for the zipper of his pants. Within seconds, her hands were inside his boxers and working the kind of magic that only a woman with some experience could do. The next thing he knew, a condom was tightly clamped to his dick, the door shut and she was sitting facing him.

Deborah barely had her eyes closed as she leaned into him, her hot breath touched his face as she moved him inside her and let out a soft moan and he gasped in pleasure as she moved on top of him, the sound of muffled music from the nightclub could be heard from outside the walls. She started off slow but quickly picked up the pace as he reached out and held on to her hips, feeling lost in strong desires as she began to make more noise and wiggle around almost driving him around the bend as she let out a loud moan and gasped as she roughly bounced on his lap causing waves of pleasure to shoot through his groin.

It had been a long time. Way too long, he realized as their encounter ended.

"I always wanted to do that," she whispered in his ear. "Now, where do you live?"

CHAPTER NINETEEN

It didn't end in the car. Chase was relieved that Diego didn't return until Sunday evening since Deborah didn't leave until early that afternoon. Sleep was infrequent but sex appeared to be her main priority, their conversation limited to her asking if the condo was 'his place' and if he had more condoms. At the time, high on pleasure, Chase didn't think about the fact that her focus was only on sex. However later, after she left, the entire night seemed surreal and strange. He wasn't sure how he felt about seeing her at work the next day.

The weekend left him feeling drained and unsettled. His fling with Deborah felt like the symptom of a bigger problem, a sign that his life was quickly sliding off track and into a territory that wasn't quite right. The longer he lived with Diego, the more he felt as though he no longer knew himself. Then again, was that a bad thing? Personal evolution was something to strive toward but how did you know if it was a more authentic you or the results of someone else's design? How much influence did the Silvas have on his life?

The truth was it was loyalty. His connection to Diego was strong and in essence didn't allow him much room to move. In many ways, when Diego insisted that he and Jolene were his family now, it was true. Barely in contact with his relatives, Chase felt as though his past was long out of sight. His own mother hadn't been in contact with him in months, his sister occasionally sent him a text but that was about it. Even his aunt Maureen did little more than send him an occasional email.

The most distressing relationship was the one he had with his three sons. Although they still talked to him on Skype, it reminded him of the obligatory conversations, as if they would rather be doing almost anything else. Although he attempted to act normal and upbeat, Chase felt his heart breaking with each conversation. He could see it in their dismissive eyes; he wasn't their father anymore. It was clear that his ex-wife was making every attempt to keep the children in contact with him but it was a battle of wills; three energetic children against one woman was never a fair fight. She would make excuses, apologize and genuinely show regret when her attempts appeared futile but the reality was always there; he just wasn't ready to face it yet. He was another one of *those* fathers but for the first time, he understood how it was sometimes easier to distance yourself, especially when the children didn't appear to need you any longer.

Sunday was no different.

"I'm sorry, Chase," Audrey spoke gently from the other end of the line. "Albert took the twins to the park and Leland is at your mom's house."

A double sense of dread filled him; not only would he not get the opportunity to speak to his kids, he didn't like the fact that any of them were spending time alone with his mother. Although she had been a thoughtful and nurturing mother during his childhood, she had also been abusive; her temperament often complicated by what he believed were some serious emotional issues. However, since Audrey worked in the mental health field, his own concerns were often brushed off as being exaggerated. It was as if what had happened to him growing up was inconsequential and sometimes, Chase wondered if Audrey thought he was only making it up.

"And I know what you're thinking," Audrey continued on the other end of the line in a soft voice. "But I think your mother is great with the kids, trust me, I've been watching her all these years. She would sacrifice her own life for theirs, so you needn't worry. Leland loves his time with grandma."

Deciding it wasn't a fight he wanted to have that day, he instead asked how the children were doing, listened to a few short stories, glimpses into what he was missing now that he moved out; some of it pulled at his heartstrings while at the same time, he remembered the hell of living with Audrey and the misery they provoked in one another. She was a whole other person since he left; much happier, their relationship better than he would've ever expected but at the same time, Chase often wondered what it would be like if he was still in Hennessey and available to his children in person.

Then again, he knew there was nothing for him in that dead-end town. He would feel like a stranger if he returned. He wasn't the Chase Jacobs he was in those days. Unfortunately, he didn't know who he was at this point. His identity limited to employee, friend to Diego and little else. Even his boxing was starting to disappear even though he continued to work out at the gym, his passion for everything seemed to fade away.

Diego, however, had enough passion for the entire building. Always full of energy and light, he eventually returned to the condo later that day, looking no worse for wear considering he probably had no sleep. His clothes wrinkled, his jacket in hand, he waltzed in as Chase lay on the couch, feeling heavy and drained at the same time.

"*Amigo*!! What are you doing lying around on the couch?" Diego asked with a shot of enthusiasm in his voice as he approached Chase, his eyes scanning over his body. "Didn't you get enough sleep last night?"

With that, he let out a loud burst of laughter as he headed toward the kitchen and proceeded to make coffee. Chase didn't reply, wondering if that was a sign that he somehow knew about his night with Deborah, something he didn't want to talk about. His thoughts were still on his earlier conversation with Audrey and the general depression that was creeping in.

"Hey, great party last night," Diego continued as he hit the button on the coffee maker and turned around to refocus on Chase. "I think I slept like three hours today."

Although he was curious where he had been, he didn't ask. Chase suspected Diego had many affairs but didn't want to know the details and certainly didn't want to open the pandora's box about his own sorted evening. Instead, he sat up on the couch and yawned.

"Yeah, it was a long night," Chase added as he heard Diego rush by, whistling as he walked toward his bedroom. Looking around, deciding that he didn't want to deal with much more that day, Chase decided to go into his own room and take a nap. But sleep was difficult and he quickly regretted not washing his sheets after his fling with Deborah the night before but to do so at that point, would only manage to grab Diego's attention and Chase wasn't in the mood for a question and answer period. Besides, he just wanted to sleep, blocking his mind of everything that haunted him.

The next day wasn't much better. Seeing Deborah at work was awkward and Diego's words about 'not fucking' coworkers haunted him, especially when the group gathered in the board room for an impromptu meeting that including a celebratory drink over the 'huge success' of their first party for gay men. Although the parties for women had always been their trademark, the fact that they were launching into a whole new area would double business and even a modest Benjamin seemed encouraged about this latest move. Everyone was happy. Everyone was drinking. Chase instead enjoyed some coffee and tried to avoid conversation with Deborah, who acted as if nothing was out of the ordinary between them. To Chase's relief, she offered little more than a quaint smile and eyebrow flash when he first passed her that morning. Clearly, this wasn't her first time doing something like this so maybe she was better at concealing it.

In fact, only Gracie talked to him during their little party that morning; Diego was chatting with Benjamin about numbers, while Jolene and Sylvana had a passionate discussion about cosmetics sold at the local department store, Deborah quietly sat and took it all in while Beverly ducked out of the room shortly after the celebration started and went back to her desk. It was, overall, a strange vibe in the room.

While Gracie rattled on about her birthday weekend that had just passed, nearby, Jolene's loud voice seemed to override everybody else.

"He says, 'don't you think you are worth it?' as if the makeup is so valuable and I'm just this pathetic immigrant that will take anything," Jolene sharply remarked as she pushed a strand of hair behind her ear. "Like I'm all sad and lonely, you know? And I look at him and say, 'I *am* worth it but is *it* worth *me?*" With that she let out a loud laugh which was infectious, as Sylvana followed suit, glancing at Chase and Gracie, who did the same.

"He did not know what to say to that," Jolene continued, this time directing her comment to Chase who had witnessed her confront many people in the past and wasn't surprised by her abrupt comment.

"My sister," Diego started, suddenly alerted to the conversation, "Always so polite."

"Hey, I do not like how men talk to women as if we are all sad and lonely if we aren't married, like that cosmetic person at the mall talk to me," Jolene said and made a face. "Nobody ever talks to a man that way. Chase, am I right?"

"What?"

"Do you have people talk to you like you're lonely, sitting home on Saturday night, waiting for the phone to ring?" Jolene prompted, tapping her fingers on the boardroom table. "No, of course not. No one says that to a man."

"He wasn't sad and lonely this weekend," Diego piped up and gave a smug smile and quickly covered it up. "We were working really late then we went to a party."

Chase purposely didn't look in Deborah's direction.

"How late were you?" Jolene asked and glanced from Chase to Diego. "That is a good sign if no one wanted to leave."

"After 4."

"We have to be careful. We cannot serve liquor after 2," Jolene reminded him.

"Oh, I know," Diego shared an indulgent smile with Chase. "Who would do that?"

"We have to be careful," Jolene reminded him. "We already have some religious groups watching us closely. We do not want to give them a reason to make our lives difficult."

"The religious should worry about what they're going to wear to church on Sunday, not what we're doing," Diego said with a shrug. "Who cares? We aren't hurting anyone?"

"You know that is not how these religious people work," Jolene reminded him. "They're all about telling everybody else how to live." She rolled her eyes and took a deep breath and slowly rose from her chair. "Anyway, I should get back to work now."

"You know, we could get involved in a charity," Sylvana suggested, her eyes on Jolene. "It would look good for the company and it would show we are giving back to the community."

"Oh, I *like* that," Diego said and let out a laugh, pointing toward Sylvana as Jolene nodded. "This one, always got a plan."

"It's my job," Sylvana spoke with confidence and stood up. "I'll give it some thought and meet with Beverly later to discuss some ideas."

"Perfecto!" Diego said and leaned back in his chair while everyone else seemed to follow Jolene's lead as she headed toward the door. Chase and Diego were the only people left.

The door now closed and everyone was gone, Diego smiled and poured himself another glass of champagne.

"So, that freak on a leash, Deborah, did she seduce you or what?"

The question threw him off guard. He had expected it on Sunday, in the car that morning or even later during their lunch break, but not at that point in the morning. In fact, Chase was hoping the weekend was water under the bridge but he should've known better. "What?"

"She was looking for you with those horny eyes on Saturday night... er....Sunday morning, I figured she was probably looking for her fix," Diego snickered and sunk the drink. "Is that how sex addiction works? Maybe this could work out for the two of you. She seems uncommitted and that's what you want, no?"

His accent was creeping in which meant he was upset.

"I don't know, Diego," Chase spoke honestly. "I would rather keep my distance from Deborah."

"Remember what I told you about people fucking coworkers, it's never a good thing," Diego sent him warning glances that seemed to be a direct order and not a suggestion. Since Chase was hardly interested in pursuing anything more with Deborah, it wouldn't be difficult to agree with him.

"You're right," Chase replied and silently wondered how Diego figured it out. Did he see them leave together? "I certainly have no intentions of hooking up with her again."

But things were about to get much more complicated.

CHAPTER TWENTY

They arrived at the restaurant before the dinner rush and as usual, Diego insisted they sit at the back of the room. Originally Chase assumed this choice had to do with private meetings that they were having about their business but now, it kind of made him curious. In fact, many things about Diego were making him suspicious and although he would never say it out loud, Chase was forming a mental list that created a sinister profile when put together. It was the little things along with the bigger events - like hitting someone with a baseball bat in the condo - that were making him feel as if he were missing a piece of the puzzle.

"Jolene, she will be here soon," Diego commented as they opened their menus and Chase felt his stomach rumble as the smell of barbecue filled the air. The restaurant specialized in food that supposedly tasted the same as what you would grill at home which immediately brought back memories from Chase's childhood, when his father would barbecue on the weekends. Perhaps, he considered, that was what the restaurant was really about; the association more than the food itself.

"I think she went to get her hair done or something?" Chase commented and quickly decided on what to order. He noted that Diego was making a face as he went through the menu as if he wasn't fully happy with the selections.

"I dunno, some kind of lady beauty thing," Diego replied and held the menu back and squinted. "I think I'll be like you and have chicken for a change. The ribs, they sure look good in the picture but too messy when you're wearing a suit."

"I was thinking the same thing," Chase agreed with a quick laugh as he pushed the menu aside and sat back in the booth. "Actually, I think I might get a steak. It's been a long week."

After the waitress came and got their drink orders, Diego brought up the very topic that Chase had hoped he wouldn't.

"So what was that about? Back at the office?" He referred to a conversation Deborah had pulled Chase into just as they were about to leave for the weekend. Although Diego pretended to not notice, it was pretty clear that he had.

Chase briefly considered not telling him. He didn't want to talk about it but at the same time, knew Diego wouldn't let it go until he found the answer. It would be better to tell him now than be mid-conversation when Jolene arrived. The last thing he wanted was her to know about his fling with Deborah the previous weekend.

"She wants me to go to the counselor with her," Chase said as he rubbed a hand over his eyes and through his short hair. Diego had an amused look on his face as if waiting for him to continue. "Apparently she goes to a counselor about her sex addiction and in their session earlier this week, Deborah claims that I took advantage of her when I knew she had a problem."

Diego let out a short laugh but appeared somewhat anxious as Chase continued to talk.

"So she wants me to go with her for her next session so we can discuss it."

"Okay, so first, she thinks this sex addiction thing is real, then?" Diego asked as he leaned in, his eyebrows raised. "Cause me, I do not. I think she uses it as an excuse, just like those celebrities on TV who run off to clinics because they were caught and suddenly have a 'problem' so they don't have to be accountable. This girl, she is the same."

"She seems to think it's real."

"Do you want me to talk to her?" Diego leaned in even further, his eyes were fiery. "Because me, I will set her straight."

Chase noted that his accent was creeping in so he knew Diego was upset.

"No, no I would rather she didn't even know that we were talking about it," Chase admitted dismissively. "Whatever, I guess I will go..."

"Okay, Chase, two things," Diego started as he laid his hand on the table, his expensive watch caught the light and sparkled. "Do you think she is going to sue us for sexual harassment or something like that, should I get a lawyer?"

"No," Chase shook his head, although he hadn't considered it until that point. "I think she just has guilt over what she did and seeing me every day is a constant reminder. I don't think she's even thinking of sexual harassment."

Diego thought for a moment. "You're right, she wouldn't have a leg to stand on. You're technically not her supervisor, you just fill in when we aren't there and she instigated this fling, which I can verify and make sure some others do too," He slowly nodded and shrugged it off. "Okay, so here is the second thing that I wanted to point out. Chase, why are you going to this appointment with her? Do you want to?"

"God no!"

"Then don't go," Diego said with a shrug and relaxed in the booth, turning more in Chase's direction. "You owe her nothing."

"But she asked...."

"So, I asked you to dinner with me and Jolene today but technically, you could've said no," Diego reminded him. "But you're here. Do you want to be here?"

"Yes, of course."

"That is what I mean, you," Diego pointed toward him and leaned in closer. "You have to start doing the things you want, not the things others ask you to do. You, *amigo*, are a follower, not a leader and that is fine in some situations but you can't be a sheep your whole life. Sometimes, you have to be a wolf. Something you have to decide what you actually want, not just what others would like you to do."

Chase opened his mouth to reply but wasn't sure what to say. Diego was right, he often allowed others to make decisions for him.

"I just feel, I guess I just feel that sometimes it's easier to go with the flow," Chase admitted as his fingers started to nervously roll around the spoon on the table.

"Said every sheep ever," Diego pointed out, his eyes narrowed in on Chase. "There are two kinds of people in this world; the sheep and the wolf. The sheep go along with what others want and never live the life they really want, they are compliant and in the end, miserable. Whereas, the wolf, he takes what he wants. He decides what is best for him."

The waitress returned with their drink order and a smile on her face. As usual, Diego flirted but as soon as she left, he was back to business as usual.

"I don't have to tell you, Chase, that I am a wolf," He spoke smoothly before taking a drink of his cocktail while his eyes stared through Chase. "I've never been interested in following a flock of sheep and I can tell you one thing, you would be much happier if you didn't either."

"But maybe," Chase spoke slowly. "That's just me."

"Are you happy?" Diego asked with raised eyebrows and before Chase could answer, he quickly continued. "Then, *amigo*, that is *not* you."

It was just then that Jolene's heels could be heard approaching the booth, her presence so powerful that it alerted the entire room, something she was oblivious to as she sat down at their table.

"There you are, always in the back of the room," She commented as she sat her purse in the booth and slid in beside it. "Diego, would it kill you to not sit somewhere that isn't hidden for a change, no?"

"I like it at the back," Diego insisted and gestured toward the room. "You can watch the world from the back of the room, it's a position of power."

"See, I do not think," Jolene commented as she grabbed Diego's menu. "I see it as hiding."

"You see it as you want to see it."

"So did you order? What is going on here?" Jolene asked, her eyes momentarily looking up from the menu. "You both look seriously right now."

"Serious," Diego corrected her grammar and Jolene shot him a dirty look.

"We decided but did not order. We waited for you," Diego insisted, his lips pouting briefly. "And then we were talking about how Chase is a follower, not a leader."

"Oh, I do not think!" Jolene commented sharply and sat the menu down. "He does not do just because someone says."

"Really?" Diego posed the question and Jolene gave a shy shrug.

"Well," She made eye contact with Chase and gave him an apologetic smile, just as the waitress approached to take their order. After she left, Jolene continued.

"Chase, I'm sorry but yes, he is right, sometimes you do tend to follow and not lead. You seem, I don't know how you say, insecurity?"

Diego cringed as she spoke but didn't bother to correct her this time.

"I find it easier to go along with what others think," Chase admitted. "I've always been that way."

"But why? I do not understand," Jolene asked and the two Silvas watched him attentively.

"I guess," Chase hesitated and thought about the question. "I don't know, when I was a kid, my mother had a bad temper, so I went along with her so she wouldn't lash out and now, I find it's...I guess it's just how I am with everyone."

"Lash out?" Jolene asked as she flickered her eyelashes rapidly for a second. "I do not understand."

"Oh, it means, to get angry and attack," Chase spoke apologetically, knowing that slangs were never a good idea with Jolene. Beside her, Diego listened attentively.

"You mean, hit you?" Jolene asked in a lowered voice, her face crestfallen and Chase immediately felt like he shouldn't have said anything.

"Yes," Chase reluctantly answered.

"Come on, Jolene," Diego jumped in. "Mom, she did not hit us sometimes when we were kids?"

"A little slap, maybe, but it was never anything bad," Jolene commented and shrugged. "Was you, was yours bad, Chase?"

"It...I..."

"Wait," Diego leaned in again. "Did your mother beat you? Like as in *beat* you with bruises? You don't mean just a little slap, do you?"

Chase wasn't sure what to say. No one had ever asked him that before; his teachers when he went to school with bruises, his relatives, friends, not even his ex-wife when he was blatantly suggesting it when discussing his estranged relationship with Louise Jacobs. Now, as an adult, in a crowded restaurant in Toronto, he sat across from two people who's eyes were full of concern and compassion; Chase felt himself grow weak as if he were suddenly a child again.

"Yes," He heard himself answer in a hushed tone. "She beat me."

The words were surprisingly freeing; even though his heart raced when he said them, it was easier than he expected to make this confession; a weight dropped from his heart. Diego's expression was angry while Jolene's eyes briefly watered in compassion.

"That is not right Chase," She quickly blinked away her tears and made a face. "I cannot believe that in this country, Canada, it is so.... how do you say? It is like supposed to be a top country that looks after it's people and this, this happens here?"

"Jolene, that happens everywhere," Diego spoke in a quiet voice. "It doesn't matter where you live, people do these kinds of things."

"I know, I don't feel like it is right here, you know," Jolene insisted. "I'm learning a lot about Canada, now that I am trying to be a citizen and they talk like it is the best country in the world and they look after their people but then, why, Diego, does a little boy get hurt by his own parents? That is not right!"

"Jolene, come on, even the most advanced countries in the world have problems," Diego gently reminded her. "No country is perfect."

"But Diego, we come from a violent country," Jolene reminded him. "Look at Colombia's history. The drugs, the violence, so many problems but yet our parents never hit us, they would not do such a thing. You know? It seems backward. It seems like we would be the ones who would live that way, not someone in Canada, a country that was safe, where the government looks after the people, a country so many admire. You know?"

"Jolene, it is what it is," Diego shook his head. "Maybe they are idealists."

"I do not understand."

"In an ideal world, they want to be all these great things but it is like...I don't know, me making a New Year's Resolution to start running every day but then I get up the next morning and there's a storm outside. Sometimes, there are things that make life challenging."

Jolene appeared to accept his answer and turned back to Chase.

"I am sorry, I do not mean to say bad things about your country," Jolene spoke gently. "I had higher expectations. You know? I thought this was a country where people could not get away with doing this."

Chase wasn't sure how to answer.

CHAPTER TWENTY-ONE

"My lime tree, look at it," Diego spoke lovingly from the other side of the room and Chase turned to see a ridiculously jubilant smile on his face as he gently touched the leaves. "It's growing!"

"I see that," Chase managed to suppress a grin and nodded. "Hope it endures the winter."

"It will be fine, I'm doing some research," Diego commented as he leaned in to sniff the plant.

Chase quickly turned away, wanting to laugh but managing to keep it together. It was so strange that someone like Diego would have such an affection for a lime tree of all things. He even had the cleaning lady trained on how to properly take care of it in the event that neither of them was around.

"I'm thinking of getting a second one if this one continues to do so well," Diego added as Chase made his way into the kitchen to pour some coffee.

It was a bright Saturday morning, the long weekend in September and everything felt unusually relaxed. Although there were a few parties scheduled for that weekend, both in and out of Toronto, none of them required either Diego or Chase to do anything unless something came up at the last-minute. For that reason, both were on call but for the most part, these things tended to go pretty smoothly now that the party planning staff had found their groove.

The business had grown quickly over the few months they were in Toronto and already expanded to more private parties. Although Chase suggested that it might be better to be mainstream rather than specialized - which had a bit of a seedy nature - Diego and Jolene continued to insist that they had found their ideal market and were already looking at new ideas including one Chase had suggested to add Boudoir photography into the mix.

Where he felt a little embarrassed about the kind of company he worked for, Diego and Jolene had no shame. They felt it was perfectly acceptable and didn't understand what the big deal was about especially when the religious group started a petition against their business. The group claimed that they were just another example of a business ruining the moral fiber of the community and that they 'encouraged' promiscuous behavior. The Bible thumpers wanted the company to either plan parties that were 'wholesome' in nature or close their doors and move out of the city.

Of course, the petition made Jolene anxious; she feared it would have negative repercussions on the company while Diego remained unconcerned, insisting that it would only bring them free publicity. Meanwhile, to take some of the heat off the company, Sylvana set up the option for each customer to donate a few dollars to a pre-chosen charity. In the case of private parties, the client would pick the cause of their choice.

Things were rolling along and for the first time since arriving in Toronto, Chase was starting to feel at home. He was slowly learning the city, feeling comfortable in his new surroundings and getting into a routine. Work had its issues but overall, things were running smoothly and life had fallen into a predictable pattern as he grew to understand and like his coworkers, even Deborah, who was slowly starting to get over his refusal to join her for a counseling appointment.

"So what are your plans for the long weekend?" Diego asked as he joined Chase in the kitchen, grabbing his full coffee mug from the counter.

"Not much," Chase admitted with a shrug. "I'm going to the gym this morning and that's about it so far."

"Hey we should go on a road trip," Diego suggested, his eyes expanding in size as he pointed toward the window. "Beautiful, sunny day, we should take off."

"I have a feeling that everyone else is thinking the same thing," Chase suggested before taking a drink of his coffee. "Traffic will be a mess."

"Oh yeah," Diego said with a frown, almost as if he forgot that the rest of the world existed and might be thinking the same thing. "But later today, we could go. I mean, by then most people will be gone if they are going, right?"

Chase slowly nodded. He did have a point.

"Montreal? Maybe we crash one of our own parties to see that it's going well?" Diego frowned again. "Nah, I don't feel like thinking about work. Let's just take off and see where we end up? It will be an adventure."

"Yeah, maybe. I should stop by the mall too and get some gift cards for the kids," Chase said with reluctance. "Audrey mentioned that they might need some extra stuff. I'm always sending money but maybe gift cards are more thoughtful. I'm never really sure what they need."

"Communication, my friend, that's the only way you'll know," Diego commented as he leaned against the counter and drank his coffee. Still wearing his t-shirt and oversized gym pants, he looked like a teenager and not a 40-year-old man. The only hint was the subtle traces of gray close to his ears and in his stubble; a rarity for a man who was always concerned about his grooming habits.

"We talk all the time," Chase replied and pulled a carton of eggs out of the fridge. "She never really tells me."

"What about the kids?" Diego asked as he continued to drink his coffee, jumping up on the cupboard, his bare feet dangling in the air, as he watched Chase gather everything needed to make scrambled eggs. "Have you talked to them lately?"

"It's hard," Chase quietly commented. "They seem to be available less and less. If they are, it's never all at once. For example, I Skyped them last night and the twins were home but Leland was apparently at mom's for the weekend again."

"Three kids, all so young, you're a machine," Diego teased as he finished his coffee and slid back down to the floor and Chase laughed.

"Want an egg?" He offered.

"Nah, I'm going to take a shower," Diego headed toward his room. "Give the road trip some thought and get back to me."

"Will do."

After having a quick breakfast, Chase was out the door and on the way to the gym when he got a text. It was from Deborah. She wanted him to go to her apartment.

Chase quickly dismissed the idea, telling her that he didn't want to cause any friction at work and as long as this affair continued, that it might cause an awkward environment.

Then she sent him a suggestive picture that indicated her current state of arousal.

Come now. My door will be unlocked and I will be waiting.

Feeling his own desires creep in, Chase decided that a little detour mightn't be such a bad idea. Of course, had he decided against it, apparently, it wouldn't have mattered. Deborah continued to send him pictures of herself and one short video that was hard to ignore. By the time he arrived at her apartment, he wasn't thinking about the discomfort between them at work or any ill effects from his decision, he reluctantly entered the apartment and she called out from the bedroom.

"Lock the door," She spoke breathlessly. Following her orders, walking toward her room, he immediately saw her lying naked on the bed. He quickly undressed, his breath increasing as he watched her spread her legs in waiting. As usual, foreplay was almost non-existent, her demands aggressive, Chase followed her every instruction without saying a word.

Grabbing one of the condoms on her nightstand, he put it on and with no emotion, slid between her legs. Deborah gasped as he thrust into her, tightening her legs around him, she cried out in pleasure, her fingernails digging into his back as she continued to instruct him; Push harder. Touch here. Lick there. Finally, letting out a loud, extended moan before loosening her grip, he collapsed on her body.

It was hardly a romantic moment between the two of them, as she almost appeared disengaged immediately after their encounter. She didn't even speak. Finally, he pulling out of her, removed the condom while her eyes studied him and she finally spoke.

"Thanks, you can leave now."

Feeling slightly awkward, he didn't reply but stood up and quickly dressed.

"If I need you again, I will text you." She commented vaguely and closed her eyes.

It was weird but certainly not the weirdest situation he had ever been in, definitely not when it came to sex. Had he ever had a normal relationship? Maybe in high school when he was with his first girlfriend Lucy, but definitely not since. His marriage had been a joke, his affairs on the side were passionate but limited and now, here he was again.

Heading to the gym, he felt defeated. Diego was constantly lecturing him to stop being a follower and become a leader. He insisted Chase decide what he wanted in life and go after it and yet, here he was, once again following someone else's wishes.

Feeling melancholy, his time at the gym was pitiful. Chase finally decided to just take a quick shower and go home. If Diego was up for a road trip, maybe that was exactly what he needed. Maybe getting out of the city would give him some clarity.

He was just outside his building when the phone rang. Seeing that it was Audrey, he was somewhat frustrated that she would call with the kids that early in the day and not their pre-established time but decided to count his blessing that the kids wanted to talk to him at all. Having difficulty hearing, he instructed Audrey to hold on until he got inside the building, where there was much less noise to distract him. It was once inside, standing beside the mailboxes that he finally could hear clearly. She was crying.

CHAPTER TWENTY-TWO

Chase's heart pounded frantically and he leaned against the nearest wall for support and closed his eyes. Leland was missing. His oldest son had been at his mother's house for the weekend and had somehow got out of the house that morning and couldn't be found. The police were searching the wooded area directly behind his mom's as well as throughout the community. They weren't sure when he left but there was no sign he had been kidnapped. However, all possibilities would be considered.

Her words were too much. Overwhelmed, Chase felt as though he couldn't breathe by the time their call ended, as he continued to lean against the wall, attempting to calm enough to make it to the elevator. His legs were weak and when he finally did move, it was almost as if they were about to give out beneath him as his mind shot in a million directions. Had Leland left the house on his own and simply wandered away or had his mother been negligent, not properly looking after him? Was he taken? Kidnapped? Was he hurt? He was only 4 years old.

By the time he reached the condo, Chase was a mess. His thoughts were erratic while his legs now grew heavy with each step as if walking through quicksand. He couldn't deal with this and yet, he had no other choice. A million thoughts jumbled his mind; all incoherent and screaming all at once.

Rubbing his face, it took him a minute to realize that Diego was talking to him, his voice only added to the many thoughts racing through his head.

"....or we could," Diego abruptly stopped and when Chase finally managed to focus again, he saw his friend standing close by, his eyes widened in surprise, his mouth open slightly ajar and a cup of coffee in hand. "What's wrong?"

Chase opened his mouth but couldn't speak. He felt Diego's hand on his wrist, directing him to the couch, where he felt some relief as he sat down. The sound of Diego's cup being placed on a nearby table was amplified, suddenly the loudest thing in the room; louder than the dryer running nearby, the radio that was playing somewhere in the condo, louder than even his own thoughts.

"Audrey just called," Chase finally managed as Diego sat beside him, attentively turned in his direction. "Leland, my oldest son, is missing."

"We will find him!" Diego insisted, jumping up from the couch. "Come on, let's go!"

"What? I don't know if."

"No, we must go," Diego insisted. "Even if they find him in the next 5 minutes, you will feel better. Let's go!"

"Oh, ok," Chase thought about it for a minute, feeling slightly calmer now that the words were spoken out loud, a task that seemed painful in the moment but relieving now that he had confessed the truth. "I...I mean, I..."

"Don't worry about the details, *amigo*, go pack and I will take care of it," Diego rushed to the other side of the room and grabbed his laptop. "We will go and make sure everything is okay and by the time we get there, he will be found, it'll be okay."

Chase slowly stood up and shook his head. "Diego, you don't have to do this. I can make the arrangements and you don't have to come."

"I want to, Chase," Diego insisted, waving his hand in the air as his eyes scanned a laptop screen. "You're in no shape to travel alone and it gives me something productive to do for the weekend. Also, I want to see this redneck town you come from, it will be fun, you know, once your son is found."

"I don't know about that," Chase slowly started toward his bedroom.

"They *will* find him," Diego insisted. "He's just a little boy who wandered off. Probably on an adventure and doesn't even realize he is scaring the entire community. I did it once as a kid and I was fine."

Chase considered what he said and although it didn't give him much relief, it did give him something to consider. Kids wandered off all the time.

In his room, he packed mechanically, as Audrey's words continued to haunt him. He sat on the edge of his bed and texted her that he was going to Hennessey as soon as he could get there. She replied by saying that the community was aware of the missing child and attempting to find him. So far, there was no luck but she would keep him updated.

His suitcase packed, Chase wandered back into the living room, where Diego was on the phone, speaking in Spanish to someone; Chase assumed he had phoned Jolene to let her know but after ending the call, he announced that the cleaner would be in to take care of his lime tree. For the first time since receiving the news, he couldn't help but smile.

They rushed to the airport, able to book a flight that was only a couple of hours away, they had to check in and it was during that time that Chase learned that Diego had arranged for a rental car when they arrived Calgary for the drive to Hennessey.

Everything was going in slow motion and yet his mind continued to race as he constantly checked his phone for updates. There was nothing. He sent a few text messages to Audrey from the airport but there was no news. His sister, who hadn't reached out to him in months, was texting him but her reaction seemed obligatory. It wasn't until he was on the plane that he grew angry, thinking that it was his mother's fault; why hadn't she watched Leland closer? Was she off in her own little dream world and not paying attention? Although deep down, he knew that wasn't a fair assumption, it didn't stop the anger from rising inside of him. Children were quick and it could've happened on anyone's watch: but that it was hers was particularly unsettling.

Diego did everything in attempts to distract him during the 4-hour flight from Toronto to Calgary. He asked questions about Hennessey, told him the detailed story about the time he got lost as a child in

Colombia and with some hesitation, suggested Chase have a drink to relax.

"That's probably the last thing I need now," Chase admitted as he turned his head to look out at the clouds that surrounded the plane. It was like flying through heaven and oddly that little thought almost made him break. What if Leland was dead? What if he got hurt? What if they didn't find him?

"I have something for you," Diego quietly commented and when Chase turned, he noted a small, white pill in his hand.

"What is that?"

"It's an Ativan."

"A what?"

"It's for anxiety," Diego replied. "You put it under your tongue."

"I'm not big on pills..."

"Chase, neither am I but sometimes, this is what you need in situations like this, you know?" Diego insisted as his accent seemed to creep in. "You'll be a basket case until we get there and it's still hours away between the plane and the drive afterward."

Chase reluctantly took the pill and followed his instructions before asking, "Why did you have it?"

"Sometimes, you know, I have a little anxiety," Diego said and puckered his lips and glanced in the other direction.

"I thought you were on high energy all the time," Chase quietly commented and closed his eyes for a moment.

"Nah, it's a lot of anxiety but I just choose to channel it as energy. It works better that way," Diego commented and waved down the flight attendant for a drink. "You have a pill, I have a drink. It'll be fine, Chase, you'll see. Everything will be fine. By the time we get to Calgary, Leland will be home, you'll see."

Sometime during the flight, Chase drifted off and had dreams of his son. He saw him eating birthday cake, the entire thing by himself, scooping it up in his hands and giggling. Audrey was attempting to clean up the mess and Chase laughed and said, "Nah, just let him do it, let a child be a child."

When he woke up, Diego announced that they were almost in Calgary, much to Chase's relief. When they arrived in Hennessey, he'd be able to take part in the search to find his son. Until he got there, he would feel helpless.

The pill helped with his anxiety and he could finally think clearly again, rather than the emotion-filled clutter that was going on in his head before they left Toronto; logically, Leland was just missing. Chances were good he would be found playing in the nearby woods, unaware of the fear he caused throughout the community. He was a little wilder than the other two children, very active, always climbing, exploring and excitedly running through the house, the park, wherever he was at the time. It made sense that he would wander away to explore.

There were so many potential dangers for children. So many things that could go wrong that kids didn't understand; even if parents warned them a million times, these warnings were often ignored by high energy children like Leland and for the most part, he escaped with nothing more than a minor cut or bruise but what if this time were different? What if he was face-to-face with a wild animal in the woods? What if he fell and got hurt? What if someone kidnapped him or he got hit by a car?

Parents often obsessed about what could go wrong and yet, wasn't that a part of life? Didn't everyone take a chance every day, especially after leaving the house? An accident, a terrorist attack, anything was possible in the world today. Perhaps Diego had been right and it was better to keep calm and wait. Chances were good that Leland would be fine.

When the plane finally landed and everyone was getting off, Chase felt frustrated by the slow-moving group, casually taking their carry-ons off the overhead rack, as if they had all the time in the world while meanwhile, he felt like shoving everyone out of his way, tackling them like a football player that was storming ahead with only one goal in mind.

He sent another text to Audrey, as he had been repeatedly since she first delivered the news but she said she had nothing to report. RCMP were talking about having an Amber Alert while locals were searching nearby woods, assuming the child probably just wandered off, pointing out at least the weather was warm and everyone was searching, therefore the odds were good he would be found.

It didn't help the unsettling feeling that was creeping back into Chase's chest as they made their way through the airport, collected their bags and headed toward the car rental area, where Diego took care of everything while Chase stood nearby. He felt some relief when they finally got in the car and heading toward Hennessey; although he gave specific instructions on how to get there, Diego still had the GPS turned on, concerned that in his current state, Chase would miss something.

They drove in silence for a while until Diego finally spoke.

"It won't be much longer, *amigo*, we will be there," His comment was casual, relaxed as he took in all the surroundings as they drove along. "At least with the time difference, it's before dinner here in Alberta, so there's still a good chance they will find him before dark tonight."

Chase nodded and bit his lip. It had been hours. He couldn't say it out loud but in his heart, he knew this wasn't a good sign. The longer a child was gone, the bleaker the situation could be. If he was still missing by the end of the day, Chase would search for him all night if he had to; he couldn't take the chance of his little boy being lost in the woods with hungry animals roaming around. It would be worth the risk of being in danger himself if it meant saving his son. He would do anything.

Guilt was creeping in as they drew closer. What if he had still been in town? What if he had never left? What if he had forbidden his mother from spending time alone with the kids? What if he was still with Audrey? Would it have made a difference?

Diego occasionally spoke, calmly asking a question or making comments as they drew closer to Hennessey but Chase felt as though he couldn't focus on a word. The pill was wearing off and anxiety once again clutched every part of his body as they entered the town he had grown up in. As they drew closer to his childhood home, cars lined up on either side of the road long before their arrival, making it difficult to find a parking spot, Diego finally said he would drop him off at the house and then find a place to park.

His childhood home felt like a distant memory as he got out of the car, his legs wobbly as he looked around. Strangers were everywhere, police in the yard, while all Chase could do was look for Audrey. He sent another text to her as they were getting close but she hadn't replied. Chaos surrounded him, as a few familiar faces drifted by without acknowledging him, he hadn't noticed at first but it was because their heads were down. They were crying.

NO!

It wasn't until he overheard an officer speaking to another that he knew it for sure. He felt the blood drain from his face, while his body felt weak, limp as if it would fall to the ground and never move again. It was as Albert walked toward him, with tears in his eyes that Chase broke down. Leland was dead.

CHAPTER TWENTY-THREE

Everything happened fast. It was as if the world picked up the pace and he was unable to keep up with it; the anguish, the voices, the people all around and yet he couldn't hear a thing. It was as if they were speaking a different language. Nothing made sense. It wasn't until he was alone with Audrey that he felt himself coming out of his bubble and suddenly everything was in a different dimension. He could hear the blood pumping through his body and feel every breath; his eyes were suddenly more focused while his throat and lips were dry, his emotions came roaring through his body and he heard himself let out a small moan, followed by a weak, pathetic, 'No." It held no emotion, no strength, but weakly fell from his lips.

Audrey's tear-stained face was red, her blonde hair pulled back in a disheveled ponytail, she was wearing an old t-shirt and stretch pants, two different colored socks; it was as if she had weakly disembarked from a highly emotional session and no longer had it in her to even cry. He had never seen Audrey like this other than the day she told him that the marriage was over, when she collapsed on the floor in tears, children crying all around her, admitting that she had tried to force something that was never there. Now, her face filled with disbelief, she crossed the floor and gave him a gentle hug, as if she barely had the strength to even lift her arms.

"He was shot," She whispered in his ear, a sniff quickly followed and although he fought it, Chase felt tears filling his eyes. "He wandered into the woods and someone shot him."

Chase racked his brain; was it hunting season? Had someone been out searching for an animal and accidentally killed his son? Was that what Audrey was trying to say? Who had done it? Did they know? There were so many things that didn't make sense; then again, he wasn't ready for it to make sense. He couldn't get past the reality that his oldest son was dead. It couldn't be real. This couldn't be happening. It felt surreal. Maybe it was a nightmare. It couldn't be happening. There was no way his active, 4-year-old son was dead. It couldn't be right. They made a mistake. It was someone else's child. It wasn't Leland. It was someone else.

As Audrey let go of him and moved away, a calamity took over her face and filled her green eyes, as if a light suddenly surrounded her and she looked momentarily at peace, as if she had accepted the news as a fact.

"It can't.." Chase started to speak, his tongue suddenly felt double its size and he couldn't talk, his mouth slowly closed. He shook his head as her eyes started to water again and she nodded.

"It is, Chase," She whispered and shook her head as tears rapidly fell down her face and dripped from her chin. "I didn't want to believe it either. I didn't want to think it was true. I didn't even believe Albert when he identified the body. I was so angry at him and yelled at him for trying to hurt me. I couldn't believe. I didn't *want* to believe it."

"Well, maybe..."

She shook her head and reached out to touch his hand. Her body suddenly was overcome by waves of sobs. "I saw," She moaned and clutched his hand. "I saw it was him. I swear I thought I was going to die too, right there. I would've done anything to trade places with him. *Anything.*"

Chase used his spare hand to wipe his eyes, the tears now fell so fast that he didn't think he could handle the intense emotion behind them. It was too much.

As he started to accept what he had, only moments earlier denied, Audrey led him toward the bed in the middle of the room. The same room he had as a child; Leland's age and that lone fact only tore him apart more as he sat on the edge of the bed and Audrey joined him, passing a box of Kleenex that was on the nightstand. Leland's clothes were across the room, scattered over the floor along with his favorite stuffed animal. This was his room when he came to visit his grandmother.

They sat in silence and suddenly overwhelmed with nausea, Chase jumped up from the bed and tore out of the room, just making it to the bathroom in time. Slamming the door behind him, he vomited into the toilet until there was nothing left in his stomach, his body went through dry heaves and tear dripped from his face, hitting the rim. He flushed and felt like he couldn't move. He didn't want to move.

A knock at the door was gentle and he immediately recognized it as Audrey's.

"Chase, are you okay?" Her voice was soft, caring, in a way it hadn't been when they were together. "Do you need me to come in?"

"No," He replied, his voice was weak, as he slowly pulled his body back up again and went to the sink. His eyes were bloodshot, his face, red, blotchy and he leaned against the sink and closed his eyes. What now? How did he get through the rest of the day? How were you supposed to live after such devastating news? How did you put one foot in front of the other, how did you eat, sleep, function, after learning your child was dead? It seemed impossible.

He threw water on his face but it gave him no relief. Finding mouthwash under the sink, he rinsed his mouth before slowly walking toward the door, feeling dead inside.

Returning to the bedroom, he gently closed the door behind him. Audrey stood at the window, looking toward the wooded area where their son had died. Downstairs, the roar of voices could be heard, some of which were comforting his mother, who unlike him and Audrey, wanted everyone to surround her. He couldn't look her in the eye. Audrey would eventually come around with Louise Jacobs but Chase would not.

"They think someone was hunting and accidentally shot him," She calmly said as Chase approached her. She had stopped crying and was looking in the distance. "I don't even know if it is hunting season or not, I don't even care, how could they not know? Did that person check and then run away? Did they not realize? I don't understand."

Feeling calmer, if even just slightly, Chase cleared his throat. "Was he far from the house?"

"A bit," Audrey replied, her fingers gently touching the window pane a serenity surrounded them. "He's so small that it was hard to see him. It took a little time but then again, every minute seemed to stretch for me. Everything was so slow. It was almost as if they had to spend more time asking questions and not just getting out there and *looking*. I was so frustrated, I wanted to scream because they weren't doing anything. Asking stupid questions. I wanted to walk out of the room and look myself but they said to stay here."

"I don't blame you. I would feel the same way," Chase admitted, he oddly felt strong beside her, in a way he never had before. Something had changed inside of him since walking out of that bathroom. He felt different. He felt almost as if his son's death was somehow making him feel more alive.

"But I guess it wouldn't have mattered," Audrey continued as she leaned closer to the window. "He was already gone."

"I think..." Chase started slowly and she turned as if his words beckoned her. "I think I should see his body."

"No!" Audrey said with panic in her voice and she grasped his arm. "Don't do it Chase! Trust me, don't do it," Tears began to fill her eyes again. "I wish I hadn't. Please, don't do it." She begged while grasping his arm tightly and she shook her head. The look in her eyes said it all and he felt the strength from moments before drain from his body, replaced by more nausea.

"I think I'm going to be sick again," His voice was barely a whisper and she let him go and watched as he left the room, heading toward the bathroom. He closed the door and leaned against it as the volume downstairs continued to increase. Why was his mother making this into a fucking circus? He didn't want the entire neighborhood in the house.

Moving toward the toilet, he slowly sat on the floor beside it, expecting to be sick again but nothing happened. A cold sweat grasped his body, he suddenly was so hot that Chase felt like he was suffocating and couldn't breathe. He closed his eyes and attempted to calm himself. He wanted to die in that very spot, sitting on the bathroom floor so he didn't have to feel the pain for another second.

An echoed, hollow-sounding knock came from the door and he wanted to tell whoever it was to go away but he instead said nothing. Forgetting it wasn't locked, he was slightly alarmed when it opened and everything was blurry as the room seemed to spin, his heart raced erratically and an echoed voice spoke to him. It was Diego.

The next thing he knew, he was being pulled up and led back to the bedroom. Audrey's face was full of anguish as she looked into his eyes. Chase felt his cold sweats end and suddenly, he was freezing. Diego saw him shake and grabbed a throw from the chair to wrap about him. He looked anxious, as if unsure of what to say.

"Audrey said you were in the bathroom for some time and she was worried," His accent was strong when he spoke, indicating that Diego was quite upset. Clearly, he had introduced himself to Chase's ex-wife. "I didn't want to intrude but we were both concerned." He gestured toward Audrey who nodded.

Chase hadn't been aware of how long he was in the bathroom but it felt as though time continued to either accelerate or slow to a crawl. It was unbelievable that his morning had started off so normal; that he had stood in the kitchen at Diego's, discussing a potential road trip. Little did he know how that same day would end.

"I hadn't realized," Chase replied and cleared his throat. "Diego, would you mind getting me some water?"

"Of course!" Diego appeared relieved to have something to do, as he anxiously bounced toward the door before turning toward Audrey. "Can I get you something? Anything?"

"I will have some water too," She replied and gave him a compassionate smile. "Thank you."

Diego nodded and slid out of the room, gently closing the door behind him.

"I don't want to go down there," Chase finally commented and turned toward Audrey. "I can't deal with all those people."

"I know, me neither," Audrey replied. "That's why I came up here and said I didn't want to see anyone except you or family. My mother is at my house with the twins now," She hesitated for a moment. "I can't even look at your mother. I know it's not her fault but..."

"I blame her," Chase spoke honestly and turned toward his ex-wife as she moved awkwardly beside the bed. "I blame her for not watching him. You have three kids all the time and you managed to keep an eye on them. She had one child. Only one to look after. There's no excuse."

"Accidents happen, Chase," Audrey replied calmly and sat on the other side of the bed. "I know she didn't mean to do this and she's as upset as us now, but.."

"No one, *no one,* is as upset as us now," Chase calmly corrected her and saw tears fill her eyes but she quickly looked away and nodded, grabbing another tissue. "I don't even know how to....do this, I don't know how we get through this, Aud. I don't even know where to start or how to process this. Nothing makes sense. I woke up this morning and everything was fine."

Audrey sniffed and wiped her eyes as Diego returned with two bottles of water in hand. He didn't say anything but gave Chase a sympathetic look as he passed them each a bottle.

"I ah...I know it's not my place," Diego slowly started. "But, I suggested to Albert? Your boyfriend," He gestured toward Audrey who nodded. "I thought maybe we needed to have some of the people downstairs leave. There are a couple of reporters floating around asking questions and I...I don't think that's right."

"Thank you," Audrey said and nodded. "All I want right now is to go home and I don't even want to go downstairs and face those people. I can't."

Chase nodded as he opened his bottle and took a long drink. The water felt as if it were floating throughout his entire chest, a cool sensation filled his upper body and he felt at peace; if even for that moment, as if everything would be fine.

"Albert is taking care of it," Diego anxiously stood beside the bed, his eyes carefully checking Chase and immediately looking away. "If there's anything else I can do?"

"Make this all stop," Audrey whispered as she started to cry again. Opening her mouth to continue, she quickly pressed her lips together and looked away.

Chase watched as Diego's eyes jumped from Audrey's to his own. He didn't say a thing. He didn't have to.

CHAPTER TWENTY-FOUR

Their eyes probed him for his entire stay in Hennessey. Everywhere he went, they looked at him as if he were an alien, a freak who wandered into town by error and couldn't find his way out again. They didn't want his kind in their small town and he could see it in their eyes: but he didn't care. He wasn't there for them. He was there for Chase.

Diego Silva was a clown that people didn't take seriously. He was the joker that had an unsettling combination of erratic energy while other times, an unexpected calamity that was disturbing to those who never seen him off his usual high energy state. His light side could brighten an entire room but his dark side could bring it to a crashing halt. These extremes in his personality made some people uncomfortable and for that reason, he decided at a young age that staying in people's lives for a short period was the most rational answer. It was a lot better than being rejected. He rejected them first.

Chase was different. He seemed to accept, if not understand his brand of insanity that perplexed almost everyone else. It was the same impulsive nature that once caused Diego to kiss him even though the two had just met and Chase clearly had no idea of his homosexual urges. He hadn't berated, humiliated or punched him, as other men had done in the past. When Diego suddenly decided to uproot his entire company and start fresh, *legally*, in another city, Chase did not protest or question him. There was an assumption that it was a well-thought out decision and that Diego had his reasons. Even when he purchased an expensive sports car only to return it the next day, Chase merely shrugged and laughed, while Jolene flipped out.

"That's just Diego," he later overheard him tell Jolene. "It's his lizard brain."

Of course, Jolene hadn't understood the term, her English was still absolutely terrible and she stubbornly wouldn't do anything to improve it but was content to just get by; but at any rate, Chase attempted to explain her own brother's impulsive nature, something that she still didn't seem to understand. True, the two hadn't always been close or in regular communication over the years, but shouldn't your family know you like no one else?

Chase knew him like no one else. It was the small, inconsequential details that were just matter-of-fact with him, while others treated Diego like a circus freak and the people of Hennessey were no exception. They looked at him strangely. As if there were something wrong with him. He didn't think it was blatantly obvious that he was gay. He dressed like most other businessmen and in fact, he hated gay men who were 'faggoty' and wouldn't even associate with them. He liked men who *were* men, not those who tried to display the actions and features of a woman. You would never catch Diego Silva wearing makeup, nail polish or talking in a feminine way, flipping his hand around like a careless moron. Fuck that. He wasn't that kind of gay.

No, there was no way the people in this hick town knew he was a homosexual; which meant they were a bunch of racist pricks who recognized that he was Colombian. His dark eyes that were almost black, as was his hair, his skin a 'warm white' as he liked to refer to it since he was hardly brown nor was he really white either. He was something in between and it was that in between that they didn't like in these predominantly white towns.

Chase insisted that it was because he wasn't familiar. Small towns, he explained, were full of people who recognized everyone and when someone wasn't familiar, they stared at him in an attempt to figure out 'who' he was; to which, Diego said, it was none of their fucking business.

That made Chase smile. It was one of the few times he did for the 5 days they were in Hennessey. Diego stayed with him; throughout the entire funeral proceedings, which ended up being a closed casket, something that seemed to create more of emotional reaction from the mother than had they allowed everyone see the child's now, distorted face after the bullet hit it. The bullet, they eventually realized, was from some redneck hunter, out on an early morning excursion near the Jacobs' home. He claimed to have had no idea that he hit 'anything' that morning, in completely disbelief when the police questioned him the day after the accident occurred.

It was the word *anything* that haunted Diego. It was a word that appeared to not have relevance to the mother, who appeared frozen in time, unable to process that her child was referred to in the same content as an animal, a tree, a piece of dog shit in the woods. *Anything.* Not a 4-year-old child, a little boy, who was out on an adventure, perhaps lost and scared, but an *anything*. Chase, however, flinched when he heard that word but he said nothing. Diego knew it hit him hard, he could see his face tighten up, the same youthful boy of yesterday was now a disgruntled man who would never see the world the same way again. Diego knew. He knew all too well.

All the while, Diego remained silent, drinking a cup of coffee - some terrible slop made by the local, popular coffee chain that should've been burnt to the ground for passing this *mierda* off as coffee. What the fuck? He had been to some of the poorest places in Colombia and they had better coffee than this *shit,* so Chase's explanation that it was because it was a poor community wasn't going to fly with Diego.

At any rate, Diego quietly drank his coffee and said nothing. It was better that he kept his thoughts to himself. It wasn't necessary that either Audrey or Chase be privy to what was roaming through his brain, the emotions exploding in his chest, raging through his veins; they did not have to know. He was there to support them as best he could. Although he didn't know Audrey well, he immediately sensed that she thought as he did; he could see it in her eyes. She was a grieving mother first. She was a vengeful mother second: but no one would ever see that side of her. No one would ever suspect because she was clever and clever people, knew when to keep their mouth shut.

Chase went through a series of panic attacks while in Hennessey, the most prevalent took place shortly after learning of his son's death.

Diego was startled to find him on the bathroom floor, curled up like a wounded animal, his eyes glazed over in shock. It was incredibly difficult to watch and made him feel helpless, unsure on how to comfort someone going through such intense pain.

Audrey understood and explained to Diego that Chase wasn't good at dealing with his emotions because he grew up in a home where it hadn't felt safe to express himself. She shared this information in a gentle manner, her therapist's voice, going on to say that Chase's mother had changed a lot since that time, otherwise she never would've allowed her own children to be alone with her. Diego wasn't so sure. The woman he saw on his first day in Hennessey, as well as at the funeral, was anything but sane. True, she had just lost her grandson but at the same time, her reaction was over the top, borderline lunacy as she loudly sobbed throughout the proceedings, screaming in fits of tears, it was about halfway through when Chase jumped up and stormed out of the church.

Diego felt his heart pounding in his ears as he rushed out behind him, fearful of what he would do in such a state of fury. Instead he found Chase slumped over on church step, wearing the suit that he had instinctively brought along on their trip, shaking. It took Diego a minute to realize that he was crying. Sobbing, almost in the same intense way as his mother but somehow it seemed more heartbreaking to see a man who was usually strong, both physically and emotionally, falling apart before his eyes. Feeling helpless, Diego sat beside him, unsure of what to say or do; he wanted to touch him, put his arm around him, somehow show him comfort but feared that Chase would take it the wrong way as if some pathetic attempt to take advantage of his weak state.

The worst part was that he did feel something for Chase as he watched him fall apart that morning, as Diego gingerly placed his hand on Chase's arm to show his support. There was a surge of emotion that flowed through him, as he watched a man he had longed for many times show more vulnerability than anyone else had ever shown him in his life. He felt an unwelcomed desire flow through him as he slowly slid his arm over his back, as he attempted to silently show Chase that he was there for him. It was a beautiful moment that he somehow knew would define their friendship: then it was interrupted.

One of the local women, some little *puta* from Chase's past came flying out the doors, with tears in her eyes, her large breasts almost flying out of her dress as she leaned down to wrap her arms around Chase from behind, she proceeded to bawl like a lunatic only making the entire situation worse with her dramatics. Diego felt all but pushed away as he pulled back and rose from the step. He wanted to tell her to fuck off and stop trying to make a play for Chase during his moment of weakness but quickly wondered if he was actually doing the same thing.

Suddenly depressed for so many reasons, Diego started to walk away but turned in time to see Chase's reaction to the whorish woman who clung to him. Abruptly standing up, he pushed her, almost a little too hard and told her to go away. Stunned as he watched the scene play out, Diego remained frozen on the spot as the young woman continued to howl and insist she was 'only trying to help' while it was clear Chase had rejected her, walking away with a hand up in the air, as if telling her to stop.

Glaring at Diego, as if he had any part in any of this, she ran back into the church, almost knocking over Maggie Telips on her way out. Jolene's former employee was appropriately dressed in a simple, black dress, as she wiped a tear from her eye and attempted to smile at Chase while ignoring Diego. He watched as she timidly moved forward and embraced Chase in a loving way, while Diego slowly eased away, feeling that neither of them even noticed.

Back in the car, he felt weak and helpless. What could he do for Chase? He couldn't bring his son back. He couldn't comfort him in the way he needed or wanted. He didn't seem to know what to say or how to act in this situation so offered no words of wisdom or reassurance. He had nothing to give.

He called Jolene. She would know what to do.

"Diego!" Her voice was soft, comforting like their mother's had been at one time. "*Como fue el funeral?*"

At first, he didn't reply. Feeling his own emotions explode like a tidal wave, Diego couldn't talk.

"Diego!!" Jolene asked with a sniff. "What is it? Please tell! You're scaring me."

"It's fine Jolene, it's just...it's hard," Diego managed to harness his emotions, although his eyes were wet as he stared in Chase's direction. "I just...I don't know what to say, Jolene, I don't know what to do, you know?"

"No one would, Diego," Jolene spoke softly and he could hear a door closing. "It is not, how do you say, it is not easy to do. It is a hard situation. No one knows what to do or say, you know?"

"Yeah," He replied sadly.

"Diego, your heart, it is big," Jolene surprised him with her comment. "You are there. You took him there, to that town, you know? You're with him. That's enough."

"It doesn't feel like much."

"Trust me, it is a lot," Jolene insisted. "What more can you do?"

"That's what I wish I knew," Diego spoke bluntly. "This, here, this is not enough." He heard his accent growing thicker by the moment and silently chastised himself for letting it escape. Even after all these years in America and now in Canada, it came creeping out when he was upset. Really upset.

"It *is* enough," She insisted.

He didn't reply.

"We will talk more," She continued, her voice growing low and husky. "We will talk more about this later when you come home."

"We will."

"But for now," She continued. "You're doing the right thing. Chase, he is family. We do anything for family."

"We do."

"*Anything*," She said one last time before ending the call.

He contemplated in silence.

It was after the proceedings when they were back at the hotel and Chase was picking at some takeout that Diego bought him, that Jolene's words continued to sink in. He thought about them again and again. People assumed he never listened to anyone but that wasn't true. Diego took in everything and allowed it to absorb, dissecting the meaning behind it all, asking himself if it rang true or if it had any meaning at all.

"You know Chase," Diego started and cleared his throat. "If there's anything I can ever do, I want you to tell me."

"Diego," Chase said, as he pushed the food around a styrofoam tray, still wearing his suit, while the tie had long ago been removed, the first few buttons of his shirt open, he looked like a little boy, defeated by the world, lost in a way that few could ever understand. "You've already done so much. You didn't have to come here, you've been helping me through this since day one, what more could you do?"

"Of course, you know," Diego sniffed, attempting to appear casual as he twisted his lips in his usual, arrogant fashion. "You, me, Jolene, we're all family. That's what we do."

Chase merely nodded, sadly returning his gaze to the tray. The nauseating scent of chicken poured through the room, almost making Diego sick, but he hid his impulses just as he always did in every situation with Chase.

"That girl today, at the church?"

"Which one?" Chase let out a sharp laugh. "The crazy one or the normal one?"

"I guess..either," Diego smirked. "Women are all crazy to me."

Chase raised his eyebrows and grinned. "The first one was Kelsey...

"Ah, yes, Jolene told me about her," Diego let out a laugh. "I think she refers to her as the *puta*."

"She's not that bad," Chase shrugged and appeared defeated. "I can't deal with her and her craziness now. The other girl is Maggie."

He knew all about Maggie.

"The lesbian?"

"Yes."

"The one you wanted?"

"Yes," Chase nodded. "God I wanted that girl, just wanted her to give me one shot, one chance to change her mind, you know?"

Diego didn't respond. His lips clasped shut, his heart pounding erratically and Diego didn't say a thing. The heavy silence filled the room as the realization hit them both.

CHAPTER TWENTY-FIVE

His heart raced. His entire body shook with fear and anticipation: an unlikely combination that somehow didn't fit together but in another way, fit together perfectly. His hand gripped to the closest thing he could find: a hard, plastic object, he grasped it with complete desperation as his legs shook and pleasure rang through his body.

He was in a car and it was speeding down the road; an empty highway that fortunately didn't have another person in sight, as the vehicle raced along at an alarming rate that caused his stomach to heave, despite the desires that shot through his body. Diego was in the driver's seat, his eyes hidden behind sunglasses but a determined expression on his face that couldn't be missed; his lips twisted in their usual expression that implied he was giving something a lot of thought, while his face was tight, as he concentrated on the road.

Chase wanted to say something. He wanted to warn Diego that he was going too fast; that his erratic nature was out of control, that it was time to slow down before they got hurt or killed but when he opened his mouth, he couldn't speak. The words were trapped in his chest, unable to move, stuck between his heart and lips. Then again, if he said anything, would it only make matters worse? Would his fear only cause Diego to laugh at him, drive faster, scare him more as if it were a big joke?

It was when he saw something on the road ahead that he panicked. It was a child. A little boy, running out to meet the car. He opened his mouth to scream but nothing came out.

Awake in his bed, he sprang up as sweat covered his forehead and upper body. His throat so dry that he couldn't speak, his heart pounding hard against his chest wall. Diego suddenly came flying through the adjoining door, wearing only a pair of boxers that almost looked too large on his small frame, his figure highlighted by the street light that flowed through the window.

"What's wrong?" Diego rushed to his bedside, his eyes appearing twice as large in the dark, his face full of concern. When Chase didn't respond, still processing that it had only been a horrible dream, Diego rushed to continue. "Chase, you were yelling. You wanted someone to stop? I thought someone was in here killing you, for God sakes."

"Ah, I...oh shit," Chase said as he closed his eyes and took a deep breath. "I was having a nightmare and...oh fuck, I hope everyone in the building didn't hear me." He referred to the small hotel they were staying at, off the main highway, 20 minutes outside of Hennessey.

"Chase, I seriously doubt that anyone else is *in* the building," Diego let out a short laugh. "We're not exactly at a top-notch hotel in a tourist friendly area. Come on!"

Following his lead, Chase began to relax and shrugged. "A lot of people come here to hunt in the fall and..."

His words suddenly halted when realizing what he had said. Suddenly reminded why they were there in the first place, his emotions weighed him back down, pulling him into the same place he had been for days. In fact, Chase was doubtful he would ever leave there again, seeing it more of a permanent home, not a brief visit. He would never be the same again and it was that in itself that made this experience even more difficult.

Diego looked sorrowful, reaching out, he patted his arm and quickly moved away. Chase knew why and for a moment, he really wanted him to stay. It was merely a quick thought that went against his usual desires but there was a part of himself that wanted, *needed* an escape from his current reality. It had crossed his mind the day of the funeral when Kelsey hugged him but then, it only made him angry. Now, as he thought about the warmth that had spread through his body, there was a part of him that wanted to call her, to be with her that night. But he knew better. If he caved to any desires now, it wouldn't end in that room.

"It's just a dream, *amigo*," Diego assured him and started toward the door. "You've been through a lot the last few days but tomorrow, we leave and I think that will help you. Going back to your life, getting out of this town, it will help you heal."

Chase nodded but he had his doubts. Nothing would take this heaviness away. It was weighing him down like nothing ever had before; all the miseries he had experienced in life before his son's death felt minor in comparison, in fact, they were a joke. His problems in the past now seemed silly, stupid and irrelevant. He was certain going back to Toronto wouldn't help. He didn't want to return to work, that first day when everyone met him with sympathy in their eyes, telling him they were sorry; he dreaded that day. It would only bring everything back up again and force him to think about it and he just couldn't.

Diego said a last good night but lingered in the doorway as if he wanted to ask Chase something and if he had, perhaps he would've been surprised by the answer. It was after he left and Chase lay back down that he realized that not only was he a different person from only a week earlier, his tendencies may have changed. Perhaps he wouldn't be as cautious as before and maybe Diego had it right when he followed his desires, and not think logically about what the consequences were for his actions. Just like the speeding car in the dream, Diego didn't think about what was ahead or the possible dangers. Chase *always* thought ahead and yet, here he was, with one less son.

He fell asleep with this new reality of the world around him. Nothing would be the same again. He knew it. Food would never taste as good. His eyes would never see the world as he had before and his temptations, he wouldn't fight off but accept without thinking of the consequences.

The next morning, Chase moved mechanically around the hotel room. He took a shower, brushed his teeth, got dressed and organized his stuff for the trip home. Glancing at his phone, he ignored texts from his sister, Maggie, and Kelsey; he grew tired of accepting condolences, telling people he was 'ok' and turning down their offers to talk. He didn't want to talk. He didn't want to think about death anymore. He just wanted to go home and Hennessey was no longer home. Maybe it never had been.

Diego was unusually quiet that morning too. His eyes probing Chase, as if he wasn't sure of what to say but there was an unspoken conversation that was transmitting between them. They silently got in the rental car and jumped on the highway before there was much traffic, anticipating more before getting to Calgary. A part of Chase never wanted to come back to Alberta again and if it wasn't for his two youngest children, he never would.

The twins were far too young to understand what was going on. On top of their miseries of losing a child, Audrey now had the two little boys asking her where Leland was and couldn't understand why their older brother was not coming back. Although she was a counselor by profession, she admitted to Chase that this situation was too much for her to handle. Her relationship with Albert was strong but she saw herself pushing him away and although she understood why she also couldn't stop herself. It didn't matter that he was like a father to the children, it wasn't the same. No one could understand how it felt for a mother who lost a child. It wasn't even the same for Chase.

He had so much compassion for Audrey but yet, he was not in a place to help her. Chase was an empty vessel and all he could think about was how he hadn't wanted to have a baby after originally learning about Audrey's pregnancy years earlier. He hadn't wanted to be a father and then when they broke up, his son seem to have little interested in talking to him and so, the disconnect sent him into an empty road of guilt that only weighed him down.

"Do you want to get some food?" Diego's voice was quiet, gentle, "We have time."

"I'm not hungry but if you want anything....." Chase answered with no emotion as his eyes stared ahead at the empty road.

"No, I'm fine," Diego replied and paused for a moment. "There is somewhere I would like to stop though if you don't mind."

"Sure," Chase said with a shrug. "Where? There's nothing here."

"That trailer park that's coming up," Diego answered as if it were the most obvious answer.

"The what?"

"The trailer park ahead."

"What? Why?" Chase asked in stunned disbelief. "Why do you want to go to a trailer park?"

"I've never been to one."

Chase didn't reply but turned his head to look at Diego. Their eyes met and a grin appeared on his face.

"I always wanted to see a trailer park."

"You've never seen a trailer park before?" Chase asked. "Seriously?"

"No, I haven't," Diego confirmed and the mood in the car seemed to relax. "I was curious ever since that Eminem song."

"An Eminem song makes you want to go to a trailer park?" Chase couldn't help but laugh. "What the hell are you talking about?"

"You're too young, you don't know his music," Diego said with a shrug. "He has this song where he talks about two trailer park girls..."

"I'm familiar with the song," Chase replied and started to laugh. "*That* song, that song makes you want to go to a trailer park? Are you kidding me?"

"Not *just* that song," Diego insisted and made a face. "I see them on television all the time, movies, I want to see what one looks like for real. Are the people in them all white trash like on television?"

"It's not the same," Chase replied and continued to laugh and then quipped, "Do you want two trailer park girls..wait, how does that song go again?"

"You *know* that's not what I want," Diego smirked and continued to focus on the road ahead as a car passed them and Chase briefly thought about his dream from the night before and opened his mouth to tell Diego but decided against it.

"I think you'll be disappointed by the trailer park," Chase insisted. "It's just a bunch of low-income families, not an episode of *Jerry Springer.*"

"After meeting your friends and relatives in Hennessey, I'm starting to think your *life* was a Springer episode back there," He teased, bringing a welcomed, if not brief, collapse in tension, "No offense."

"None taken, you're not that far off the mark on this one," Chase replied and let out a laugh as he looked out the passenger side window as they moved closer to the trailer park and Diego turned into it, slowly driving through, observing with fascination. For the most part, there was nothing to see. Appearing bored and slightly disappointed, he turned at the end and drove back through, showing less interest.

"You know, most of the time, things never are as exciting as we have them built up to be in our heads," Chase commented as he looked into the windows of the trailers, seeing mostly young people.

"Sometimes, but not always," Diego's comment was matter-of-fact but his eyes shot through Chase and left him silent. "Sometimes we underestimate and it's all about timing, my friend. If we came back here on a hot summer night, we might find this same trailer park is anything but boring. Life is like that. Like I say, it's all about timing."

Chase knew he wasn't just talking about the trailer park.

CHAPTER TWENTY-SIX

His son's death changed him. Moment by moment, Chase was seeing the world through a different set of eyes. Broke wide open, he had no choice but to view everything he had once denied. It reminded him of a scene in a popular television show where a subdivision burned to the ground and neighbours were left in disbelief; looking each other in the eye for the first time, the same neighbours who didn't know or care who lived next door before the fire, were suddenly huddled together, crying about all they had lost. The same people who walked around with masks of confidence were as vulnerable as children. It was as horrifying as it was beautiful.

Chase began to see things different on way to the airport. The lines on Diego's face, the signs of worry in his eyes, the vulnerability that he hadn't noticed before that day. But there was something else. When he removed his sunglasses to make a complaint about the coffee at the airport, there was a coldness in his eyes that he hadn't noticed since their first meeting; back when Diego came flying through Jolene's makeshift office in Calgary, ordering her assistant to get him an Americano.

"Does anyone in this God forsaken state known how to make a decent cup of coffee?" Diego complained to Chase, turning away from the young server. "I mean, really, is it so difficult?"

With that, he rushed away and Chase was left giving the cashier an apologetic smile.

Following behind, Chase didn't bother to explain that it wasn't the server's fault. Clearly, Diego's frustrations weren't really with the coffee. He was anxious since arriving at the airport. As usual, he sat as far away from anyone, always concerned that their conversations would be overheard, even when they talked about nothing at all.

A Korean teenage boy walked past them wearing a pair of ear buds, the music of Marilyn Manson flowed through and Chase recognized the song 'Disassociative' which ironically would seep through his brain a million times in the upcoming months. He would later realize that it was one of many synchronicities that would enter his life during his most vulnerable state.

"Are you okay?"

This time it was Chase asking Diego the question and not the other way around. It felt empowering on the other side.

"Ah...yeah, don't worry about me," Diego said and cleared his throat, pulling himself together and shrugged. "Just this coffee is terrible, it's no big deal."

"It seemed like a big deal a minute ago when you were ripping into that guy," Chase nodded toward the cashier at the lunch counter. "What's going on?"

"Nothing," His answer was too fast, too quick to seem sincere. "Don't worry about me."

"Why not? You worry about me?" Chase retorted and noticed Diego's eyes warm to a deep brown, his face relax as his fingers fiddled with the coffee cup lid.

"It's just, you know, been a *tense* week," He shrugged and took a deep breath. "I'm not used to dealing with this heavy stuff. I'm not good at it."

"No one is good at it, Diego."

"No, but I mean, I don't know what to say," Diego quietly replied and turned a bit in his chair. "To you, to your family, I feel like this is one thing that I can't fix."

"No one can fix this and no one expects you to fix everything," Chase quietly commented, his body felt light in the chair as if he could float away. His eyes shifted to a little boy who was around Leland's age and he felt a sharp pain in his chest. He could barely handle his other two children while in Hennessey and now, he didn't even want to look at someone else's child.

"I know but, I still, I feel I should," Diego's words were confusing but heartfelt. "I feel that...I don't know, we're family, Chase and with family, I always try to do whatever I can to fix something. And this time, I feel, helpless."

"I appreciate it," Chase replied, his voice soft, relaxed, he felt defeated and unsure of how to even begin to explain that it wasn't necessary that Diego worry. "I do, I appreciate it but...it is what it is. We have no choice but to move forward."

Diego nodded and didn't reply, his lips tightened up and he finally said, "I told them, at the office, not to talk to you about any of this."

"Really?"

"Yeah, I spoke to Jolene about it last night," Diego abruptly turned and touched Chase's arm. "Not that you have to rush back, I mean that when you do return, Jolene will instruct people to not bring any of this up. I know how you feel about that..."

Chase hadn't confessed that this was one of his concerns so was impressed by his friend's instincts. "Thank you, Diego. I definitely don't want to rehash this at work."

"And you won't," Diego insisted. "If anyone brings it up, I will fire them!"

"You don't have to go that far," Chase said with a little laugh, a small drop of joy filled him as he saw Diego's usual feistiness return. "I was actually thinking of the same thing but wasn't sure if I should bring it up."

"You didn't have to," Diego insisted. "I know you, Chase, I know you don't want people fussing over you and I know it would be awkward and difficult. You want to go back and preoccupy your mind. I get that."

"Sometimes," Chase started slowly, unsure if he should continue his thoughts. "I feel like you know me better than I know you."

"What do you want to know?" Diego shrugged. "I have no secrets from you."

"I feel like I'm not supposed to ask for some reason," Chase picked his words carefully but didn't fail to humor Diego, who's face lit up with a smile.

"You think I'm a gangster, don't you?" Diego said as he leaned toward Chase, a sinister glint shone through his eyes. "I'm Colombian, the drugs, Escobar, I know I know....that's what people think when they hear where I'm from, I'm a gangster. I'm surprised when I get through the airport without a cavity search, for Christ sakes."

"I didn't mean that," Chase automatically felt bad even though Diego appeared humored by the concept. "I mean, you know, when I worked for Jolene in Calgary, I hadn't realized that we weren't a legit business..."

"Freelance party planners, nothing illegal there," Diego scrunched up his lips and shrugged. He crossed his legs and his right foot began to jiggle around. "You know, to see how it worked before starting anything officially."

"The guns? You guys both have guns? The baseball bat incident?"

Diego shrugged again, his foot continued to bop around. "As I said before, we're from Colombia. We didn't grow up in a safe place. There was a lot of violence and we, as kids, learned very early that you have no one else to protect you but yourself. It's different for you. You lived in a safe country."

"But you're in that safe country now."

"Old instincts, they never die," Diego leaned away from Chase, his eyes studied him carefully. "As for the baseball bat, I'm not exactly The Rock, I need to protect myself."

"The gun doesn't do that?" Chase calmly asked even though Diego appeared slightly defensive.

"You shoot someone, it's pretty messy," Diego replied with a shrug. "The police get involved and all that...but if you hit an intruder with a baseball bat, it's different. You know, bruises and broken bones can come about in many ways. A bullet, it can only come from a gun."

Chase nodded and remained silent.

"I got no secrets, Chase," Diego said and leaned closer to him. "I tell you anything. *Anything*. I would tell you about the first time I put a man in the hospital and the last time I jerked off. But only you, no one else, cause you're *family* to me. I tell you anything."

"I would rather hear about the guy you put in the hospital," Chase spoke matter of fact tone and Diego let out a short laugh.

"Are you sure? He replied with a sanctimonious grin. "The other story is pretty good too."

"So how many men have you put in the hospital?" Chase asked, ignoring his last comment. "Do you even know?"

"One can never be sure," Diego replied. "But I beat the living shit out of a guy from high school when I was 15 or 16 and before you feel bad for him, I will tell you, he beat me up first. Him and a gang of guys."

"Why?"

"In their words? Cause I was a *maricón,*" He shuffled uncomfortably in his chair and briefly looked away. "It's faggot in Spanish."

Chase studied his face, as he turned back with a spark of anger in his eyes.

"It was confusing cause that boy and me, we were messing around but he must've felt ashamed of it later," Diego continued and turned toward Chase. "He told his friends that he *heard* I was gay and they grabbed me after school, beat the shit out of me. So when I got better, I found him, when he was alone." A mischievous grin formed on his lips. "My mother, she thought it was nice when I left the house with a baseball bat cause she assumed I was going to play with some of the local kids. I wasn't going to play no baseball."

"You put him in the hospital?" Chase quietly asked, as someone passed by talking on a cell phone.

Diego leaned on his hand and nodded. "I damn near killed the fucker. I broke his arm and fucked up his leg. I would've done more damage but instead, I threatened him. If he ever told anyone I did this, I would kill him next time."

Chase wasn't surprised. This was the same man he had watched attack a stranger in the condo earlier that year. It was clear that it wasn't his first time attacking someone. He wasn't sure what to say so continued to listen as Diego's accent became stronger as he spoke.

"No one ever bothered me again," Diego continued and leaned back in his chair, briefly closing his eyes. They suddenly sprang open again.

"Until I got to California but there, it wasn't just because I was gay, it was because people there, there's a lot of racism."

"I can relate, at least, a bit," Chase joined in and Diego looked intrigued. "I never thought about being native until I moved to Calgary and people were looking at me differently. I never had that happen before and it took me a while to learn it was because they thought I was dangerous. At first, I thought it was because of my size until I was at the corner store one day and overheard some woman whispering to the owner to 'keep an eye on the fucking Indian'. I guess I was a little naïve before."

"People, they want you to think they aren't racist but they are," Diego insisted. "Whites, they think they are superior more than they don't."

"I don't know about that," Chase disagreed. "Not all white people are like that."

"A lot are," Diego commented and pressed his lips together. "I saw it more in the states than here, I will admit but it might be the circles I traveled in."

"I'm half white," Chase commented.

"Phew! Barely," Diego teased and rolled his eyes. "I'm whiter than you, *amigo*."

"I have another question," Chase asked boldly and Diego looked comfortable, only raising his eyebrows. "How did you get your money?"

A grin swept over his face and he waited for a moment before answering.

"From my daddy."

"Your father?"

Diego let out a sharp laugh. "My *father?* He won't even speak to me since he found out I'm gay," he sat his coffee cup on the floor beside his chair leg. "No, my *daddy*, amigo, the man I started having an affair with shortly after I moved to the states. Remember, I told you."

"An older man?"

"Yeah, I mean, he was a little older than I am now," Diego said with a shrug. "Established, rich, he was from the old school so he hid the fact that he was gay from everyone but yet, everyone knew, you know?

Some thought he was divorced because his wife was a bitch but his wife got tired of catching him getting sucked off by other guys."

"That might but a strain in a relationship," Chase quipped and Diego merely grinned and looked away.

"He was....handsome and saw a naïve 20-year-old, an inexperienced man who needed someone to take him under his wing. Teach him things; you know, in and out of the bedroom and that was me."

For a brief second, Chase had a glimmer of a previous conversation with Diego where he admitted that Jolene had concerns that he was doing the same with him since they shared a living space.

"People thought that I was just some kid he took in, was helping out, a homeless immigrant learning English," Diego's eyes were staring at the floor as if deep in thought. "He groomed me, made me into the man I am today. Helped me with my English since he was bilingual and ah...taught me to have some class and I, in exchange taught him about good coffee and kept him satisfied in bed."

"Did you love him?" Chase asked boldly.

"In a way," Diego replied. "But not 'in love' that's a rare and special thing. It doesn't happen every day and if you're lucky, once in a lifetime. Not all relationships are about the romantic love that you see on television, sometimes they are more of a business arrangement."

His dark eyes met with Chase's and quickly looked away.

"Anyway, he died a few years ago and left me a lot of money," Diego said and tensed up. "It was...awkward since he had children my age who didn't exactly appreciate it but, there wasn't much they could do."

"Were you expecting it?"

"No, not at all," Diego replied. "I mean, he kept me, you know, I guess you would call it a 'sugar daddy' and gave me jobs, so I had something on a résumé, made me take courses to learn business skills, made me a US citizen with his connections and those same connections are now working on making me a Canadian citizen."

It was a stunning confession. It was difficult to envision Diego ever being in an imbalanced relationship where he had little or no control but relied so much on someone else. It made him think of his own relationship with Audrey when they first married and he immediately had compassion. He knew what a weak position that was and he also knew that Diego was holding back. There was more, he sensed it.

"Powerful man?"

"Very much so," Diego suggested with a nod. "Very very much so but, you know, he was good to me, I was attracted to him so it wasn't like he had to force me into his bed but I wanted to explore and so, I cheated on him a lot. I slept with a lot of men. I was rebellious and didn't appreciate being tied down and he understood that about me."

"And now?"

"I guess we mellow with age," Diego seemed lost in thought as he leaned back in his chair, he suddenly looked depressed. "But you know, we never really get what we want. We take what we can get and hope for the best."

Chase didn't reply.

CHAPTER TWENTY-SEVEN

He felt haunted by his son's ghost during the day, plagued by nightmares when he tried to sleep. Chase was restless, exhausted and felt as though the funeral was somehow supposed to sweep everything under the rug. It didn't happen that way. He couldn't stop thinking about Leland for a moment. Sometimes he would smile over something Diego said but it was as if he suddenly caught himself and stopped; how could he smile when his son was dead? Did he have a right to be happy?

After returning to Toronto, he briefly avoided Audrey. Talking to his ex-wife was far too painful. However, after a few days, Chase realized that he was only hurting himself because she was the only other person who knew what he was going through. And yet, they weren't really going through the same thing because she was the mother; she carried Leland for nine months and she was with Leland for every day of his life while Chase had faded into the background.

They started to have many late night conversations. It was usually just after Audrey put the twins to bed, forcing her to think about the one son she would never read a bedtime story to again. She would call Chase in tears, sometimes unable to speak but eventually talking about her own personal hell.

"How is Albert doing?" Chase asked one day, wondering if maybe her husband would be a better source of comfort than himself. It was understandable that they would connect with this experience but her current partner was in the same house, so it made more sense that she be with him and not to call her ex-husband.

"He doesn't understand," She sniffed. "He doesn't get it."

"I think he does," Chase spoke in a gentle tone, concerned that Albert might get the wrong idea about these very regular conversations. "He saw Leland like a son too."

"I just can't look at him," Audrey quietly admitted. "I can't look into his eyes and see the same man who seemed more concerned about comforting your mother that day than his own wife. And I can't look at *her* either. I will never forgive your mother."

Chase understood that but as the days went by, now over a week since Leland's death, his anger subsided. Not that he didn't hold his mother responsible in any way but because it didn't make a difference. Being angry with her didn't bring Leland back and getting through the day was enough of a struggle without gathering enough energy to be angry with his mother.

"Audrey, for what it's worth, I think you need to give Albert a break," Chase replied softly. "Don't be angry with him. You need each other now. Talk to him."

She reluctantly agreed after some more coaxing and their daily conversations were soon replaced by regular text messages.

Although everyone from Hennessey attempted to keep up with Chase after the funeral, he didn't have it in him to meet them half way. He would reply to their messages but didn't go in-depth when answering their questions. He was 'fine' when they asked because he refused to talk about the emotional tornado that was ripping through his heart because it simply wasn't somewhere he wanted to go. And did he want to connect with these people? Maggie, Kelsey, his sister, everyone who had almost forgotten him since leaving the province were suddenly back in his life with a vengeance? It didn't fit for him. It was as if they were doing it out of a sense of duty.

It was on the Thursday afternoon after returning from Hennessey that Chase decided to return to work the next morning. Getting that first day in would be the hardest and at least it would be followed by the weekend, so it would cushion his return. Diego seemed pleased with this decision.

"You're right, *amigo*," He replied as he fussed over his lime tree, checking the soil carefully to make sure it had enough water. "I think that it is best that you get back into a regular routine and sitting around here by yourself all day, it's not good, you know?"

"I know," Chase agreed and took a deep breath. "I'm more tired than if I was at work."

"Grief is exhausting," Diego replied as he gently pushed his lime tree into its regular spot. "It will be okay."

Chase got up the next morning and followed his usual routine, as he had before Leland died. In a way, it felt mechanical but at least he was taking action. On some level, he knew that this was important and that timing was everything. You couldn't let things slip away too far otherwise it might be impossible to ever get them back again.

He dreaded the first few minutes back at the office. He didn't want to see a hint of sadness in anyone's eyes, those sympathetic looks that suggested they were silently waiting for him to fall apart but most of all, he didn't want to be pitied. However, he should've realized that Diego would be all over it.

Walking ahead of Chase, he swung open the door much like a cowboy strutting into a saloon, with a sharp, warning look in his eyes, he took in the office. Deborah was on the phone. She barely glanced in their direction. They met Sylvana in the hallway, who stopped to talk to Diego about something, ignoring Chase, who slipped by, almost running into Gracie coming out of the staff room; she gave him a kind, yet enthused smile that suggested she was happy to see him. Next was Benjamin who merely smiled and said, 'Good to see you back," shook his hand then walked away.

A huge weight fell from his shoulders and he thought about Diego's recent comments on how work was your 'other family' and like real families, there was dysfunction combined with angst but at the end of the day, everyone was in your corner. He appreciated it more than he had before, suddenly feeling that connection that he had simply ignored in the past.

Now rushing to catch up to him, Diego followed Chase into Jolene's office and closed the door, noting that Beverly wasn't in the room. Unlike the others, she appeared stunned to see him back to the office, her eyes immediately filled with tears as she jumped up from her desk and ran toward him, her full bosom squashed against his chest as she gave him a tight hug. "Oh, Chase! I am so sorry, oh my goodness, your heart, it must be so broken."

"Jolene!!" Diego snapped beside them. "For fuck sakes! I told you not to do this!"

"It's, it's ok," Chase gently replied, surprised that he wasn't feeling emotional as he looked into Jolene's eyes as she backed away, wiping a stray tear away and clearing her throat. "I'm fine. It's fine."

Diego didn't appear convinced and took a deep breath, looking toward the door. "I will go get you a coffee."

With that, he awkwardly slid out of the room, softly closing the door behind him.

"I'm sorry, Chase, I didn't mean to cry all over you," Jolene sniffed and reached for a Kleenex on her desk. "I didn't mean to but as soon as I see you, I could not help it. I just am so sad for you.I cannot imagine, you know? I cannot imagine how you must feel."

"I know," Chase shared a sincere smile with her. "It's ok, Jolene."

She leaned against her desk and nodded. "You and I, we've been together for a long time now. You're family to me and I know Diego, he feels the same. We are so sad for you. He may not show it, but he, he's very depressed for you too. He try to make it better but he does not know how, you know?"

"I know," Chase nodded. "There's really not much anyone can do."

"I know, I know," She waved her hand in the air and walked behind her desk again and sat down. "I cannot believe this has happened to you."

Diego returned with two cups of coffee on a tray.

"Diego, a tray, you really needed a tray?" Jolene reached for her own coffee cup, already sitting on the desk.

"Yes, Jolene, I *really* needed a tray," Diego commented and dramatically continued. "See me, I only have two hands and I can't open the door and hold two cups without making a mess."

"Okay, you do not have to be snippy, Diego."

He brought the tray over to Chase and gestured toward his cup.

"Thank you," Chase said and graciously took it while Diego took the other and sat the tray on Jolene's desk. The two of them sat down.

"Do they know who did this to your son?" Jolene abruptly asked.

"Jolene!" Diego snapped. "For God sakes, woman, can you leave it alone!"

"It's okay," Chase said and put up his hand. "It's okay, Diego, I don't mind answering."

"You shouldn't have to," Diego muttered and continued to look frustrated with his sister.

Jolene appeared stunned by her brothers remark.

"They know who did it but it seems it was an accident," Chase quietly answered. "I don't want to get into it a lot but I think he's going to just get a slap on the wrist."

"What?" Jolene appeared confused. "A slap? What?"

"I mean," Chase hesitated for a moment, as if he suddenly couldn't think, he noted that Diego appeared concerned. "It means, he won't be punished much for it. At least, I don't think he will."

"What?" Jolene snapped. "Are you joking with me, Chase? That is not right! He must go to prison and die there!"

Diego gave her a sharp warning glance and she immediately shrunk in her chair.

"I'm sorry, Chase," She sounded regretful. "I keep saying wrong thing. I just mean, he should be punished for what he did."

"I agree but I know how the court system works," Chase spoke honestly, feeling defeated by the same topic he and Audrey had discussed many times. "The worst part is that everything is played down. I mean, the guy is the town drunk, he was probably drunk at the time."

He noted the anger in Diego's eyes as he exchanged looks with his sister.

"Also, he has a tendency of hunting when he wants, where he wants and not following the rules," Chase continued and bit his lower lip. "He claims he was practicing on bottles and didn't see Leland. Everyone in Hennessey knows what he is like but when it comes to court, none of that will come up cause it's what we know about him in general, not about that morning."

"Who is this man?" Jolene asked and made a face as she picked up her coffee.

"His name is Luke Prince."

"Prince?" She curled up her lips in a similar fashion as Diego often did then made a fist and slammed it on the desk. "Well, Luke Prince, may you *rot* in *hell.*"

"Can we not talk about this anymore?" Diego cut in awkwardly and the siblings exchanged looks, Jolene giving a quick nod.

"Yes, I know you are right," She cleared her throat. "Let's not talk on this no more."

"Oh God," Diego rushed in to change the topic. "Jolene, your English is so bad. I cringe every time you talk."

"I speak fine," She snapped. "You, you do not worry about me."

There was an awkward silence and when Chase glanced toward Diego, he noted that he was biting his bottom lip, his eyes a million miles away.

CHAPTER TWENTY-EIGHT

What started off as an intense pain slowly evolved into anger; another kind of misery that ate at his soul every day and although Chase hid it well, he constantly thought about his son.

Already out on bail, Luke Prince claimed to not know he had shot anything - *anything* as if Leland wasn't even a child, just another animal wandering through the woods. Of course, there were complaints about where the shooting took place since it was too close to private property but somehow that seemed inconsequential. The justice system was more concerned about the accused's rights, stating that he was apparently 'disorientated' at the time and that his gun 'accidentally' discharged. He had no idea that there was anyone in the woods and in fact, his lawyers were questioning why Leland wasn't being monitored better; how did the child escape Louise Jacobs' house without her knowing? Was she a neglectful guardian?

It was a game Leland liked to play. While savages like Luke Prince wandered through the wooded area shooting at defenseless animals and slapping themselves on the chest when they made a 'kill', Chase's son ran through the edge of the woods looking to capture various animals to bring home. In the child's world, he was merely playing cops and robbers; the small animals were the robbers and he was capturing them, much like a cat after its prey. He rarely was successful, more thrilled by the chase than the capture but he had been known to snatch up a wiggly toad before it managed to escape and hop away. There were also snakes but he hadn't been allowed to capture them since scaring his mother when he brought one into the house. Most of the time it was a butterfly and on one occasion, Audrey found him sitting on the ground with a small bird perched on his hand.

He was a daredevil and as such, often put himself in dangerous positions - climbing on unstable furniture, hanging from the banister, jumping off the bed and on top of his brothers - the list was endless and yet, their fears were usually that he would just break an arm or leg. It never occurred to them that he would wander into the woods and get shot.

The worst part was that Luke Prince didn't seem to think he was accountable. He appeared to have no remorse. Audrey insisted that his lawyer probably told him to keep a stiff upper lip to not seem weak but when before the judge, show regret and disbelief that he committed such a crime. It seemed unreal that people were even taking his claims seriously but they were.

Luke Prince was older than Chase. Always on the football team during high school, he was part of the unofficial alpha dog club of Hennessey; the same one that had rejected Chase, yet because of his size and strength, generally kept their distance too. He was the kind who thought being a man was in direct correlation to how much liquor you could drink and still stand up and how big of an animal you could kill. This time, he got the biggest kill of all, Chase bitterly thought.

Luke worked in the oil fields for weeks at a time and had just returned home a few days before shooting Leland: something that locals knew meant that he was 'on a drunk' since that was his regular routine. Chase had seen it with his own eyes while working at Bud's bar years earlier. So many times had he watched Luke - or 'the Prince' as some called him - strut up to the door, already smelling of alcohol either with a 'lady friend' or some of 'the boys' showing off his money, paying for drinks and being an overall jackass. Bud had been the icon for white trash and yet he looked down at Luke as if he were the dirt below his feet. He always instructed Chase to be ready for a fight or some tense situation if 'that fucking hillbilly started something' and it wasn't uncommon for Chase and Bud to find any reason to escort him out.

Chase didn't talk about it much with Diego. The few questions he did ask were carefully worded as if he didn't want to kick the hornet's nest but gently tap it. His reactions were always calm, his face tense even though he rarely said anything, it was clear Diego shared his anger but yet, never expressed it. Perhaps, they didn't have to since they shared a bond that was stronger than any words that could be spoken.

The weeks went by and somehow got a little easier and in some ways, more difficult. Audrey grew angrier, while Chase heard that his own mother had aged overnight. She no longer took the children to her house. Audrey didn't offer them and Louise Jacobs didn't ask. Chase felt numb. No longer sad or angry, he felt nothing.

His actions were mechanical. Work was a distraction and where he once was the 'nice' one in the office, he discovered himself to become tougher, even grabbing Sylvana's attention when he snapped at her one day. Stunned, she quickly apologized and scurried away but he instantly saw a change in how she acted around him. He felt stronger, powerful, and not just Diego's lackey, dutifully following behind.

While he avoided Deborah upon returning to work, something between them changed over the weeks. Where he originally had no interest in hooking up with her, a couple of weeks after returning, a gentle brush up against him in the staff room prompted a fast hookup in the public washroom two floors down. It was a release that seemed to remove him from his current life, if only just for a short few minutes and it was the start of an affair that was pretty regular, if only for selfish reasons. It was an emotionally void and ideal for both because neither had anything to give.

Fortunately, no one at the office was aware of their affair. Diego knew that Chase was spending much more time at the gym, releasing his anger on the heavy bag and certainly had no idea of the sexual relationship he often shared with Deborah after going to the gym. The fierceness he released on the punching bag was nothing compared to the passion that sprung between the sheets after the gym, the only way he could escape the dark thoughts that followed him every day. It was the only time that he wasn't thinking of his deceased child.

Grief has many stages. Where Audrey was once full of anger, she was falling into a depression as the holidays grew near. She dreaded Christmas. They both did. It was too painful and although Chase's ex-wife was speaking to a counselor, Chase was starting to wonder if it was working. She was doing worse, not better. Then again, was he doing any better either?

Diego insisted that the best way to move forward was to get involved in a new project.

"At first, I thought it would be boxing," Diego commented one day while they were at work. Chase was sitting at his desk, feeling ill after learning that the charges against Luke Prince would probably be minimal. The police finding little reason to not believe his story of shooting a child in error. It was like a nightmare. Diego knew about this and insisted the best way to get through it was to preoccupy his mind. Chase was surprised he was the voice of reason.

"But now," Diego continued, "I think, we need to work on some new ideas for next year. You know, the parties are still popular but you can't let things get stale. We got to keep moving forward."

Chase silently nodded.

"We have a meeting soon, you and I, with someone who is very important to this company," Diego commented as he closed his laptop and relaxed in his chair. Dark eyes shone from across the room as he pressed his lips together and rocked back in the chair while staring at Chase, "An important investor, a silent partner."

"We have a silent partner?" Chase was surprised. "I guess, I just thought..."

"That it was only me and Jolene running the show?" Diego grinned and slowly shook his head back and forth before sitting upright again and pulling his chair closer to the desk. "No, but in fairness, it's not something I talk about and most people around here, they know better than to ask too many questions. That's how I like my employees. I want them to do their job and not worry about these things."

"How long has this person been a partner?"

"From day one," Diego raised his eyebrows and tapped a finger on his laptop. "He and you will meet sometime soon. I think it's time you get more involved in this business, the behind the scene stuff, not just the office."

Chase silently nodded. A strange sensation seemed to creep up inside of him, causing his heart to lurch. He shared a look with Diego that was strong. The truth hidden in dark corners was about to be exposed and he was ready.

CHAPTER TWENTY-NINE

"Fuck its cold!" Diego complained as they made their way to his car on a late November morning. The temperatures were slightly unseasonable but yet, Chase didn't have the heart to tell him that the worst was yet to come, that the chill of that morning was minor compared to the bitterly cold days in January and February. Granted, he was also new to Ontario and someone told him that it wasn't as bad in Toronto as Calgary, regardless he knew Diego would hate it. Having lived in Colombia and then California, winter was a foreign concept. "How do you people stand it?"

"We're used to it," Chase gently replied as he got into the passenger side and buckled his seatbelt. "Wait till it starts snowing."

Starting the car, Diego didn't respond as he turned up the heat and flew out of the parking garage. Their daily ritual had formed throughout the months and although Chase was now looking at buying a car, he knew he would continue to go to work with Diego in the mornings. Even though he would've preferred to arrive at the office a little earlier, he learned to go with the flow and not say anything.

As they drove to work, Chase felt his heart grow heavy as he noticed the Christmas decorations in the windows of various shops throughout the city and he automatically thought about Audrey and the twins. How would they get through this holiday season? Although they all were doing a little better since Leland's death, it was still a hole in everyone's heart that would never go away.

"Today is the day," Diego interrupted his thoughts, an appreciated gesture at that moment. "Today, you will meet our major investor, our silent partner."

Slightly unprepared, Chase opened his mouth to respond but wasn't sure what to say. Not that it mattered, Diego was already talking again.

"I told him that we can trust you," Diego airily commented, as if there were no suggestion behind his words. Chase felt the hairs stand up on the back of his neck but ignored it. At one time, this would've unnerved him. Now, nothing could throw him off course. After losing a child, anything seemed manageable in comparison. Nothing scared him like it once did; now that he had faced his worst fear.

Chase made eye contact with Diego as they sat at a red light and gave a quick nod, a vague smile on his lips.

"He's Mexican but we, we get along okay," Diego wrinkled his nose as he spoke, almost as if there were something tickling it and quickly shifted his attention back to the road as the car moved forward.

"You make it sound as if that's a surprise," Chase commented and grinned to himself.

"Nah, you know, sometimes, you can't trust those Mexicans," Diego spoke skeptically, his body shifted uncomfortably in the seat. "But, I got to give credit where its due and this man you will meet today, is a clever business man."

"Where did you meet him?"

"When I was in California," Diego answered, appearing slightly more comfortable. "He was....a business contact of my *daddy*. He contacted me after he heard that I was thinking of starting a business and said to keep him in mind, that maybe we could work together. The rest is history."

"Does he live in California?"

"No, he lives in Mexico but he travels some with his work, throughout North America, I don't know where else," Diego began to twitch again. "I don't ask."

Arriving at the office, everything about the day seemed relatively normal. The meeting with the mystery investor was to take place at 10 a.m. at a luxury hotel in the downtown area. Chase was as eager to see inside the building as he was to meet this man, having never visited a pricey hotel, he wanted to compare it to some of the places he had stayed as a kid.

As it turns out, there was no comparison. The hotel was beautiful from the outside alone, while the inside was nothing short of spectacular. Chase could almost smell money as he walked through the doors; everything from the decor, to the courteous staff that made him feel like a king returning to his palace; it was easy to see how someone could get used to this lifestyle. He often wondered if that was how Diego's 'daddy' had lured him in so many years ago; was the promise of living a charmed life with all the comforts too much to deny? Chase wasn't so sure he would've been able to deny it either if he was in his shoes.

Not that Diego had specifically said that he lived an elegant life but it appeared that he was pretty carefree, without the worry of paying rent, for school or anything else but in other ways, Chase recognized that maybe it did affect him. There was a vulnerable side to him that he rarely displayed but for some reason, he was showing it that morning. Did this man, the investor, intimidate Diego? Had they had a relationship of some kind? There was something odd about his body language all morning that Chase couldn't put his finger on. There was something off about this entire situation.

An 'associate' of the investor met them in the lobby; a large, burly Mexican man who looked more like private security than someone who was merely working for the mystery man. He didn't smile but said something in Spanish to Diego, who merely nodded and gestured for Chase to follow as they approached the elevator. No one talked until they arrived at the hotel suite, when Diego said *gracias* and the large man merely nodded, only glancing at Chase as Diego knocked on the door.

The man appearing on the other side was nothing like Chase expected. About the same height as Diego, he looked more like a movie star than an average business man. With a sparkling smile, friendly, dark eyes and perfectly styled shiny, black hair, Chase briefly wondered if this was the reason Diego seemed a bit nervous about this meeting. He wore an expensive suit and gestured for them to come in and as he closed the door, he immediately began to speak in Spanish and then suddenly stopped.

"Ah wait, does your associate speak Spanish?" He gestured toward Chase and continued to smile, his English very precise, his accent distinct.

"No," Chase answered for himself but quickly added. "That's fine if you two need to discuss something..."

"Nah, you're here for a reason," The Mexican man extended his hand and continued to smile. "I'm Jorge Hernandez, nice to make your acquaintance."

"Nice to meet you, I'm Chase Jacobs," He noted that Jorge's handshake was strong, his eye contact friendly yet intense, sending a message that was quite clear. He let go of his hand and gestured toward a nearby table, where there was a pot of coffee along with a tray full of pastries. "Please join me."

They gathered around the table and Diego appeared unusually quiet, if not restrained as he reached for a strawberry tart, something that Jorge seemed to note, a smirk appeared on his face. He reached for the pot of coffee and poured a cup for Diego, then turned his attention to Chase.

"Coffee? I'm afraid that it's not the best coffee around but it is sufficient."

"Yes, thanks," Chase replied and considered how this was a very casual meeting. He noted that Diego made a bit of a face when he took a sip of his coffee and quickly added a little more cream. Upon tasting his own, he saw why.

"Chase, have something to eat," Jorge continued to smile and gestured toward the food. Please, I wouldn't be much of a host if you didn't eat something."

"Thank you," Chase replied and reached for a fancy cinnamon roll, which had a drizzle of icing and pecans sprinkled on top of it. Nothing like the ones his mother used to make. The aroma combined with the texture and flavor was beyond impressive, as he nodded his head as if to answer an unasked question.

"It is good?" Jorge's eyes lit up and Diego curiously glanced in his direction. "They make the best food in this hotel. It's what keeps me coming back, despite the outrageous inflation, I still enjoy it when I'm in Toronto."

"Delicious, thanks," Chase replied and took another drink of coffee. It was clear that Jorge took pride in impressing his guests and gave an unpretentious nod before continuing.

"I believe in quality," He replied and turned his attention toward Diego. "What is the use of money if you can't enjoy the finer things, am I right?"

"You're right, *amigo*," Diego replied, the confidence returning in his voice. "I did not have such things growing up so if I can have them now, I certainly enjoy them."

"Ah, me as well," Jorge agreed. "We lived in poor conditions when I was a child but life, it has been good to me."

"So Diego," he continued, turning slightly while sipping his coffee. "How is that sister of yours?"

Diego seemed to tense up with this question but quickly shrugged it off. "She's great, as usual."

"That is not a surprise," Jorge reached for an elaborate pastry that reminded Chase of an upscale version of a cake he used to see at the convenience stores. "How could a woman who is that beautiful be anything short of perfection? Those Colombian women, you can't beat them," He turned his attention back to Chase. "The most beautiful women in the world, if you ask me."

Diego appeared slightly perturbed as he bit his lip. Chase smiled but didn't respond.

"So Chase, I am happy to meet with you today. I hear such wonderful things from Diego," Jorge spoke with ease, his face continued to show friendliness as if a smile was always around the corner. He took a bite of his dessert, just as Chase finished his and Diego seemed to only eat half of his own. "It appears you were with the company even before it really was a company at all? Back when Jolene looked after things in Calgary? That pitiful little office, oh my, do you remember that, Diego?"

"I know, when you tell Jolene to keep costs down, she keeps costs down," Diego sat back in his chair, coffee cup in hand. "That much you can be assured of."

"She made me a lot of money in Calgary and you're both making me a lot of money now too," Jorge said with a sniff and suddenly, something changed. The two men made eye contact and Chase sensed a message passing between them, a dark brooding look appeared in Jorge's eyes as he turned back to Chase. "And now, we will continue to make money but we must be careful."

Remaining silent, Chase was waiting for the other shoe to drop. He sensed that it was coming and remained silent.

"Diego, how much does he know?" The Mexican man shifted his eyes across the table. "About what we do."

Shaking his head, Diego didn't reply at first. "Nothing."

"Well now, that's about to change," Jorge replied, his eyes became darker as he spoke, his face suddenly more serious, as the charming side seemed to all but disappear. "What Diego has told you is that I invest? I do, that is correct. I invest money into this business, I'm satisfied with the return but we also have something else that has gone on all along. Something that you aren't aware of but that was for your own good. But now, it seems you are becoming a larger part of this company so it's important that you know all the plays going on behind the scenes. It's important that you are aware because we will need more help in the future."

Chase nodded, his expression stoic, he didn't say a word.

"See, I'm like the invisible man. The silent partner, in a way," Jorge continued and Chase noted that Diego was watching him closely. "I'm a normal businessman from Mexico, officially I work in the coffee industry but behind the scenes, I have other interests. And those business interests connect nicely with the parties your company holds. A little something to make the nervous relax and the anxious to show themselves, to enjoy life, just like the finer things we are enjoying here today," He gestured toward the food on the table. "Life is too short to not enjoy everything it has to offer and in my opinion, everything is fine in moderation; food, overpriced hotel rooms, these are things that we can have sometimes and why not? We deserve it."

Chase tilted his head and continued to listen.

"But some things, our society say we shouldn't enjoy because they are *bad*," Jorge made a face and glanced toward Diego and back and Chase. "Alcohol, sex, drugs. These things, we're told are bad, some may even say evil, but you know what I say, Chase? I say just like with food and other nice things, everything in moderation is fine. And if someone goes to one of your parties, intrigued with the possibilities, perhaps aroused and yet, a little piece of them is nervous, perhaps slightly restrained, they want a little something to take the edge off, as you say here. A pill, a little cocaine, never hurt no one."

Chase didn't say a thing. He got the picture.

CHAPTER THIRTY

Drugs. Jorge Hernandez wasn't only an investor. He worked with one of the biggest drug dealers in Mexico and at Diego's parties, he was making a killing.

Not that he could blame him. It was the ideal place to sell drugs. Chances were good that people who were willing to pay to get into such expensive parties with the sole intention of hooking up for their pleasure, probably wouldn't be opposed to paying a little extra for something to enhance the experience. After all, they were barely balancing between the garden of good and evil, why stop there? It made perfect sense and really, Chase wasn't surprised. It was something he considered in the early days, back when they were still in Calgary and he had to rush a woman who had overdosed to the emergency room. Of course, it had been an isolated incident so he hadn't given it more thought.

Now he knew better.

Diego was quiet when they left the hotel that day. After being educated by Jorge on exactly how the process worked, Chase was left with a lot to think about. It was very carefully orchestrated and in fact, it would be easy, had any of their parties been raided, to plead ignorance. As far as he knew, Jorge was merely their investor and although that made him privy to the time and places of these parties, there was no reason to believe he was in the drug trade. Although it was in client agreements that no drugs be brought to the parties, it was merely a legal document prepared only for show. In the end, anyone could bring and sell drugs in the parties and who would know the difference?

"Do you not think that there are drugs everywhere?" Jorge had asked with a shrug, he had poured himself a second cup of coffee and shared a smile with a hesitant Diego. "I mean, come on? Political functions? Big fundraisers? All these celebrity parties and awards? You mean to tell me that people naïvely believe there are no drugs at any of these events? Come on! They are everywhere. Television leads people to believe that there are only drugs with the kids, with the rock stars, the bums on the street and that the drug dealers, they look like me and Diego."

The two men shared a laugh.

"In reality, you would never suspect the people selling at your parties. They look as wholesome as your neighbor growing up. No one would ever suspect and that is how we like it."

Chase learned that it was often the same officials supposedly against the illegal substances that were letting them in. It was a secret though and if it came down to it, these same people would turn on people like Jorge, if the truth ever got out. Chase felt naïve and yet, wasn't it just more proof that society wore a bright, beautiful mask to cover its shameful secrets. Hadn't he had this lesson many times in his young life? The media told you what was right and wrong and yet, it was only a fantasy that people chose to believe.

It wasn't until they were almost back to the office that day, just as they were about to pull into the underground parking, that Diego said something.

"You're awfully quiet," his comment was casual. "Should I be worried?"

"No."

"Are you sure?" Diego was hesitant, his dark eyes were a warm brown as he turned toward Chase, inspecting his face closely. "I hope us telling you this wasn't a mistake."

"Why would you say that?"

"You aren't saying much."

"Do I ever?"

"True," Diego nodded and seemed to relax as they pulled into a parking spot. "I want you to know that we are protected. We are in no danger and we aren't doing anything wrong."

"We're taking money from the drugs, aren't we?" Chase inquired.

"It's not that simple," Diego replied as he put the car in park and turned it off. They sat in silence for a moment.

"The only way Jorge would invest is if we would allow him to sell at the parties," Diego began as he turned in his seat. "So technically, the only thing we are doing wrong is allowing him. But on paper, it looks like we only have him as an investor."

"There's no kickback?" Chase asked skeptically.

"Not yet," Diego admitted. "But there will be, there's something coming. He has a lot of people in his pockets, that is why he comes here with no suspicions on him. He's untouchable."

"But are we?"

"Yes, he will protect us," Diego spoke confidently although there was something in his face that said otherwise; a minor twitch, here and there, an evasive look in his eyes as they glanced away. "It is what it is."

"But how protected is he, really?" Chase asked, suddenly regretful that he didn't know more about such things. Then again, did he ever expect to be in this position?

"He's got protection from the top in both his country and here," Diego insisted with a nod. "You have *no idea* how much. People speak of corruption in Mexico but they don't always know about the corruption here. You don't think these politicians, the police, they don't like their drugs too? They don't enjoy the good life? Everybody's got a secret vice no matter how professional they look in a suit or how educated they are, there's always far more going on behind the scenes in any situation than you realize. Don't matter if it's a businessman or a politician. There's so much that the people don't know and really, do they want to?"

Chase considered his question and decided the answer was no. People wanted to believe the world was a good place full of leaders who had only the best intentions but at the end of the day, they were only human too regardless of how society chose to paint them.

It was an unexpected lesson but one that he took in stride as they got out of the car and headed for the elevator. Once inside, Diego spoke again.

"The thing is that with Jorge, they found their right *hermosa rostro,* their handsome face that people want to believe the best about. Do you think that it's a coincidence that he looks like a celebrity on television? The handsome ones are meant to distract. The loud, obnoxious ones that offend us are also meant to distract. It's the bland, boring ones that you got to watch out for because they, my friend, are often the ones that are behind the scenes doing the dirty work."

These words stuck with Chase and he would start to look at the world very differently. He would watch the news with a new set of eyes, viewing reporters with skepticism and the rich and powerful with disdain. He knew their secret.

Back in the office, all was running as normal. Deborah was working on a laptop, her eyes briefly scanning over Chase's body as he walked in and he pretended to not notice. The last thing he wanted was for Diego to be suspicious although, after the morning he just had, there was a part of him that craved a quick hook up to take the edge off.

They immediately went to the boardroom, Diego silently tilting his head as they passed Jolene's office, letting her know to join them. Chase walked past just as she jumped up from her seat, closing her laptop, she muttered something to Beverly as she walked into the hallway, her eyes carefully inspecting Chase as if silently asking him a question. He could tell that she didn't like any of this and yet, hadn't she known about it all along?

Jolene closed the door and they all sat down, with Diego at the end of the table and Jolene across from Chase. She didn't open her laptop but folded her hands on top of it, her brown eyes searching his face.

"So?" She finally asked. "Chase, what do you think? It's not good?"

"Jolene, he's okay with it," Diego said as he gestured toward Chase. "I told you he wouldn't care and he didn't."

"Is this true, Chase?" her accent seemed heavier, thicker than usual. "Are you sure you feel this way?"

"I do," Chase spoke honestly, shrugging, he wasn't sure how to tell them that he really didn't care in light of what had happened a few weeks earlier. Life seemed less relevant by the day and unlike before, he was content flying by the seat of his pants. "If you guys aren't worried, then

I'm not worried. As long as I'm not going to be arrested for something, I don't care."

"Really?" Jolene asked skeptically. "Cause I'm not sure that I'm always comfortable with this, you know?"

"Jolene, why are you trying to put words in his mouth?" Diego asked. "I told him and I tell you, we are fine. To us, he is an investor, end of story. Even if this is caught, they have no proof. We are no more in the wrong than if we owned a nightclub where people sold drugs, you don't think that happens every day? Come on! It happens in every nightclub in this country, I am sure of that."

"Yes, I suppose this is true," Jolene agreed and turned her attention to Chase. "I always felt as though I was wrong to hide this from you but I thought it would be better, you know?"

He silently nodded.

"Jorge is the reason we have all this," Diego gestured around the room. "He put his money on us and we...we let him do his own thing and everything is fine. There's nothing to worry about."

"Oh, and in the future," Diego continued. "We never speak of this again in this office. I don't want to seem paranoid but those people out there, they work for us but do we really know them?"

"It is better we don't speak of this here," Jolene agreed and then as if to convince Chase. "You know, to be safe."

"You, Chase, you are different," Diego said as he stood up from his chair and pointed toward the clear glass door as they watched Sylvana walk by. "We're family. They are just employees. They know nothing. If they ever seem suspicious and ask, you know nothing."

Chase silently nodded.

"Chase, he knows, he doesn't speak," Jolene commented as she got up from her chair and Chase slowly followed her lead, a warm smile passed between the two of them. "He knows about secrets."

Diego gave him a short, pleading glance then quickly looked away as he grabbed his laptop.

"So what did you think, of Jorge?" Jolene asked curiously, her words light as if she had immediately forgotten the more serious side of their conversation. "He's nice, no?"

"He's nice," Chase agreed. "I would never suspect..."

"I know! He is so *handsome*," Jolene's eyes grew in size as she spoke, a smile formed on her burgundy lips as she made her way toward the door. "Diego, he thinks he's handsome too."

"He's ok," Diego sniffed and showed no commitment as he held his laptop close to his chest.

"He thinks he's so handsome," Jolene continued to tease, winking at Chase as she reached for the door and the two men followed her. "He gets all weird around him."

"I do not Jolene," Diego was insistent. "It's business, you can't be drooling over someone you are doing business with, at least, *I* don't think so."

"You don't worry about me," Jolene commented as she opened the door. "I have a meeting with him later today. Did he say why, Diego?"

"No," his reply was abrupt as he passed both Jolene and Chase and went into the office.

Jolene merely shrugged and went into her own office.

Chase glanced back toward Deborah.

It was almost lunchtime.

CHAPTER THIRTY-ONE

While growing up in Hennessey, Chase remembered his father once telling him that there often was an eerie calmness before a storm. It was a tranquil, beautiful silence that only people in the country grew to recognize as a subtle warning of what was to come; creating an inner calmness that was about to erupt and fade away.

It was difficult to hear in the city; where noise loomed all around, the vehicles alone filling the atmosphere with the sound of engines purring, music blaring and horns beeping would be enough to cause anyone to feel like silence simply didn't exist. It was a distraction and like most distractions, if done properly, no one ever realized what was about to take place.

Chase would have many distractions that week. After his meeting with Jorge Hernandez, it almost seemed as though everything picked up the pace. The mood in the office shifted from calm to a more impatient, nervous energy that was hard to miss. Suddenly, everyone seemed more snappy with one another and the worst contributor of all to this air of frustration was Diego, who was upset with his sister.

"She says," Diego complained after slamming the office door closed and stomping toward his desk. "That she is supposedly going to have meetings with Jorge about business but I know better. Clearly, there is something more going on between the two of them and she's hiding it from me. If they really had business to discuss, wouldn't I be part of the discussion?"

"It would make sense," Chase was hesitant to offer his opinion, feeling like a child that had to take sides after his parents argued. It was unsettling but at the same time, Diego did have a valid point. Why was Jolene meeting Jorge in private? It seemed unusual. "But I don't know. I mean, what did she say?"

"What did she say?" Diego plunked down in his chair and made a face. "She says that I have talked to him privately in the past, so why is this any different? She claims that she would feel better if she could be reassured that we were safe in this situation, which by the way, has been going on for some time but now, what? It worries her? I don't understand."

Chase didn't reply. His brain searched for an answer but he simply didn't know. He could see that Diego had his own suspicions.

"I told her that we will be fine but she said that to feel reassured that she had to talk to him herself, to look into his eyes and she would know," Diego shrugged. "I mean, I know they talk about women's intuition but us men also have instincts and I think I would know if he suddenly couldn't be trusted. What do you think?"

Chase considered his lone meeting with Hernandez and shrugged. "I don't know what to tell you. I went along with what you thought and trusted it."

"Exactly!" Diego commented as he pulled his chair closer to the desk. "That's what I say but no, she won't believe me and now she has this meeting with him and I think that it's total bullshit. I think it's an excuse to hang out with the 'handsome man' rather than what she is telling me."

"But you know, even if so, is it a big deal?" Chase hesitantly countered.

"Ah yeah, you don't shit where you eat," Diego insisted, his eyes grew in size as if it were the most obvious thing in the world and Chase was suddenly brought back to his days in Hennessey, hadn't Bud told him the same thing at one time? Then again, hadn't *Jolene* told him the same thing too? Diego often said it but did he mean it? "Especially when the person you're working with is in the line of business that this man is in if you know what I mean? He's not the kind of man she wants to get involved with for so many reasons but she won't listen to me. I told her that and she insists that nothing is going on. But I know better. I know Jolene."

Chase thought for a moment and shrugged. "I can't see Jolene doing that," He spoke honestly but saw the doubt in Diego's eyes.

"You, you only see one side of Jolene," Diego insisted and pointed toward the wall between their offices. "Here, she is another person from the outside world. You only know her work personality, you don't know her outside of work."

"Is it really that different?"

"It's really *that* different," Diego insisted but didn't elaborate instead opening his laptop and went back to work.

Diego was miserable for the rest of the day and into the weekend. He disappeared for a few hours on Friday night and Chase wondered if he had gone to talk to Jolene out of whatever he thought she was doing. He somehow didn't think it was what Diego suspected and yet, he couldn't help but be intrigued by his words earlier in the week. What was Jolene like outside of work? Did she have a lot of affairs? She certainly had the femme fatale vibe and the fantasies of her seducing him shamefully filled most of his own daydreams for the rest of the weekend, including when he was having sex with Deborah on Saturday night. He envisioned Jolene moaning in ecstasy, touching herself, engrossed in ever second.

He had to end his affair with Deborah. It was simply getting out of hand and those fantasies alone were suggesting that he wasn't even attracted to her; not that she appeared to be attracted to him either. They used one another. It made him feel disgusted with himself and wondered how he became this person? Why he allowed it at all? It wasn't just because of Leland dying - although that hadn't helped - but that he let life happen to him and not ever going after what he wanted. But what did he want?

After arriving home late on Saturday night, he noted that Diego wasn't around and was about to take a shower when his phone rang. It was Audrey. She was crying.

"What happened? Is it one of the boys?" Chase felt panic fill his heart as he broke out in a cold sweat. Closing his eyes, he attempted to calm himself but felt like he was sinking.

"No," Audrey sniffed and took a deep breath. She was silent for a moment. "They're all saying that it's me."

With that, she let out a loud cry and her voice shook uncontrollably. "They're saying it's my fault that Leland died. That I allowed him to stay with your mother and everyone knows she isn't all there. That I was sick of listening to three kids crying and I sent him there for the weekend."

"That's ridiculous!" Chase snapped, his anger crept up immediately replacing his anxieties. "Who the hell would say that?"

"Everyone around town," She sobbed and hesitated for a moment. "They're saying that your mother should be investigated for not looking after Leland properly because he was her responsibility. I feel like everyone in town has turned against us. They don't blame Luke Prince and say it's our fault for letting our kids always 'run wild' and that Leland shouldn't have been in the woods in the first place. That Luke had no way of knowing that a child would be there, alone, so early in the morning. They're turning it against us."

"Who? It obviously can't be everyone in town," Chase attempted to correct her. "That doesn't make sense. It's probably his family trying to make him sound like the innocent victim in this situation but there's no way that the court will see it that way."

"His lawyer, though," Audrey continued to sniff. "His lawyer wants to have social services investigate us because they say there was obviously something wrong that a child was out wandering by himself so early in the morning, that maybe he wasn't being taken care of properly."

"That's fucked up!" Chase felt anger rise in him and he started to pace as he talked. "First of all, he wasn't at home and second, little kids wander all the time. Parents do the best they can but sometimes, things happen. I can't believe they're saying such cruel things."

"They are, though," Audrey replied as her voice calmed and she cleared her throat. "It doesn't seem to matter that he was at your mom's place. We *allowed* him to go there and now, they're trying to gather people who say they've seen us be neglectful in the past. We allowed Kelsey to babysit the kids and then she ended up being in underground porn, for fuck sakes! How does that look? It looks like we're terrible parents who don't care."

"Unreal," Chase snapped. "This whole situation is insane! This is obviously Luke's lawyer attempting to take some of the heat off him before the trial. He knows that small towns thrive on rumors and he's hoping to sway things in their favor. As if Luke was innocently out practising that morning, sober, and has no idea he shot Leland. That's fucking insane!"

Silence followed. At first, he thought Audrey hung up on him because she wasn't speaking or crying.

"I think you're right," She finally replied and with heavy emotion in her voice, she finally replied. "Chase, I don't have it in me to do this anymore. I don't have it in me to go to trial and to fight. I don't have it in me to tell people that these rumors aren't true and now when I take the kids anywhere, I feel like everyone is watching us as if they want to see us make a mistake. It's like a popularity contest and Luke wins, so we have to lose. I just can't do it. I don't want to even live here anymore. I want to get out of this fucking town. I never thought everyone would turn against at the worst time of my life."

Chase felt his original anger deflate as she spoke. It wasn't right. It was unbelievable to him that people would turn against Audrey at that moment. Even he, who had a lot of issues with his ex-wife over the years, would never hold this against her. Even if Leland had left her house that morning and snuck out, any original anger would've quickly faded away upon seeing her face the day their son died. Her heart was completely broken and the fact that her town turned against Audrey was unbelievable to him. It made Chase sick to even consider.

"Are you sure, Audrey?" He gently asked, hoping that maybe she was actually exaggerating or paranoid. He took a deep breath. "Maybe there's a part of you that blames yourself and you think people are blaming you too. I know I kind of blamed myself at first."

"No Chase, this is the crown prosecutor," She replied simply and hesitated to continue. "He told me because he wants us to take this case to another district so we will get fair treatment. He said Luke Prince has too many family and friends in the community and none of them want to believe he's guilty. Get this, they don't think it's right that his freedom be taken away because he made a 'mistake' that they claim was our fault for not properly looking after Leland."

Hearing Devin crying, she ended the call and left Chase with his thoughts. He sat on the couch in disbelief, feeling as though he had to tell someone this horrible news and yet, he couldn't move. His brain raced and he couldn't think of a single person to share this with other than Diego and who knew where he was that night. He was probably on his own rendezvous. Then again, who else was there to confide in?

He sent Diego a quick message and didn't receive a reply. Just then the door flew open and his cranky roommate of earlier in the day strode in as if nothing were wrong in his world.

"You rang?" He said in a haunting voice with a smile on his face as he closed the door behind him. As he approached Chase, the smile fell from his face.

"What's wrong, amigo?"

Chase opened his mouth to say something but hesitated and shook his head. Diego silently nodded.

CHAPTER THIRTY-TWO

Where most people in Luke Prince's situation might try to keep a low profile after being arrested for a crime as heinous as shooting a child, he was contrary. Rather than being apologetic, he was defensive. Instead of being tight-lipped on the subject, he was vocal on his innocence and was insistent that he was a scapegoat for Louise Jacobs' irresponsibility. The real kicker was when Chase started to hear that he was hinting to many residents in the small town that Leland's grandmother had a 'problem with the alcohol'. The ironic statement sent Chase into a rage and he found himself at the gym, blindly pounding on the heavy bag in the basement; fortunately, no one was around to witness his fury or they may have questioned his sanity.

The real issue, as Diego would later point out, was personality. Some people, he insisted, flocked to strong personalities who said what people secretly wanted to hear or expressed their own dark thoughts and fears, therefore, making them feel it was acceptable to do the same. Many, he insisted were the sheep and lead by a few, lone wolves.

"But me," Diego added during that particular conversation that followed the frustrating news from Audrey. "That's why I make sure to always be a wolf; sly, strategic, ready for anything and never turning away from a fight. I was like that as a teenager when those boys beat me up and I'm like that to this day. And you, Chase, you need to learn to do the same."

"As I always tell you," Diego continued, his eyes sympathetic while his voice full of unexpected compassion as he sat beside Chase on the couch. "You're a follower, not a leader. You must be careful because some people will lead you to greatness and some people will lead you astray. You can't let life happen to you, *you* need to take on life and go after what you want, not just take what you can get. Only beggars take what they can get and no beggar has ever owned a condo like this," He swung his arms around without breaking eye contact with Chase. "No beggar drove their dream car or went to bed with the person they really wanted. No beggar has the life they truly desire because they don't know what that is and they underestimate their own value."

"I don't think I'm that bad," Chase muttered as he slumped over, feeling defeated.

"No but it's a slippery slope, my friend, trust me on that one," Diego continued as he turned toward Chase, his accent becoming stronger as he spoke. "I've watched you, observed you since we first met. You've got so much potential and you can't let a tragedy like your son's death pull you under. And it can happen fast."

"When my father disowned me as a kid back in Colombia," He continued as Chase turned in his direction. "That could've pulled me under but I wouldn't let it. I made plans. I made decisions and this is my life now. I didn't allow his shame of me become my shame too. You can't let that redneck town or their decisions on you or your ex-wife's parenting skills shame you. That's what they want. That's what this Luke asshole wants. He wants you to believe his story along with the rest of them but *you*, you know better. You must be stronger than him and trust that eventually, he will get what's coming."

Diego was right. It was so easy to fall down and not get up again and he was starting to see that Audrey was doing just that; to the point that he received a phone call from Albert a few days later to discuss how she was slowly moving away from the person she had always been. No longer strong, defiant and aggressive, she was now encompassed by a depression. It was understandable but at the same time, as Albert pointed out, she still had two children who were very much alive.

"She doesn't even want to leave the house now," Albert spoke honestly and it was those words that haunted Chase the most. Long after the call, he thought about the woman he had met years ago; the same woman who was very aggressive with him, making it clear that she wanted him and him alone. Audrey had controlled his life for years before she finally realized that it wasn't giving her the results she craved; it didn't make him love her and in fact, had the opposite effect. It was a painful realization but she got through it. What if she didn't get through this one?

Christmas was around the corner and some of Audrey's family had apparently decorated the house, helped to buy gifts for the boys and attempted to bring some spirit to the household. Chase was grateful for their help. Other than money, he had nothing to give. There was no way he could return to Hennessey at that point. His anger was too intense and if put in the wrong situation, he feared he would become the same animal he was at the gym when standing before a heavy bag. He would stay in Toronto.

Jolene hosted a dinner for Diego and Chase on Christmas, inviting the two to her apartment for a traditional meal. Wearing a dress and heels, she didn't seem to think it was unusual to strut around the kitchen in such formal attire for a relaxed meal at home. Although very much like she was at work, there was a more relaxed presence as she joked, often bursting out in laughter. Diego had even accused her of being drunk.

"Drunk, I am not drunk," She was insistent, even though she was drinking one of many glasses of wine that evening. "It is Christmas, you know how I love celebrating. I thought this year, I would do as you Canadians do it with this turkey and stuffing. I do not know. I just talk to Beverly and it sounded very nice so I thought, I will try."

"This isn't how you celebrate in Colombia?" Chase asked and watched as both Diego and Jolene shook their head no.

"I have done both," Diego replied with a shrug. "I mean, in America, of course, we did all your traditional things but it's still kind of new to Jolene, who hasn't been in North America as long"

"Yes, I spend Christmas with Diego in America but we did our own traditions those years," She commented as she sat down at the table. "It was fine but I wanted to learn what you do here. You know, how you celebrate."

"Why wouldn't you just do Colombian traditions this year?" Chase was curious and actually, would've welcomed learning how his two friends celebrated in their home country.

Jolene and Diego exchanged looks across the table and smiled, before shifting their attention back to Chase.

"We did it for you," Jolene spoke quietly with a shy shrug. "We thought maybe, maybe this would make you happy. You know, something traditional with your family."

Chase wanted to reply but the words wouldn't come out as he shared a gentle smile with Jolene. A warmth filled him and for a second, he felt emotional as he looked away and considered that these people truly were his family.

As if sensing the strong emotions filling the room, Diego nervously jumped up from his seat and rushed into the kitchen.

"The food, Jolene! Are you trying to burn the building down?" He quipped as he went to the stove and removed the cover from a pot while at the table, Jolene reached over and gently tapped Chase's hand. She then rose from her seat, her heels clicked into the kitchen.

"Diego! Get out of my food!" Jolene called out as she rushed up behind him. "It is not for you to make a comment for my cooking. I only start one fire ever and it was manageable, ok?"

"With the fire department, it was manageable," Diego spoke jovially, clearly enjoying the moment, he grabbed a fork to reach into something in the pot and Jolene slapped his hand.

"No no no!! You do not try, go sit!" She spoke abruptly but there was a hint of teasing in her voice. "Go sit down! Be good for a change, Diego. You're like a hyper child waiting for your gifts, go sit and talk to Chase. Leave me be!"

"Now you sound like our mother," Diego started to inch away with a mischievous look in her eyes, as Jolene turned around and glared at him.

"You compare me to our mother one more time, I will put you in this oven and cook you!"

"He'd probably fit," Chase called out and took a drink of his wine.

200

"Hey! Come on," Diego returned to the table and gave Chase a warning glance, while a smirk erupted from his lips. "It's Christmas, don't be mean."

The three had an enjoyable meal and although Chase had spoken to his kids earlier that day, he made a point to check in again that night after arriving home. Full of turkey and a traditional Colombia dessert that was mouth-watering, he slumped in his bed and talked to the boys on Skype. He felt relief that they expressed excitement over the day and didn't carry even a hint of sadness; children were so adaptable. His only wish was that day would help lift Audrey out of her depression to embrace life again. Devin and Chet needed her.

"It's been a long day," She commented after the two hyper children ran off. Her face was pale and tired, her eyes slightly brighter than they had been in recent weeks. "I managed to get through and I actually enjoyed most of it. There were a few moments that I had to rush away so the kids wouldn't see me upset but it was a little easier than I thought. My family helped a lot."

"That's what family do," Chase couldn't help but to think of his own evening and the love and support the Silva's had shown him. It was almost foreign to him, having never felt that with his biological family. "This wasn't an easy year."

"It will get a little easier, though," She acknowledged hesitantly. "It already has but I still have days when I don't want to get out of bed. I will never be the same person again. I don't know how any parent could be in this situation."

Chase nodded, unsure of what to say. She was right. Neither of them would be the same but he hoped that she would learn to swim the tainted waters of the small town that turned against her, even though he was sure some wished that she would sink.

"It'll be okay, Audrey," He replied gently. "We have to trust it will get better."

She silently nodded.

Life moved forward and the mood at the office was joyous as they planned the last-minute details for the sold-out New Year's Eve parties. Still on a high from Christmas, the office was calm until Jolene announced another mystery meeting with Jorge Hernandez and once again, Diego lost his mind.

"I can't believe it!" He fumed on the way home from work a couple of days before New Year's Eve. "I told her to stay away from him because he is not safe and now, it seems they're spending the holiday together in Whistler! We need her here and she'll be off with Jorge Hernandez, of all people, drinking wine and sitting in a hot tub."

Chase wasn't sure what to say. He definitely understood why Diego was upset but didn't want to get in the middle of this ongoing battle between the siblings.

"Jolene, she never listens," Diego shook his head as they sat in traffic. "It's like she hears what I say, then does the opposite. She puts herself in danger."

"I don't think she's necessarily in danger right this moment," Chase tried to counter. "I mean, I don't know..."

"Trust me, I know she's putting herself in a vulnerable situation," Diego replied, his face began to twitch and he clamped his mouth shut. Appearing frustrated, he shut down and appeared tense for the rest of the night.

Just as Diego suggested, Jolene wasn't at work the following morning. Beverly sat alone in their shared office, causing Diego to make a face as he passed. His anxiety only increased throughout the morning, drinking more coffee than usual, his face scrunched up in anguish and although Chase wanted to offer him words of comfort, he wasn't sure what to say. In fact, he didn't believe Jolene was in danger. Chances were good the affair would end shortly after the holidays, once everything got back to normal.

Chase's phone rang just before lunch and he felt his heart race when seeing the number. It was Audrey. Jumping up from the desk, he headed for the boardroom. Briefly glancing at Diego, he noted a dark look in his eyes as Chase answered.

"Chase," He immediately heard something different in his ex-wife's voice. It carried a little more strength than it had in months, a hint of confidence and yet, an uneasiness that made him nervous as he stepped into the silent boardroom. "I can't believe it."

His thoughts sprang back to an earlier fear that social services had been called, arriving during the holidays to harass the family. He felt anger crawling up his spine, his heart pounding with ferociously as he reached for the first chair he saw and sat down.

"I can't believe what happened," She repeated as if in shock and Chase felt his stomach churn in anticipation. "He's gone."

"Who's gone?" Chase asked and closed his eyes and he felt a tightness in his chest.

"Luke."

"He left town?" Chase asked as he felt fury fill him up. Of course! The bastard skipped town. The courts had allowed him out on bail and now Luke Prince had left the country.

"No, I mean...he's dead."

"What?" Chase snapped, stunned by such news and a burning started in his stomach and slowly crawled up his body.

"He was shot?" Audrey replied as if asking him a question rather than supplying him with an answer. "Someone shot him. When he was out in the same woods. I don't know why or if he was hunting but someone shot him."

Chase felt weak as he rose from the chair and slowly walking back to the office as she continued to speak. "I think it was another hunter that did it," She took a deep breath and started to cry just as Chase returned to the doorway of the office. Diego immediately looked up and their eyes met as Audrey suddenly calmed down and continued. "He was shot right between the eyes and they said it had to be an experienced shooter, someone who knew exactly what they were doing."

Chase opened his mouth but couldn't speak.

The world started to spin and he knew it wasn't about to stop.

CHAPTER THIRTY-THREE

Everything started to shift after that call. It was as if his entire world suddenly looked different; the blinders were taken off, showing a reality that hadn't been obvious to him before that day. It wasn't as if anything had been carefully hidden but more like a gift that was loosely wrapped, the label still displayed. Then again, there was a huge difference between knowing something and suspecting it and up until that point, Chase was only doing the latter.

His original reaction was to go to the washroom and throw water on his face. In there, he found Benjamin washing his hands, a look of concern on his face.

"Are you ok, Chase?"

"Ah, yeah, I'm fine," he managed an unconvincing smile and Benjamin appeared satisfied with this answer and walked out of the room.

A warmth swept over his torso, swooping up from a place deep inside of him, squeezing his lungs until he could barely breathe as his heart raced frantically, pain shooting through his chest. He felt nauseous and rushed into an empty stall, immediately kneeling down before it, allowing the waves of heat to flow through him as his throat went dry and his limbs felt weak. Not allowing himself to get caught up in the attack, Chase attempted to calm, breathing slowly, he felt heat and agitation begin to extract from his body, as a chill ran up his spine and he involuntarily shook.

After a few minutes, he felt his body slowly return to normal as he stood up, quickly wiping dust from his pants, he walked out of the stall, met with Diego's brooding eyes. Neither of them said a thing at first, a shared silence that could be interpreted in more ways than one, it was finally Diego that spoke.

"What's going on?" His eyes were huge, full of curiosity and yet kind, leaving no question that he was sincerely concerned. "I thought something was wrong but then, I didn't want to intrude but Benjamin stopped by my office and mentioned that you didn't look well. What's going on, *amigo*?"

Chase opened his mouth but almost felt as if the news were a guarded secret and yet, shouldn't he be happy? Shouldn't he be relieved that the man that took his son's life was now dead? Instead, a new set of problems had risen up, leaving him with a complication that made his life before that day seem much simpler in comparison.

Hesitant at first, Chase began to speak slowly, as if not sure of what words to use. "He....I mean, Luke Prince, he's dead."

A stunned silence filled the room, as a nearby tap dripped so loudly, it almost sent a tremor through Chase. Diego stepped back.

"Wait, isn't that the guy..." He muttered.

"Yes."

"He's dead?" Diego asked as his voice indicated more surprise than his eyes. Wasn't there something that didn't sit quite right? It was like going for a haircut and having one small fragment fall down the back of your shirt, causing a slight discomfort for the rest of the day. It was almost impossible to shake until you later took a shower before bed and yet, something told Chase that nothing was going to wash this feeling away. It was something a little more permanent lodged in his soul.

Diego examined his eyes as if evaluating Chase's reaction.

Realizing he hadn't answered Diego's question, he slowly nodded.

"I'm not going to lie, Chase," Diego spoke gently. "This man, he didn't deserve to live after what he did to your son. So I hope however it happened, it was painful for him. I hope he suffered just as he's made you suffer."

"If you had told me a few weeks ago that this was going to happen," Chase started and hesitated to clear his throat, shaking his head. "I would've thought it was justified, the same way as you. But now, you know what? I feel nothing. I don't feel better. Doesn't bring my son back. It feels....senseless..maybe even a little hopeless."

"Why hopeless," Diego tilted his head as if he couldn't understand.

"I don't know," Chase answered honestly and took a deep breath. "I guess cause he will never go to jail but then again, I guess the other side of it is that he's not going to put my family through a trial since he wanted to plead not guilty for most of the charges. I don't know. It doesn't feel like I would've expected."

"It's a win, Chase," Diego muttered as if he didn't want anyone else to hear him.

"Maybe," Chase quietly replied and leaned in closer to Diego. "But it doesn't feel like a win."

Diego nodded in understanding.

"We'll talk later," Diego replied as his eyes showed signs of compassion, he swiftly turned around and left the room.

It was after he left that Chase realized that he never asked how Luke Prince died.

Although Diego attempted to distract him all afternoon, Chase found his mind wandering back to his haunting conversation with Audrey. She sent a local newspaper article on the death, which merely said that the circumstances were what police referred to as 'suspicious' but they didn't get into much detail. Clearly, there would be a lot of questions asked and he secretly feared that his own family would be pulled into a mess. He just wasn't sure which family.

News started to spread and by the end of the day, Chase received messages from his sister and aunt Maureen but didn't feel inclined to reply. It would've been almost effortless to send a response to their text messages and yet, he felt no initiative. Since Leland's death, he felt more separated from his family, as if Leland was one of the last ties to his former home and they were left severed, blowing in the wind. Although there was a part of him that knew this was the time to reconnect, an even bigger part of him felt like family was only a technicality but in reality, these people had never been there for him during the course of his life. They wandered in from time to time but weren't a regular fixture. How was that family?

By contrast, it was Diego and Jolene that were there for him. He knew that he could lean on them when needed and they would support him and not simply make a casual appearance when it was convenient or out of obligation. It was something reliable and although people loved the idea of independence, there was an even deeper part that he believed needed a connection; something that didn't allow him to sway in the wind but connect with something more stable. His birth family, unfortunately, had never been stable.

It was a concept they discussed again that night when him and Diego decided to go for dinner after work. It was an impromptu idea after leaving the office, they instead walked to a nearby restaurant that was family owned, serving mostly business class in the downtown area. Upon walking in, Diego started to wrinkle his nose, his eyes automatically shooting to the back of the room.

"I hope we can sit away from everyone," He spoke in a low voice as the waitress approached them. "These people are practically on top of one another."

"For two?" The young woman asked after greeting them.

"Yeah, something in the back, maybe away from people," Diego instructed with a charming smile. "We got business to discuss, you know?"

"Of course," She smiled and gestured them to followed her.

She put them in a small booth at the back of the room as requested, dimly lit and with candles on the table, Diego looked satisfied with the location. Chase said nothing but merely gave an appreciative smile toward the waitress as he sat down. Passing them each a menu, she quickly let them know what the specials were before rushing away.

A somber David Bowie song filled the room, although it was barely audible over the murmur of voices and clatter of dishes. Most of the people around them didn't even seem to notice them at all. It was just another day. It was another day where Luke Prince just happened to die.

Neither said a word at first, Diego studied his menu while Chase only took a brief glimpse of his own. He suddenly felt exhausted, drained and the last thing he wanted to do was eat, however, he ordered a chicken caesar wrap and salad and listened as Diego did the same.

"So, what's going on in that pretty little head of yours," Diego attempted to tease but quickly saw that it wasn't working and looked away. "Look. I don't know what you want me to say. I'm not disappointed that this man is dead. For what he did to you," he made a face and shook his head. "He doesn't deserve to live. No one who hurts a child does as far as I'm concerned."

Chase didn't respond at first and finally shrugged.

"It doesn't change anything," His reply seemed to leave Diego disappointed, deflated in response.

"It's still fresh," Diego commented as the waitress brought their drinks; a glass of wine each, even though Chase had no interest in drinking. After she left, he continued, "Wait until tomorrow, you'll see, you'll wake up feeling like a new man. You'll wake up feeling like a man who controls his own destiny."

"I'll wake up feeling like a wolf?"

A smirk formed on Diego's lips. "Like I say, if you can, always be a wolf. Everyone else can be the sheep but life is too short. So don't waste your time dwelling, over thinking, only dream big or don't dream at all. Wake up strong cause the world, it wants you to be weak. And you cannot allow it. You simply can't."

Chase contemplated his words as they swept through his brain, sinking deeper and deeper, he almost didn't hear Diego when he continued.

"It's like my father always said, one of the *few* things he said that was right, you cannot allow the world to tell you what you can't have and you cannot allow the world to win when it gives you a losing hand. You have a choice. There's always another move that can be made, you just have to decide, do you want it to be strong or do you want it to be weak."

"Your family had different values than mine," Chase countered and sighed.

"And has that served you well?" Diego twisted his mouth, his dark eyes focusing on Chase. "Tell me, has that made your life as you wanted it?"

"Did I ever tell you what happened to me when I was a teenager?" Chase replied, "When I got Audrey pregnant."

"You were forced to marry her, to fulfill everyone else's wishes," Diego answered and slowly nodded. "And how did that serve you?"

"It made me angry," Chase answered honestly, slowly starting to see what Diego was suggesting. "I felt hopeless. Like I had no choices."

"Exactly," Diego replied. "Things worked well as long as you complied with everyone else's wishes. You weren't your own person. And when you left, moved away?"

"You saw how it was at the funeral," Chase replied and took a sip of his wine; it was bitter, which was appropriate. "They were like strangers."

"That's because they are strangers, they don't know you," Diego insisted and relaxed in his seat. "Family, it is not the people who you are born from, the people who wipe your ass when you're a baby or go to your high school graduation, they're the people who would do anything for you. They're the people who would run into a burning building for you and think nothing of it. Wouldn't give it a second thought. It's the people who defend you no matter what and the people who would cut their heart out themselves and give it to you if needed. Do you understand?"

His words were full of passion, strength and there was no denying, not even for a second, that the intensity behind them was stronger than anything anyone had offered Chase before that day. Chase felt his apathy start to dissolve like wax melting beneath a flame, with an equally passionate fire that would burn through anything.

"Yes," Chase slowly nodded. "I understand perfectly."

Diego seemed to ease off as their meal arrived and as if sensing the tension, the waitress politely smiled and instructed them to call her back if they needed anything.

They ate in silence while Chase mulled over his words and as the truth sunk further and further in, he decided it was best to not ask questions. It was not until they were almost done eating that he finally spoke.

"How is Jolene?"

"Terrific," Diego replied, a subtle sense of sarcasm rang in his voice. "She's with Jorge Hernandez, probably cozying up by a fire."

"That's good," Chase gently replied as he sat his fork down. "It's gets really cold in Hennessey this time of year."

Diego looked up from his food, his expression calm, if not slightly relaxed. A small grin crossed his lips but he said nothing.

CHAPTER THIRTY-FOUR

People want to believe that things work out in the end; that good prevails over evil but sometimes that isn't the case. It only takes one tragedy to make those lines in the sand blurry. The idealism of a child disappears with adulthood. People can attempt to justify anything but it doesn't make it right. It's human nature at its best and it's worst.

Diego was right. Chase awoke the next morning with a brand new set of eyes. The room gave him an unexpected comfort that he had never felt before, like a child in a womb, he was safe, as if nothing could hurt him. There was a security that never existed, a sense that he was invincible, powerful and more alive than he had felt in years. Although in theory, it was wrong that someone's death brought about feelings of strength, it somehow did. It removed the vulnerability that crept in after Leland died; that heavy, unsettling feeling as if he had crawled in a dark hole and could never escape.

His eyes fixated on a window nearby, Chase felt compelled to rise from the comfort of his sheets and go toward it. Ignoring the chill in the late December air, he looked outside into a whole new world. It was a place that no longer intimidated him. The last few months had been pure hell and yet, here he was, feeling renewed in a way that he had never thought was possible. It was New Year's Eve and he was ready to move forward and push everything behind him. It served no one to focus on the son he had lost so tragically but instead, he would honor Leland's life by being a stronger man. It was time to refocus.

It was clear that Jolene and Diego would expect more from him now. Not that he ever hesitated to show loyalty but without being told,

Chase knew he would be pulled into their world a little further than would've made him comfortable at one time - at *one* time - but the world was no longer the same place and he was no longer the same man.

He had a new reason to live and that reason was his family. They had shown loyalty to him and now, Chase was about to do the same for them. His life had meaning, a reason to get out of bed in the morning.

After showering and getting ready, he found Diego in the living room, slowly moving his lime tree in front of the balcony doors. He didn't care that it hadn't produced any limes yet, he remained insistent that it soon would give him a 'great bounty'. Patience was the key.

Barely looking up from his tree as Chase said good morning and headed toward the kitchen, Diego finally seemed satisfied and followed him. Chase was pouring a cup of coffee when he looked up to see Diego silently looking into his eyes, as if inspecting him in the same way he had his overgrown plant.

"So?"

"So?" Chase put the pot back and sat down his cup.

"How are you today?" Diego tilted his head and leaned back against the counter, almost as if he were checking his face a little more carefully from a different angle. "You look different."

"I don't know if I'd go that far," Chase grinned. "But you were right, I feel very differently about everything today. The world is not the same."

"Like you're in control and not being controlled?" Diego asked as he reached for his own cup that sat on the island. He walked to the coffee pot and topped up his mug. "Like you're the wolf and not the sheep? Was I right?"

"You were right," Chase quietly replied and took a drink as Diego turned back to face him. "I'm not sure if it's right to feel this way, but I do."

"Hey," Diego said as he tapped his fingers on the counter. "What he did to your son, that was not right. As much as the Bible talks about turning the other cheek and all that shit, I believe in something different. I believe that every crime has a punishment and that every wrong also has a right. We all owe others for our debts and if you leave it up to the judges, no debt is ever paid. They throw those they see as less desirable away and let idiots away with their crimes. It's the way it is, Chase. I use to date a cop. He told me that they arrest, work hard to give the criminals no wiggle room and then the judge tosses it aside and does what they want anyway. We don't want to believe this is true, but it is."

Chase couldn't argue. It was on the news all the time. Criminals were all but walking away from their crimes. Women were raped. Men were tortured. Children were killed. Judges let them go and often blamed the victim. The woman should've kept her legs together. The man provoked the situation. The child should've been watched more carefully.

Not people who looked like him though. Natives filled the jails. He was a teenager when first discovering that fact in a documentary television program, leaving him with mixed feelings that were hard to understand. It made him fearful of becoming one of those statistics and made him wary of ever pushing back when pushed.

"I'm not saying that this would've been the case with this Luke guy but I'm not saying it wouldn't have been either," Diego continued and raised his eyebrow before turning to unplug the coffee maker. Taking another drink, he swung around and completely changed gears. "Just a short day at the office, I promise. I think most people have the day off, as per Jolene of course, not me. I would've made them come in for a half day but hey, I can't be the bad guy all the time, you know?"

"If given the option, most won't show up," Chase replied as the other comments Diego made were simmering in his head. "Probably just us."

"Nah, Benjamin will come in," Diego predicted and took a long gulp of his coffee. "The Italian, she'll be in and.....Gracie and Deb are party girls, so they won't, I know that already and Beverly will pop in and get stuck at reception since Deborah is probably home planning a gang bang or something."

"She's not that bad," Chase laughed in spite of himself. "At least, I don't think so."

"Really?" Diego asked and finished his cup of coffee. "I don't know about that."

"It doesn't matter," Chase replied. "I don't want to have anything to do with her."

"Ah, see, it's happening already," Diego's voice rose as he pointed a finger toward Chase before wandering back to the sink and rinsing his cup. "You aren't being her sheep anymore cause you never wanted her to begin with."

Chase didn't reply but finished his coffee.

At the office, it was exactly as Diego predicted. Beverly was on the phone at Deborah's desk, looking slightly annoyed. As they walked down the hallways, they met Benjamin leaving the kitchen, biting into a donut, he pointed back into the room to indicate there was a box on the counter. Diego thanked him and slid into the kitchen, Chase was behind him.

"Ah, no coffee, I guess that's what happens when Jolene isn't here," Diego reached for the pot and began to prepare it while Chase hesitantly grabbed a chocolate donut and bit into it. "Everything goes to hell."

"Having to make a pot of coffee is hardly hell," Chase said between bites as he leaned against the counter and watched Diego measuring out the water and finally, his special brand of coffee. "Besides, if anyone else made the coffee, you wouldn't be happy with it anyway."

"Hey, this is the second pot of the day," Diego joked. "That's two, Chase, what am I, the fucking servant?"

Chase laughed and finished his donut just as Sylvana entered the room, with a paper bag in hand, she crossed the room and placed it in the fridge.

"See! I told you!" Diego gestured in her direction. "I was right about the people who would be here today."

"Of course I am here," Sylvana spoke abruptly but her face revealed a glimmer of humor. "Some of us have work to do."

"I'm working," Diego insisted as he turned on the coffee pot. "This place wouldn't run at all without my fabulous coffee."

Sylvana merely grinned before walking out of the room.

"Cold as ice, that one," Diego gestured in her direction as he opened the box of donuts and grabbed the most decorated of them all, covered with icing and candy. "She should have one of these, apparently she needs some sweetness in her life."

The morning went quickly and before long they were all heading out, satisfied that everything was in order for that night's parties, however Diego would have to keep his phone close at hand in case of any emergencies or issues. They had four private parties and two major events: one in Toronto and another in Vancouver. They had hired some temporary staff during the holidays but the two planners, Cleo and Raymond, would oversee all the parties. Things generally went smoothly but there were sometimes questions or confirmations to make.

For that reason, Diego settled on a quiet evening in. He, however, hadn't thought about it one way or another. Holidays had always been irrelevant to him. They had no meaning and that particular year certainly gave him little reason to celebrate.

Audrey called him later that evening. Chase immediately recognized something different in her voice. She was calm, tranquil, in a way he hadn't expected.

"Sorry, Chase, I totally forgot to get the boys on Skype earlier to say Happy New Year," She started the conversation off awkwardly, as if realizing what she had done. "I was rushing around all day and the media keeps calling me, its crazy. My mom thought it might be better if she take the kids for the next few days to get them away from this insanity and I was so rushed to get them ready, I never even thought."

"It's fine," he assured her and sat on his bed. "I totally understand. How bad is the media?"

"They're around," She muttered and he could hear a cupboard door closing as he envisioned the kitchen in his former home. "I don't have a comment and I *won't* have a comment. At least, nothing that is politically correct to say."

"Yeah, I hear you there," Chase replied.

"I obviously can't tell them that I hope he rots in hell," Audrey continued and Chase smiled to himself as he heard the woman he once knew slowly return. "I don't care who did it and I don't care why. That's how I feel. I don't care about his family because they certainly slung mud at us when we were down. I don't care if he suffered."

"Probably things you shouldn't tell the media," Chase admitted and secretly shared her feelings. "Any more news on it?"

"Just what I told you before," Audrey sounded more confident as she spoke. "He was shot by someone who knew what they were doing. It was from a distance and they still got him right between the eyes. Shot him down like the animal. Ironically, I don't think it's hunting season either, so why was he out there, wandering through the woods? Of course, no one is talking about that."

Chase didn't reply.

"I think it was a local hunter. A lot of them were pretty mad when this happened especially when Luke got cocky about everything."

"Really?"

"Yeah, that's what one of them told Albert last week but the funny thing is that the police haven't arrested anyone," She commented calmly. "The police are still there investigating the scene but nothing seems to be coming up, from what I'm told."

Chase didn't reply.

CHAPTER THIRTY-FIVE

Reporters had a difficult time finding Chase but a few days later, they did. When asked for a comment, he held back all emotions and merely said that it had been a very sad year for his family, one he wouldn't wish on anyone and that he hoped that everyone could move forward. He avoided addressing Luke Prince's death directly, knowing that the reporter was attempting to get a reaction out of him and when unsuccessful, she muttered something about 'not getting a good quote' before rudely hanging up on him.

"Fucking bitch," Diego muttered when Chase repeated the story to him the following morning on their way to work. "You know, I respect the media but I kind of hate the media too. They are soulless. They create unnecessary drama that gets everyone upset and angry. You know, it's almost like they don't feel they are successful if they don't have people raging at the television or crying at the end of one of their stories."

"It's because if people aren't emotionally involved, they don't care and if they don't care, they don't keep watching," Chase commented as he glanced out the passenger side window. "And if we keep watching, they keep their ratings and if they keep their ratings, they keep their jobs."

"Nah, we would watch even if they didn't pull that shit," Diego made a face and gave a loud sigh as they stopped at a light. "I respect the real reporters, the ones who get into a dicey situation and show us first hand what is going on but the reporter that called you the other day, she was being a cunt. Did she even say she was sorry for your loss? Show any compassion? Of course not! She wanted you angry and make some off the cuff remark so that she would have this insane quote and get the lead story or whatever the fuck they call it."

Chase couldn't deny that the reporter showed no compassion and was on a mission more than anything else. Perhaps in her place, he would be an asshole too. It didn't really matter and he hadn't brought all this up just to have a car ride rant with Diego but, then again, there they were, doing just that. The idea made him grin, something that Diego caught.

"What's that big smile for?" Diego bellowed out jokingly, a touch of accent crept in.

"You, when you get on a rant, it's funny to me," Chase replied as the car started to move again, as they eased closer to work. "Anyway, it doesn't matter, she didn't get a good quote from me and she won't. I don't want any attention."

"See, you're a good student," Diego said with a self-satisfied smile. "Always keep under the radar. Stand out from the crowd but only in your presence never your words. Words, they come back to haunt you so if you say nothing, they got nothing."

They arrived at work slightly early compared to most days, not to mention the first day back after New Year's, which was fine by Chase. He knew it would be Jolene's first day back and he was anxiously awaiting her return. There was so much to say and yet, he felt as though he couldn't say a thing. As Diego said in the car, words can come back to haunt you, so say nothing.

As it turns out, it wasn't necessary. Beverly, who was once again answering phones that morning since Deborah wasn't yet at work, immediately told Chase that Jolene would like to speak to him alone. Diego's face automatically softened as he patted Chase on the arm and headed toward the staff room while Beverly returned her attention to the phone.

Although he certainly had no reason to feel nervous, Chase felt a familiar anxiety in his stomach as he headed toward Jolene's office and walked inside. She immediately looked up from her laptop, her face fell into a relaxed smile as she instructed him to close the door behind him. Without replying he did so and when he turned around, she was rising from her desk, wearing a fitted blue dress and long, smooth black boots, her heels clicked on the floor as she rushed toward him and pulled him into a warm embrace.

"Happy New Year, Chase," Her words were gentle like a mother to her baby, her embrace warm, loving while a gentle scent filled his lungs. He felt his original nervousness ease as he hugged her back. She let go and stepped back, her smile carried a hint of tears as she patted his shoulder and turned away. "It is over now."

"Happy New Year to you too," He finally found his voice after the intense moment eased, allowing him to speak again. A warm glow filled his body and he felt temporarily frozen to the spot. Unspoken words filled the air around them but he couldn't have said any of them, even if he had tried. His legs felt weak as Chase found a chair and sat down on the other side of her desk, while she was once again seated.

"I trust that we can start a new page, no?" She spoke quietly, as she pushed her laptop aside. "I think we are ready for a new beginning. I think we all deserve it, especially you."

Chase nodded and felt overwhelmed with emotion and didn't dare speak, fearing that it would open a can of worms. Staring into her eyes, he sensed she was fighting the same battle on the other side of the desk. She took a breath, blinking rapidly, Jolene cleared her throat.

"This year, it will be different," Her smile appeared forced as she nodded, glancing out the window before turning back to Chase. "You will see, it will be different for you. You are part of the family and with family, there's a loyalty and love, but there is also working together for what we all want. This year, we expand, grow, you will see. We will make more money, be very successful. Everything will be perfect."

Chase nodded and felt she was waiting for a reply. "I agree."

Grabbing her phone, she began to text rapidly and then sat it down again.

"Diego, he will meet us now and with the rest of the staff a little later," Jolene took a deep breath, pushing her breasts up and Chase quickly looked away, just as Diego walked in the door, closing it behind him.

"Did you two play catch up?" Diego bellowed out as he walked toward them, coffee in hand, appearing reluctant to sit down. He seemed joyful unlike their drive into work earlier but Chase noted that he glanced in his direction with some curiosity.

"We did," Jolene replied and gestured for Diego to sit down while she grabbed a nearby newspaper and pointed toward an article. "Did you see this?"

Moving his chair forward, Diego squinted his eyes and read out loud, "Greek men that are flavorful and hearty".

"No! No! No!" Jolene shot back, pulling the paper back a bit. "It say, 'A Greek *menu* that *is* flavorful and hearty. You see with your pervert, sex eyes again! Ah! Ah! Ah!"

Diego grinned and shot Chase a mischievous look. "I like what I said better."

"No! No! We are not going to this topic, Diego," Jolene retorted. "That was not what I was pointing at in first place but also, this year, you need glasses."

"I don't need glasses, Jolene," Diego insisted. "I was just having some fun with you."

"You *need* glasses," She insisted again and pointed at another article. "This is the article I am speaking of, here!"

"*Sex club supports immoral behavior in Toronto,*" Diego read out loud and shrug. "Oh, like Toronto had morals, to begin with! So, who cares, Jolene. This is just in the opinion section anyway, no one gives a shit about anyone's opinion."

"They might, it shows that these religious people, they aren't going to go away," Jolene complained. "This, it could be a problem."

"Whatever, I'm not worried," Diego shrugged and sat back in his chair. "A new abortion clinic will pop up and they'll be too busy protesting *that* and forget about us in no time. You'll see. Plus, no one cares. It's not like we have them in school gymnasiums for fuck sakes. People are allowed to express their sexuality in a party. They have to agree to the contract before they pay for the party and so, legally, we are covered."

"And morally," Diego continued as an impish grin lit up his face. "Let's face it, none of us have morals here."

Chase couldn't help but laugh and Jolene reluctantly followed suit.

"I just, you know, don't enjoy this attention on us," Jolene pointed out.

"I know, keep under the radar," Diego agreed. "We had this exact conversation on the way to work this morning. Some lady reporter was calling Chase for comments on what happened back home."

"Oh," Jolene quietly replied. "What do you say to them, Chase?"

"Nothing really," He shrugged. "That it was a sad year for everyone involved and that was basically it."

She appeared satisfied with his reply and nodded.

"This reporter, total bitch, was mad he wasn't ranting and raving like a lunatic so she could get some radical comment and hung up on him," Diego complained, his face scrunched up in frustration.

"No!" Jolene appeared shocked. "So rude!"

"Media," Diego shrugged and sniffed. "Psychopaths out for blood."

"Yes, speaking of that, Chase, is there any lead or any news from where you are from?" She asked in a quiet voice, her composure stern as she wove her fingers together and sat them on the desk. "About this.... person who shot your baby?"

Chase shook his head. "Other than the bullet and even that, they can't seem to find anything."

"No suspect?"

"No, nothing," Chase replied and the two continued eye contact. "They don't have the area closed off anymore and when I spoke to Audrey last, it didn't seem like they had any leads."

She nodded and looked toward Diego, who merely raised an eyebrow.

"I say, what's done is done," He cleared his throat, continuing to stare at his sister. "We move on. Am I right, Chase?"

Both sets of eyes were on him and he nodded. "Yes, I agree."

"Then let's not speak of this no more," Jolene replied in a gentle voice. "It is a sad topic and we are about happy times. We don't talk sad. That is last year and now, we are here."

"And now, we are here," Diego repeated and gave Chase a quick smile. "We must call a meeting to discuss our lucrative holiday parties. We made a killing."

It was as if the entire room fell silent. Chase felt his throat tighten while Jolene had a perturbed expression on her face.

"I...ah, poor choice of words," Diego stuttered for a moment but seemed to grin in spite of himself and carried on as if he had said nothing out of sorts. "At any rate, we were *successful* on this weekend. While you were off canoodling with Jorge Hernandez, Jolene, we were here overseeing the parties and all went exceptionally well. Even the venue owners are begging to have us back."

"What is a canoodle? I do not understand?" Jolene looked confused. "Is that a perverted sex thing?"

"Sorry," Diego replied. "Off falling in love."

"I do not fall in love this weekend and furthermore, what if I did?" Jolene snapped back. "You, you like meaningless affairs and I say nothing. You do not tell me what, who or if I can love. As someone once said to me, 'I will be happy in love or I will be happy to die'."

Diego made a face and didn't respond.

"Do you remember saying that? Diego?" Jolene pushed a little farther. "Do you remember?"

He didn't respond for a moment, merely rubbing his face with one hand while closing his eyes. "Things, they change sometimes, Jolene. And you know I don't like you saying that especially considering the company you're keeping now."

Chase bit his lip and attempted to ignore the tension in the room. There was apparently so much more that he didn't know about Hernandez and he had a bad feeling that he was about to find out.

CHAPTER THIRTY-SIX

January was a temperamental month that consisted of impromptu and erratic storms that seemed to put the city at a standstill. Diego constantly complained about the 'unliveable' temperatures and even spent half of one morning wearing leather gloves in the office, repeatedly asking Chase why Canadians 'put up with this weather' as if anyone had a choice, whereas Jolene merely draped her Christmas green winter coat over her shoulders and cranked up the heat.

"What are you hot-blooded?" Diego commented on one of those days, nearing the end of January. Rubbing his gloved hands together as if they were both sitting in the middle of a snow bank and not his office. "It's freezing cold in this office. How are we expected to work?" Chase shook his head and with a humored grin, crossed the room, turned up the thermostat and returned to his desk. "It's not cold in here, Diego. Haven't you ever experienced a real winter before?"

"Sometimes, when I was in California."

"No, a *real* winter, come on, Diego," Chase sat back down on his chair and attempted to return his attention to work. They were coming up on their busiest season since starting the business; Valentine's Day. Although it was a holiday that never had any meaning to him, he could see how it would bring out the right mood for their parties, requiring them to hire two more party planners. Chase was in the process of going through resumes with what he called his 'Diego eyes' in attempts to figure out who he would like.

"It was a real winter there too, amigo, sometimes I had to wear a sweater," Diego's dark eyes stared in his direction. "And you know me,

I don't like sweaters. I find them bulky and uncomfortable and they, you know, they're not a good look for me."

Chase looked up from his work to catch Diego with his lips twisted as he stared at the thermostat.

"I think I will get another coffee," He said and jumped up from his chair, grabbing his coffee cup, he rushed toward the kitchen, almost running into Deborah on her way in.

"Chase I need to talk to you," She airily commented while pushing the door slightly, managing to leave it open ajar. Glancing over her shoulder as if she expected to find Diego listening on the other side, dropped her voice as she moved toward him. "Why aren't you answering my texts? I thought we had..an arrangement."

"Deborah, it's not a good idea," Chase replied while leaning back in his chair. "We work together. Plus my life, it's been pretty complicated lately, I'm not in a good place for anything."

"As if you've ever been in a good place," She complained as she swept her hand over his desk. "Suddenly the fact that we work together is an issue? I talked to my therapist about this and she said the most interesting thing, she.."

"Nah nah nah," Chase waved his hand in the air and shook his head. "We aren't going there, Deborah. I don't need to know what your therapist says or thinks. Things get complicated when people have to work together and...I'm, I'm sorry."

"It's Jolene, isn't it?" Her eyes suddenly became smaller, darker behind her glasses, as her pale face formed into a frown. Deborah leaned against his desk, her voice rising slightly, making Chase nervous. "You're having an affair with her, aren't you? I see how you look at one another and she's stacked and hot, I get it. You're throwing me over to satisfy the boss."

Just then, Diego hurried in the door, his eyes huge and full of anger. His strong presence caused Deborah to jump, startled by his brooding glare as he approached her, it was clear that she had crossed a line this time. Chase felt compelled to say something to cut the tension but also recognized when it was probably best to not say anything, as Diego pointed at her with his free, gloved finger.

"You, I've had it with you," Diego snapped, his voice turned cold, his eyes darting through Deborah, who actually appeared nervous, her original confidence long gone. "Always leaving your station, showing up late for work, now you suggest that Chase is having sex with me! You're hardly one to question anyone's morals little girl, I think its time we have a talk."

"Diego, I think she means..."

"Chase, can you leave us alone?" Diego didn't even allow him to finish his comment and deciding that perhaps it was better he didn't, Chase stood up from his chair and picked up his laptop. "I'll be in Jolene's office."

Just as he reached the doorway, Diego could be heard calling out for Beverly to take over reception, something that she appeared unhappy about as she rose from her desk. Jolene glanced up from her laptop and her eyes jumped back and forth between her assistant and Chase.

"Thank you, Beverly."

Diego slammed his door so hard that it caused Chase to jump just as he was entering Jolene's office.

"Close the door," She instructed and he followed her order before walking toward the empty chairs on the other side of her desk.

"Is it Deborah, what did she do?" Jolene asked innocently and although Chase didn't want to tell her about the affair he briefly had with the administrative assistant, he wasn't sure how to avoid it either.

Slightly embarrassed by the entire story, he sheepishly confessed the truth, "I had a...thing with Deborah for a while. I wasn't probably in a good place and it happened and now she wants to know why we haven't continued."

"Oh.." Jolene appeared intrigued. "Is that why Diego is mad?"

"Well, not really," Chase replied. "I think it's a lot of things, the fact that she's always late or leaving her desk and...he kind of overheard something when he walked in."

"What?"

"Well, Deborah was kind of suggesting that the real reason I wasn't showing her any interest was because I was...with you," Chase finished hesitantly and saw Jolene's face tighten in an unpleasant expression.

"Diego walked in at the end of it and heard her suggest that I was sleeping with 'the boss' and assumed it was him and flipped out."

"He think, *he* the boss?" Jolene spoke abruptly, her finger pointed toward the next office. "And she think that we..."

"Pretty much," Chase replied with some hesitation, seeing the anger burning behind her eyes.

"This office gossip, it has to stop," Jolene said and shook her head. "Terrible, these people who make up stories. When did we ever do anything to suggest such a thing?"

Chase answered with a shrug.

"It is funny that Diego thought she meant him," Jolene started to grin as she playfully swirled her chair around. "He don't like gossip."

"I think he might fire her."

"I think *I* might fire her," Jolene countered. "This is too much. These stories at work are not right."

"It's not right," Chase agreed and wondered if she was also thinking the same as him; he somehow doubted it. He quickly pushed his own intriguing thoughts aside, as he had done more and more lately, his attraction to Jolene somehow had grown in recent weeks to shamefully fill his fantasy life during times that required it.

Diego flew in the office shortly after proclaiming it done. He fired Deborah and walked her to the exit.

"But what we will do?" Jolene suddenly was aware of the consequences. "We need someone to take care of the desk."

"Beverly's got it covered."

"Beverly has a lot of other work to do," Jolene complained. "She doesn't have time."

"Relax, she's taking care of it," Diego insisted and sat beside Chase and he noted that the gloves were off. "I told her to go through some resumes and pick someone."

"We can't just pick anyone here," Jolene complained. "We need someone we can trust."

"It's answering phones, Jolene," Diego said and shrugged. "We need someone who shows up to work and answers a couple of calls."

"There's a little more to it than that," Jolene insisted but Diego merely shrugged, as if it were of little consequence.

"So, she thought you and Chase," Jolene started quietly and winked in Chase's direction.

"Apparently, she thought *you* and Chase but I just heard her say, 'the boss' and assumed she meant me, since, you know, we live together," Diego sniffed and curled his lips. "I wanted to stop any rumors right away but after a short talk, I decided it's better to let her go. She isn't good at her job and I think we should replace her."

"I am the boss too," Jolene commented. "It's my name on that door out there too."

"I know, I know!" Diego put his hands up in the air. "Either way, it's not right. Can we both agree on this?"

Jolene reluctantly nodded and glanced at Chase.

"Chase, what did you see with her? I don't understand," Jolene asked. "She's so..I don't know, not attractive."

"It was a situation where the timing was...not great," Chase said in attempts to carefully reply and hopefully move on.

"He means he was horny when she came along," Diego jumped in with a laugh. "Kind of like with you and Hernandez."

"Diego!" Jolene snapped. "That is not right for you to say."

"It's true though," Diego said with humor in his voice. "Hey you two can be all secretive of the fact that you want to get some, but me, I'm always horny and I'm not afraid to admit it."

"Diego, we don't need to know, ok?" Jolene sternly commented. "You are very rude."

"Hey, I'm just honest," He countered. "And in fairness, Hernandez wouldn't even have to ask me twice and I'd be naked. He wouldn't even have to have the question out of his mouth and I'd be on my knees, so I get it but Deborah," Diego turned his attention to Chase. "God, are you sure you're not into men cause that girl, with her shape, I don't know, she's almost not a woman, you know?"

"Diego!" Jolene snapped. "Enough of you! Stop it!"

Diego fell silent but with an evil grin on his face.

"You cannot fire Deborah for her talk at the office and then turn around to do the same," Jolene chided.

"I'm just stating my opinion," Diego spoke defensively. "I'm from Colombia and women there, they got a shape, you know. Here is America, your women strive to be a shapeless size zero. It's gross. I'm just stating what every man is thinking - gay or straight - we like a little shape, you know?"

"Canada, Diego, not America," Jolene corrected, as she often did when her brother brought it up. "We are in Canada and not all women are super skinny here."

"But they *want* to be," Diego complained, ignoring her correction and moving on to the second comment. "It's like they want to look like a bunch of shapeless 12-year-old boys, it's gross. Men too. I met a man last week that looked like I should've been babysitting him, he was so thin, I couldn't...you know? It was creepy I told him no, not happening," Diego twisted his lips and shook his head. "I would think straight men would feel the same about their women."

"Maybe men here have a little more respect and actually like the woman as a person and not just tits and ass," Jolene was clearly growing frustrated. "Do you think I like men staring at my breasts all day? Do you think I don't know they stare at my bum when I walk away? Do you think we like that?"

"Oh I know," Diego rolled his eyes. "Women want to be treated like queens."

"Hey!" Jolene snapped. "*I* treat *me* like a queen and when you see yourself that way, others do too."

Diego rolled his eyes.

"Whatever, Jolene, whatever," He mocked her.

"Chase, what do you think?" Jolene turned in his direction.

"I think I have a lot of work to do," He started to rise from his chair.

"Coward," Diego accused with a grin on his face. "Go ahead."

Chase was happy to leave the office as the sister and brother continued to debate the issue. That was, until he returned to his own desk to find Sylvana sitting behind it.

CHAPTER THIRTY-SEVEN

"I saw you were behind closed doors with Jolene and Diego and I had to wonder," Sylvana boldly crossed her legs, as if to show that she wasn't about to move. Expressionless, her eyes fixated on Chase. "Were you in there discussing how Diego just fired Deb for calling you out on screwing him....or is it Jolene? I don't even know which one it is, there's a pretty solid case for both."

"Sylvana, get out of my chair," Chase chose to not dignify her remark. Ignoring him, she merely shrugged as if what his demand was nothing more than a suggestion, her eyes roaming over his body.

"You know, Deborah has some great stories about you," She continued, her fingers weaving together, she tilted her head slightly. "Apparently you had no problem using her even though you knew she was a sex addict and her therapist suggested you were a toxic person in her life. It's like that didn't matter and now to learn about what is going on with....whichever one you are doing," She pointed her finger toward the wall between his and Jolene's office. "Although, you have been with Jolene for a while and she made sure you came to Toronto with her, but at the same time, you *live* with Diego, so that's kind of weird too. I can't quite figure you out."

"There's nothing to figure out," Chase replied in a calm voice despite the fact that his heart was racing a mile a minute. He wanted nothing more than to pound his fist against the desk but forced himself to stay composed. She was trying to push his buttons, just as she always did and he wouldn't let her win. "There's nothing going on and as for

Deborah's sex addiction, maybe she should take some accountability for her own choices."

"True," Sylvana agreed, causing Chase to drop his defenses slightly, if not for long. "But you knew her weakness and played on it for your own selfish pleasures. That's pretty low if you ask me."

"That's the thing," Chase spoke abruptly. "*No one* asked you."

"Sometimes these things must be pointed out especially if someone is fired," Sylvana replied as she uncrossed her legs. "Especially after Diego completely degraded her in their meeting. She called Gracie in the elevator, crying, saying Diego called her 'the office whore' and told her to go work a street corner somewhere. A little harsh, isn't it?"

"Deborah wasn't always doing her job, she was showing up late and constantly gossiping," Chase spoke evenly. "It had nothing to do with anything else. Insinuating, falsely, that I was sleeping with the boss was the last straw for Diego and he fired her."

"Please, he fired her because you were sick of having her around now that you're done with her."

"When she was here earlier today," Chase felt his patience waning, his heart picking up the pace. "She was angry because I *wouldn't* sleep with her anymore. You can't have it both ways, Sylvana, you can't give me shit for 'using' her then turn around and give me shit for telling her that it wasn't a good idea to hook up anymore. This isn't even about her, it's about me. You clearly have an issue with me and always have. What's your fucking problem?"

Chase wasn't sure which of them was more surprised by his comment but he remained stoic, while Sylvana's eyes widened and for a moment, he thought she was going to admit defeat and leave. However, he had misread the situation.

"You're right, I don't like you," Sylvana agreed and finally stood up and crossed her arms in front of her chest. "You're their pet. You don't have to do a damn thing around here and meanwhile, I'm doing two people's jobs and Diego just calls me 'the Italian' all the time as if I don't even have a name. So it's pretty clear you have special treatment for some reason."

With that, she finally left.

It was unsettling that Deborah was still spreading office gossip and even more unsettling that people thought he was getting favouritism at work. Then again, was he? Did he get special treatment from Diego and Jolene? True, they considered him family but in everyone else's eyes, he was merely another employee, so maybe Sylvana wasn't completely wrong.

Unfortunately, his attempt to explain the truth behind Deborah's stories was to no avail. Although the office was small, the stories spread through like rapid fire; everything from how cruel Diego was to Deborah when he fired her, to the alleged affair with one of the two bosses in the workplace, but the last straw came when he found out that Deborah was planning to sue the company for wrongful dismissal. As soon as Chase learned this story, he went directly to Diego with his concerns.

Diego laughed.

"Yeah, our lawyers will knock her on her ass over that one" Diego grinned from ear to ear. "Considering she is spreading gossip throughout the office about these wild affairs you are supposedly having with me and Jolene, not to mention that I have a record of all the times she was late that I made her sign....she's got nothing, Chase."

Shortly after, Beverly found a new administrative assistant, an older lady in her 50s named Verna. Unlike the younger people at work, she had little interest in office gossip. Everyone seemed to like her, she was a good fit and most of all, Diego thought she was perfect.

"We need more Vernas and less of these young kids," Diego commented airily one day in the staff room when it was just him, Chase and the newest edition to the staff. Sitting at the table, enjoying her lunch break with a cup of Diego's coffee and a muffin, she let out a little laugh. "People who actually understand professionalism."

"It's a different world now," Verna insisted as she swallowed her food, sharing a smile with both Diego and Chase. Pushing a strand of her dark, curly hair behind her ear, her blue eyes seemed to dazzle when she spoke. "When I started out, there was no Internet or smartphones to distract everyone. You had work to do and you did it because you needed the job. Now, there's a different attitude with young people. I find my son is the same way. I practically had to push him out the door to get a job and we certainly didn't raise him to be like that."

"Well, they aren't all like that," Diego pointed at Chase as they both made their way to the door. "But many are, unfortunately."

Although Chase would've like to get to know Verna better, he immediately had the sense that Diego preferred he didn't and at that point, perhaps it was best to steer clear of any personal conversations at work. That's what got him in trouble in the first place.

Things were getting back to normal and everything appeared fine until one morning when Jolene came roaring into Diego's office, abruptly closing the door behind her, she looked as if she were about to explode.

"That *puta* Deborah, I want to *kill* her," She raged, immediately causing Chase to jump up from his chair and Diego's eyes to widen as his sister approached the desk. "I just get off the phone with our lawyer, he claim that her lawyer call him and say we fire her illegally because she knew about sketchy things we were doing here and if we do not pay her off, she will go to the CRA and get us audited."

"What? She doesn't have a leg to stand on," Diego shook his head but appearing a little mortified at the same time. "We fired her cause she was always late, I have the proof."

"It don't matter, Diego," Jolene snapped at him. "The point is that she is threatening to cause shit for us unless we give her money. She wants revenge and even though our lawyer, he say we would probably win in court, that it don't matter because it would bring too much attention Diego, we can't get the government and police in here snooping around."

"Jolene, that's not going to happen," Diego assured her. "We need to talk to our lawyer, set up a meeting."

"I did," Jolene sat down. "It is in the morning. Oh, Diego, what will we do?"

"Look, guys, we aren't doing anything illegal," Chase started to speak as he walked toward Diego's desk and sat beside Jolene. "Benjamin is taking care of the books and our parties are legal." They both gave him a long look and he remembered Hernandez. "Look, regardless, she has nothing. I think she's trying to milk this situation."

"Milk? I do not understand," Jolene shook her head, suddenly appearing exhausted.

"Take advantage," Chase replied and glanced toward Diego, who appeared tense. "Right?"

"We can't talk about this now, Chase," Diego replied. "I think the three of us need to go out and have a calming lunch."

Diego was insistent that they never speak of anything shady in the office, so it was clear their lunch was to discuss details that were best not spoken about at work. Did they think that the walls had ears? Chase decided it was best to not ask.

Calmly, the three of them left the office, announcing that they had a meeting and would return a little later. Verna gave a short nod as they walked out the door and to the nearest elevator.

"I don't trust her," Diego announced as soon as they were inside, the three of them alone.

"Verna?" Chase asked.

"No, I don't trust anyone but there's something off about her," Diego shrugged and made a face.

"You said how great she was just the other day," Chase recalled their conversation in the staff room.

"I say a lot of things, Chase," Diego replied while Jolene quietly listened, her face full of worry. "You're the only person we trust at work and to be honest and that's why we never talk about anything much at that place. We act as if all is normal."

"No, we do trust Benjamin," Jolene quietly added.

"He does the books," Diego shrugged as the door opened and the three walked out while a group of strangers walked in.

Chase didn't ask for an elaboration.

"He's paid...very well," Jolene muttered to Chase as the three of them made their way toward Diego's car: another place they weren't allowed to speak of anything about work.

Once at a restaurant that was known for its chicken, more of a family establishment, the three sat at the back of the room and Jolene immediately ordered a glass of wine. After the waitress left, Jolene closed her eyes and rubbed her forehead. "Bad day."

"So here's what we are going to do," Diego started to speak immediately, ignoring the menu in front of him. "We talk to the lawyer and find out our options then we take it from there."

"What does she know exactly?" Chase asked just as the waitress returned with Jolene's wine. Diego and Chase ordered the special while Jolene shook her head and said she couldn't eat.

"Don't pick at my food," Diego insisted after the waitress left. "I hate when you do that."

"I will not do," Jolene moaned. "Diego, what are we going to do? Our lawyer, he say that she might have us in a bad situation. Even though we do nothing wrong, she can still pull us through the mud."

"But what does she know?" Chase repeated his earlier question.

"I think she know about drugs," Jolene barely muttered, as if speaking into her drink. "She applied with us after one of the parties she attended. She saw the drugs and maybe know something was going on. That is what she told her lawyer but ours, of course, said no, that was not going on."

"Maybe we need to get Hernandez into this," Diego spoke cautiously. "He might have to step in."

Jolene made a face and her body tensed up. "I don't think it come to that, do you?"

"He won't like this," Diego's eyes blazed. "I could also speak to her."

"We cannot," Jolene said with a shrug. "Not if she has legal issues with us, we cannot because it will look bad. Like we are harassing her, you know?"

"Do you think Hernandez can talk to her?" Chase asked but immediately felt naïve when both Jolene and Diego gave him a look.

"If he steps in," Jolene traced her fingers along the edge of her wine glass. "She might be in a lot of trouble. He works for people who do not mess around, Chase. They don't like problems."

Diego frowned and shook his head.

"And neither do we."

CHAPTER THIRTY-EIGHT

It amazed Chase how food had the power to lighten the mood at work; People automatically dropped their defenses as their eyes lit up at the sight of anything covered in icing or with the aroma of something fresh out of the oven. Knowing Diego as he did, Chase sensed that their impromptu meeting with a supply of donuts and cheap pizzas was merely a way to lure the sheep in before a mass slaughtering, since he was completely infuriated with at least two of their small staff.

On the outside, this pre-Valentine's Day meeting was a way to thank the staff for their diligent work during their busiest season since opening the office. It was a way to thank everyone for their efforts and of course, they fell for it; gorging on food, casually chatting, as if the work day had already ended. Meanwhile, Diego drank his coffee, ate his one slice of pizza while watching everyone carefully. Jolene did the same, occasionally exchanging menacing looks with Diego. Sylvana and Gracie chatted enthusiastically, completely unaware of the tension in the room, while Beverly and Benjamin had a quiet conversation and Verna ate her food, saying nothing.

It was about the time that Chase finished his second slice of vegetarian pizza that he noticed that Diego's eyes growing darker, his expression more fierce by the moment, much like an animal about to sink his teeth into a victim. It carried the same intensity as he saw the day Diego attacked the man with a baseball bat and more recently, the day he learned of Luke Prince's death. It was a look that was unforgiving, uncaring and ferocious.

Slowly rising from his seat, Diego's eyes scanned the many faces that sat around the table, immediately grabbing Verna and Jolene's attention. Opening his mouth as if to speak, he closed it again and continued to watch everyone, his face tense. Chase exchanged apprehensive glances with Jolene who shook her head no, as if to tell him to not say anything.

"I have something to say," Diego started in his normal tone, attempting to gather everyone's attention. This time, he captured a respectful nod from Benjamin as he turned his chair slightly and Beverly did the same, her face serious and calm. Meanwhile, Sylvana and Gracie continued to chat away as if their boss hadn't spoken.

Diego's grim face grew darker by the second and with one sudden move, his hand abruptly came down on the table with a loud bang, causing Gracie to jump, her eyes full of shock as she turned around while Sylvana looked slightly alarmed by the unmistakable anger behind the action. Everyone turned their attention to Jolene as if expecting her to tell Diego to calm down but she remained tight-lipped, apathetic and ignored their glances.

"I *said,*" Diego's voice had risen to express anger as his cold glare fixated on Gracie, who was blinking back tears in reaction to his hostility, "I have something to say and I would appreciate it if everyone would listen."

Standing upright, he was silent for a moment before continuing.

"This lunch was a little treat to thank everyone for the extra efforts you've all taken during what has been our busiest season yet," Diego stood taller as he spoke, ignoring Gracie as she casually wiped away a tear, he stepped away from the table, his black eyes inspecting each of their faces as he spoke. "I appreciate all the effort made and I want to thank you."

He ended with a relaxed tone that momentarily sent a brief serenity through the boardroom that perhaps lowered everyone's defenses: but it shouldn't have.

Diego didn't speak for a moment as if he were weighing words in his head. He walked around the table to close the conference room door and returned to the head of the table. Rubbing a hand over his face, his eyes darted toward Sylvana and Gracie and just as quickly jumped to the back of the room.

"As you know, we recently had to let Deborah go." He hesitated and his lips curled into an angry pout, "I know *you* all know because you've been gossiping about it non-stop."

"Lots of stories going around," He continued. "Lots of *fucking* bullshit going around. Insinuations she was fired for anything other than not doing her job, which she didn't do well. Often late, sometimes not coming in at all, leaving Beverly to cover for her, therefore putting her own work behind. *Fucking* a delivery guy in our staff washroom. But the day I walked in on her making false accusations about other staff members, I said that's *it*."

His nostrils widened as fury continued to fill his face, while Chase noted some hints of his accent creeping in. Diego had everyone's full attention.

"I have no tolerance for gossip. I have no tolerance for disloyalty. I have no tolerance for anyone trying to tear down this business or each other," He hid no anger in his voice. Shaking his head, he pointed around the room. "This here, this is not high school. This is a business. It's work. If any of you want to spread rumors, tell lies around the office, then you should get off your ass and get the *fuck out* of this office right *now!*"

The speech that started as if spoken from a docile lamb ended in a roar that filled the room, causing the guilty parties to sit up a bit straighter, almost as if to admit their wrongdoing. Those who hadn't taken part in the gossip carried a serious expression, if not a hint of fear in their eyes. Benjamin merely nodded in understanding, as if he appreciated Diego's speech, while Jolene continued to sit in silence.

"Consider this a warning," Diego bellowed out, once again ignoring the tears in Gracie's eyes. "Next time, there will be no fucking warning. Next time I hear gossip in this office, you'll be asked to leave immediately."

The meeting ended on a tense note and after the chatter and joyousness of the surprise lunch, the mood of the office changed as everyone rushed back to their desks, leaving Chase and Jolene behind with Diego. Once they were alone and the door closed, Diego sat back down and cleared his throat.

"That was a little much, no?" Jolene finally spoke, as she reached for the last piece of pizza. "I mean, did you have to scream and yell at them."

"No," Diego calmly replied. "But you know what, it made them listen."

"This is true," Jolene bit into the pizza. "I have not seen you like this for a long time."

Appearing completely spent, Diego rubbed his eyes and didn't reply.

"I talked to Hernandez earlier today, he wants to go see Deborah,"

"No! Oh no, Diego, has it come to that?"

"It has."

Diego made eye contact with Chase and for a moment but didn't say anything. When he did, it was in a hushed tone. "He wants you to go with him."

Chase felt a chill crawl up his spine and although he didn't know exactly what would take place during this meeting with Deborah, he somehow guessed that it wasn't something he wanted to take part in. He didn't reply but nodded in agreement.

"When will this happen, Diego?" Jolene asked between bites. "And why? Maybe she will go away, no? I mean, the lawyer said that..."

"It doesn't matter what the lawyer said," Diego replied as he took a drink of his coffee. "She keeps threatening to call the government, the police, everyone. We did nothing wrong but do we want to invite trouble?"

"We could tell them the truth that she's mad for being fired," Chase offered. "She clearly has emotional problems if she goes to a shrink, I mean it's not a stretch."

"No no," Diego shook his head. "We do not want the police here under any circumstances. The three people you never want poking around unless necessary are your doctor, the government, and the police. Otherwise, they start sniffing around, looking for problems that aren't there. And me, I don't trust these people we work with to not talk too much."

"Yeah, we have to stop her now," Jolene agreed. "She wants trouble."

"She wants revenge," Diego corrected her. "Hernandez will speak to her."

"Should we....be talking about this..." Chase allowed his words to drift off and pointed around the room, knowing that they usually avoided such conversations at the office. Diego merely shrugged.

It wasn't until after work when the three of them met Hernandez in his hotel room that things were more openly discussed. Anxiety was at an all-time high while Hernandez merely observed everyone giving their thoughts with a smirk on his face, his eyes shifting from person to person, mostly Diego and Jolene arguing over how to deal with Deborah. Chase remained quiet and noticed Jorge looking his way with a humoured expression.

"There's no question," Jorge finally cut in, appearing relaxed as if they were merely discussing what color to paint the office walls and not whatever he had planned for Deborah; something Chase suspected would be unpleasant. Although he didn't want to see her get hurt, his loyalty was with Jolene and Diego.

"No question? I do not understand," Jolene appeared confused and the two exchanged looks that didn't suggest they were lovers as Chase had been lead to believe. In fact, he sensed nothing between them, rather than the sexual overtones he had expected.

"There's no question," Jorge replied with a casual shrug. "I have to speak with her. There's nothing else we can do now and when I've finished, she will back off."

"What will you say?" Jolene apprehensively asked.

Jorge didn't reply but lifted his eyebrows, his chocolate-brown eyes falling into a pensive stare as if deep in thought, then he glanced away.

"Chase, I need you to come with me," He sat forward in his chair. "She will not see you but I need your help with something."

The room fell into an awkward silence and Chase felt his throat grow dry.

"We are, what day? Thursday?" Jorge calmly glanced at his phone. "I will be in touch with you tomorrow and by then I will have the details worked out. I already have looked into this young woman and I have a pretty good idea how to deal with this situation."

Chase nodded in silence.

"I don't want Chase in a weird situation, you know?" Jolene's voice lowered and she tilted her head down, her eyes looking up at Jorge.

"He won't even get his hands dirty," Jorge's eyes met with Jolene's before shooting a look back at Chase. Unlike the day they met, he no longer saw the Hollywood smile or the charm that was disarming but instead, there was a darkness in his eyes, a cunning, ruthless stare that challenged Chase's earlier assumption. There was no question that this was a man who would sink his teeth in until he tasted blood and have no conscience, no regret, and no remorse.

CHAPTER THIRTY-NINE

Having no conscience would've been convenient, especially as they approached the weekend and more specifically, the time when Jorge Hernandez would need Chase's help with the Deborah situation. The problem was that he wasn't so sure how they were going to take care of her; he didn't want to think that Hernandez was planning to kill her but at the same time, he had no doubt that the charming Mexican could slither into anyone's life and seduce them into thinking he was harmless. Then again, perhaps he would only serve her with a warning to back off Diego and Jolene Inc. He wasn't sharing details with Chase and if life had taught him anything, it was that it was best to not ask.

Jorge arranged to pick him up on a late Saturday night and much to Chase's surprise, he drove a basic SUV; a rental that he obtained for his time in Toronto. Only saying hello, he remained silent, focusing his attention on the GPS until they arrived outside a popular nightclub. There he parked the vehicle nearby and smoked cigarettes, his eyes fixated on the small crowd that waited outside until he spotted Deborah.

"There she is, in the red coat."

Chase immediately recognizing Deborah and nodded. She was alone, her eyes on her phone as she waited to get inside the club.

"So this is what we are going to do," Jorge hesitated for a moment as he reached for his coffee and took a drink. "I'm taking you back to the condo but when I text you later, you've got to get your ass over to Deborah's place. Tell Diego to take you and wait outside until we go inside. Then I want you to stay downstairs and keep an eye out for people. If anyone comes along, I want you to distract them if you can and if not, send me a text immediately."

"How do I distract them?" Chase nervously asked.

Jorge turned toward him and gave a casual shrug. "Don't worry, no one will be around. I've already checked out her building and it's pretty small. Most of the occupants are lights out by ten kind of people. The tenant living beside her works nights and the other side is vacant. I'm not worried."

Chase didn't reply. He recognized a confident man who had been in this kind of situation before and successfully walked away unscathed. He was in a trance-like state as he stared at the nightclub that Deborah was about to enter, finally breaking free, he glanced back in Chase's direction.

"Aren't you going to ask me what I'm going to do?" He pointedly asked Chase.

"No."

"Good," Jorge turned the ignition, raised an eyebrow and turned onto the street. "Because I wasn't going to tell you anyway."

Back at the apartment, Diego was sitting on the couch, apparently waiting for Chase to return. Assuming he was expecting a rundown, Chase immediately began to talk but was quickly cut off.

"I know,"

"You know?" Chase hesitated, feeling a heaviness fill his chest. "So…"

"Tell me when you receive the text," Diego spoke with no emotion as he rose from the couch and walked toward his room.

"What's he going to do?" Chase felt reluctant to ask.

Diego turned around and shrugged. "Just going to talk to her." His eyes were full of innocence and for a moment, Chase almost believe him.

Every minute he waited for the text was full of anxiety. Chase felt like he shouldn't become involved in this mess. What if Jorge killed her? Was he being paranoid? Had Hernandez been involved in Luke Prince's death? So many questions ran through his head and yet, he felt he couldn't discuss this with anyone. There was an unspoken assumption of silence on everyone's part. Almost as if you didn't say it out loud, then nothing happened.

It was almost midnight when the text arrived and they headed to Deborah's apartment building. Waiting across the street, he saw Jorge's rental SUV park alongside her building and the two of them got out. She was clearly drunk as she stumbled on the sidewalk, laughing at herself as if she were an absolute delight. Chase grimaced from his seat. Jorge rushed around with his perfect smile, he made the gentlemanly gesture of reaching for Deborah's arm to help her inside. Charm was clearly his most disarming feature, as she hooked arms and they walked through the entrance.

"Go," Diego quietly instructed. "I will see you at home later."

"But aren't you..."

"Jorge said he would take you home," Diego commented as he kept his eyes on the building. "If not, text me."

Slowly getting out of the vehicle, his legs were rubbery beneath him and for a moment he wasn't sure if he could walk toward the building. His heart raced frantically, everything inside of him said to run away; but where would he go? Easing across the street and toward the entrance, he found a business card stuck in the door to keep it from locking and he graciously moved inside, sliding the card into his pocket.

He could hear the couple as they walked upstairs, Jorge teasing Deborah about not being able to handle her alcohol while she giggled. Their loud whispers were moving farther away and glancing around, Chase edged toward the bottom of the stairs and wondered if he should stay by the entrance or perhaps it would be better to follow them? Reluctant, he decided to do nothing.

After a few minutes and no sign of anyone attempting to come into the silent building, Chase quietly eased up the stairs, taking each step slowly, making sure to stay alert in case someone opened the front door. As he arrived at the second level, he could barely hear the sound of Deborah's giggles, softly echoing through the hallway.

Chase continued to walk carefully, alert to every sound and detail in the small building. He wondered what to do if anyone walked out of their apartment, although that seemed unlikely at that time of night. His heart rate continued to increase and as much as fear absorbed him, there was something else he was feeling; excitement combined with and anxiety that shot adrenaline through his veins. It was shamefully invigorating. A pleasurable high filled him as he made his way up the third flight of stairs and he finally caught sight of Jorge and Deborah from the distance. They were standing beside the steps on the fourth floor, close to her apartment, their voices a flirtatious whisper.

Her hands were running over his body as he whispered something in Deborah's ear and she giggled and teased him, acting as if she hadn't decided if Jorge could join her in the apartment. It was strategic. This was a game to Deborah; the seduction, the trouble she had created at work, it was the thrill of playing people that she thrived on. It disgusted him. *She* disgusted him.

Jorge Hernandez knew how to play the game. Rather than begging for her to give into her desires, he suggested that she be a good girl and go to sleep, perhaps she was too drunk to make a respectful decision. He then coyly hinted that he could *maybe* come with her but he wouldn't try anything, out of respect, something that made Chase grin to himself as she fell for it. She insisted he come inside.

Backing off slightly, Hernandez gestured for her to lead the way and it was only then, as she turned her back that his dark eyes shot a quick glance in Chase's direction. It was a look he would never forget, full of anger and hatred, full of vengeance and fury, full of pure evil. In one quick motion, his hand went around her throat and swiftly pulled her back as she gasped for air, then with one quick move, threw her against the wall next to the stairway. As if trying to catch her breath, a stifled moan escaped, sounding like that of a wounded animal; full of fear, even from the dark corner where she could not see him, Chase recognized the sound of panic.

Trapping her against the wall with one hand, Jorge continued to hold the other against her throat, as tears flooded her eyes and she struggled for her breath.

In a voice that started off as calm and rapidly increased in speed and intensity, Jorge could be heard speaking.

"Look, little girl, you're going to let this shit with Diego and Jolene go and I mean *now*. Drop everything, drop the lawyer and don't ever go to the CRA or the police because if anyone starts to investigate today, tomorrow, ten years from now, I'm going to fucking kill you. And I'm going to get away with it cause I always do. And if you go to the RCMP, your best friend or anyone else about our conversation, I guarantee it will be the last fucking confession you will ever have, got it?"

Shivering, Deborah absolutely frantic, as tears poured down her face, her fear unmistakable, as she nodded, attempting to say yes, her voice shook so badly that she was unable to say that one word. Chase felt some compassion creep in for her and had to look away, unable to witness anymore. He could hear Jorge continue to threaten her and she quietly sobbed, gasping for air, Chase decided that it would be best that he start down the third flight of stairs, his legs felt heavy as he walked.

It was when he heard a loud thud that he stopped, his heart pounding in fear as a sharp spark ran through his veins. He heard a few quiet steps behind him and turned to see Jorge calmly walking past him as if he had done nothing out of the ordinary. His eyes were menacing and yet tranquil at the same time, as he gestured for Chase to follow him. Tempted to go back, feeling as though he should check, he knew better. He didn't want to make the mistake of being the next person that Jorge Hernandez turned his rage on.

Feeling shell-shocked, he followed Jorge downstairs and it was only after they were outside in the cold night air, as they headed to his SUV that he finally spoke.

"Is she..."

Realizing what he was asking, Jorge gave a self-satisfying grin as he climbed in the SUV and Chase reluctantly did the same.

"I'm guessing a broken arm, maybe a leg," He replied casually as he started the vehicle and grabbed a cigarettes from a pack that sat on the dash. He lit it up and inhaled deeply before releasing the smoke into the vehicle. He put on his seatbelt and glanced in the rearview mirror before pulling onto the street. "She'll be fine but I guarantee, she won't fucking talk. In fact, I think I just taught her a valuable lesson about talking too much."

Relieved that he hadn't killed her, it took a moment to fully digest everything Chase had just saw. He wanted to talk but wasn't sure of what to say.

"Are you sure she's not..." He couldn't finish the sentence but instead, glanced toward Jorge who was continuing to puff on a cigarette as if it were his treat after a violent mission.

"Ha?" He seemed to come out of his daze. "Her? Oh, she's fine. Trust me. I've been doing this a while, I know how to shake people up. She won't talk and when they find her, they'll assume she was drunk and tripped. I mean, did you see those shoes she was wearing? Hardly practical."

"But what if she does?" Chase couldn't help but ask.

Hernandez didn't reply at first but simply glanced in his direction, an ominous grin on his face. "My friend, you worry too much. You remind me of a woman. I think you've been hanging out with Diego too much."

Chase felt himself start to calm slightly, a little apprehensive to accept the excitement he felt following this brutal attack. It reminded him of a fight he had been to with Diego months earlier, a boxing match that ended with the opponent being put in an ambulance; he hated it but loved it at the same time. There was a ruthless side of himself that enjoyed watching someone getting hurt and he wasn't sure why or what that said about him.

"Now Jolene," He continued as they glided down the street, heading toward the condo. "She's nervous but she knows what must be done. When her mind is made, I don't think anyone would want to get in the way."

Feeling calmer as they drove farther away, he felt engulfed in an unexpected bond with Jorge Hernandez. They shared a moment that was almost as intimate as one would with a lover; a shared, dark secret that inflamed the night, a trusted moment that was stronger than Chase had ever felt with anyone before; not a girlfriend, not family, not even Diego. It was unexpected. He felt himself open up and ask a question that had burned on his lips for weeks.

"Do you know about my son that was shot? About the man who shot him?" His voice filled the otherwise silent vehicle. "Luke Prince, he was killed a few weeks ago?"

An unexpected look of compassion was in Jorge's eyes as they only briefly looked away from the road. "I know about it, yes."

"Do you know who did it?" Chase asked in a quiet voice.

He didn't answer, his solemn eyes glancing once again at Chase and looked away.

"Chase, its best to not think about the past," Jorge sternly informed him. "Everything that falls behind us, should be left in its place. Does it matter who did it?"

Shaking his head, he didn't know what to say.

"You know what is wrong with the world today, Chase?" Jorge replied as they pulled up in front of his building. "There's no loyalty. People are fickle. They say they will do anything for those they love, for those who have shown them loyalty, they talk, talk, talk and yet, when needed, few stick around."

Shifting the SUV into park, he turned toward Chase, his eyes watching him carefully. "You have two people who are very protective of you and at first, I wasn't sure. I didn't trust this kid that they had working for them, I was suspicious."

"Of me?" Chase asked.

"Yeah, of you," Jorge confirmed as he studied his face. "It's amazing what someone can learn when they talk to the right people, ask the right questions. But that's my thing, Chase, I'm *really* good with people."

Chase briefly considered the episode with Deborah.

"Hennessey is an interesting little town," Jorge said as he put out his cigarette and reached for another one. "Very colourful bunch but they sure love to talk. Especially that girl, Kelsey? The one with the tits?" He grinned and then in a sudden moment of mock seriousness added. "She liked you a lot Chase."

Feeling slightly unnerved by the fact that Hernandez was in his former town and talking to people he knew, Chase didn't say anything.

Laughing, Jorge turned back toward the steering wheel as if preparing to leave. "Don't worry about the shooter that got Luke Prince. Just be glad that someone did."

Chase took that as his warning to stop asking questions and got out of the SUV.

CHAPTER FORTY

It wasn't until a breakfast meeting with Hernandez, Jolene, and Diego a couple of days later, that the topic of Deborah came up again. The four once again met in Jorge's hotel room, where an array of sugary treats and traditional breakfast foods along with coffee awaited them when they arrived. Diego was on his second strawberry tart, cringing at the bland coffee while Jorge and Chase were finishing up a more traditional, Canadian breakfast of bacon and eggs and Jolene took a few bites of her whole grain toast, that they eased into the topic.

"So our lawyer, he contacted me yesterday and he say that Deborah is backing off," Her eyes met with Jorge's and he nodded, appearing intrigued and surprised, as if this were news to him. A fine actor, he raised an eyebrow as Jolene continued to speak. "Apparently, she had a little slip fall on the weekend and she now feels there's a perspective on things."

"She had a slip *and* fall and now has a *new* perspective on things," Diego corrected her in between bites of his strawberry tart and cringed.

'Do not correct me like a child!"

"Hey now," Jorge butted into the conversation, a smile easing on his face. "Diego, she's still learning English, let it go."

"She's been here long enough, she sounds like...like..."

"An idiot?" Jolene snapped. "An immigrant just learning the language?"

"Well, look at Jorge," Diego pointed at the Mexican. "He doesn't even live in Canada and his English is perfect, he barely has an accent."

"I am not ashamed of my accent," Jolene spoke defiantly. "If you are, that is too bad."

ALWAYS BE A WOLF

"Hey, don't get me in the middle," Jorge cut in with a hand in the air. "I spend a lot of time in North America and made a point to perfect my English and downplay my accent. It helps me get mixed in the crowd easier and we know that in this line of work, that's necessary. But I don't see an issue with how Jolene speaks. Now, can we get back to the topic at hand?"

"As I was saying," Jolene glared at her brother. "Her *new* perspective is very different and she does not feel that we are any longer at fault and maybe it is time to let it go. We send her flowers and hoped that she got well soon. I think that she see we hold compassion for her."

Diego had a lopsided grin on his face as he raised one eyebrow while Jorge gave Jolene his full attention, his head leaned forward and eyes looking up, his head giving a slow nod. Had Chase not been there to witness the attack, there was nothing in his composure that suggested Jorge had anything to do with it.

"A broken arm? Leg?" Jorge asked as he reached for his coffee while making eye contact with Chase.

"A fractured arm and bruised ribs? I think?" Jolene replied and reached for a pastry. "I do not know. I think maybe some bruises and stuff? Especially around her neck area? I guess it is how she fall, no?"

Her innocent eyes met with Jorge's equally innocent eyes and he merely shrugged.

"Some people bruise easily," He cleared his throat, sniffed and reached for the pot of coffee. "Anyone want some more?"

Diego turned up his nose and shook his head while Jolene gave a tight smile and did the same.

"Ah Colombians! They think they have the best coffee, the best cocaine..." He teased.

"Your Mexican food, it is nice," Jolene offered.

Jorge laughed and showed off his movie star smile and the four of them moved on to other business.

The meeting lasted a couple of hours before all four stood up and started toward the door. It was there that Hernandez commented on how he would be returning to Mexico but would be coming back soon.

"I've got some business to take care of at home but I'm thinking that we should look into a more permanent location and not go from venue to venue," His comment created interest from both Jolene and Diego. "I have some leads on a few places but we won't get into that until I have more details."

"I like," Jolene commented while Diego nodded. "We were discussing this just the other day how we need to consider such things."

"I think it would make more sense to invest in a building and not give any of our profits away to the venue owners" Diego agreed and nodded.

"Good," Jorge said and his eyes jumped back at Chase. "I have something important for you to help me with too. Now that I see what you are made of, I think there's someone you need to take care of for me."

Chase froze on the spot and couldn't speak. *Take care of?*

"But I won't get into that today," Jorge casually commented with his usual, smooth voice, as if they were merely discussing the food selection for their next meeting, he showed no expression.

Chase didn't respond while neither Jolene or Diego reacted.

If there was an awkwardness, only he noticed as everyone said their good-byes and the three of them exited the room, while Jorge went back inside.

It wasn't until they were in Diego's car that Chase expressed his concerns. "What did he mean back there?"

"What do you mean?" Jolene turned around in her seat while Diego stared ahead at the road, clearly in his own thoughts. "About looking for a location for our parties?"

"No, what he said to me...about taking care of someone?"

"Ah, I do not know," Jolene replied and turned back in her seat and pointed at an abandoned building as they passed by. "What about that place, Diego? It's pretty big, no?"

"It looks kind of scummy and plus, look at this neighborhood," Diego gestured toward the street. "Not a good location for us. We'll have to give it some more thought."

"I guess he, Jorge, has something in mind," Jolene replied.

"Hernandez *always* has something in mind," Diego shook his head. "Why do you not like?"

"I like Hernandez fine but I think he's out for numero uno and no one else," Diego replied.

"Hmm...maybe..." Jolene dreamily looked out the window, as if envisioning this new location while in the back of the car, Chase worried about his future.

Jorge's words continued to haunt him for the next few days. He envisioned all kinds of scenarios including one where Hernandez insisted that he kill Deborah; although, that didn't make sense considering she had completely backed off since her 'fall' the previous weekend. Regardless, his brain continually contemplated the possibilities and when he brought up the topic to Diego a few times, he merely made a face and grinned.

"Come on, Hernandez doesn't tell other people to do his dirty work," He shook his head as if Chase's concerns were ridiculous. "Like he trust anyone else to do a thing. That's why we weren't allowed to even approach Deborah in this whole mess because he's so arrogant, he thinks no one can fix a situation like him."

Chase didn't feel too assured and Jorge's words continued to haunt him in both his sleep and waking life. The nightmares were plentiful while his fears were almost debilitating and although he wasn't one to normally get too caught up in fear, he knew that if Jorge or either of his bosses asked, he had no choice but to do as they wished. They weren't the kind of people you said no to and if he hadn't known that before, the last few weeks had proven it.

As the month moved forward and February turned into March, Chase began to find some relief as time slipped away. Perhaps Jorge had changed his mind or maybe he wasn't coming back to Canada for a few weeks or months. Maybe it was a misunderstanding? Perhaps he misunderstood what Jorge said and he needed Chase to take care of *something* for him. Maybe he needed help looking at locations?

The days moved forward and his birthday was quickly approaching and although this had no significance to Chase, it did to everyone else.

His boys were excited about it and asked him in their Skype conversations if he was having a party with balloons and cake. He continually said no and attempted to explain that adults didn't do those kind of things until it became abundantly clear that this wasn't the answer they wanted to hear, so he finally relented and said yes, that Jolene and Diego were having a party for him. The kids asked if they could come and didn't understand why they couldn't, even though their mother went to great efforts to explain that they were too far away.

The twins were getting close to the same age as Leland when he died and a fear crawled into his heart when he thought about it. Although it wasn't logical to worry that something would happen to them, what if it did? Hernandez could turn on him and now that he knew where to find his family, would he ever threaten them to get what he wanted? There was no doubt that he was a dangerous man and who knew the lengths he would go to if he ever found himself in a bind.

Ironically, Jorge was returning to Toronto on Chase's birthday. If he had ever wanted to proof that he was an unlucky person, this made for a compelling argument. So as much as Diego and Jolene rattled on about how they were going to take him out for a 'family' celebration that night, it was difficult to get too enthused knowing that Hernandez would probably show up and ask him to do something despicable that same day.

Chase started to go to the gym more often as he got closer to his birthday, spending hours a week pounding on a heavy bag while his mind raced in every direction. It had been an overwhelming year full of big opportunities and big heart breaks. How did people move ahead so casually, as if the past could not catch up to them? He still thought about his son and the gruesome way he died every day. The death of Luke Prince hadn't taken that away. It gave him no relief. He would always wonder if it was Jolene who killed Prince or Hernandez?

On the morning of his birthday, Diego excitedly flew in his bedroom door just as Chase was waking up, half asleep, an enthused roommate sang him Happy Birthday, forgetting the lyrics halfway through and stopped.

"Ah, you know the rest," He shrugged and stood at the end of his bed. "I would give you an early morning birthday present that would make you very happy but I somehow don't think you want it from me." He winked and let out a boisterous laugh as he headed back out the door and into the kitchen.

Chase couldn't help but laugh and stretched. "Thank you anyway, Diego."

"I would spoil you for women," Diego called out and turned on the water and then suddenly turned it off and just as Chase was about to get out of bed and head for the bathroom, he heard the words that got his day off to a disturbing start.

"Hernandez wants us to meet him at his hotel before we go to the office," Diego sang out. "A quick meeting? Hmmm...maybe he has a birthday gift for you, *amigo*. But I guarantee, it wouldn't be as good as mine!"

With that, he let out another boisterous laugh and Chase froze in the spot.

CHAPTER FORTY-ONE

"Please, come in," Jorge stepped aside, his perfect movie star smile in place, he pointed across the room to the usual array of food and of course, coffee. Chase could hear the shower running and wonder if Jolene was his guest. If Diego was thinking the same thing, he didn't show any signs but instead focused on the food.

"No strawberry tarts today?"

"Ah! I am sorry Diego but someone got to it before you arrived," Jorge grinned and glanced toward the bathroom. "Who can say no to a beautiful *señorita*?"

Diego grimaced than shrugged, grabbing a pastry instead and pouring a cup of coffee. Chase hesitantly moved toward the tray and grabbed a muffin. Once the three sat at the table, Jorge immediately began to speak.

"Jolene will not be attending today," Jorge announced as he poured himself a coffee and reached for a muffin. "I had a project for her to work on and the matter is quite urgent so I preferred that she get started right away."

"Oh yeah?" Diego asked between bites while in the next room, the shower stopped. Chase glanced at the bathroom door and wondered who was on the other side.

"We may have found a venue," Jorge grabbed his laptop and excitedly showed them a popular downtown location. It had once housed a well-known nightclub that had phased out over the years but remained opened, although stagnant in business, he explained. "Not that the guy really wanted to sell but I manage to persuade him."

Diego merely nodded while Chase noted the devilish grin on Jorge's face as he went on to explain the finer details of the building as he showed more images, commenting on changes he would like to make, things he felt were ideal for their parties and the timeline for this project.

"My goal is to open sooner than later," Jorge commented as he shut the laptop and returned his attention to the muffin on his plate. "That is why Jolene is not here this morning, she's doing some research for me, making some calls."

"So, he didn't want to sell?" Diego appeared confused as he took a drink of his coffee. "I mean, I know it's not the hot spot they say it used to be but it's still a pretty popular place."

Jorge shrugged. "He recently had an accident and is unable to keep up with demands."

Both Diego and Chase stopped and stared at Hernandez but neither said a word.

"I actually got it at a very fair price," Hernandez continued with a lopsided grin on his face and shifted his attention to Chase, "You Canadians, always so accommodating."

Chase didn't respond. He had a feeling that it wasn't a matter of choice in this situation.

"And so," Jorge continued as Diego reached for another pastry. "That brings me to another piece of business. Chase, I need your help with something. Diego and me will be tied up most of the day sorting out a few details about this property, so I need you to take care of someone for me."

Shit.

"She won't give you a problem," He spoke casually and took a drink of coffee. "But I know I can trust you and Chase, I don't trust a lot of people."

For the first time, Chase began to wonder if he meant the woman in the bathroom but he somehow doubted Jorge Hernandez wanted him anywhere near his girlfriend, so his thoughts returned to the original concern; he wanted him to attack or intimidate someone in the same way he would, in a way he clearly had normalized over time.

Diego glanced at Chase but didn't appear worried. Continuing to eat, he seemed more interested in the food than the conversation.

"Ok," Chase managed to say with some hesitation.

"Don't worry, it will be fine," Jorge casually assured him and moved on to Diego, discussing their agenda for the day regarding switching the property to the company, the details they would have to take care of immediately and a meeting with their lawyer later that morning.

Chase couldn't focus on their words however, his mind was going in several directions, wondering if this had to do with Deborah. Was he planning to ask Chase to go hurt her again? Maybe she relented in her earlier decision to not go after Diego and Jolene inc. and he would have to persuade her in an unsavory way.

The sound of a hair dryer in the bathroom was a momentary distraction, as Diego and Jorge continued to talk about the day ahead. It was clear that violence and crime were part of a normal existence to Hernandez and Chase momentarily wondered if he would someday be the same. Was he in too deep? Should he get out now? Move back to Hennessey? Return to his old life? Was this a mistake?

The questions flowed through his mind until the bathroom door finally opened and a little girl stepped out. Chase assumed she was no more than 8 or 9, the child was undoubtedly Jorge's daughter, with the same eyes and smile, she wore her hair back in a ponytail as she hesitantly wandered out wearing a little blue dress over her tiny frame. Although sheepish at first, her shyness didn't last as she walked over and climbed up on Jorge's lap and reached for a cookie on the tray.

"*No mi querido,*" Jorge spoke gently and she automatically pulled her hand back.

"*Papá, tuve una tarta de fresa,*"

"That is not breakfast," Jorge sternly insisted. "You took that before I could stop you and that was supposed to be Diego's, now he is very disappointed."

Her eyes drifted toward the only other Latino in the room, appearing apprehensive, she reached for the toast. "Papa..."

"English, Maria, we talked about this," Jorge interrupted. "You need to practice your English and you have a lot of opportunities while we are in Canada."

"Now this is Diego and this is Chase," He introduced the two men and his daughter glanced from one to the other.

"Chase, is that a name?" Maria asked him with perfect English and before receiving a response, turned toward her father. "Is that a name or, how do you say?"

"Nickname?"

"Yes," She replied and turned toward Chase. "Is that your nickname? Do you have a real name?"

"That is my real name," He gently replied, suddenly having a feeling who he was 'looking after' that day.

"Oh," Maria reached for a small container of jam. "That name is weird."

"Don't be rude," Jorge warned and she offered Chase an apologetic smile.

"Now Chase," He continued to speak over the little girl's head. "I need you to look after Maria today. You have children and I know you can do this...I thought about asking Jolene but, I don't know."

"She is *not* good with children," Diego replied as he relaxed in the chair, sipping on his coffee. "That's why she has none."

"Is that the lady with the big boobies?" Maria sang out, her mouth full of toast.

"Hey! You do not say that!" Jorge warned but Maria merely made a face, wiggling her nose to show dislike.

"Chase, you can take her out maybe," Jorge stopped for a moment to think. "I don't know, is there a place for children around here?"

"I want to go to the Eaton's Centre," Maria insisted.

"Already a teenager," Jorge said as he shook his head. "Not even 10 years old and this is what I hear, everywhere we go, she researches the malls in that city and insists we go see."

Maria giggled, her large brown eyes shyly searched Chase's face.

Although it wasn't the task he had feared for the day, it certainly scared him almost as much. What did he know about little girls? He had three boys. *Had.*

Later that morning, Jorge and Diego dropped the two off at the mall with a handful of cash and Maria excitedly entered the building as if it were paradise. Pulling an iPhone from her little purse, she immediately did a search and pointed toward a popular ladies store. "I want to go there."

And so that was how the day went. While Diego and Jorge were off doing business, Chase was escorting the child around the mall. He noticed a lot of women smiling as he followed an enthusiastic little Mexican girl from store to store, to the point that he felt exhausted and begged her to take a break. She insisted they go to MacDonald's. After ordering their food, the two sat down to eat.

"So, I notice you haven't bought anything yet," Chase attempted to make conversation. Jorge certainly gave him enough money for the little girl to shop however because the difference in currency, he would have to help her if she wanted to buy anything.

"Neither have you," She countered.

"I'm not the one who wanted to come to the mall," Chase pointed out and she giggled.

"I go to all the stores and then I decide what I want and I go back," She spoke confidently of her strategy. "I take a picture with my phone so I remember and then I go back later."

He had wondered why she had taken so many pictures along the way but assumed she was posting on social media and not strategizing. Perhaps she wasn't so different from her father.

"So did you decide yet?" Chase asked hopefully.

"No, I haven't gone to all the store yet." She replied as she bit into a fry. "It could take hours."

He smiled stiffly.

"Papa says you have kids," Maria tilted her head curiously. "Do you have girls or boys."

"Boys."

"Papa says I can't ask you about them, why?"

Chase wasn't sure how to answer but her eyes were watching him curiously, as she continued to nibble on a fry, her Chicken McNuggets still untouched.

"I...I think because one of my children died," Chase spoke hesitantly, feeling reluctant to even broach the subject.

"How did he die?"

"It was an accident," Chase decided to not get into the details, however, she didn't let go.

"What kind of accident? Like in a car?" She asked innocently and took a sip of her juice.

"No, it's probably better we don't talk about it," Chase spoke diplomatically. "It might scare you if I tell you."

"I don't get scared."

"You don't get scared?" Chase grinned.

"No, I watch scary shows all the time," She replied with a matter-of-fact expression on her face "They don't scare me."

"Like scary movies?"

"Like *Sons of Anarchy.*"

"*You* watch *Sons of Anarchy?*" Chase couldn't help but be a little surprised. "Is that show even on in Mexico?"

"I don't know, I watch it on dad's computer. I sometimes watch when he is busy and doesn't know," She replied with a giggle. "And *Breaking Bad.* I like the boy on that show." She giggled shyly and blushed.

Chase grinned and nodded. "Those shows are more for...adults."

"I know cause there's a lot of violence and sexy stuff too," She continued to nibble on her fries while Chase finished the last of his salad and opened up his coffee. "But it's not a big deal."

"So how did your son die?" She pushed on, her eyes fixated on his face.

"It's probably better we don't talk about it," Chase replied, hoping to get off the topic.

"Does it make you sad?" The little girl continued to push on and tilted her head as she listened.

"Yes," Chase answered honestly.

"Do you cry for him?" Maria asked as her eyes widened and she sipped on her drink.

"Sometimes," Chase replied, feeling grief fill his heart as he spoke. Leland would never be this girl's age.

"How old was he?

"Almost five."

"What was his name?"

"Leland."

"Can I see a picture?"

Chase reached for his phone and found one from the previous summer. Passing it to her, she held the phone carefully as she stared at the image, her finger running over the screen.

"I'm sorry for your loss," Maria frowned with a hint of tears in her eyes. "I will say a prayer for you so you won't be so sad anymore."

Chase opened his mouth to say something but couldn't speak. It took everything he had to not break down over this heartfelt, innocent comment, something he would never expect from anyone let alone a little girl he had just met.

"Thank you," He finally managed in a quiet voice as he felt his whole body become incredibly hot, his throat tighten and his heart race. The entire room had an echo and a cold sweat grasped his body.

Closing his eyes, he attempted to calm himself but instead thought of what Jorge Hernandez would say if he passed out while babysitting his daughter. The cold sweats seemed to get worse, his body felt like rubber in the chair.

"Chase, are you ok?" Maria had panic in her voice, her small fingers touched his hand and he found himself slowly coming out of the dark tunnel and returning to the present moment. She looked upset. "Are you going to be sick?"

"No, I'm fine," He responded and took a drink of his coffee, his shaky hand managed to spill some on his shirt. He grabbed a napkin with his other hand and wiped it off.

"That's going to stain," She spoke earnestly. "I can get it out for you though, I get papa's coffee stains out all the time."

Chase smiled.

CHAPTER FORTY-TWO

It was a really long day at the mall. Chase enjoyed spending time with the enthusiastic little girl but quickly grew tired of wandering from store to store. Maria had granted his wishes for many breaks but it was usually during that time that she polluted him with questions about his children, his former marriage and if he thought he would ever marry again.

"Why do you say, 'I don't know' to all my questions?" Maria asked him mid-afternoon, shortly after the pair sat on a bench that faced a cosmetic store. A welcoming fragrance flowed toward them as they watched women having their makeup applied, causing Chase to hope Maria didn't get the idea to go in and do the same. It was clear that she viewed herself as more of a young lady than a child but he suspected Hernandez wouldn't appreciate his daughter having a full face of makeup when he picked them up.

"I answer your questions the best I can," Chase gently replied. "I just don't always know the answer myself. For example, I don't know when or if I will get married again and things like breakups are complicated."

Maria considered his reply but seemed unsatisfied. "But would you like to get married again *maybe*?"

"I guess, maybe," Chase shrugged. "I don't know."

"Papa says if you don't know what you want, you'll never get it," Maria commented airily as she turned away from him and crossed her legs in a ladylike fashion. "Me, I know I want to get married someday. A huge, amazing wedding with lots of flowers and pretty dresses, hundreds of guests and the perfect husband."

"Aren't you a little young to be thinking about all that?" Chase asked as a grin curved his lips.

"Aren't you a little old *not* to be thinking about it?" She countered stubbornly, her brown eyes narrowing in on his face. "Your life will go nowhere without a plan."

"Does you father say that too?" Chase grinned, humored by their conversation.

"Yes, he does."

"Well, in many regards, he is right," Chase admitted and felt a little awkward about explaining himself to a 9 year-old-girl, let alone one he just met that day. "I should have my life together more but I feel like it's been off track for a long time."

Maria nodded in understanding.

"My father likes you or you wouldn't be with me today," Maria offered as she tilted her head and gave him a curious stare. "My father doesn't trust anyone to look after me but he likes you. He said you were good with kids."

"Your father has never seen me with kids," Chase quietly replied.

"He said he could tell plus he interviewed people where you used to live," Maria said and turned more in his direction. "They all said you were a really good father."

"They did?" Chase attempted to hide his surprise but the clever little girl caught it right away.

"Yes, you did not know?" She asked pointedly. "Didn't you think you were a good father?"

Chase looked away and didn't reply. Fortunately, he didn't have to because Maria's phone beeped and after checking the message, she quickly jumped off the bench.

"We must hurry, papa is on his way to get us."

Chase was full of relief as he followed her to one last stop, followed by the main entrance, where Jorge and Diego waited outside.

"Did you buy me anything?" Diego automatically asked and Jorge laughed.

"I didn't buy *me* anything," Chase replied as he climbed into the SUV behind Maria, as she quickly fastened her seatbelt.

"Let me guess," Jorge looked into the rearview mirror, his eyes glancing from Chase to Maria. "She went to every store in the mall, took a lot of pictures of things she wanted and ended up buying something from the first store she went into."

"Yes," Chase replied and Maria giggled.

"I liked the mall but it's not my favorite," Maria replied and then went on to name all the shopping centers she had been to on their travels, in the order of her preference. This conversation carried them back to the hotel, where Diego had left his car.

The four got out in the parking area with Chase helping Maria down from the SUV. Her feet barely had hit the ground, when she put her arms up in the air to show that she wanted to hug him. Awkwardly, he leaned over and the little girl grasped him around the neck and gave him a rushed kiss on each cheek, then stood back.

"Thank you, Chase," She gave him a bright smile. "I had a wonderful day."

Standing upright, he noticed an appreciative smile on Jorge's face while Diego looked slightly stunned, he returned the compliment to Maria.

"You're welcome," Chase affectionately replied. "It was nice getting to know you."

With that, Maria took her father's hand, the two said their goodbyes, as they made their way toward a nearby elevator. Diego pointed toward his car and him and Chase silently headed there.

"I bet you had a better day than I did," Diego muttered once they were inside the car. "Roaming around the mall while I got dragged from meeting to meeting. I'm not even sure buying this building is a great idea but he seems to think we could have a regular spot. I'm not so sure I like that. I want to keep it exclusive but this sounds like anyone can come in at any time. I'm not sure Jolene is going to like this either."

Chase remained silent as they made their way out of the parking area and on the side street. "I'm sure it won't be as easy to get in as a normal, everyday club, right?"

"I don't know, Chase," Diego shook his head and appeared frustrated. "The problem is you can't say no to this guy. He owns us. I think Jolene may have better luck talking to him. I think they're meeting tomorrow."

Chase nodded and briefly considered the idea when Diego cut into his thoughts.

"Which means you'll be babysitting again."

"What? Really?" Chase asked. "Doesn't he have a nanny or something?"

"Nope," Diego replied. "His wife had Maria up until recently."

"What happened?"

Diego didn't reply but shook his head.

"Did he get custody or something?"

"Do you think someone like Jorge Hernandez goes to court when he wants something?" Diego countered. "Not likely."

"But it sounds like she travels with him a lot..."

"Nah," Diego replied as his lips twisted into a stubborn frown. "They travel together on vacations but not while he's on business. I believe he is trying to get a nanny. Just hope that's not *you* or you might be living in Mexico next week."

"Hey, no no," Chase replied. "I'm not moving to Mexico to be a nanny."

"If Jorge Hernandez says you're moving to Mexico to be a nanny, even temporarily, you're gonna be doing it. You don't say no to this guy."

"But my life is here...."

"I know that and he knows that but do you think he cares?" Diego replied. "That little girl clearly *loves* you and she is the only person he cares about, other than himself."

Chase didn't know what to say.

"Just wait and see, that is all I'm saying," Diego continued.

"But I don't even speak Spanish," Chase countered. "I don't know anything about Mexico, wouldn't he prefer someone who can speak their first language or a woman, at least?"

"Yes, of course, he would, but he could see you as a temporary fix while they look for someone suitable."

"He didn't say that did he?"

"No," Diego replied. "But I've known this man for years."

His accent was creeping in which wasn't a good sign. Chase felt like he was smothering as he processed the news of what might be around the corner. He fell silent with only his thoughts.

"What a birthday for you," Diego cut in and reminded him of something Chase had somehow forgotten with his busy day. "But that is fine, Jolene and me, we are taking you out to for dinner. So let's not think about this stuff now. It's too soon to say anyway."

Chase reluctantly agreed but wasn't in the mood to celebrate.

Back at home, he had a quick conversation with Audrey and the kids before getting ready for his dinner with Jolene and Diego. He couldn't help but note that no one else in his 'real' family bothered to text or call him that day, only clarifying the fact that family wasn't necessarily the people who brought you up.

The Silvas took him to a well-known restaurant in the city's downtown area, one that was given terrific reviews by foodies and reviewers alike; it was elegant, distinguished and the food was tremendous. Diego and Jolene made a huge deal over him, insisting he drink glass after glass of wine, something that seemed to lighten his dark mood until he felt comfortable enough to broach the subject of the company's future. He asked what Jolene thought of buying the former nightclub.

"I think it might be good," Jolene replied thoughtfully while Diego made a face. "My brother, no, he do not think it will be good but I, I think it will be good."

"Jolene, you're so naïve," Diego shook his head. "Part of what people like is the exclusivity."

"Then tell this to Jorge," She insisted. "Don't be scared. He will not shoot you because you have a different opinion."

Diego looked skeptical and made a face.

"Get Chase to talk to him," She suggested. "He likes Chase! You know he don't let just anyone look after his daughter."

With that, Chase took another long drink as his head swirled around with the events of the day. So many questions arose in his mind, springing to life, they echoed through his head and were only fading with each glass of wine. Until he got up to leave, it hadn't occurred to him how much he had to drink, as he stumbled out of the restaurant and into the car. The last thing he remembered was Diego helping him inside the condo.

CHAPTER FORTY-THREE

From the moment he opened his eyes, the room spun. For some reason, turning to his left seemed to slow down the disturbing merry-go-round in his bed but when accompanied by so many other unpleasant sensations, it was hardly much of an improvement. His eyes alone felt as though he had a beach full of sand in them while his throat was so dry that he feared a single glass of water would be overwhelming to the senses. Not that his stomach would welcome anything at that moment, as it angrily churned with even the slightest movement. He felt disgusting and disgusted with himself. It wasn't like Chase to get drunk and the embarrassment over his behavior was nothing compared to how he felt when the sheets rustled, gently floating over his naked body.

Blinking rapidly, Chase managed to focus his eyes on a nearby chair where the clothes from the previous day were neatly placed. Carefully folded pants and underwear, his shirt and jacket on a hanger, his wallet, and phone on the nearby dresser. There was no way he did that.

Rubbing one hand over his face, Chase attempted to remember the previous night. Flickers of conversations and visions scattered through his brain, like a confusing dream that didn't make sense the next morning. He vaguely recalled getting home. Hadn't Diego helped him to his room? Did something happen between them? Would Diego take advantage of him in a vulnerable situation?

Unfortunately, his memory wasn't cooperating. Even his instincts were a little blurry that morning as he rose from his bed and slowly made his way into the shower. The hot water brought him little relief and in fact, he felt more nausea creep up as the steam surrounded him, his mind a million miles away. He finished and stepped back out of the shower, pulled on his robe and sat on the edge of the tub. His thoughts continued to roam back to the previous night but his recollection wasn't improving and in fact, it seemed to fade even farther away.

Finally, he stood up and started to get ready for work in a mechanical fashion. Knowing that the upset stomach wasn't likely to settle anytime soon, he briefly considered taking something for it but changed his mind. Perhaps he deserved to suffer for drinking too much. The last thing he wanted was to end up like his mother and so many others in his former community, who used alcohol as a crutch. People like Luke Prince.

Feeling apprehensive, Chase made his way toward the kitchen, the smell of brewing coffee met him at the door, causing his stomach to stir a little more before the wave of nausea passed. Diego wasn't anywhere in sight and unsure of what else to do, Chase automatically wandered toward the lime tree and decided to move it out before the sun started to rise.

It was as he pulled the awkward ceramic pot across the floor to the patio doors that something caught his eye. A small, round lime was growing on the tree. He almost hadn't noticed the piece of fruit but it was definitely there. Diego had purchased this plant almost a year ago and this was its first lime.

"Diego," He called out excitedly. "You got to come see this!"

Rushing from his bedroom, Diego's eyes doubled in size when he saw Chase inspecting the tree and for a moment he froze before silently moving toward him.

"I can explain," Diego's voice was full of apprehension as he approached, his dark eyes grew in size and he nervously inspected Chase's face. "I didn't know if I should say anything..."

"What do you mean?" Chase immediately realized they weren't talking about the same thing.

Diego clamped his mouth shut and he glanced toward the plant, his face suddenly filling with excitement.

"Oh my God!" He exclaimed, pouncing toward the miniature lime tree and carefully inspected the piece of fruit. "My first lime is here!"

Chase stepped back and watched Diego diligently check the rest of the tree. He finally appeared satisfied and turned the side with the lime toward the window and carefully adjusting the plant. With a big smile on his face, he swung around and clapped his hands together.

"It's going to be a beautiful day!"

As if he had a bolt of electricity run through him, Diego flew into the kitchen and poured himself a cup of coffee. It was as if the sudden appearance of that one lime revived him and gave Chase a reminder of the man he had been many months earlier when they first moved to Toronto. A certain spark that had faded was now back and yet, there was an unmistakable elephant in the room.

"Diego, what were you going to say when you first came out of your room?" Chase asked as he slowly made his way into the kitchen. "You were going to explain something to me?"

Diego abruptly swung around with a deadpan expression on his face. "I don't know what you mean."

"You were going to say something," Chase coaxed as he joined him in the kitchen. "Was it about last night."

"I wasn't going to say anything about last night."

"Are you sure?" Chase asked as Diego turned his back to him and stirred some cream into his coffee.

"Yes."

Chase hesitated for a moment, feeling another bout of nausea pass over him, he was about to ask again when Diego's phone began to ring. Rushing away from Chase, his tone was quite serious when answering it and his words quickly jumped to Spanish.

Feeling like absolute shit, Chase decided to have a cup of coffee and try to eat something. Finding a slice of cold pizza in the fridge, he nibbled on it and found it helped; until five minutes later when he rushed to his bathroom and threw it back up. He found some relief and once again returned to the kitchen and sipped on his coffee.

Hearing Diego's hands clap together, Chase turned around to see him return to the room, a look of satisfaction on his face.

"It's a good sign, this lime," He insisted excitedly. "All good things will come our way. I just got off the phone with Jorge. He wants to meet me and Jolene this morning and has some ideas on the club. I guess he did research and wants to continue with the exclusivity and considering possible memberships and other exciting things. This is *perfecto*!"

"When are you meeting?" Chase asked as if his thoughts were even in the present moment, rather than the night before and his desperate recollection of what did and didn't happen.

"Soon, he says, soon," Diego rushed to his cup of coffee and took a long drink. "He wants us to meet him and of course, we will drop you off at his hotel to stay with Maria. She's doing schoolwork this morning. We will be out for a breakfast meeting."

Chase pushed aside his concerns and decided instead to focus on the moment. His memories of the previous night would eventually return and he would deal with them at that time. Instead, he took a deep breath and followed Diego out the door.

In the car, they didn't have a chance to talk, as Diego was on the phone with Jolene, who was also in her car. Her voice loudly echoed through the Lexus, half in Spanish, half in English, they discussed what they wanted for the new venue and prepared for the meeting with Jorge. Feeling empty and depressed, Chase was only half listening.

Pulled back into the conversation, he heard Jolene question how he was feeling today, followed by a loud shot of laughter.

"He's looking a little sick today," Diego snickered. "He definitely isn't feeling as *good* as he was last night."

Diego's comment came across innocently enough but there was something about how he emphasized *good* that rattled Chase. Perhaps it was just his imagination. He remained tight-lipped as they arrived at the hotel.

By the time they got to Hernandez's door, Chase decided that nothing had happened between him and Diego. Clearly, there would've been an awkwardness between them if anything had, so he was just being paranoid. Perhaps he had removed his own clothes and threw them on the floor and Diego, being a neat freak, followed behind to pick them up and neatly fold and place them on the chair.

Jorge answered the door and quickly ushered them inside, with his usual Hollywood smile. Maria sat on the couch, surrounded by books and papers, a laptop beside her, she was clearly unhappy doing schoolwork. Fortunately, Chase had brought his own laptop so he could also get some work done that morning.

"I hear it was your birthday yesterday," Jorge commented off the bat and pointed toward an array of pastries and breakfast food on a nearby table. "I invite you to help yourself to some food, unfortunately, I was not able to get a cake on such short notice."

"Oh, that's fine," Chase let out a laugh. "The last thing I want now is cake."

Jorge laughed and nodded. "Yes, I hear you three celebrated last night. Unfortunately, I was unable to make it."

"I could've gone," Maria piped up as she reached for a small plate behind her, she nibbled on a strawberry tart. "I was free last evening."

"It was a grown up night," Jorge reminded his daughter.

"I'm a grown up."

"You are *not* a grown up." His voice was flat and he returned his attention to Diego. "Shall we go? We don't want to keep Jolene waiting."

"Let's go," Diego grabbed a pastry off the tray and the two headed toward the door. Jorge turned back momentarily to remind Maria to finish her school work before following Diego out of the room.

"OH God, I've been doing school work since last night," Maria complained after they left. "What good is any of this to me anyway?"

"I would do it and get it out of the way," Chase advised. "I always left my homework until the last-minute and then had to rush to catch up."

"I know but I get bored with it," Maria insisted as she stood up from the couch. "I try to make papa happy and he likes if I have nice grades."

Chase nodded and a thought crossed his mind.

"What about your mom?" Chase asked calmly as if it were nothing more than a casual question. "I bet she wants you to have good grades too?"

Maria shrugged. "I don't know. I haven't seen her in a while."

"Oh, is she on vacation or something?"

"No," Maria calmly replied. "She disappeared."

Chase opened his mouth to reply but nothing came out. A trickle of fear raced to his heart and he felt his mind racing.

"But I think she is upset and avoiding us," Maria continued as she reached into the tray of food for a piece of toast. "Papa and her had a bad argument one day and then she went away. I think probably because she was embarrassed and upset. Kind of like if I argue with papa and then hide in my room until I'm not mad at him anymore."

Although he appreciated her logic, Chase somehow felt that the reality wasn't quite so innocent.

CHAPTER FORTY-FOUR

It wasn't the first time Chase wondered how his life had spun out of control. The last time it happened was in Hennessey when he was in a loveless marriage, working two jobs, having multiple affairs and somehow found himself in the underground porn industry. He hadn't been happy and yet, it was as if he blindly went along with things until one day, he suddenly opened his eyes and looked around.

It was that day once again. Rather than being a sheep as Diego often suggested, he had to learn to be a wolf. Unfortunately, it seemed almost impossible to shift gears. Much like being caught up in a strong current, he only knew how to allow the tide to sweep him away into an unforgiving ocean.

It hit him as he sat across from an innocent child who believed that her mother had gone away over an embarrassing argument with Jorge Hernandez. It seemed unlikely that Maria would have any suspicions about her mother's extended disappearance and he pitied the day when she recognized that her father was dangerous. It would be a huge blow to her current, loving perception of a man that she looked at with idealizing eyes. Perhaps it was his own naïvety toward life that Chase saw in Maria and he regretted the day it would be lost, just as his own had been.

Where would he be that day? Chase feared the answer. Things were becoming more dangerous and yet, hadn't there been many warnings he chose to ignore? His instincts, the little things Chase noticed over time and yet, he had chosen to turn a blind eye to everything. Accepting his new and loving *familia* was the trade-off for him. It was something he hadn't had before and clearly, it was something that his heart craved above everything. Even if that meant getting caught up on the dark side.

He often had wondered how young men found themselves caught up in the 'gangster' lifestyle of crime and violence. He no longer wondered. The only difference between him and someone in a street gang was that he dressed a little better, looked slightly less conspicuous to strangers but underneath it all, he was the same. Jorge, Diego, Jolene, hadn't they all demonstrated that they weren't beyond committing a violent act to get what they wanted? Didn't they seek their own justice? Then again, weren't their justifications resonating with him? Was the entire world corrupt?

Rubbing his face with both hands, Chase suddenly felt completely exhausted and closed his eyes. Physically, mentally, he had nothing left to give. He wasn't even able to rationalize this situation or comprehend what it meant to him. Technically, he didn't 'know' anything for certain. Jolene and Diego had only openly revealed that drugs were sold at their parties. As for Jorge, other than seeing him threaten Deborah and shove her downstairs, he only had suspicions. Then there was Luke Prince.

"Chase?" Maria was suddenly beside him, her hand placed on his shoulder as he abruptly opened his eyes. "Are you okay?"

After hesitating for a moment, Chase took a deep breath and shook his head. "I can honestly say that I'm not sure."

She frowned, her huge chocolate eyes inspected his face before silently walking to the tray of food and bringing back the pot of coffee, lovingly filling his cup.

"This will make you feel better," She commented before returning it to the tray. "Chase, is it because you were drinking last night?"

"Thank you," He leaned forward in his chair, sitting the laptop on the table and reaching for the cup of coffee. "It's in part because I had a bit too much to drink last night but I also didn't sleep so well."

"I wish I knew yesterday that it was your birthday," Maria returned to her place on the couch and pulled her legs beneath her. "I would've bought you a present!"

"That's fine, Maria," Chase gently replied. "I don't need any gifts but thank you, you're very sweet."

"You're my friend, Chase," Maria confidently replied. "My one Canadian friend. I never had a Canadian friend before."

"No? Were you ever here before?"

She shook her head no.

"Mommy wouldn't let me travel a lot just sometimes," She continued. "Daddy thinks it's a great opportunity to learn about other cultures and real world stuff."

Chase let out a short laugh as he scratched his chin, wishing he had shaved that morning. Maria tilted her head and watched him.

"Do you agree?" She calmly asked. "Do you think I will learn more by traveling?"

"I'm sure you will," Chase nodded and took a drink of his coffee. "You're a very perceptive young lady."

"Chase, do you think my father is a bad man?"

The question couldn't have been more unexpected and he struggled with keeping a stoic expression.

"Of course not," He said in an unconvincing voice. "I think your father loves you and would do anything to give you the best life possible."

"But do you think he's a good person?" Maria asked as she pressed her lips together. "Mama used to say he was a bad man."

"Are your parents separated?" Chase calmly asked even though on the inside, he felt his heart racing. If he answered anything wrong, she could tell Hernandez and that was the last thing he wanted.

"Yes, they broke up last year."

"When relationships don't work," Chase started slowly, carefully weighing each word. "Sometimes people say mean things about one another because they are angry. Your mother was probably the same."

"But my father isn't a bad man," Maria scrunched up her forehead and shifted uncomfortably in her seat. "I cried when she told me that and when I told papa, he was upset. I thought he was going to cry too."

"People sometimes say things to hurt one another," Chase calmly tried to explain. "When my ex-wife and I broke up, we said some horrible things to and about one another. I'm sure it was the same with your parents."

"My papa, he never said anything bad about mama," Maria spoke proudly. "He only said nice things about her to me, even when she was being so mean."

"Your father is a good man," Chase managed to say the words with complete conviction, breaking eye contact and looking back into his coffee.

"I don't think she's coming back," Maria continued to speak and Chase felt a heaviness fill his limbs, his soul pulled down by the words. It broke his heart to hear because although she clearly favored her father, her instincts told her something was wrong that her mother had disappeared.

Chase returned his gaze to Maria as she shifted uncomfortably in her seat, his voice was soft yet strong when he replied, "I'm sure she will."

"She never left me before," Maria sniffed and blinked back her tears. "What if she is gone forever like your son?"

Instinctively, he crossed the room when the little girl started to cry. Sitting beside her, he pulled her into a hug and didn't reply at first, unsure of what to say.

"That's different, Maria," He slowly let go of her and looked into her eyes as she wiped the tears away. Reaching for a nearby tissue box, he pulled one out and handed it to her. "My son died. Your mother, she probably is just gone to see a friend or to do some traveling."

"She hasn't called or texted," Maria sniffed as she wiped her tears away. "She sent me a text from the airport and then went away. Daddy says he talked to her but I think he says that to make me feel better."

Chase didn't reply.

"What if she died?"

"She didn't die," Chase attempted to assure her. "Your dad would've told you if anything happened to her."

"I think he's scared of upsetting me," Maria was insistent as she pulled a blanket over her shoulders suddenly looking younger than her actual age. "So he's hiding something from me."

"I really don't think that's the case," Chase was insistent, relieved that her tears had stopped. "But maybe you should let him know how you feel. Personally, I think he would tell you if something was wrong."

She didn't reply but pulled the blanket closer.

Chase awkwardly stood up and walked toward the cart of food. "Can I get you something?"

She shook her head no.

It was while on his way back to the chair opposite Maria that she asked the question.

"Chase if you knew anything about my mother, you would tell me, right?"

An unmistakable confidence filled his voice as he turned and looked her in the eye. "Of course I would."

CHAPTER FORTY-FIVE

"What's with you?" Diego asked as they drove home that afternoon. The day had dragged by and all Chase wanted to do was jump in the shower and go to bed. His body felt heavy, his head ached and the many thoughts that plagued him were getting louder. Had Maria's mother been killed? As much as he had moments of sheer hatred toward his own ex-wife, times when his anger almost took over, he never would've killed her but Hernandez was different.

"I'm just tired," Chase replied and took a deep breath, glancing out the window at rush hour traffic as they slowly made their way home. "Today was a total write off for me."

"You looked after Hernandez's kid so some would say," Diego cleared his throat and Chase turned to look at him. "Some would say you might've had the most important job of the day."

"I don't know about that," Chase replied and reached for his bottle of water. "I think that kid could look after herself. She's pretty smart."

"Yeah but we aren't talking just anyone's kid," Diego sniffed. "We're talking about Hernandez's kid. If the right person thought she was alone and had a beef with him, they would think nothing of kidnapping her."

Chase felt incredibly naïve when this reality hit him because he certainly hadn't even considered it. Then again, no one had ever indicated that Hernandez was well known or sought after man in Mexico, so how was he to know? How prominent was this guy and were Canadian officials aware he was in the country? Was he being watched? A whole new level of fear grasped him, causing a tightness to grip his chest. Was *he* in danger?

"I didn't know that," He finally replied as his heart raced. "How big is this guy back in Mexico?"

"He's known," Diego replied, giving no further information. "The point is that he picked you for a reason. He sees you as someone he can trust. He sees you as someone who would do anything to protect his daughter. Plus you have that intimidating, bodyguard look that makes him feel safer, I dunno."

"I'm not sure how safe I feel right about now."

"That's why he wants to get you a gun," Diego spoke casually, making a face, he shrugged his shoulders. "I think he mentioned something about a taser as well."

'A gun? I've never used a gun," Chase spoke sharply, causing Diego to raise his eyebrows slightly, only taking his eyes off the road momentarily. "And a taser? Are those even legal to have in Canada?"

"Do you think Hernandez cares if they are illegal?" Diego let out a short laugh. "Trust me, in the right situation, you won't give a fuck if they're legal. You'll be goddamn happy to have access to either one and Jolene is going to teach you how to shoot."

"What? When?" Chase couldn't believe what he was hearing. "My son was shot and you guys think I seriously want to learn how to use a gun?"

"If it were my son," Diego spoke in a quiet, respectful voice. "That would make me *want* to learn. It's a dangerous world, Chase and we can only protect ourselves and our loved ones. No one else will do it for us."

Chase didn't reply. Obviously, his own circumstances were substantially different from that of an average Canadian. There was no going back now, that ship had sailed. Even if he tried, Chase had a feeling that he would never be able to escape this world he now lived in. He thought about it all afternoon and although in some ways it made him feel more protected, that was perhaps irrelevant in the face of the potentials dangers that these people had introduced into his life.

"So the kid, she really likes you," Diego commented as he reached for a bag beside him and pulled out a piece of red licorice and started to eat it. "Hernandez said she talked on and on about what a great day you had, everything you did, all the stores you went to and he was quite pleased. That's good, we want him pleased."

"It was cool. She's a nice kid," Chase felt himself going along with the conversation even though he couldn't quite get past the upcoming shooting lessons he was apparently about to take.

Of course, he also didn't count on it being the very next day either.

"Me and you," Jolene pointed at him as soon as he walked in the door. "We have a lesson later."

"*We* do?" Chase asked absently, still not feeling well since his drinking escapade two days earlier. Then again, after all the information he had swimming in his mind, it had been impossible to sleep.

"Yes, you and me, *we,*" She affectionately tapped his arm as they passed in the hallway and Chase immediately went into the staff room for a cup of coffee. Sylvana was standing at the counter, eating a cookie and immediately began to laugh when she saw him.

"So I hear you can add 'professional babysitter' to the list of your useless skills," Her comment was sharp, her eyes glared through him as he made his way to the coffee pot. "The rest of us are here working our asses off and you're out playing with someone kid all day." She started to walk away and Chase's eyes immediately focused on her full butt as she did so, he felt a surge of anger flow through him.

"Apparently, you didn't work much of your ass off," His voice was unexpectedly sharp as she turned around with a stunned look on her face and Chase felt an unexpected desire flow through him. Her full, round ass and how it wiggled slightly as she walked, the hint of cleavage that always tantalizing him when she bent over nearby, her aggressive nature that challenged him, teased him, taunted him. There was something different in her expression when their eyes met, a lust that flowed between them that he never would've expected. It was how Sylvana's lips gently fell opened as her eyes roamed his body for a long, intense silence that told him that something had changed.

While Diego, Jolene, Benjamin, and Beverly had a meeting to discuss the new venue, Verna worked diligently and Grace did research, Chase and Sylvana slipped out of the office with the excuse that he was checking something in her car. Instead, they breathlessly slipped into a vacant washroom on the first floor and proceeded to share a hungry kiss.

"We only have a few minutes," She instructed with some vulnerability in her voice, as she unbuttoned her blouse to show her full breast pouring out of a push-up bra, lifting her skirt, she wore a skimpy thong and Chase felt his breath only increase as he quickly grew hard. Her mouth covered his and she pulled him close, immediately moaning when he pushed her against the wall.

Not surprisingly, she called out a series of instructions; where to touch, how to caress, how fast, how slow and for some reason, he felt himself get more horny with each order, as his tongue made it's way down to her breasts, sliding into the front of her bra to tease her nipple while she gasped.

"Suck it," She cried as he followed her instructions and she loudly moaned. "I want you inside me...now..."

She gasped as he entered her, panting loudly, as he grabbed her ass and pulled her up, she tightly wrapped her legs around him as he moved deeper inside her, she continued to instruct him on the pace and forcefulness until she starting panting, 'Oh God' in his ear and unable to hold back for another second, he finally came inside her.

After a short recovery, they got themselves back together, both of their faces flushed, she suggested they return to the office as if in midst of an argument so that no one would suspect anything. It worked.

"Stupid redneck, I figured someone from Alberta would know about cars," She snapped as she returned while Verna ignored them as they entered the room, they quickly separated and Chase noticed the meeting was still on in the conference room.

Unfortunately, rather than satisfying him, his quick encounter seemed to instead make his body highly sensitive for the rest of the day. Especially later that morning at the gun range when Jolene was leaning up behind him, in attempts to show him how to hold and point the gun, her breasts pushed against his back, her hot breath on his neck, causing him to feel strong urges that were distracting him from the task at hand. His lack of ability was simply written off as being unsure of how to use a gun as well as being slightly off his game after his drunken birthday night.

"You will do great tomorrow," Jolene insisted after the lesson. "It will be fine."

"I'm not sure how comfortable I am with having a gun," Chase smoothly broached the subject as they walked to her car. "I mean, my son was shot."

"Do you not see, Chase, that is why you need to know," Jolene was as insistent as she unlocked the car as they got closer. "After all, you are looking after Maria. You must know how to protect her if anything were to happen."

It wasn't until they got in the car that he asked something that had been on his mind since the day before.

"Jolene, can I ask you something," Chase asked as she put on her seatbelt. "What happened to Maria's mother?"

"I don't know? She left, *maybe?*" Jolene spoke innocently and shrugged. "What did she say?"

"Vacation?" Chase asked skeptically.

"Then it is a vacation."

"Maria is scared something happened to her," Chase continued. "She saw her parents argue and then....her mother went missing."

"Chase, come on," Jolene made a face and started the car. "He probably tell her to go away for a while but she's fine. She was a bit of a princess, he tells me, so she probably is lying on a beach somewhere with drinks being served to her."

"Really?"

"Really!" Jolene was insistent. "The little girl, she has a wild imagination. That is all."

"Are you sure?"

"Yes, Chase, I am sure."

"I have one more question," Chase continued. "What about Luke Prince?"

"What about?" Jolene grabbed and pulled on her sunglasses. "He's gone."

"Do you know how?"

"Some hunter? Isn't that what your ex-wife say?" She replied but there was something in her voice, a distinct sound that faded out when she finished her sentence. "I do not worry about these things and you, neither should you. That man, he got what he deserve. That is what I say."

Chase opened his mouth to reply but promptly closed it instead.

"Has Diego say anything to you?" She finally continued. "About this?"

"No," Chase replied.

"Ok," She replied simply and focused on the road. "Then do not worry."

CHAPTER FORTY-SIX

"Diego, he cannot be in the dark no longer," Jolene's muffled voice could be heard through the walls as Chase opened his eyes and glanced at the clock. It was almost 7:30, which means he slept for over an hour since getting home from work. Closing them again, he simply wanted to escape; perhaps open his eyes to a different time, a different life, something that was easier than what he was dealing with at that point. Did he really have sex with a coworker he hated then go for shooting lessons with his boss? Was that a dream? A bizarre, *insane* dream?

Diego didn't reply and a long silence followed.

"Is it, you know, ok to talk about this?" Jolene asked and Diego could be heard moving around the living room. "Was she here today?"

"Yeah, she left earlier when we got home."

The only person that left earlier that day was the cleaning lady which led Chase to believe that he was dreaming and not actually overhearing a conversation. It didn't make sense that Diego would care if his housekeeper had been around or had someone else been in their apartment? What was he talking about?

"It is fine then?" Jolene asked and without waiting for a reply, she continued. "It is not fair for him to know so little when he could be in danger. I say we tell him everything."

"I don't think we should," Diego replied. "It should be a need to know basis. That way, he can honestly say he had no idea if anything were to happen. I don't want him involved in this mess."

"I say we tell," Jolene continued as if Diego hadn't spoken at all. "He needs to know. What if something happens and he's unprepared."

Silence followed.

"Okay, but not everything," Diego finally agreed.

"Today he ask about Luke Prince and Hernandez's ex? The girl's mother?"

"We don't tell him anything on Prince, it's too close to home," Diego insisted quietly and fell silent. "I don't know about Hernandez's ex but we know that he plays by his own rules."

"Do you think she is dead?" Jolene lowered her voice.

No reply could be heard.

Chase didn't move. He barely breathed upon hearing these words and although a part of him wanted to rise from the bed and interrupt the conversation, he waited instead and let the words sift through his mind. They felt heavy like a huge weight on his chest. Their conversation confirmed what he believed, the truth glaringly bright in his eyes. It didn't matter who killed Luke Prince; the reality was that it was Jolene and Diego that put the wheels in motion. Hernandez's ex might be alive but she was certainly in danger, and not laying on a beach somewhere, sipping on drinks.

It was after Jolene left that he got out of bed and took a shower. After changing into some comfortable clothing, he reluctantly wandered into the living room where he found Diego in the kitchen, unloading the dishwasher.

"Hey, I thought you were out for the night," Diego commented casually, a hint of something unfamiliar in his voice.

Shrugging, indifferent to the comment, Chase yawned and took a quick look into the fridge. Shutting the door, he decided against eating.

"Jolene said that the shooting lesson went ok today," Diego broke the awkward silence as he continued to put the rest of the dishes away. He turned toward Chase and their eyes briefly met before Diego looked away again. "She said that tomorrow you were getting down to business."

"I guess so," Chase replied and licked his lips. Moving toward the couch, his legs felt heavier with each step as if he were forcing them through a mountain of snow. Sitting, he wondered how to broach the topic. "I'm still not comfortable learning, though. Using a gun doesn't feel right to me."

Diego finished what he was doing and turned around. Standing behind the island that separated them, he didn't reply at first. "You might never need it but if you do, wouldn't you like to know how? Guns are more about security than they are about using them. Knowing they are there. It's kind of like a house alarm. You hope you never need it but there's a certain comfort knowing it is in place if you ever do."

"I suppose," Chase reluctantly agreed. "It seems like a stretch."

"It's not a stretch," Diego assured him. "Look, Chase, we must be vigilant. Now that Hernandez is getting more involved in this business, it does increase the potential for danger. We might not see or touch it but a lot of drugs are going through our parties. And with that, there's always a chance that things will take a bad turn."

"Is it worth it?" Chase asked, feeling slightly naïve. "I mean, why not have the parties as they are and keep the drugs out of it?"

"If we don't then we don't have an investor and we don't have a business," Diego spoke honestly. "Everything is expensive and we are new. We need the help and no one else was ever interested, regardless of how well we were doing, most potential investors were only interested in putting a minimal amount because they didn't fully trust our longevity."

"And Hernandez felt differently?"

"Hernandez knew differently," Diego corrected him. "He's been in from day one. Even in Alberta, you and Jolene running the office? Jorge was investing in us. We had attendees on the inside making sales. We weren't even sure that it would work but it took off immediately. Other than that OD once, the woman you drove to the hospital? We never had any other problems. We insist in our contract be signed before attending the parties that no drugs be brought in so instead, it's assumed that we have no idea, which protects us."

"So the contract is there to protect us, not the client?"

"It's never been about protecting the client," Diego assumed him. "It *never* is in these cases. Companies are out to make money and not be sued."

"So how do you work the money in,"

"We exaggerate our numbers. Fake clients so it looks like we are busier than we are. There are all kinds of ways to filter it in. Jorge wants our own establishment because we can increase our potential of doing this in various ways with fewer eyes watching so we don't have to worry about venue owners figuring things out. By the way, that's another reason we don't tend to use the same venues too often. We don't want any of these guys catching on."

Chase nodded as he considered these words. Everything was slowly coming together.

"Don't think that other nightclubs don't do this, by the way? It happens all the time," Diego added. "Bars aren't just selling you a drink and a good time, they often have drugs dealers in place, prostitutes, you name it. Those places are expensive to run in power alone, they need whatever brings people in and what makes them leave feeling satisfied with their night."

"It's not about the club but the experience," Chase calmly replied as Diego made his way from the kitchen to the living room, a cup of coffee in hand. Plunking on a nearby chair, he turned in Chase's direction.

"Nothing ever is how it seems in business," Diego took a deep breath. "And that's the kind of thing they *don't* teach you in business school."

"Wouldn't having our own venue shine more of a light on us?" Chase wondered. "Especially with religious groups complaining now?"

"Maybe, but even if someone was caught, we can honestly say we don't know them," Diego insisted. "We have a lot of drug dealers and most have a small amount on hand, which makes them less of a target if they're caught. They usually make it sound like it's their own stash that they're selling as if they are 'helping' the other person out. It's manipulative, but it works. It's all in the wording and believe me, Hernandez has them well-trained on how to proposition someone for drugs or anything else."

"Are there prostitutes at our parties?"

"There are a few in place to seem like guests, yes," Diego replied and made solid eye contact with Chase. "That has been the case from day one as well. Hernandez also takes care of that and these guests have to show interest in the less....we'll say, desirable or popular guests. They're paid well to do so."

"How do we know none of these people will talk if they're caught?"

"Hernandez picks them carefully and he makes it very clear that if they open their mouths," He hesitated for a moment. "Let's just say, they know better than to talk. They can walk away if they don't want to do it but they must never tell anyone. Trust me, he knows everyone has a weak point and he's not beyond taking care of it."

Chase felt his heart race and he looked away.

"Don't worry, you're in good with Hernandez," Diego appeared to read his mind. "And that's exactly what you want."

"So why do I need a gun?" Chase got back to his original point. "What kind of danger is he in?"

"It's not that he's in danger necessarily," Diego replied. "He's well protected. He has a lot of government contacts back home as he did in the US and here in Canada. How do you think me and Jolene are getting our citizenship pushed ahead without waiting years? The man is well-connected. He's untouchable."

"But how?"

Diego shook his head. "Look, his family, they're protected. They've always been protected in Mexico and elsewhere. As much as the government tries to say that drugs are the root of all evil to the public, in private, they know that they add to the economy. Look at me. I created more jobs because of drugs. I buy nice things and spend money because of drugs. I put money back into the economy because of drugs. As much as we want to make them the problem with society, they are merely a symptom and most of the time, people are only casual users. That is how I see it. As long as Jorge keeps out of the news, keeps under the radar, no one cares what he does. The minute someone complains, they will arrest his ass and pretend that they always have known about him and were 'investigating'. That is how the police work. But with his lawyers, they'd have him out of it in no time. He makes it very hard to connect him to this case."

"And he tells people he works in coffee?" Chase asked, still attempting to process all this information. "Isn't that his cover up?"

"He *technically does* works for his father," Diego grinned and held up his cup. "They are in coffee."

"Why didn't you tell me all this before?"

"I figured, you know, the less you know, the better. You know me, I'm a little protective of you," Diego gave a shy smile and shrugged. "But Jolene, she thinks we need to tell you more to cover yourself."

"So the police?"

"Some care, some don't," Diego shook his head. "What difference? Even crime creates jobs. Even if all the illegal drugs were off the market tomorrow, it would only give the big pharma companies more power because addicts are their bread and butter. But that's ok cause they wear nice suits and have expensive lawyers."

Chase couldn't help but grin at this comment.

"That is why *we* wear nice suit and hire expensive lawyers," Diego spoke smugly. "Two can play at that game, *amigo.*"

CHAPTER FORTY-SEVEN

After Diego told him the truth, Chase began to think about all the little things that happened since he started to work with Jolene and suddenly, so many things made sense. The clues had always been there for him but yet, he had never been one to make assumptions. Although he once thought himself as naïve, he now felt it was because he had always viewed the world in black and white. Diego brought out a lot of grey.

He thought back to the woman who overdosed a year earlier while he was still working in Calgary. At the time it occurred to him that maybe dealers might be in place at the party but then felt ashamed for assuming that his Colombian boss would necessarily be involved in such a thing. It also explained why his former friend Maggie quit her job as a hostess, especially in her pursuit to join the RCMP. How much did she know? Being inside the party gave her a lot more opportunities to see, an advantage Chase never had while working at the door.

It took him a few days to accept this new reality. Although it made him a little nervous, it also was strangely intriguing. It seemed as though every detail was considered; from how to get the drugs in the bars, to how to sell them and cover everyone's ass in the process. Diego didn't talk to him about how they got drugs into the country but from the sounds of it, it didn't seem like Jorge Hernandez would have any trouble especially when he was so politically connected. It was an eye-opening conversation for Chase, one that would change his view on business, society, and government.

He now watched the news with cynical eyes. His brain constantly analyzing the words, dissecting the information given, putting it together in light of his new perception. Politicians were merely robots wearing starched suits, their lips repeating words written by someone else after careful analysis on the topic by a third-party, burned to the memory of the talking head. Business news made him laugh. The fake concern about community matters and charity was so overblown, insincere, only in place to remove attention away from the evil many were doing; polluting the environment, poisoning customers with questionable ingredients in their products and intimidating their employees to go with the flow. Society was a fucking mess and yet, he worried about working for Diego, Jolene, and Hernandez? At least he felt loyalty and could most people say that about their employer?

It was about a week after his conversation with Diego that they had another one that was just as eye-opening. It was almost as if he wanted to give Chase enough time to allow the information to absorb before handing him more details. The two had just walked in the condo on a Friday night and while Chase smiled at the housekeeper, Diego immediately started speaking to her in Spanish in a lively exchange. The two laughed and glanced in Chase's direction as he checked the mail and threw it on the island. Their conversation continued before she said *buenos noches* and left.

Chase sat on the couch and was about to check a message on his phone when Diego walked past him and plunked down in his usual chair. It was small, expensive and apparently imported from somewhere or another; a luxury Diego would insist on while shopping for something as basic as a chair. His eyes fixated on Chase, he looked as if he wanted to speak but didn't know what to say.

"What's up, Diego?" Chase sat back on the couch, sliding the phone in his pocket, his body relaxed. "What did the cleaning lady say?"

"Her?" Diego pointed toward the door. "Ah nothing, well, not really anyway. I do want to tell you something about her though."

"Is she a drug dealer too?" Chase joked and Diego's face fell into an evil smirk and he shook his head.

"No, *amigo* but she's no normal cleaning lady either," He seemed to relax slightly, his arm leaning against one side of the chair. "That woman there, she cleans, yes, but she also does a little extra work for me too."

"Her?" Chase glanced toward the door as if it somehow represented the Latino woman who dropped by every Friday afternoon.

"She checks the apartment for cameras, listening devices, that kind of thing," Diego spoke casually as if it were the normal 'extra duty' of a housecleaner. "She knows where to look, what to look for, all of that and she makes sure we are secure here and also, we have her go into the office a couple of days a week. That is why Jolene goes in so early, so she can meet up with her before the rest of the staff gets there."

Although stunned by this news, the situation was so absurd that it made him laugh. "You're joking, right? This sounds like something out of one of my mother's soap operas."

"I do not joke about this kind of thing," Diego insisted with a serious expression. "So far, nothing here in Toronto but one must always be careful."

"Isn't this a little paranoid?" Chase wondered out loud.

"No because we have found something in Jolene's old office," Diego shuffled uncomfortably in his chair. "That was another reason we left Calgary. We didn't feel as secure there. Toronto had always been good to us business-wise, so we come here."

"So there was something in Jolene's office?"

"A small listening device, yes," Diego nodded. "The time that I met you? That time, something was found during a routine search that Hernandez insisted on. Even we thought it was extreme until we actually found something. That is why we are iffy about talking about this kind of business at the office and try to take it to a public place, somewhere away from others."

"So you came to Calgary to talk to Jolene about what she found?"

"Yes and to meet you, of course," Diego insisted. "I was a little concerned it was you who planted it but right away, we figure it was your little friend, Maggie. Perhaps trying to get in good with the RCMP, she was pretty desperate for them to accept her, so it made sense."

"I don't think Maggie would do that," Chase interjected but Diego was already nodded.

"Oh yes, she did and I made her confess," He spoke honestly. "That is why she left. She had nothing, just a hunch and both me and Jolene had a very *stern* conversation with her and that is why she not only stays away from us now, she probably stays away from you."

This news shocked Chase. He knew Maggie had her suspicions and hinted to that effect but she was trying to build proof against Jolene and Diego? He felt betrayed as a combination of deceit and anger filled him. Even though they had been friends for years, it seemed obvious that she was willing to throw him under the bus without a second thought. He thought about how the police once paid a visit to their office asking to speak to Maggie about her sister, who was missing at the time. He thought it was weird that they would even know where to find her, especially since she was only part-time and rarely at the office during weekdays. It was all coming together and he didn't like the picture.

"I didn't know if I should tell you at first," Diego quietly admitted. "Jolene said you were close to her growing up and she felt it would hurt you, that it was better to not say anything but we talked it over and decided that you had to know the truth. There is a possibility that she will return to your life and if she does, at least you will know why."

Stunned, Chase never would've thought she would be involved with something like that.

"But if she wasn't in the RCMP, why would they let her get involved?" Chase asked as he attempted to sort out the details. "Plus, didn't you say we are protected?"

"We are protected at the top but not from every officer out there. It's our job to keep off the radar," Diego shook his head with a neutral expression on his face. "As for Maggie, why do you think she disappeared? She was training. They must've liked that she was proactive and trying to help with a case against us. Needless to say, she could be a huge problem."

"Hernandez went to your hometown to talk to her sister," Diego continued. "Not just because he was researching you to make sure you could be trusted but because he wanted to learn more about Maggie, through Kelsey. He knew that the younger sister liked to talk a lot, had issues with the law and so he set it up that they would have a nice, drunken chat. When he did, he found out everything he had to know to put the pieces together."

"But why would Kelsey tell this stranger anything?"

"He found out she was on a dating site and decided to make his move that way," Diego spoke calmly and folded his hands together. "And he's handsome, so of course, he charmed her, went to visit her town, got her drunk, asked a lot of casual questions and here we are.... we know Maggie is in the RCMP, that she did a 'special favor' to help earn brownie points? I think that is what she said."

"Wow," Chase shook his head. "I can't believe she would do that."

"Believe it," Diego insisted. "You, however, checked out perfectly. You always have. Hernandez said she talked about missing you, about what a great father you were, how great you were with the kids and that is when he got the idea that maybe you should keep an eye on Maria for him. He also heard about you threatening that bar owner very forcefully, I might add, when you learned about the underaged porn Kelsey was in. He thought that spoke to your character and loyalty and that is why, my friend, you're in such high regards to Hernandez. He wants to think you would do the same if anyone ever came near his little girl. He wants to know you would go to great lengths to protect her."

Chase silently thought about his words before finally replying. "I would. Even if it wasn't Hernandez's kid, I wouldn't let anyone hurt her."

"He sees that with you," Diego insisted. "You, my friend, will always be protected too as long as he feels that the loyalty goes both ways."

Chase nodded and allowed these new revelations to gently fall into his consciousness and he felt stronger than he ever had before as if the door to the truth had finally been opened.

"That is why your son's killer, he is cold in his grave," Diego admitted, his eyes grew softer. "We would never allow someone to hurt one of our own and not pay. You're our brother, our family."

Chase felt his emotions weighing heavy on his heart. He had never had this kind of connection with his real family. Sadly, he didn't even feel this strong connection with his own sons, regardless of how hard he tried. No one had ever risked anything for him before and no one had ever let him know that he mattered. Swallowing back the lump in his throat he looked in Diego's eyes and nodded. There was a deeper understanding that no words could express.

"Unfortunately, we live in a world where loyalty means so little that when we find it, we must respect it," Diego continued and sat forward in his chair. "So, we keep in contact, we keep our eyes open and we stay vigilant. This condo, Jolene's, the office, we check everything regularly because we can never be too careful. We also have our own camera so we can check all three places when we wish. We place them near the doors to keep an eye for anyone who might come in that is unfamiliar."

"So the camera is by the door here?" Chase asked and glanced around the room. "Like, in the lights?"

Diego shook his head.

"Picture?" He pointed toward a photo of him and Jolene.

Diego shook his head.

"The mirror?"

"No."

"Where then?"

Diego rose from his seat and walked toward the lime tree, turning it around in a way that hid the pieces of fruit forming and pointed in the tree. Chase rose from the couch and briskly walked over, he got very close and at first, he couldn't see a thing. Then he saw it. Small, almost completely hidden, it was in the direction that Diego always insisted when they left the house.

"Your lime tree?" Chase grinned as he stood back up. "You've had a camera hidden in your *lime* tree all this time? Is that why you have it?"

Diego twisted his lips and made a face. "Who would suspect? No one!" He grinned and then his expression grew serious. "But, you know, I really do like limes."

CHAPTER FORTY-EIGHT

"I did not think that you would want to know," Jolene gently commented over a glass of wine. Her eyes sparkled when met with the dim lights of the small Italian restaurant, as the three of them joined together on a Saturday night. Diego sat in silence, a pensive expression on his face. The enticing aromas from the kitchen filled the room, tantalizing Chase as he attempting to focus on her words and in a way, he didn't want to talk about it anymore. Hidden cameras, drugs, deception, loyalty or lack thereof; it was a lot to process. His life was starting to feel like a television series.

"I am sorry about Maggie," Jolene continued and stared into her glass of wine for a moment before continuing. "But you know I never like her. I always had a bad feeling, you know? She had walls up and that made me suspicious. I couldn't put my finger on it but I knew something was not right."

"You were right," Diego cut in and the two made eye contact then both shifted their attention to Chase. "But I don't understand something, Chase. If she was suspicious of us and she thought of you as a good friend, why would she bring you in on all of this? Why would she recommend you to Jolene?"

Chase considered his words for a moment, fearing they were possibly suspicious of him. Parting his lips slowly, he clamped them shut again and mused.

"We weren't close after she moved," Chase considered as he reached for his own glass of wine, hoping it would take the edge off the conversation. "She thought something was going on with me and her sister Kelsey and it pissed her off. She barely even spoke to me anymore."

"But why would she care?" Jolene gently coaxed. "She is gay. It's not like she wanted you herself."

"Kelsey was young, she wasn't even 18 and was already a trainwreck," Chase smirked when he thought about it and shook his head. "Not that I was much better at that time but I did the right thing. I tried to be Kelsey's friend and keep it that way but it didn't seem to matter because both women weren't happy. Kelsey was mad that I wouldn't hook up. Maggie was mad at me....I don't even know why. I guess she assumed I was taking advantage of Kelsey."

"Yes, I was surprised when you moved to Calgary and you weren't spending time with Maggie," Jolene said and twisted her lips. "It was as if you were a stranger to her, you know?"

"That's how I felt," Chase replied and noted that Diego was listening carefully. "Even when I left Calgary, she wished me luck, said goodbye and that was it. But still, I can't believe that she was trying to help the RCMP."

"She admitted it," Diego repeated the same fact he had told Chase the previous night. "I was pretty forceful on the subject but the truth, it came out."

The waitress interrupted their conversation to take their orders. After she left, Diego finally spoke.

"I'm wondering if somewhere down the line, she could come in handy," He twisted his lips while lifting a glass of wine. "I mean, we can always feed her lies as well as the truth."

'Nah nah, we keep away from her," Jolene shook her head. "I say, Chase, you get a new phone number. If I were you, I would keep her and that Kelsey good and far away. Both of them are trouble. We don't need the girl who talks too much or a police girl anywhere near us. Keep them both far, far away."

Chase nodded and felt his phone vibrate. Glancing at it quickly, he saw another text from Sylvana. Since their original hookup at work, she had gone out of her way to avoid him until earlier that day, when she suggested that they talk. He ignored the text. As the truth came out, the more certain he was that it was best to keep a safe distance from his coworkers. It was necessary to separate work from play.

"Is there anything else I need to know?" Chase was hesitant to continue with this topic because he felt as though all these new facts continued to accumulate.

Diego and Jolene exchanged looks and he immediately knew the answer.

"We talk to you about this now because when we open new place, you will take on more responsibility," Jolene confessed sheepishly. "Rather than going place to place, having our little parties, we will now be working at a regular location and therefore, we will be moving more product. We must be ready for anything."

Chase remained quiet and looked away. Although there was a part of him that felt as though he were sinking in quicksand with no way out, another part of him felt his loyalty to Jolene and Diego strengthen. They were his family now. His sister and mother had no contact with him since Leland's death and his remaining children appeared less and less interested in their Skype conversations. To them, Albert was their daddy.

His attention shifted back to Jolene then Diego's as they quietly watched him. Rubbing his eyes, Chase exhaled loudly and shrugged. "Just tell me what I gotta do."

Sensing their relief, Chase felt himself relax, knowing that they had his back.

Hernandez had a way to slinking in and out of town without either a hello or goodbye, returning the following Monday, he sent direct orders to Diego to drop Chase off at his hotel. Assuming he was back to babysitting duty, Chase didn't hide his disappointment when Maria wasn't in the hotel suite but was back in Mexico.

"Ah, I love that!" Jorge's face lit up and he pointed toward Chase upon seeing his disappointed reaction. "I love that my daughter means this much to you. It means you will treat her as your own and that is my wish. She will always be safe with you."

Without skipping a beat, he pointed toward the nearby couch. "Please, sit down, Chase."

Following his instructions, Chase felt compelled to react to Jorge's comments. He sought his approval in the same way he did with Diego and Jolene. In fact, he needed it.

"You're right, Maria will always be safe when she's with me," Chase remained stoic as he watched Jorge sit across from him, his dark eyes carefully watching him. "I lost a child. There's no way I would ever let anyone go through the same thing."

"I know," Jorge replied, his eyes narrowed in on Chase, as if analyzing every line on his face, he slowly continued. "I'm counting on it."

A chill ran through Chase's body and he felt his heart pick up the pace, pounding like a mad bull in his chest, he suddenly felt a cruel possibility pass through his head and he quickly pushed it away. It was much too cruel to even consider. It would suggest that Jorge Hernandez was more dangerous than he originally thought. He couldn't, he wouldn't think about it. Instead, he glanced at the floor and took a deep breath.

"Today, we have something to take care of," His comment was sharp and quickly pulled Chase back into the conversation. "We must have a conversation with someone. We're having a bit of difficulty with the former owner of our new club. Everything else is in place and the sale went through but he isn't getting some of his shit out of the venue. I told him originally to have it completely cleaned before we took over and the place is a fucking dump. We need to go pay him a visit and reaffirm this information."

Chase had a feeling that he was the one who would be taking care of things. Was this a test? He felt as though Hernandez was still questioning his loyalty.

"Ok," Chase replied without any hesitation. "Tell me what you need."

"I need you to let him know that we aren't fucking around," Jorge tilted his head and twisted his eyes up, in doing so, he projected a less charming side but instead, a dark, penetrating look that was like that of an animal about to attack. "I need you to remind him that we are in charge here, not him."

"I know you can, Chase," he continued. "I know you have it in you. Just remember that this guy is a fucking lowlife. He isn't a classy businessman, he's some bum that happened to take over his father's nightclub and almost sunk it into the ground cause he was too busy snorting coke in his office to look after his business and now, it's gone. It's time for him to take his shit and get the fuck out."

Jorge wasn't exaggerating. The former owner met them at the bar and not only was he kind of sketchy looking, dressed like a 80s rock star wannabe, he wore sunglasses inside as they walked through and Hernandez pointed out all the issues he had with his new club, including rat traps in the corners, boxes or crap piled everywhere and old equipment that was no longer functional, which appeared to be dragged into the middle of the floor for no other reason other than to aggravate. The place was filthy with garbage thrown everywhere, including half-eaten food, which was probably where the rat traps came in. Needless to say, the smell was reprehensible; the stench of piss and rotting rat carcasses filled the air.

"This is a fucking mess. I want it cleaned, I want an exterminator in here and I want it done this week. No more fucking around," Hernandez spoke directly, glancing at his legs. "And if this place isn't in mint condition this time next week, you may have some mobility issues."

"What are you fucking threatening me again?" The rock star wannabe started to laugh, shoving his hands in his jacket pockets. "You don't get it, you fucking wetback, you already forced this club out of my hands, you didn't even give me a fair price and now you think I'm going to clean it for you? If you want it clean, get your errand boy to fucking clean it."

His last comment directed at Chase, who didn't even see it coming; a storm of rage gathered as he walked over and ripped off his sunglasses and threw them on the floor. Underneath, the man's blue eyes were suddenly wide open and full of fear, the same fear he had attempted to hide when using tough talk moments earlier, the fear that only made Chase feel stronger.

"I want to look in your fucking eyes and hear you say all that one more time," His last words dragged out, the brave no longer spoke but shrunk under Chase's powerful gaze. It was then that he reached forward, grabbing hold of the man's cheap leather jacket and pulled him forward. The man smelled of coffee, cigarettes and rank breath.

"We want this place clean, so fucking clean that you can eat off the floor and we want it done by next week or I'm going to find you, and I'm going to beat you so bad that you will wish you were dead and they're going to find you outside in the trash, with all this other shit," He saw the man attempt to squirm away and grasped him even harder. "You racist, redneck piece of shit. Don't you ever disrespect either of us again. When we tell you to do something, you better fucking do it."

Chase suddenly pushed him to the floor as he cried out in pain, holding his arm.

"Oh," Jorge piped up as Chase stepped back. "And don't get any crazy ideas cause I also know where your family lives and works." He shoved both hands in his pockets then turned his attention toward Chase with a sinister smile on his face. "His mother in the North end, she seems like a lovely woman but you know, sometimes these nursing homes, they make mistakes."

Without going into more detail, Hernandez turned and started toward the door. Chase looked back at the former owner on the floor, attempting to slowly get up, his eyes full of fear.

"Leave her out of it, I got this," His voice was suddenly accommodating and as much as Chase hated to admit it, there was something in that moment that he enjoyed. It was the power. And it was at that moment, he knew he was in the most trouble of all because there was no greater high than he felt as he looked into the eyes of a man who was fearing for his life. Nothing else had ever made him feel this way; not love, not lust, no pleasure was as intense as how he felt that moment. He was now the wolf.

CHAPTER FORTY-NINE

One week later, the new venue was immaculate. Garbage was removed and the entire place sparkled, leaving Hernandez satisfied with the results. A cleaning woman was finishing up when the two men arrived, an older, Chinese woman personally took them for a tour through the building to prove that everything was exactly how they wanted it. At one point Hernandez squatted down to the floor and rose his eyebrows, a huge grin crossed his face as he looked at Chase and pointed down.

"I can literally see my reflection," He slowly stood up while the cleaning lady beamed at his compliment and Chase merely nodded, showing little expression.

"He told me to get your approval and give you the keys before I leave," She reached into her pocket and pulled out the spare set and Jorge took them with a smile on his face then shrugged.

"It don't matter. We got someone coming over to change the locks shortly." He gestured toward the exit. "But thank you."

After complimenting the Chinese woman again and walking her to the door, Hernandez dropped his Hollywood smile and made his way back toward Chase, raising his eyebrows. "Looks like you did good. Your threat worked well. Now we gotta get Diego's cleaning lady in here to check it a little closer. One can never be too careful"

He reached into his pocket and pulled out a pack of gum. He offered a piece of Chase who shook his head no, saying he didn't chew gum.

"You shouldn't," Jorge insisted as he shoved two pieces in his mouth. "I'm trying to quit smoking and so I picked up another disgusting habit. I made a promise to Maria to stop."

"She's a smart lady," Chase commented as he shoved his hands in his pockets. "You should listen to her."

"The only woman I would ever listen to," Jorge commented casually as he walked toward the window and gazed out then walked back, looking around the former nightclub. "I wonder how many people met here, fell in love or...or lust, had kids, married, divorced, hated one another and came back to start it all over again."

"That's kind of depressing, isn't it?" Chase shrugged. "I dunno, I always thought people saw bars as more of an escape from their real lives. A way to forget about their problems for a while, to dance, to have fun."

"Maybe," Jorge forcefully chewed his gum. "But when you think about it, is any of it real? Life, it's a series of experiences and the only ones that mean anything are the ones that we decide should. You are right, people see it as an escape, just like Jolene and Diego's business. It's like a secret, naughty fantasy they want to experience and feel it's ok because others want to do the same. It's like they share the same secret and secrets, they are very powerful."

Chase considered the secret that had been silently sitting in a corner since Luke Prince's murder. The police had all but given up on the case, deciding that there were no leads to who murdered the murder. Perhaps, they cast a blind eye as well. Cops were human too and no one wanted to see a child die. Chase felt there was compelling evidence that Jolene was the shooter and other times, he suspected it was Hernandez or someone he hired that did the deed. Maybe it didn't matter and in the end, perhaps he would never know the truth.

"I'm going to get Jolene and Diego over here," Jorge commented as he continued to chomp on his gum and he point around the room. "We have to wait for the locksmith anyway and by the way, the four of us will have a set of keys; you, me, Jolene and Diego."

"Me?" Caught off guard by this remark, Chase turned toward Jorge, who was texting. "I'm going to have a set of keys too?"

"Of course you are," Jorge replied as he finished the text and looked up. "You're as much a part of this as the rest of us and you've earned it. We want you to help oversee the bar, didn't they tell you? I mean, unless you'd rather be stuck in the office with Diego all day." He laughed. "And let's face it, no one wants to be stuck anywhere with Diego all day."

"But me?" Chase felt skeptical. "Can I run a bar? I mean I don't know."

"There's nothing to know," Jorge shrugged. "Benjamin will work with you to set up the books but generally, he will be overseeing them. Jolene and Diego will still be your bosses, telling you what is going on and basically, you make sure no one burns this place down and that you scare the staff enough that you can keep them under your thumb. At least, that would be my recommendation. Order stuff, sign papers when it arrives, its pretty basic. Jolene will be here awhile to show you what to do. Diego will drop by to scare your staff because, let's face it, he looks pretty menacing."

Laughing at his own joke, Jorge glanced at his phone. "Oh, they're on their way. Perfect." Sliding the phone in his pocket, he continued to chomp on his gum. "Hey, you'll be given a raise too. Don't get me wrong, there's a lot of responsibility. You have to keep your eyes open and be alert. If the police ever show up, you know nothing and call our lawyer. But we will get into that more later."

As much as a part of him wanted to protest, fearing he wouldn't be capable of doing the job, another part of Chase wanted it. He wanted to be the boss. He wanted Jolene, Diego, and Jorge to know they could count on him. He wanted to make them proud.

"Wow, I'm really grateful," Chase struggled with his words and still wasn't sure if he picked the right ones as he watched Jorge remove the gum from his mouth, place it in a nearby garbage can and take out another two pieces. "I'm just a bit...shocked..."

"I thought you knew we were going to get your more involved," Jorge said as he shoved fresh gum in his mouth. "This is part of it and we've only just begun."

It was as if time sped up after that conversation, as if the hours and days flew by as they prepared for the opening of the new venue which would simply be called JD Exclusive Club. Heavily advertised, the first few weeks were booked solid. One of the many intriguing points to potential and former customers was that it was difficult to get in; you had to have the money and sign a very detailed agreement before being considered. In fact, the exclusivity was stronger than ever before and gave the company a right to say no, if they felt someone wasn't a good fit. They did so with the claim that they wanted their customers to feel safe and comfortable.

Of course, in reality, their main concern was not allowing people of a suspicious nature in the door. They were especially careful now that they were bringing in more drugs; what Diego referred to as 'mountains of cocaine'. Everything would be done with ease and carefulness. It seemed pretty solid but there was still some worries of the police getting involved but as Diego would often point out, there were always risks.

Life moved forward. The grand opening happened and was a special invite to former customers, a way of encouraging future patronage with free food and drinks, the ability to socialize and see the new venue and everything it had to offer. It received rave reviews on their Facebook page and website, indicating that they were professional, creating a luxurious and safe environment for those who wanted to explore their sensual side in a less conventional way; although Chase would later learn that many of the more over the top reviews were actually bought, overall people appeared pretty excited about their new venue and this was proven by the increase in bookings and events. Life, as Diego would say, was beautiful.

And as much as Chase loved the club, he missed the office. He missed seeing his coworkers regularly, the same people he was with for a year, the meetings in the boardroom and the constant ranting of Diego about everything from the coffee to his frustrations with 'the Italian' but endings were a normal part of life and for Chase, there had been many, but there were some that were harder than others.

One day Audrey contacted him about her future marriage to Albert and tactfully asked him if her new husband could adopt Chase's two boys. It was like his heart sank right to the floor when she quietly confirmed how they now saw this man as their father and even though she had a lot of wonderful things to say about Chase, nothing sank in after those first few words. They instead floated on top while he felt brokenhearted over her request.

He ended the conversation feeling stunned, as he sat alone in his new office, Chase suddenly began to go over the last few years in his mind. There had been a slow, careful unraveling of his relationship with the boys that he blamed himself for but at the same time, hadn't Audrey also contributed? How many times had she promised he could talk to them only to have a last-minute excuse? Hadn't she convinced him that it would be better for the boys if they bonded with Albert? If he stayed away for periods of time?

He attempted to work. He attempted to preoccupy himself but Audrey's words continued to resurface throughout the day, asking him to allow Albert to adopt his two remaining sons. It was like a kick in the stomach especially having lost Leland. Audrey somehow managed to spin the entire situation, using that tragedy as a way to emphasize how important it was for their family unit to have more stability. Chase wasn't stable in her eyes and she wanted him to step back.

His thoughts were so cluttered and confused, his mind so haunted, that Chase didn't hear Diego and Jorge walk in the club and jumped when they entered his office.

"You were a million miles away just now," Hernandez pulled up a chair as he chomped on a mouthful of bubble gum while beside him, Diego appeared troubled upon seeing Chase's face. The two had been friends and roommates for over a year now and without a doubt, he was the one person that knew Chase better than anyone. Slowly pulling his chair over, his dark eyes met with Chase's and immediately looked away, a sullen expression on his face.

"I guess you could say I was," Chase replied honestly. "Just some shit from back home."

"Back home? You mean that redneck town you're from?" Jorge asked as his eyes zeroed in on Chase, taking in everything carefully, he suddenly seemed concerned. "Oh yeah, what's going on there?"

"You know," Chase replied as he shook his head. "It don't matter."

Jorge tilted his head forward, his eyes gazed up and he continued to inspect Chase's face while chewing his gum. Diego bit his lip and shrugged.

"What's up? I'm family. Tell me." Diego insisted.

"He's your family," Jorge attempted to lighten the mood with a sarcastic quip. "What more could you want?"

Chase grinned and took a breath as the two sets of eyes zeroed in on him.

"My ex-wife wants her new man to adopt my kids," Chase said with a shaking voice, something that seemed to surprise him as much as the two men who sat across from him. He noted that while Diego looked sympathetic, his eyes reaching out to Chase, a shot of fury ran through Hernandez's face.

"No fucking way," Jorge snapped and he sat ahead in the chair, his forehead wrinkled and his eyes became small, dark, full of anger. "You tell her that those are your kids and you aren't fucking signing anything."

"Chase, I gotta tell you," Diego calmly added. "I'm not surprised. She's been pulling them away from you for months and even during the funeral, I kinda sensed she...I dunno, it was weird, it was as if she wanted to put a wall up between you and the twins. It didn't feel right but at the time, I didn't feel I should say."

"Ex-fucking wives and girlfriends," Jorge shook his head. "They take and take and take. Maria's mother tried to pull this kind of shit on me and I said no fucking way. And this, this isn't going to happen either."

"I don't understand," Chase attempted to make sense of it. "We don't have a bad relationship. It's not like we fight. In fact, we get along better than we ever did."

"Women are always playing games," Hernandez shook his head and continued to chomp on his gum, now with more aggression. "Fucking crazy shit."

"Nah," Diego shook his head slowly. "I was there. I mean, during the funeral. They do have a good relationship. In fact, I was surprised about how warmly she was with you, Chase. I hadn't expected that. She even told me to look out for you after the funeral cause she was worried. So, it's not out of anger toward you."

"Maybe she feels it's a good idea," Chase shrugged apathetically. "Maybe she's right."

Jorge didn't take his eyes off Chase. In fact, he didn't even blink as he took everything in and finally, he eased his hand out in front of him and in an eerily calm voice said. "Don't sign anything yet. This don't add up. Let me look into this for you."

Diego shuffled uncomfortably in his chair and Chase quietly nodded.

CHAPTER FIFTY

If there was a crazy train, Chase Jacobs was on it. Where he once was a passenger, watching as the train moved along the track, easing through tunnels and passing through small towns, he was now in the driver's seat. He spent his entire life being compliant, going along with everyone's wishes and not chasing after his own desires. As a child, his mother had taught him that he was not in control of his own life but merely an actor that followed a director's instructions, unable or incapable of creating his own destiny. The scary part was that he believed it.

Working with Diego, Jolene and now Jorge Hernandez had brought to light that in a world full of sheep, always be a wolf. He had zero doubt that no one could or ever would control any of their destinies and for that, he had admiration and sometimes fear. His fear, however, wasn't because he worried any of them would hurt him but rather, he wondered about the path he might be headed on. Although it felt completely natural, he was brought up to never hurt anyone and to do the 'right thing' however that definition differed from person to person. To the Silvas and Jorge Hernandez, some things justified a barbaric punishment. Real life was not a politically correct television series that ended with the 'good' guys winning and the 'bad' guys losing. Only the naïve believed that Hollywood bullshit.

Everything was changing so fast. But with those changes, sometimes something familiar from the past rises again. A certain person, place or thing that brings you back to another time and place, when you were less jaded about the world, perhaps a little less tough, back to a day when you believed in a certain magic that no longer seemed possible.

Maybe it had never been real at all or maybe, it stopped being possible when you stopped believing. Chase wasn't sure but it was the dreary morning that he heard a soft voice say his name, just as he was about to walk in the club to start his workday, that he turned around to see her.

"Wow, small world!" Maggie was walking toward him wearing a long coat and heels as she approached casually as if it were a mere coincidence that she was in this particular city and on the club's street that morning. He felt his heart race and he was suddenly back in Hennessey, during a time when he would've done anything to make her fall in love with him. It was the same girl who took him home from a disastrous party on the night that their friendship formed but yet, where was she? No longer the girl in cut-off jeans and t-shirt, no longer the gentle, sweet teenager, the woman who walked toward him may have had a smile on her face but her eyes were sizing him up, analyzing him carefully, as if preparing her next move. Like an animal about to quietly pounce on something she viewed as inferior to herself, she moved toward him and swept him up into a cold hug.

As she moved away, the smile falling from her lips, she stepped back and was silent for a moment, as if to re-evaluate the situation. Chase ignored the part of him that was heartbroken over the girl she had once been, on those hot days when only his hormones ruled, knowing that she wasn't interested in him or any man at all. Hadn't she always manipulated him? Hadn't she always known how he felt about her and took advantage of it until it wasn't convenient? Wasn't that exactly what she was doing again?

"What are you doing here?" Chase quietly asked her as she awkwardly bit her lip. Her blue eyes searching his, she finally looked away.

"We should talk," She spoke honestly. "It's important. Can we go somewhere?"

"I don't have time to talk," His answer was abrupt and he could see she was a little shocked by his reaction. "I have work to do."

"It's important."

"I *don't* have time."

"Chase, these people you're working with," Maggie started carefully. "You have to get away from them. Hernandez is a very dangerous man. I know he doesn't seem it but he is. Diego, Jolene, they are no better."

"And suddenly you're concerned about my well-being?" Chase spoke boldly, thinking back to when he originally moved to Calgary and how cold she had been to him. He thought of all the information he had recently learned about her connection to the RCMP and started to turn away. "Look, I don't need your help."

"You have to listen to me," She insisted. "I came to warn you..."

The club door suddenly opened and Hernandez stood beaming on the other side. The song 'December '63 (Oh What A Night)' loudly flowed through the club behind him.

His eyes were cold but his Hollywood smile was strong as he gestured behind him. "Let the lady in, please, I would love to meet your old friend."

Although his words sounded friendly, welcoming, Chase knew better. There was a look they exchanged after Maggie reluctantly passed through the entrance as he did the same and closed the door behind him. It was the same look Jorge had when he pulled out a gun and placed it next to Maggie's head. She remained calm but there was unmistakable fear in her eyes.

Stunned, Chase stepped back, his mouth fell open and he was unable to speak. He felt his heart race as he looked into Maggie's frightened face as she put her hands in the air to indicate surrendering.

"What a coincidence! I come here to warn Chase about *you* and you come here to warn him about *me*," Jorge said in a mocking voice as his dark eyes stared through her. "So tell me a story, little girl. I'm fascinated to hear what you came here to say."

"I was trying to help," Maggie's voice was shaking. "Chase, please!"

Hernandez suddenly backhanded Maggie, causing her to fall to the floor and although his old instincts would've been to help her, something stopped Chase this time as he stepped further back. Hernandez continued to point the gun at her head as her fingers reached for the spot he hit her. "The truth *now!* I'm not fucking around princess, start talking."

"I set you up," Her voice was small, barely audible. "When I had you hired by Jolene, I set you up."

"*Why?*" Hernandez's eyes blazed in anger and she shrunk beneath his powerful stare.

"I was angry with you, Chase," Maggie continued her confession as she attempted to pull her body away from Jorge. "I...I wanted to get in the RCMP and I knew Jolene didn't trust me but she would trust you. Everyone does. I thought once you got in I would persuade you to turn on them."

"What?" Chase shook his head in disbelief and glanced at Hernandez who didn't take his eyes off Maggie for a second.

"She used you," Jorge commented, his face growing more tense with the moment. "She misjudged your loyalties. She misjudged *you*, Chase."

"I was wrong," Maggie spoke again, her eyes begged him for help. "But don't be mistaken. These people are criminals. All of them! They are loyal to no one. They are dangerous."

Shaking his head, Chase felt sick as he backed further away not accepting her words. Glancing at Jorge, they had a brief, intense moment of eye contact leaving Chase feeling incredibly gullible, he secretly feared that Hernandez thought he was involved in this mess. However, it quickly became clear that this was not the case.

"You're about to see how dangerous. Tell him what you told his ex-wife," Jorge calmly instructed and Chase felt his heart sink. "Tell him about the little visit you paid to Audrey. I think he might like to know."

She was silent for a moment, her eyes glanced up at Chase's and shamefully looked away. He felt his heart racing, while his eyes stung as he stared at her. Suddenly the song 'Break my Stride' came on the radio.

Tears poured down her face as she started to sob uncontrollably, her head down, she didn't even look in his eyes. Her voice was barely a whisper. "I told her that you worked with criminals and she needed to keep you as far away from the kids as possible. I told her to keep pulling them back for their own good." She took a deep breath and with desperate eyes looked up at Chase. "I was trying to protect your kids."

Covering her face, Maggie's sobs were loud, her voice begging as she finally looked into his eyes. "I'm sorry Chase, please forgive me but I only did what I thought was right."

Anger seemed to vibrate from Jorge, his breathing was loud, as if he were struggling to hold back his fury. His cold eyes finally looked away from Maggie and met with Chase's for a split second but in that split second, a silent communication connected them in a way that only another parent could understand. No words could've been more powerful. No words were needed. It wasn't necessary.

"You tried to have my kids taken away from me?" Stunned to hear the innocent calamity in his own voice, as if Chase were, for that moment, eighteen once again and talking to the girl he was so much in love with. He felt weightless as if this were a dream that couldn't possibly be real. "You actually went to Audrey and told her I was...dangerous?"

Maggie nodded, continuing to weep, she avoided his eyes. "After I quit with Jolene, I went back home and saw Audrey. She mentioned the kids were bonding with Albert a lot since you left and I suggested that it might be for the best to keep away from you. I didn't say anything more until Leland died."

She stopped crying but still didn't look into his eyes, choosing instead to pick at her nail polish, reminding him briefly of her younger sister, Kelsey.

"She commented how nice Diego was and I told her to not be fooled, he was a dangerous man," She started to cry again. "That they are all dangerous and you were too. I told her to keep the kids away from you, for their safety. I couldn't see her lose another child after that day."

"But you had no issue with *me* losing my kids," Chase softly replied as he stared down at her, he felt a lump in his throat and shook his head. Suddenly hit by a wave of rage, his voice rose and his next words were full of aggression, bubbled with intense fury. "You actually told her that I was *dangerous*. That my kids were in *danger* because of me. That she should keep them away from me. All this time, I keep seeing them less and less..."

Chase couldn't even finish his sentence. He felt panic as his heart raced erratically but he fought it off. "I already lost a child and you wanted me lose the two I had left," He hesitated for a moment and his voice was suddenly full of emotions. "Who *are* you?"

He didn't care that Hernandez was easing the gun closer to Maggie's head, her hair a mass of tangles as her body shook from fear and anguish.

Chase turned around and started to walk away when he heard the shot. For a moment he closed his eyes and saw a million memories pass through his head, almost as if his own life was passing before his eyes but instead it was Maggie's. It was the times they spent together that now felt as though it never meant a thing. It was the love he felt for her, a woman he didn't know. She was a manipulator and now he saw clearly how cunning she had always been. He had been so naïve but he wouldn't be again.

He decided to not turn around. Instead Chase walked outside into the crisp, spring air, and took a deep breath as if it were the first day of a new life. It was a life where his eyes were wide open; alert and ready, he could take on the world. Nothing would ever be the same again. *He* would never be the same again. He was no longer the naïve boy. He was no longer the compliant man. He was the wolf and his story was just starting. This was not the end but a new beginning.

Love the book? Check out the We're All Animals to learn more about Chase Jacobs and to follow along on his adventures!

Send some LOVE - Write a review :-)

Printed in the United States
By Bookmasters